*FIRE FLASHED THROUGH
HER VEINS . . .*

Roger pulled her against his body. Innocent though
she was, her feminine instincts sensed his sudden lust.
She could feel his heart beating against her breasts.
"No," she whispered as he bent his head to kiss her.
His response was a low laugh. "Would you please be
still, Alexandra sweetling."

Then his tongue was in her mouth and her arms wrapped
themselves around his neck. Desire was softening her
body. She wanted to feel more, know more. . . .

Her lips were still warm from the imprint of his kiss, but now Silvia knew there was nothing to protect her from the terror of Serpent Tree Hall. Not even love. Especially not love. . . .

ANDREA PARNELL

Lovely young Silvia Bradstreet had come from London to Colonial America to be a bondservant on an isolated island estate off the Georgia coast. But a far different fate awaited her at the castle-like manor: a man whose lips moved like a hot flame over her flesh . . . whose relentless passion and incredible strength aroused feelings she could not control. And as a whirlpool of intrigue and violence sucked her into the depths of evil . . . flames of desire melted all her power to resist. . . .

Coming in September from Signet!

Fires of Destiny

LINDA BARLOW

AN ONYX BOOK

NEW AMERICAN LIBRARY

NAL BOOKS ARE AVAILABLE AT QUANTITY DISCOUNTS WHEN USED TO
PROMOTE PRODUCTS OR SERVICES. FOR INFORMATION PLEASE WRITE TO
PREMIUM MARKETING DIVISION, NEW AMERICAN LIBRARY,
1633 BROADWAY, NEW YORK, NEW YORK 10019.

 ONYX IS A TRADEMARK OF NEW AMERICAN LIBRARY.

SIGNET, SIGNET CLASSIC, MENTOR, ONYX, PLUME, MERIDIAN
and NAL BOOKS are published by New American Library,
1633 Broadway, New York, New York 10019

First Printing, August, 1986

1 2 3 4 5 6 7 8 9

PRINTED IN THE UNITED STATES OF AMERICA

To Halûk, my husband, my lover, and my inspiration

Acknowledgments

I wish to thank several people who have helped me in various ways over the many years that have gone into the creation of my characters and the writing of this novel. They include my first readers—back in junior high school—Sharon Sidebotham Nash and Heather and Chris Barlow; my more recent readers, Vicki Iritsky, Sema Özkaynak, and Ulya Özkaynak; the members of my writing group—Debra Stark, Jack Ormsbee, Pamela Moriarty, Mark Roegner, Paula Kwon, Steve Campbell, Sam Fisk, and Karen Paradies; Nancy Martin and Carla Neggers for their helpful critiques and constant friendship; my parents, Bob and Babs Barlow, for all their enthusiasm; and my former baby-sitter, Marcia Sadlow, who took care of my daughter so I could write. A special word of appreciation also goes out to Miriam Freidin for helping me understand the psychology of an author's relationship with her characters.

I also want to express my gratitude to my editors, Susanne Jaffe, Claire Zion, and Jeanne Tiedge, for their help at various stages of the writing of this novel, and to my agent, Larry Moulter, for his valuable advice and friendship.

Last, a big thank-you to my daughter, Dilek, who lets Mummy work, and my husband, Halûk, who has gracefully accepted that "I'll be there as soon as I finish this sentence" really means "Don't wait up for me." Without their love and encouragement this book would never have been finished.

Prologue
The Mediterranean, June 1555

Two men stood side by side, staring down at the narrow bed in the ship's surgery. The younger man felt a gentle touch on his shoulder. "I'm sorry, Roger," the physician said. "There wasn't a thing more I could do for the lass."

Roger Trevor wondered vaguely why he felt no emotion as he looked upon the pale, still face of the woman who lay there. Celestine. Her apricot hair was fluffed on the pillow, glimmering and shining as it had in life. Her expression was more serene than he had ever seen it. Her eyes, mercifully, were closed, but he remembered the way they had gazed at him last night—full of pain, fear, and what he imagined to be silent accusation. He would remember those iridescent blue eyes, he knew, until the day when he too lay as stiff and cold as she.

"You did your best," he said mechanically to Tom Comstock, his surgeon and one of his oldest friends.

"In such cases the physician's arts are useless. One day, perhaps, 'twill not be so."

"Aye," said Roger flatly. She looked so young, even younger than her age. An innocent child who had been entrusted to his care, instead of a woman.

But Celestine de Montreau had proved neither innocent nor a child.

"Her family? You know 'em, I believe?"

"Her parents are dead. There's a grandmother in Marseilles and her brother Geoffrey is an attaché at the French embassy in Stamboul. He's an old acquaintance of mine." Roger stopped, then slowly added, "An enemy now, I fear. There was trouble between us already, but this will make it worse. 'Twas he who asked me to see his sister safely home." Roger's voice dropped to a whisper. "He wanted me to protect her, not seduce her. Not get my bastard upon her."

Tom did not reply, and Roger took his silence for condemnation. There was a perverse pleasure in knowing himself condemned, particularly by as tolerant a man as Tom. It was exactly what he deserved. "I killed her," he added softly.

"Don't talk rot," said Tom. "You take too much upon yourself. You always have. Come, let's get out of here. You need some fresh air and a few swigs of aqua vitae."

"I ought to cry for her."

Comstock pursed his lips.

"Why can't I cry for her?"

"Perhaps if I leave you alone?"

Roger shook his head. He stared again at the thick apricot lashes that lay against her bloodless white skin. *Bloodless.* She'd bled internally, Tom had said. Her lifeblood had drained from her veins to her abdominal cavity, and there was no way he could stop it, nothing he could do.

"It's my fault," he repeated. His wits seemed incapable of dealing with anything beyond that fact.

"Christ, man!" Tom Comstock took his arm and dragged him forcibly away from the deathbed. "You're in a fine state. 'Tis normal enough, given the circumstances, but I mistrust you, all the same. And, on second thought, I'm not leaving you alone."

Roger hardly heard him. He was thinking of Celestine, laughing huskily, tossing her golden head as she ran her fingers over his naked chest. "I, a virgin?" she'd murmured. "Did my brother tell you that? Ah, but of course he did." She seemed to think it was the greatest jest in the world. "But perhaps my brother doesn't know me. *You* know me, do you not, Roger?" Her hands moved lower on his body, arousing him with her clever, expert caresses until he pressed her down beneath him and thrust deeply into her eager, wanton body. "Oh yes," she'd laughed when he brought them both to pleasure. "I think we understand each other very well."

He fancied that Celestine's cold lips were faintly curved now, smiling still. As if she knew something he did not. He was pricked with a needle of superstitious dread. "Evil will come of this," he predicted as Tom urged him out, up on deck, into the sun.

Comstock silently made the sign of the cross.

I
England, August 1556

Reason is the greatest enemy that faith has: it
never comes to the aid of spiritual things, but—
more frequently than not—struggles against the
divine Word, treating with contempt all that
emanates from God.

—Martin Luther

1

ALEXANDRA DOUGLAS knelt in the sanctuary of the small Norman church where Will Trevor, oldest son and heir of the Baron of Chilton, had been buried several weeks before. She prayed aloud for his soul, using the familiar Latin prayers, not caring if anyone heard her, defiantly wishing that someone would. Her fingers were so tightly clasped together, her bones showed.

After a few minutes of unconsoling prayers Alexandra reminded herself that Will's grave was no place to indulge in angry passions. Anger couldn't do Will any good now. She should have been more angry, and more determined, when he was still alive.

On his deathbed Will had asked for a priest, and Alexandra considered it monstrous that his request had been denied. She, his betrothed, had been leaning over his bed, sponging his forehead and talking nonstop in an effort to get him to respond. He'd been unconscious ever since his accident three days before, but when he'd unexpectedly opened his eyes and muttered the word "priest," she had rushed out to inform his father. Outside the chamber where the baron had secluded himself in grief, Alexandra met Francis Lacklin, the Calvinist heretic who had recently converted the baron and most of his household to the reformed beliefs. "You must have misheard," he said upon learning of Will's request.

"I heard perfectly," she retorted. "Will used to tell me often enough that he wasn't confirmed in his heresy. If he's decided to recant on his deathbed, he must be allowed to do so!"

"Aye, to be sure, if such is really his desire," Lacklin agreed. He spoke in his usual slow, measured tones. "But poor Will has been as blank as death itself for three days. How could he possibly have taken such an important decision?"

Alexandra pushed an unruly lock of red hair out of her eyes and glared at him. He was a big man, tall and broad-shouldered with cold silver-gray eyes, in many ways intimidating. But Alexandra was not easily put off.

"Do you call me a liar, Mr. Lacklin? Are you so determined to convert the entire Trevor household that you would disregard the last request of a dying man?"

"You are distracted, mistress," said Lacklin. He put one arm around her shoulders and drew her toward a bench. "Come sit down for few moments. This is a difficult time for all of us, but particularly for you. Will you pray with me?"

His voice was sympathetic, but she didn't trust him. Ever since their first meeting a few weeks before, she had believed him insincere. She suspected that it was not spiritual grace that inspired him as much as ordinary earthly ambition. Pulling away, she said, "I don't require comforting yet, thank you. You will pardon me. I'm going in to his father."

She did so while Mr. Lacklin hurried to Will's bedside. But the baron had broken irrevocably with the Papist Church of Queen Mary, and he refused to summon the parish priest. Later that night Will Trevor died while Francis Lacklin solemnly read from his heretical English translation of the Holy Scriptures beside the silent bed.

Staring around at the denuded altar and the bare walls of the ancient chapel, Alexandra wished she had simply run without permission to fetch the priest. Surely they wouldn't have refused the holy father admittance. Although he had spoken only that one word, Will had clearly desired to die with the rites of the Church. It had been her duty to help him. If God was as strict and narrow in his judgments as people were, poor Will might be burning in hell for her failure.

She had failed him in so many ways. She had known him since childhood and loved him as a brother, but she had not wanted to be his wife. Of the three Trevor brothers he was her least favorite. But, being the eldest, it was he who had been chosen for her husband. She would have much preferred to marry Roger, the second son, or even Alan, the youngest.

Guiltily Alexandra stared at the slab of stone which covered the entrance to the Trevor family crypt. The absence of dust in the cracks around the stone proved that it had recently been lifted, but there was nothing else to indicate Will's passing. His name had not yet been added to the list of Trevor dead on the tablet over the altar, and no comfortable verse had been selected to commemorate his short life. The most recent inscription had been carved ten years ago in 1546 for Catherine Trevor, first wife of the baron and mother of Will, Roger, and Alan.

A vivid memory of Lady Catherine's funeral came back to her. Everybody from miles around had mourned her. The church had been crowded with the family and friends of the Trevors and with all the retainers from both Chilton and the nearby Douglas manor. No one had stayed away for fear of attending a heretical ceremony; along with most of the great families in the north of England, the Trevors had been loyal to the Church of Rome in those days.

The chapel that had been divested of all the trappings of popery for Will's burial had been a very different place ten years ago. The altar had breathed incense; the gold crucifix, shining Communion plate, and flowing garments of the priests had suggested a richness of the life of the spirit that struck a dramatic contrast to the dark and fleeting life of the body. Indeed, the occasion had seemed more a celebration of eternity than a time of mourning. At least until Roger's outburst.

Alexandra remembered standing on tiptoe next to her

parents to see over the back of the pew when her friend and adored playmate Roger Trevor had leapt up to the altar and accused his father of pushing Lady Catherine over the cliff at Thorncroft Overhang, where she had died. The congregation had gasped at this outrageous and ill-founded charge, but Alexandra had longed to join Roger up there, screaming in fury at the bitter power of death, blaming the adults around them for letting such a terrible thing happen.

Will had not raged the way Roger had over their mother's early death. Unlike Roger, Will had never seemed particularly emotional.

Poor Will. She imagined him lying frozen for all time amid the bones of his ancestors, his pleasant face forever blanked, his strong and sturdy body eroding into dust. She imagined herself lying on a stony bier beside him, as she would have done someday if she had become his wife. The chill of death rose up from below, and she shivered, wishing she had worn a warmer cloak over her simple mourning gown. She wondered if Will's shade could see her kneeling here and if he now knew that she had loved him as a brother only and had not wished to lie beside him ever, alive or dead.

Bowing her head, she began to pray again. She prayed so hard that she did not notice the stream of light which briefly poured down the center aisle of the church as the main doors opened quietly and closed again. Not until the whisper of boot leather on stone came near did she hear and lift her head to stare down into the gloomy nave.

A man was coming toward the altar, but in the shadows she could not make him out. He was tall, as Will had been, and he moved slowly. She swallowed hard. Will had died with his sins unexpiated. What if he was not at rest? What if he had returned to reproach her for her lack of love, desire, and determination? She trod on the hem of her gown as she jerked to her feet. Ghosts, she told herself firmly, do not make a practice of marching around churches in the middle of the day.

At her sudden movement the figure in the nave stopped walking, and their eyes met in the dimness. He had a stare which reached out and grabbed her, so full of life and energy were his dark eyes. This was a living, breathing man, she realized with relief, as his voice rang out across the distance that remained between them.

"Forgive me if I've disturbed your meditations, madam," he said, approaching her once again. "I didn't expect to find anybody here."

Sweet Jesu. That voice . . . those eyes . . . the way he walked . . . surely she knew him. He didn't look much like Will: he was taller, his lithe, hard-muscled body was leaner, and his features were more finely chiseled. But the family resemblance was there.

"Roger?" she whispered.

His dark eyes narrowed for an instant as he came to the bottom of the chancel steps. His gaze assessed her thoroughly, in a manner that made her flush. No, she thought. It couldn't be. Roger had never looked at her like that. But then, the last time he saw her, she was only eight years old!

His eyes came back to hers, and she saw that he was smiling. "God's blood! 'Tis Alexandra Douglas, all grown-up. Good day to you, milady." The last word was said affectionately as he mounted the steps in two quick strides and opened his arms wide for her.

She threw herself at him in a most undignified manner, her voice echoing against the disapproving walls of the church. "Roger! I don't believe it! It's been years and years. 'Tis high time you came home!"

He tipped her chin up with one lean finger and kissed her upturned mouth in a lusty manner which was new to her. It happened so swiftly that she hardly had time to note the unfamiliar tingle that shivered along her nerves at the feel of his firm lips pressing on hers. It was pleasant—very pleasant—but before there was time to savor the moment, he set her back a little to look at her. "God's bones, but you've improved. I remember you as a short, skinny little baggage."

She grinned at him from her new vantage point of a head shorter than he. She was tall—most women would come no higher than his shoulders. "You look different too." She considered the faint lines around his eyes and mouth. "Rather cynical and world-weary."

"How perceptive." He touched a finger to the end of her nose. "You're not world-weary yet, I trust?"

"Heavens, no," she said cheerfully. "How could I be? I've hardly even *lived*. Already a widow though never a bride—" She stopped speaking abruptly as the thought struck her that he might not know of his brother's death. He might have come here to visit the grave of his mother, whom he had loved. She felt her bones shake with the dread of telling him.

She glanced uneasily back toward the crypt. Watching her, the look in his eyes sobered, and he said, "You were praying for Will, I take it?"

"Then you know?"

"That my brother is dead and I'm the new heir? Aye, I heard the news when I came through London on my way home." He left her to move closer to the stone over the crypt. "Poor old Will," he added. "Sensible, sober, and sane by all accounts. I certainly never expected to look upon his grave."

He spoke without emotion, and his coldness startled her. She remembered him hot, exploding with feeling. But that was nearly ten years ago, she reminded herself. Ten very eventful years, if there was any truth to the rumors that occasionally reached Roger's family about his activities. Since that day long ago when Roger had run away to sea, he had been a mariner, a student in a monastery, a Christian warrior defending the True Faith from the Mohammedan infidels, a captive of the Turks in Stamboul, and finally a sea captain skippering his own trading vessel from port to port in the Mediterranean. Although Alexandra had never given up hope of seeing him again, he'd been gone for so long that it had seemed unlikely that he would ever return to his family in the north of England. Yet, without warning, here he was. His father was sick, his elder brother was dead without issue, and Roger stood to inherit extensive lands, a title, and a fortune.

"Weren't you and Will supposed to marry and unite our estates?" he asked. "God's blood, I'd forgotten that. Was that what you meant by . . . You're not really his widow, are you, Alix?"

His use of her old nickname made it seem as if no time at all had passed since they had last met. "No. We had a precontract but no actual wedding. We were to have been joined next spring on my nineteenth birthday."

He hesitated briefly before putting his next question. "Precontracts are binding. Was your union consummated?"

"No," she said without embarrassment. He was not the first to wonder about this. Many young couples considered the precontract a license to engage in lovemaking, but Will had never pressured her to anticipate the formal ceremony. "There'll be no posthumous heir to supplant you, Roger."

"That's not why I asked. I was only thinking of you. I don't even want the bloody barony."

This was an intriguing disclaimer. She wondered if it were true. If so, why had he returned so fast?

"We weren't lovers." Smiling ruefully, she added, "I'm a virgin."

Roger's eyebrows went up, and his dark eyes danced with amusement. "God's wounds, Alix, you say it the way someone might say, 'I'm a leper.'"

She laughed. The stone wall echoed the sound, and she endeavored to affect a more solemn mien. Surely both the subject and the levity it induced were inappropriate in this particular setting. But Roger seemed intent to pursue the matter:

"The marriage could have been solemnized a couple of years ago—you're certainly old enough. Was the disinclination on my brother's side or on yours?"

She began to feel a little uncomfortable. Disinclination—was that what it had been? "Nobody seemed to be in any particular hurry. I didn't love him, if that's what you're asking. Not that way."

"And he? Did he love you 'that way'?"

"No. It wasn't in his nature, I don't think. He wasn't passionate. He wasn't at all like . . ."—she stumbled a little—"like most people." She had been about to say "like you."

Roger's eyes were surveying her body again, frankly traveling down over the small swell of her breasts under the laces of her square-necked mourning gown; the narrow span of her waist, which was accented by the tight leather girdle that bound it; and her long legs, disguised by her voluminous kirtle and overskirts. Her slim ankles, visible because the gown was an old one that should have been lengthened long ago, received his full consideration. She shook her head in what she hoped was a careless gesture. She wasn't used to such attentions.

When his gaze returned to her face, she was smiling bravely. "I feel like a slave you're considering buying. They do buy slaves in the Mediterranean, don't they? How much would you give for me?"

"If you were on the auction block, you wouldn't be wearing so many confining garments, and neither would you be looking so saucily into my eyes. You would be properly intimidated, Alexandra." He met her saucy grin with one of his own. A moment later, though, he looked back at the gravesite, and his merriment faded. "You and Will weren't suited, of course. You were marrying out of a sense of duty. Obeying the dictates, no doubt, of my honored father."

The subtle mockery underlying his words reminded her of all the strife between the baron and his second son. She wanted to ask him if he still blamed his father for Lady Catherine's death, but she couldn't bear to open his old wounds, especially not here, where his mother was buried. Instead she returned his appraising stare. He was older, that was certain. He looked as if he might be in his mid-thirties instead of almost twenty-five. Besides the tiny lines on his face, there was a sliver or two of gray in his dark hair. His body was lean and hard, and his skin darker than she remembered it—due, no doubt, to the Mediterranean sun. He was broad across the shoulders, although by no means brawny, and slim at the waist and hips. Lithely built and graceful, while at the same time uncompromisingly masculine.

And he was handsome—rather strikingly so. His brown eyes were large and thickly lashed; expressive eyes, eyes that could fix upon you and draw your soul out of your body. And his mouth, although narrow, had an undeniably sensual twist to it. Defying fashion, he wore no beard, which further accented the well-shaped, angular lines of his face.

Alexandra also noted that he seemed prosperous: his doublet and hose were richly fashioned although rather severe in style. His sword belt, boots, and gloves were of the finest leather, but the only true ostentation about him was found in the jewels around his Spanish collar; they were deep in color and enormous.

He cocked his head a little to one side. "You like what you see?" he asked, obviously amused by her scrutiny.

"I haven't decided. I believe I expected you to be much fiercer. A gold earring or two and a scimitar held between your teeth."

"Earrings and scimitars? God's blood, you make me sound like a pirate. Is that what everybody imagines I've been up to all these years?"

"Naturally. You have a colorful reputation. Kindly don't disabuse anyone—your brother Alan and I have taken great trouble to make a legend of you."

"Is that so?" One of his hands reached out and touched a lock of her thick red hair, which, as was usual at this time of the day, was coming loose from its somewhat untidy braid. The sensation of his fingers whispering against her scalp sent a series of curious little quakings scurrying through her. "On further consideration I'll wager that I could make my fortune with you on the Candian slave markets, Alix. Red hair is very rare and much prized in the Middle Sea. And if you're really still a virgin at eighteen, that'll send the price soaring."

Alexandra managed to jerk her head free without hurting herself unduly. He was jesting, of course, but hadn't it occurred to him that all her life she had been the intended bride of the heir of Chilton? And now that Will was dead that he was that man?

He cast a more somber look around the church. "Let's get out of this dismal place, shall we?"

Perhaps he wished to mourn his brother in private. Guiltily she chastised herself for not having thought of it sooner. "Would you like to be alone here? I can wait for you outside."

But he stepped away from the altar and, taking her arm, steered her down the steps. "I've had enough of churches, thank you. They're little more than tombs. What's wrong with this one, incidentally?" He looked curiously at the bare walls as he walked her down the center aisle. "Where are the plate, the candles, the altar cloth, the sacred hangings, and the priests, for that matter? Has my father tried to save his immortal soul by erecting a newer, more elaborate house of worship?"

"No. He's trying to save his soul by practicing Luther's heresy. Or is it Calvin's? Anyway, all religious articles that smack of popery have been removed from this church. Hardly anyone comes here anymore—they hold Scripture readings every day at Chilton Hall."

"Surely you jest? I seem to recall that my father used to change his religion to suit the times, along with anyone else who had any sense. It's hardly wise to turn Protestant now while Bloody Mary's so avidly burning heretics all over the country."

"The more martyrs the ecclesiastical courts burn, the more converts the dissenters make. It's a kind of subbornness, I think."

"Have you joined them, Alix?"

She clenched her fingers, thinking of Will's unshriven soul. "No. No, I haven't, despite Mr. Lacklin's determined efforts to convince me of the error of my ways."

Roger stopped short by the baptismal font; she could feel his fingers biting into her arm. "Mr. Lacklin? Francis Lacklin?"

"Yes. You know him?"

There was a long silence. Roger seemed to have turned in upon himself. "Aye," he said finally. "Is he here?"

"He's at Chilton, yes. He's the one who persuaded your father and Lady Dorcas to become such faithful Protestants. Now he's working on Alan, who is proving to be less malleable than usual. No doubt he'll be delighted to start in on you too." She glanced down at his hand on her arm. "You're hurting me."

He released her, his lips curving briefly in an apologetic

smile. But he seemed preoccupied, and she sensed a struggle going on inside him. She was seized with curiosity, not only about his interaction with the formidable Francis Lacklin but also about everything else in his wild and dramatic life. For the first time since Will's accident she was able to think about something other than the bitter power of death. She felt her spirits leap as they stepped out into the sunlight. With Roger home she was sure they would soon see the last of Francis Lacklin and of everything else that smelled of hypocrisy and gloom.

Instead of returning through the forest to Westmor, Alexandra decided to accompany Roger to Chilton Hall. The homecoming of the prodigal was an event she didn't want to miss.

Leading his horse, they walked the mile together over the rolling fields toward the old manor. She besieged him with questions about his life abroad, which he answered good-naturedly. He hadn't been a slave, although he had been captured; he had toiled briefly as a clerk for a wealthy Turkish merchant in Smyrna, a man who became his friend and, later, his business partner. He'd learned piloting and navigation while at sea, and he'd talked his mentor into allowing him to lead a trading voyage from Turkey to Marseilles. "After that the challenge was in my blood. I had a light, fast ship built, hired an expert crew, and thereafter made two or three runs a year."

"It sounds like an exciting life."

"It has its rewards," he conceded, his dark eyes dancing.

She supposed the rewards included a woman in every port and his own personal harem back in Turkey. She imagined all those women, each exotically beautiful with black hair and almond-shaped eyes.

"Why did you give it all up to return to this gray and damp climate?" As she spoke she tried to brush a lock of burnished red hair out of her eyes. She wished she'd taken the trouble to dress more carefully today. Normally the state of her garb wouldn't bother her, but the women she had just conjured up for Roger came swathed in silken veils, cloth of gold, and curled slippers. None of them had the curse of red hair, nor were they quite so tall and flat-chested as she believed herself to be.

He seemed to hesitate. "Curiosity mostly. I don't know exactly how long I'll stay."

"You mean you're going back to the slave girls and the corsairs and the cargo holds full of figs and olives and wines and spices? But surely, now that Will's dead, you have responsibilities here." One of which, she added silently, might prove to be the match between the heir of Chilton and herself. "Your father, at least, is bound to think so."

Roger's shoulders lifted in a gesture of indifference. Alexandra noticed an unremembered hardness around his mouth. "What my father thinks and what I think are likely to be two entirely different things."

He changed the subject by asking her to tell him some of the local gossip. Since Alexandra was on friendly terms with almost everyone who lived nearby, she was able to supply him with a long series of anecdotes. She chattered on freely until they came to a place in the road that caused her to fall abruptly silent.

The trail doubled back on itself to avoid a rocky mound, skirting the edge of the dense woodland known as Westmor Forest. There were many legends associated with the forest, which lay to the south of the converted abbey now known as Westmor. The woods were said to be haunted by demons, and few of the local farmers or villagers cared to venture very far into the gloomy trees.

Alexandra paid no attention to these legends. She loved the forest. She had been playing there since childhood, and nothing unpleasant had every happened to her; nothing, at least, that could not be traced to human agency. The worst fright she'd had there had occurred when the Trevor boys tied her to a tree at nightfall and left her to the mercy of a horrible shape that crept up on her, howling and shrieking. The demon had turned out to be Roger, clad in one of his mother's fur-lined cloaks, and for once he had succeeded in making her cry.

But there *was* something ominous about the way the forest stretched out a shaggy arm, encroaching on the road at the one spot where wayfarers were hidden from the look-out tower of Chilton Hall. "This is where Will's horse took fright and threw him," she explained, pausing underneath a huge oak and pointing to a ditch on the side of the road. "It still seems so difficult to believe. He was an excellent horseman. But he wasn't riding his usual mount that night, and the physician said later that he must have been drinking."

Roger also stopped, looking at her rather than at the ditch, and gave her another of his deep, unnerving stares. He had a habit of focusing directly into her eyes, as if he wished to discern the thoughts behind her words. "Did he drink excessively?"

"No. I can't recall ever seeing him the worse for drink."

Roger went to peer into the ditch. The road curved sharply just before it.

"There was a rock in the ditch," Alexandra added. "Will struck his head on it. He died of a brain fever."

Roger jumped down into the ditch and looked around. He poked around a bit in the damp ground—the ditch had once been a stream, and the earth was muddy there—then climbed out and scraped clay off his boots. He cast his eyes up the road toward the manor, which was hidden behind the rocks. "What a perfect place for an ambush." His voice was a lazy drawl, yet Alexandra thought she could detect an odd note in it. "I trust nobody had a grudge against Will?"

He had expressed the fear which had been haunting her ever since the night Will had been carried up to Chilton Hall, his body hanging limp, his hair dark with blood. She was not the only one who thought the accident strange. She had heard that the baron had been asking questions in the village.

"Nobody that I can think of," she replied.

Her voice must have betrayed her doubts, for he touched her arm. "But?" he prodded.

"But it's peculiar the way it happened, that's all."

Roger turned and looked into the woods. The masses of dark green plants were threatening to overgrow the path. "Someone could have hidden there on the edge of the forest and frightened Will's horse at the critical moment. But it would have required precise timing, and besides..." He stopped, his body coming alert. He stared into the thick trees just across from where they stood, and one hand flew to the hilt of his sword.

"What is it?"

She felt a sharp pain in her shoulder as Roger flung her aside and dived into the undergrowth, his blade drawn and flashing. There was a scrambling sound as someone tried to run. Alexandra recovered her balance and leapt after him in time to see Roger tackle the figure who'd been lurking here.

With his sword to the fellow's throat, Roger dragged his quarry out into the open. He was an ungainly youth with straggling hair and bad teeth. He lay on his back quivering beneath Roger's blade, his eyes rolling. Sounds of alarm were squeaking out of his throat.

Alexandra dropped to her knees in the dirt beside them, unmindful of the consequences to her gown. "It's only poor Mad Ned from the village," she said, placing a restraining hand on Roger's sword arm. "Be careful. You'll cut him with that thing." To the youth she said, "We mean you no harm, Ned. You startled us, that's all."

"Mad Ned?" Roger repeated, still holding him down.

"He's the village half-wit. He can't talk, and it's not clear how much he understands, but he's quite harmless, I promise you. Put your rapier away. This isn't the Moorish coast."

"I'd like to know what the devil he was doing spying on us."

Mad Ned was shaking with fear and vainly trying to squirm away to the safety of Alexandra's skirts. "Heavens, you're suspicious, aren't you?" she said to Roger. "Let him go. He and I are friends. Come, Neddy, let's brush you off, shall we?"

Roger backed off while Alexandra helped the frightened youth to sit up. Slowly, with another wary look at Ned, he sheathed his weapon. "You have some curious friends."

"Aye, like ex-monks, ex-mercenaries, and sea captains," she taunted him. "You've scared him out of his few remaining wits."

Ned's head was twitching back and forth. He stole a closer look at Roger as Alexandra explained to him, "This is the baron's other son, Roger, who's been away for a long time. You needn't be afraid of him, Neddy."

But Ned was obviously not reassured. In fact, the more he squinted up at Roger, the more alarmed he became. As Alexandra rose to her feet, he rolled over, jumped up before either of them could stop him, and fled into the woods. Roger tensed for a second as if he might chase him, then relaxed and laughed. "He's not half-witted when it comes to saving his skin, is he?"

"I warrant he's not half-witted at all. He's very clever about some things. He knows the forest better than I do, and the birds and animals come when he whistles to them. He's gentle, and he cries when the village children throw rocks at him."

At the mention of rocks, Roger took another look into the ditch. Alexandra added, "If only he could talk! If anyone did lay an ambush for Will, Ned might have seen it. He's always in the forest, even at night."

She thought Roger's mouth tightened at this, but he said nothing more as they walked on toward Chilton Hall. Rounding the rocky mound, they could see the ancient fortresslike buildings atop their grassy hill. Although the walls of the outer enclosure were crumbling, and the hall itself was in a state of obvious disrepair, the manor was still an imposing sight, a symbol of the power and privilege which the Trevor family had long enjoyed. It seemed inconceivable to Alexandra that the eldest son of this noble house could have been done to death in a ditch.

Roger must have felt something similar, for he said, "Doubtless it was an accident, after all. Anything else would be extraordinarily farfetched."

"Aye. Accidents *do* happen." She tried to lighten the mood by teasing him. "Anyway, the only person with a true motive to murder Will was out of the country at the time."

His mouth twisted unpleasantly. "You mean me? What motive did I have?" He glanced up at the buildings on the hill. "A crumbling stronghold which will take my entire patrimony to restore? An unimpressive title at an unimportant court? Some rocky farmland, a lot of woods, and a few sheep?"

"In sooth, it does sound paltry when you put it like that."

"We might as well accuse you. You didn't want to wed him. What a fortuitous escape." He ran his eyes over her in the same lecherous manner he had employed in the church. "Will they hang you, I wonder? By that sweet neck of yours?"

Alexandra abruptly recalled the old lesson of their childhood: you don't tease Roger unless you're prepared to be repaid in the same coin.

"If you'd been clever, you'd have waited till you'd got yourself a son," he went on. "Then you'd have been a rich widow with dower rights, as well as the mother of the heir. That's what I would have done in your place."

"I'm not so cold-blooded. And neither are you."

He just looked at her. She shivered a little. Perhaps Roger *had* become cold-blooded.

They were within hailing distance of the ancient stone edifice when the gates of Chilton Hall opened and several people spilled out onto the road. "They've seen us. Imagine their faces when they realize the stranger is you!"

"Did I neglect to tell you? I sent my party on ahead. They know it's me."

Of course. A man of his position wouldn't travel without servants. "There's Alan waiting up by the gate. And this is your father coming out to greet you. Well, my Lord Prodigal, are you ready to enter the lists?"

"Girded for battle, milady." He turned to look at the slowly approaching figure of Richard Trevor, his father. His brother, Alan, and his stepmother, Dorcas, the baron's second wife, remained behind at the main gate with a crowd of excited servants while the baron advanced alone.

Roger took a deep breath and blew it out audibly. His face was calm no longer. "Body of Christ. My enemies in the Middle Sea would make merry if they could see me now, quaking in my boots because I'm about to meet a man whom I once sincerely feared and hated."

"Quaking?" Alexandra was astonished to hear him confess that he had nerves that could betray him.

"Aye, quaking. Do I look as fainthearted as I feel?"

"No, in sooth, you do not."

"Then I must be an excellent actor."

She laughed, delighted with this glimpse of the man behind the mask, this assurance that his strange and eventful life had not robbed him of his essential humanity. It had, in fact, made him more approachable, more honest. As a boy, he never would have admitted to fear of any kind.

She caught herself stealing a glance at his beautiful long-fingered hands lacing and unlacing themselves as she assured him that his once-formidable father was probably quaking far more than he. He raised his eyebrows at her, and for an instant a current ran between them. His sensual lips curled in a smile.

He is the heir of Chilton now, she thought once again, and blushed.

"Go on, Roger," she said quickly to cover her confusion. "Your faithful troops will be right behind you."

"No, I'll meet him alone. Give me a few minutes, will you?"

Roger and the baron walked the last few yards toward each other alone, like duelists meeting against the indifferent blue sky. Who spoke first was impossible to determine from the spot where Alexandra watched, but she did see Roger bow slightly, giving his father a token of respect. After a brief exchange, the baron drew his son closer and saluted him on both cheeks, then they turned and walked together through the gates of Chilton Hall.

2

ALEXANDRA sat opposite Roger on the family dais in the great hall that evening watching in fascination as he cut his meat with an ornately carved knife and speared it with a matching fork. Like everyone else at the long trestle table, Alexandra made do with her fingers, using her knife only when a slab of meat proved particularly tough.

"Are you afraid of dirtying your hands?" she asked him, glancing down at her own rather greasy fingers.

He took no offense. "Try it," he said, handing her the two-pronged fork. "It's useful for holding down a slippery piece of meat while you carve a few chunks off it. That's the idea."

Alexandra laughed as she captured a piece of meat on the tines of the fork and lifted it to her lips. Roger watched her movements intently, and for some reason, she stopped laughing and blushed instead. She passed it back to him. "Thanks, but I think I'll stick to my trusty old fingers."

He grinned, his dark eyes gleaming with merriment. Indeed, he'd been remarkably pleasant-natured all afternoon. He'd spent the hours since his arrival unpacking and giving gifts. He had presented the baron with two intricately knotted Turkey carpets, several casks of wine, and a beautifully bound volume of Aristotle for his library. Alan had received several books, which had pleased him mightily since he fancied himself something of a scholar. Printed books were rare, and Alexandra, who loved books too, frankly envied him.

But she herself had not been forgotten. Roger had given her two presents which she ordinarily would not have accepted from a man who was not a blood relation: a bolt of sea-green silk and an ivory-and-gold comb to wear in her hair. Lady Dorcas had helped her dress her hair before supper so she could wear the comb. The baroness had also lent her one of her gowns, and Alexandra had dressed with more than usual attention to the details of her appearance.

"I knew the comb would suit you," Roger had said approvingly when they sat down to eat. "Not even ten years and several thousand miles could dull my memory of your fiery hair."

Although she usually mourned the flamboyance of her dark red tresses, these words made her feel that the color might not be such a curse after all.

Supper had turned out to be an elaborate affair. Instead of taking cold meats in the small family dining room upstairs, the Trevors supped in the cavernous central hall of the manor. The boards on their trestles stretched the entire length of the smoky room, and the entire household, arranged strictly according to their degree, from the baron's body servants down to the lowliest stableboy, had gathered in Roger's honor. At the start of the meal, they had all stared with great curiosity at Roger, who rose and made a witty speech expressing his pleasure to be home. He received a rousing cheer when he finished, and Alexandra overheard a number of approving comments, particularly from the women.

The only person who did *not* seem impressed with Roger was his father. The baron was getting old, Alexandra thought, shooting a glance in his direction. His face was thin beneath the abundant gray hair, and his eyes had lost a little of their vividness since his heart seizure the previous winter. Alexandra wondered what he thought of the man his son had become, a man most fathers would have been proud of. She had always seen the baron as a strong, domineering personality, not unlike her own father in his ability to command a situation. Tonight, however, it was Roger whose charisma had everyone transfixed. The baron seemed a paler, dimmer figure in comparison.

The great hall resounded with the noises of hearty eaters toasting each other with home-brewed ale and dogs prowling around the boards, whining for scraps. The cooks had out-done themselves, preparing a veritable feast of boiled beef, roast veal, pigeon pie, rabbit stew, and roast capon. There was fresh bread to accompany the meats, and, for dessert, custards and sugar dulcets. Alexandra had to loosen the laces of the leather girdle which cinched her waist before she was halfway through the third course.

Since it was difficult to make oneself heard during the meal, the conversation lagged until the hall began to clear of the servants who had to get back to their evening chores. As the kitchen helpers removed the plates and threw bones to the waiting dogs, the Trevors moved their stools around the enormous stone hearth where they could finish their wine in comfort. Seizing her chance, Alexandra lost no time in trying to draw Roger into a discussion of politics.

"Did you come through London? What news is there of a possible war with France?"

"None that I know of, thank God." His voice was clipped and short. "Why? Are you filled with patriotic fervor for your beloved country?"

She shook her head. "Goodness, no. Nobody that I know wants a war. Why should good Englishmen march off to their deaths at the whim of Mary Tudor's Spanish husband?"

Roger stared at her lazily under hooded eyelids. "I've heard that Sir Charles, your father, is at court; that he is one of the queen's chief advisers."

"Yes, I believe that's true," she answered with some reserve. Her father's perpetual absence was a sore subject with both Alexandra and her mother. Years before, Lady Douglas had taken on the task of administering the Westmor estates herself while her husband pursued his ambitions at court. "Unfortunately, we don't see very much of my fa-ther."

Watching her intently, he went on, "Surely his position requires that you remain loyal to the queen? As I understand it, you, at least, are not a heretic." He glanced toward his father, who was. It was the first specific reference to the baron's conversion. Francis Lacklin was not present that evening—he had gone to visit a nearby manor for the day. No one seemed to know when he would return.

"The court is miles away, and anyway, I am loyal," Alexandra said. "If the queen were determined to execute everyone who disagreed with her policies, she'd be obliged to send a goodly portion of her countryfolk to the stake."

"The burnings that Mary Tudor has encouraged are a travesty of justice," said the baron. "This is England, not Spain. We want no Inquisition here."

Roger took a long quaff of wine. "Are you one of those, Father, who would like to see the queen deposed and her Protestant sister set upon the throne?" he drawled.

"Certainly I pray for the continuing health and safety of Princess Elizabeth."

"Mary Tudor could be queen for years; in fact, she might long outlive her sister. And she is, by the grace of God, our queen. What you think about her is your own affair, but since I arrived here this afternoon, I've heard treason being carelessly uttered in every quarter. It's dangerous, Father. In London people are burned for such talk."

"If a man cannot speak his conscience within his own walls—"

"If there are spies within your walls? What then? You can't trust everyone in such a large household."

"Can I not?" the baron roared. "Perhaps your years in the treacherous East have made you overly suspicious. None of my people would ever betray me."

Roger pursed his lips in anger, and Alexandra squirmed in her seat, wishing to high heaven she had not started this discussion. It struck her that Roger was merely seeking to warn his father, but the baron clearly took his words less as a warning than as an insult. Which was not, perhaps, surprising.

For as long as she could remember, Roger and his father had been at odds. They seemed to bring out the worst in each other. Roger had been a headstrong, difficult child, and whenever he got into mischief, his father's idea of discipline had been to beat him severely. Instead of teaching the boy a lesson, this treatment had only hardened Roger into a true rebel.

To make matters worse, when Roger was fourteen, the baron had threatened to divorce his wife. Roger adored his lively, passionate mother, and was devastated when he learned his father's intentions. Divorce was no simple matter, but King Henry VIII had managed it, and throughout the country, other unhappy husbands were encouraged to try their own luck with the ecclesiastical courts.

When Lady Catherine unexpectedly died, Roger had come to the conclusion that rather than struggle for years to obtain a divorce which was unlikely ever to be granted, his father had pushed his wife over a cliff. There was no evidence to support this, and nobody but Roger had ever seriously believed it. Everyone else believed she had committed suicide. The baron's quick remarriage to the young and lovely Lady Dorcas only increased the antagonism between father and son, and after a domestic battle of epic proportions, Roger left home to begin the odyssey that had kept him out of England for ten long years.

"What possible advantage can come of openly admitting your espousal of the reform beliefs?" Roger persisted. "It's mostly townsfolk who have gone to the stake, but no one is immune to the queen's justice."

"I must do as my conscience demands."

"Despite the risk to your family?"

"Ah." The baron's sharp eyes had focused on Roger's face. "You are concerned about your inheritance, perhaps? Now that you stand to gain something from your family ties, you wish to be certain I don't squander the estate and disgrace the title before they can be handed on."

Roger expelled a harsh breath and retreated behind a mask of indifference. "We misunderstand each other," he said coldly. He refilled his wine cup and stared into the fire.

"Enough of England and her dreary troubles," Dorcas interjected. Smiling pleasantly at her stepson, she went on, "Tell us something of your life in the Mediterranean. That is what we are all longing to hear."

"I fear my experiences in the importing and exporting of

goods will hold little interest for a lady like yourself," Roger said shortly. He was taking frequent sips of his wine, and his easy manner of earlier in the day seemed to have vanished. He'd been moody as a lad, Alexandra remembered. He hadn't changed in that respect.

"What we really want to know about is life in a Turkish harem. Is it true that the sultan has several hundred concubines at his beck and call? How does he decide which one he wants on a given night?"

"Alexandra!" Dorcas chided. But the baron looked slightly amused, and Alan leaned forward as if eager to hear the answer to these important questions.

Roger seemed to relax. He gave her a slow, mischievous grin. "Being a male, I don't know very much about life in a Turkish harem. I could arrange for you to find out firsthand, though, if you so desire."

Alexandra was unsubdued. "By selling me as a slave, Roger?"

He held out his wine cup, and without thinking, she reached for the jug and refilled it. He laughed at her. "You anticipate my needs very well, Alexandra. Perhaps I'll keep you for myself."

Alexandra saw the baron nod in satisfaction, a gesture which Roger did not catch. Alan's face tightened, and Alexandra flushed. But before she could think of an appropriate retort, Roger's expression changed. He was looking over her shoulder into the gloom of the great hall, and his body went tautly still.

Alexandra turned her head. Francis Lacklin, fresh from preaching the Word of God, had just come into the hall.

Lacklin stepped closer. "Please don't interrupt your conversation on my account," he said to Roger. "You were saying...?"

Roger did not reply. He simply stared at Lacklin, his fingers tight around his wine cup, his face a mask. Alexandra glanced back and forth between them, much struck by the almost palpable tension. Roger knew Lacklin, he'd told her. She'd meant to ask him how, but in all the excitement of his return, the subject had slipped her mind.

The baron rose immediately and embraced Lacklin,

greeting him in a far more friendly manner than he had received his own son. In fact, as she saw them standing together, Alexandra had the odd sensation that it was Francis Lacklin, not Roger, who truly belonged here.

Lacklin bowed courteously to them all, saying, "I've heard the happy tidings, my lord." He turned back to Roger, who had remained seated, his legs stretched casually out in front of him.

As the baron began an introduction, Roger said, "We are already acquainted." His eyes met Lacklin's. "You do remember me?"

Like Roger's, Lacklin's face was controlled, revealing no emotion. After an infinitesimal pause he replied, "Of course. Although you are greatly changed."

"It's been what—ten years?"

"Nearly that long."

Roger glanced at his father, who seemed both puzzled and annoyed at this exchange.

"You know each other?" Alan said, expressing the surprise of them all. He shook his head doubtfully. "But how?"

"We once shared an interest in the sea," said Roger. "In fact, he taught me much of what was later vital for me to know. We served aboard the same ship."

Sweet Jesu! Alexandra pondered this intelligence in silence. The pious Mr. Lacklin had been a seaman?

"You never told me." There was a note of challenge in the baron's voice. "Not once in all these weeks have you indicated that you were acquainted with my son."

Alexandra half-hoped to see Lacklin discomfited, but if he was he didn't reveal it. "I once knew a boy named Roger, but I had long forgotten his last name, if indeed I ever knew it. Certainly I never dreamed he was your son."

"I wasn't proclaiming my identity in those days," Roger said dryly. "I was trying to pass as a common sailor."

"And failing," Lacklin reminded him with a slight smile. He pulled a stool around and sat down with them, saying, "I fear I've come in at a bad moment."

"Not at all." Once again, Roger seemed at ease. "I'm being pressed for tales of my adventures." He glanced over at Alan, who'd been plaguing Roger for stories all evening long. "Alan in particular seems to believe that I've done nothing for ten years but engage in a series of hair-raising escapades and bloody battles. I hope you haven't been emulating me, brother, by rushing about challenging the neighbors to cross swords with you."

"Not me; I'd never challenge anyone." Alan shrugged his shoulders, which were rounded from the way he constantly hunched over his books. "I'm hopeless with a rapier. My last fencing master gave up on me, didn't he, Alix?"

"Perhaps you ought to ask Francis to give you some lessons," Roger suggested.

"You mean he's a swordsman as well as a sailor?"

Lacklin shot Roger an irritated glance before answering, "I once had a modest skill at the sport."

"Modest?" Roger laughed shortly. "He's one of the finest swordsmen I've ever seen."

Alexandra felt a kind of triumph: her suspicions were confirmed: Francis Lacklin was not what he appeared to be. "What a waste," she commented. "It seems that Alan and I could have been studying fencing with a master instead of listening to interminable lectures about spiritual grace."

Frowning faintly, Lacklin rose. "If you will pardon me, it's time for the evening prayers. Would anyone care to join me upstairs in the winter parlor?"

The baron at once offered his arm to his wife. Roger poured himself another cup of wine. "Not I," he said. "Alix?" She shook her head. "Alan?"

Alan hesitated before following his brother's example and helping himself to more wine. "I'd rather not, not tonight," he said, avoiding Lacklin's eyes.

"Good night then, my lady, Father," said Roger as they turned to go with Lacklin. "If you feel at all like reminiscing afterward, Francis, I'll be here for a time."

While Francis Lacklin shepherded his small flock up the winding staircase which led to the floor above, Alexandra could have sworn she saw Roger Trevor smile enigmatically into his wine.

3

*T*HE FIRE had burned down to ash, and the great hall at Chilton was growing chilly. The smells from supper lingered, mixing pleasantly with the smoke from the wood chips and the fresh scent of summer rushes on the floor. All was quiet. It was well after nightfall and most members of the household were abed.

Roger got up and threw another log on the fire. It flared up, illuminating his face. Alexandra noticed the dark circles under his eyes. She didn't think they'd been there earlier.

"So we three reprobates will go merrily to hell together," he said, sitting down again and pulling his stool closer to his brother. "Are you staying the night, Alix?"

When she nodded, he added, "Do you sleep here often?"

The question sounded casual, but Alexandra hesitated before answering. She sensed he meant something by it, although she wasn't sure what.

"She has a bedchamber here," Alan replied.

"Moved in already, my dear?"

"I've always had a place to sleep here." The way he was looking at her was making her uneasy. His mood had changed again from amiable to something slightly less attractive.

"Have some wine," he said, pouring it.

"Aren't you drunk? You've been drinking that wine for hours."

"Very likely. You disapprove?"

"That depends on how garrulous it makes you. I'd love to hear more about your acquaintance with Francis Lacklin."

"So would I," said Alan. "You really served together at sea? Somehow I can't imagine him on a ship."

"He was the second officer on the ship I ran away to all those years ago."

"Were you friends?" Alexandra persisted.

Roger shrugged. "You could say so. I was the most junior seaman aboard—a child of . . . what, fourteen, fifteen? The reality of life at sea was rather different from my expectations. Francis Lacklin was the only person on board who didn't find it amusing to take the fine young lordling below-decks and beat him black and blue. He was kind to me when I desperately needed kindness."

"He probably wanted to convert you. Heavens, imagine being trapped on a ship with him; there would be no place to go to escape. Did he convert you?"

A muscle had tightened in Roger's jaw, and his eyes looked at her as if he weren't really seeing her. "You'll remember that I entered a monastery shortly thereafter."

"So you did," she agreed, feeling foolish.

Alan started to ask something else, but Roger interrupted him, saying, "No, my friends, I've talked more than enough for one day." He turned to Alan. "You're what—seventeen? Why are you still living at Chilton? Why haven't you joined some wealthy lord's household or taken a post at court?"

"I wanted to, but Father doesn't approve of the court of Queen Mary. Even before he became a dissenter, he didn't trust the papists."

"So what? If I sent Father to the devil at fourteen, you could have done the same by now yourself."

But Alan shook his head. "No, that's just it—I'm not like you. I wish I were." When Roger did not reply, Alan doggedly went on, "You've done so many things, been so many places. Your life is filled with adventure—"

"You've been reading too many romantic tales," Roger said coldly. Which was unfair of him, Alexandra thought, considering that his own life had been as exciting as any romantic tale. She was about to say so when Alan came out with the question that she, with all her outspokenness, hadn't dared to ask:

"Do you still hate our father?"

There was a pause while Roger sipped his wine. "No," he said. He spoke in short, clipped syllables as he went on, "It was years ago, that unpleasantness—another lifetime. Why? Do you?"

He's lying, Alexandra sensed. But a moment later she checked herself, thinking: How do I know what he really feels?

"No," said Alan. Then, as Roger stared at him, he qualified, "Well, perhaps I do, sometimes."

"How unfilial."

This time Alexandra could have sworn Roger spoke ironically, particularly since he saw her watching him and raised an eyebrow.

"I can't help it. He treats me like a child."

There was a whining undertone to Alan's voice which Roger responded to immediately: "Maybe you act like a child. Have you ever thought of that?" He looked to Alexandra for confirmation. "Does he act like a child?"

If he did, she certainly wasn't going to betray it—she and Alan were unfailingly loyal to one another. But as she denied the charge, she had a flash of memory: Alan screaming with fright because Roger had locked him in the haunted tower. Sickly and delicate as a lad, Alan had been coddled by his mother—overmuch, perhaps. He had grown up timid, and even at seventeen he hadn't completely succeeded in suppressing his fears. To Alan, the world was still a very dangerous place.

Roger, on the other hand, had been too full of natural vitality to have much sympathy for his fearful younger brother. He used to tease Alan often—not with any real malice, but with enough energy to intimidate the boy thoroughly. And unlike Alexandra, Alan allowed himself to be bullied. She too had been locked in the haunted tower, but instead of bawling, she had climbed out on a ledge and in through an unlocked chamber to make her escape.

Alexandra watched unhappily as Roger filled his cup

once more. He'd definitely had too much. "You must be exhausted from your journey—perhaps we ought to retire. Alan . . ."

But Alan must have been feeling the effects of the wine himself, for he paid no attention. "What do you think I should do with my life?" he persisted. "I have no great talents or accomplishments, except translating from the Greek and composing poetry."

Roger considered him through half-shut eyes. "Poetry—ah, there's a useful skill. You used to play the lute excellently, do you still? How fortunate. The ladies will adore you. Take up the art of seduction; that ought to improve your opinion of yourself."

"I don't think I'd be very good at seducing anybody," Alan said.

"What an appalling lack of confidence. It's the perfect occupation for a younger son. I assure you, Alan, beautiful noblemen never starve."

Alan looked embarrassed. Roger glanced from one to the other and added, "Or marry this lovely lady now that she's free. She's wealthy enough to keep you, and she's certainly capable of managing Westmor Manor alone while you loaf about translating Homer."

Alan's face was crimson. "How can I? You're the heir—it's you she's supposed to marry."

The silence this comment generated was as thick as a wall. Alexandra felt her own color rise, burning her neck and cheeks. She took a gulp of wine and forced a laugh.

"Good heavens! Will the Trevors never run out of brothers? I don't wish to marry any of you, thank you very much."

"You have to," Alan insisted. "You signed a contract to wed the heir of Chilton."

She tried not to panic. Roger was staring at her in a manner that could only be described as malevolent. "That contract was nullified by Will's death."

"Why? There's still an heir," Alan persisted.

"I agreed to marry Will Trevor, not anybody else. Don't be a goose, Alan."

"You've always loved Roger much better than Will. You'll be delighted to marry him."

Alexandra was thoroughly humiliated. Roger's continued silence did not help. "I love you all, as brothers. I think you've had too much wine, Alan."

Roger shifted in his seat, and they both looked at him. His face was impassive, but when he spoke his voice was harsh. "Go to bed, Alan. I wish to speak with Alexandra alone."

Alan rose. "I didn't mean to cause difficulties," he said, shuffling his weight from one leg to the other. When no one spoke, he added defensively, "But Father has talked of it, Alix, you know he has."

"Good night, Alan," Roger said. The boy seemed to wilt under his direct stare.

"Good night," he replied and left them.

Through her embarrassment, Alexandra was thinking: I won't let him do that to me. I won't be reduced to jelly by a look and a harsh word. "You needn't worry. He was talking nonsense," she said.

"Was he?" There was no more than four or five feet between their stools, and as he spoke, he stretched out his lean, muscular legs until he could touch the hem of her kirtle with his boots. Somewhere during the course of the evening he had removed his doublet and opened the neck laces of his white lawn shirt. She could see a black smudge of hair dusting over the supple muscles of his chest. He looked relaxed . . . and yet threatening, lazing there in his trunks and hose, his dark eyes hooded, his well-shaped fingers curled around his wine cup. "Here we are, alone together in the dark, sweetling. What do they all expect? You even have a bed here. How convenient. Am I to regard you hereafter as my property?"

"You're angry," she whispered. She clenched her fingers in her lap, trying to ignore the strange tightening in her stomach that his words engendered. There was a warmth deep inside her, the significance of which she dared not contemplate. "So am I. Alan had no call to say those things."

"I'm glad he did. I must be slow-witted, since it hadn't occurred to me until now that I might inherit anything else from Will besides the claim to Chilton."

"It occurred to me," she admitted honestly. "But you

might have been dead for all we knew to the contrary. Or already married."

"Instead here I am, alive and unwed and full of exotic tales of the lush and sensual East. . . . Look at me, Alix."

Reluctantly she raised her eyes to his.

"For years you've expected to wed the next Baron of Chilton. I suppose it's natural for you to assume that I will carry through with the terms of Will's contract. And Alan's right, isn't he? You always did love me better than Will."

"Yes, I loved you better than Will, but that was a long time ago." She sent him a smile to soften her words as she added, "If you imagine I've been pining for you for the last ten years, you must have an excessively high opinion of your attractions."

She held his gaze and this time it was he who looked away. But she had recognized something in him which she had never seen before: a kind of pained resignation, as if he had suddenly realized that he must tread carefully, be courteous, but keep his distance, taking care not to injure an old friend who had grown old enough to make unwelcome demands on him. He sighed faintly, dragging a hand through his thick dark hair. Something about the gesture called up her earlier impression of the world-weariness from which he seemed to be suffering. What was wrong with him? Had he undergone some heartsickness, some tragedy? An unhappy love affair, perhaps?

"Roger, good heavens, I was eight years old! You were so much older, and yet you actually played with me—naturally I adored you. You were a hero to me."

"I'm no fit suitor for you, Alix," he said, as if she hadn't spoken. There was an odd, almost haunted look in his eyes. "Believe it. I'm no hero now. The things that happen to young women who get entangled with me are . . . " He paused, as if searching for the right words. ". . . highly unpleasant."

This made her curious, yet only half her attention was on his words. She was surreptitiously looking at his body. There was no doubt about it—he was as comely a man as she had ever seen. With his dark, lively eyes and his tough, yet gracefully masculine physique, he was much more magnetic than either of his brothers.

Averting her gaze to stare into the low-burning fire, Alexandra examined her heart. Despite her denials, she suspected that it would be easy to fall in love with him. It was not just his looks, but his entire manner: he was mysterious and exciting, even dangerous. She was already feeling his pull deep in the most secret places of her body.

She could imagine herself longing for their fathers to arrange a marriage between them, and awaiting its formalization in a breathless haze of anticipation. And yet, because she possessed very little in the way of feminine vanity, she could also imagine a lack of enthusiasm on Roger's part— an understandable desire, considering his history, for a woman more courtly and sophisticated than herself.

No, she told herself firmly. The vague thoughts on the matter that had been running through her head all day would have to be dismissed forever. A union between herself and Roger Trevor was impossible. She must accept it. Moreover, she must make sure he did not suspect that the idea held any appeal for her; rather than worry about hurting the feelings of some silly Yorkshire maiden, he would withdraw his friendship. And she certainly didn't want that.

"I really wouldn't fret, Roger," she said lightly. "I assure you, my father is not the slightest bit interested in this match. He's given up whatever designs he may have had on the barony of Chilton. And as for me"—she gave him her most earnest smile—"I never had any."

"So you've discussed the matter with Sir Charles?"

"When Father was here for Will's burial, the subject of my marriage came up," she admitted. "Actually, he seemed quite adamantly opposed to you—he said you had an unsavory reputation and that you were entirely unsuitable for me."

Roger grimaced. "Very sensible."

"So, as soon as my father secures a position for me, I'm to go to court and look for a husband there. I suspect he intends to dangle me before every titled nobleman between the ages of seventeen and seventy."

"You father knows a great many people. No doubt he'll arrange a splendid match for you."

"No doubt," she said glumly.

His dark eyes searched her expression. "You don't wish to marry?"

"I don't wish to be bartered in exchange for riches or property, no. Nor do I care to have my lifelong bedmate forced upon me by my father."

He raised his eyebrows. "What a radical view. Your father is likely to be a much better judge of men than you."

"Would you allow your father to choose a wife for you? You're up in arms at the very idea."

"I've had more experience in these matters."

"You mean because you've had all sorts of mistresses and I'm still a maiden? But I'm not convinced it makes a jot of difference. Some people are good judges of character, whatever their experience."

"Meaning yourself, I take it?"

"Yes, I believe so," she said, stating her main source of pride.

"And what does your excellent judgment tell you about my character?"

Alexandra pulled a wry face. "Now you're mocking me. Well, I suppose I deserve it. I don't know, Roger. You're a mystery. I can't see very far into your dark and twisted soul."

She spoke lightly, and she expected him to stop looking so serious, but instead his frown deepened. "I would advise you not to try, either," he snapped. He emptied his cup and poured more. "You'll only get hurt if you do, so kindly concentrate on someone—anyone—else."

"Now you're making it challenging."

He did not find this remark amusing. "I am in deadly earnest, Alix. You're an unusual young woman, and I'm fond of you, but I live in a world which is very different from your own, and I do not welcome intruders."

She stood up with a jerk. "What do you imagine—that I intend to follow you about the way I did when I was a child?"

"Sit down," he said in the same tone he had used to intimidate Alan. "I haven't finished with you yet."

Her skin was burning from her scalp to her neckline. "And I'm not one of your junior seamen. I shall pay no heed to your commands."

His mouth twisted in anger, and he rose abruptly and came to stand over her. She could feel the heat of his body, just inches from hers. An astonished cry escaped her as one of his hands reached out to wind itself into her thick red hair.

"Roger? Wh-what are you doing?"

He made no reply. There was an odd quaking in the depths of her stomach as he tilted her head back so she would have to meet his eyes. His pupils were dilated so much that the brown of his eyes was merely a rim around two black, heated centers.

They stared at one another in silence. It was an angry stare, a challenge—at least it began as such. Then something altered in the depths of his eyes. He made a growling sound in the back of his throat, then pulled her flush against the hard length of his body.

She knew she should pull away, and she would, of course, in just a moment. His embrace was most improper. He was holding her against him and she must make him stop. It would be highly wanton of her not to protest at all! "Roger, please!"

"It is your misfortune to have grown up to be a woman I could easily fancy, Alix," he said huskily. He took her chin between his fingers and allowed his thumb to rub rhythmically over her lower lip. She shivered and her heartbeat accelerated. *Was he serious?* "I desired you from the moment I saw you again this afternoon, all primly praying by your dead lover's tomb."

She was sure her eyes must be wide with surprise; she probably looked an utter idiot. She didn't know what to do or say. She tried to draw away, but his grip on her tightened. "Were you really innocent of him?" he demanded. His hand slipped down over her bodice, and she gasped as his clever fingers sought out the tip of one of her breasts through the simple homespun fabric. The sensation was intense—it ripped through her, causing tingles from head to toe. Her body arched against his, and as he stroked it, her nipple hardened. The tightening in her stomach escalated into a fiercely throbbing ache.

"No," she breathed, trying again to escape. *He couldn't be serious!*

"What, shy?" The anger flared again. "I wonder how long that would last, if I put my mind to exciting you. Red-haired women are by far the most passionate."

His head inclined as if to take her lips, and she could smell the wine on his breath. Of course! He was drunk—that was why he was doing this. If he hadn't been in his cups, he would never even have noticed her.

Hurt and furious, she tore herself away. "How dare you, Roger? I'm not some tavern wench to be toyed with in your drunken lechery!"

His entire body tensed, his nostrils flared, and for an instant it seemed that he might seize her and force her to respond. Not that he would have to exert himself too much, she admitted to herself, ashamed of the sensual excitement still churning in her blood.

He swallowed and visibly regained control. He looked momentarily abashed, regretful even, but his voice was harsh as he said, "Get away from me, little virgin. Go to bed before I throw you down on the rushes and prove to you that fine ladies like yourself are not as different from tavern wenches as you seem to think you are. I could take you, Alexandra, and make you cry out in pleasure under my caresses. But I'll be damned if I'll wed you."

"By the Mass, nobody asked you! You *do* have a high opinion of yourself, I see." She pushed back a loose red lock so violently that she knocked the comb he had given her out of her hair. It fell among the rushes at their feet. Absurdly, tears came into her eyes. "And you're a whoreson bastard when you're drunk."

Roger reached down to retrieve her comb, but because she was determined not to let him see her watery eyes, she turned away before he could hand it to her. "Good night," she mumbled, seizing one of the candles from the mantel-piece to light her way upstairs.

Without looking toward him again, she fled in the direction of the stairs.

"Alix, stay!" His voice sounded sober, as if he'd suddenly realized how vilely he'd behaved. But she pretended not to hear. With her candle casting long shadows on the stone walls around her, she flew up the winding staircase to her familiar chamber.

Lying facedown in the middle of the huge four-poster which took up most of the space in the small room, Alexandra reviewed the events which had just taken place. Her body was alive with a strange tension that increased as she relived the feel of Roger's thumb on her lip, his fingers on her breast. Lust, she told herself, a little dazed by the idea. She was lusting after Roger!

Dear heavens, she moaned, flinging herself over so she was stretched out on her back. She pushed herself up on her elbows and surveyed her breasts, belly, and hips as if she'd never seen them before. Tears forgotten, she smiled at her slender young woman's body, then abruptly broke into laughter. So this was what sexual passion felt like. For years she'd wondered what it would be like to yearn after a lover. She had felt stirrings, certainly; she had fallen madly in love with her share of cheeky grooms and handsome men-at-arms, but never had her passions been deliberately aroused by any member of the opposite sex. She was a gentlewoman, and betrothed to the heir of Chilton—no man would have dared to dally with her. Only Will Trevor had possessed the right to do so, and he had never touched her.

Before Will's death, Alexandra had often wondered what their intimate life would be like. She had not been drawn to him. Will had never aroused this aching in her loins. But Roger . . . *I could take you and make you cry out in pleasure under my caresses*. Her cheeks flamed at the image his words evoked. No doubt he was right!

Still, she reflected with no small degree of regret, it had been the wine speaking. He didn't really feel that way about her. How could he? As her mother was constantly reminding her, she was too tall, too slender, and not alluring enough.

In the morning he would be embarrassed. He would very likely apologize. She recalled his tone of voice at the end as he'd tried to call her back. He'd already realized that his treatment of her had been thoroughly reprehensible.

Perhaps she shouldn't have fled so precipitately. She certainly shouldn't have left his gift behind. He probably thought she'd torn it out of her hair on purpose, no longer wishing to keep a present from him. This was untrue, and she didn't want him to think her so petty and ungrateful. Perhaps she should go back down and claim it.

The sensual tension in her lower body tightened at the thought of going back down to that dark, cavernous hall where Roger Trevor lounged in front of the flickering fire. What if he touched her again? What if he took her in his arms and kissed her eager lips, running both hands over her breasts this time, and pressed her even closer, his loins moving against hers, his tongue thrusting into her mouth . . .

Dear heavens. She swallowed hard, then crossed herself, asking God to preserve her from lustful thoughts. She was going to retrieve her comb, that was all. He had called her back and she had discourteously ignored him. It was his first night home—she must apologize and give him the chance to do the same. Courtesy demanded that she put things right with him.

Without further examining her motives, she rose, straightened the skirts of her gown, and made her way back down the narrow stairs. At the bottom she heard voices coming from the hearth in the great hall. She had imagined him sitting there alone with his wine cup, wishing himself back in the Middle Sea, where he had only to contend with minor annoyances, like pirates. But instead it sounded as if he had found himself a companion.

Pausing on the threshold of the archway, Alexandra peered into the great hall. Through the gloom she could see Roger and Francis Lacklin sitting facing the fire with their backs to her. They gave no indication of having heard her quiet footsteps on the stairs.

Damnation! She didn't want to speak the lighthearted little speech she'd been preparing on the way down the stairs in front of the dour Mr. Lacklin. Well, there was no help for it. She was about to enter when she heard the mention of her own name.

"Don't underestimate Alexandra," Roger was saying. "She's not easily fooled. It certainly sounds as if you've been overdoing it, anyway . . . endless hours of boring prayers? Long sermons on spiritual grace? Jesus, Francis. I thought it was the earthly kingdom you cared about, not the bloody world to come."

Alexandra stood poised in the archway, ashamed to be eavesdropping, but too appalled to stop: Francis Lacklin really was the hypocrite she thought him. And Roger knew it.

"Make no mistake," Lacklin said tightly. "I believe in the doctrines I teach."

"I know. But when we were together last year you insisted that your aims were more political than religious. Now here you are at Chilton, leading my father down the garden path of righteousness. I'd be laughing at the lot of you if publicly embracing heresy weren't so dangerous."

Last year? But it had supposedly been ten years since they'd been together. Alexandra crept closer, keeping well in the shadows.

Roger paused to drink, still partaking freely of the wine. "I never expected to find you here, Francis. What happened, did things get too hot for you in London? Are you taking a breather up here, away from danger, away from intrigue?"

"It was wise for me to leave the city for a time, yes. But I will soon be going back."

"Whatever happened to your ingenious plot to assassinate Bloody Mary and put her sister on the throne?"

Francis Lacklin turned his head, and Alexandra leapt back out of sight, her heart pounding in her throat. She could hardly believe what she was hearing. Assassinate the queen? That was treason—much worse than her most extravagant imaginings. Francis Lacklin wasn't simply a heretic, he was part of a secret rebellion against Queen Mary.

Dear God, Roger had lied to her, lied to them all. It was apparent that Lacklin was not someone he had known slightly

ten years ago; no, they were well-acquainted, co-conspirators, it seemed, in treason.

"If you refuse to stop drinking that poison, at least keep
your voice down," Lacklin said. "You drink too much."

"I'm celebrating my homecoming."

"You're a devil when you drink. I felt like smashing your
teeth in earlier when you were going on about my skill as
a swordsman—Christ, man, have you no sense at all?"

"It bloody well serves you right for coming here in the
first place. I suppose you wanted to assure yourself of my
loyalty? What's the matter, don't you trust me to keep our
bargain?"

"I trust you," said Lacklin.

A silence. It was so quiet Alexandra was sure they must
be able to hear her breathing. But they were looking at each
other and not toward the place where she stood clutching
the cold stone wall and condemning herself as a *bona fide*
intruder into Roger Trevor's dark and twisted soul. She was
appalled at the implications of her discovery. Roger had
criticized his father for embracing treason and heresy, but
here he was up to his neck in it himself.

"And I, you," said Roger to the unbearable Mr. Lacklin.
"But I've no wish to be hanged, drawn and quartered as a
traitor. Or roasted as a heretic."

"I need you, Roger. You promised me your help."

Jesu! With what? Alexandra wondered.

"If you really expect help from me, you will leave Chilton. My position here is precarious enough without your
presence."

"Let me have some of that wine," said Lacklin, pouring
himself a cup. He stared into the fire, then said, "You may
be right. We cannot continue to play so dangerous a game
in front of your family, and besides, there is much to be
done in London to help our people escape the burnings."
He looked back at Roger. "But if I go, I expect you soon
to follow. I need you there," he repeated.

Roger said nothing.

Lacklin's voice dropped and Alexandra missed the next
several sentences. Then she heard another name—her fa-

ther's. "As you know, Sir Charles Douglas has achieved considerable power at court," Lacklin was saying. "In addition to his public office, he runs a considerable network of spies—papist spies, of course. But he is no devout Mass-goer."

Roger laughed harshly. "That's certain. He may pretend to be pious for the queen's benefit, but it doesn't extend to his private life. I saw him in a public house in London on May Day I think it was—with a wench on each arm and another bringing up the rear. His poor wife must get lonely sitting there at Westmor while Douglas makes the most of his freedom at court."

"I doubt if Douglas wastes very much time worrying about his wife," Francis Lacklin said dryly.

Her heart slamming, Alexandra slipped away from the archway. She felt sick—she couldn't listen anymore. She had cramps down deep in her belly at the thought of her father with a wench on each arm.

That's what you get for eavesdropping, she told herself miserably.

She crept back up the winding staircase, not daring to make the slightest sound lest they discover her. She had spied upon them; they had probably killed people for less. She had a brief vision of them catching her, forcing her to tell them how much she knew, then debating various lethal ways of silencing her. Nonsense, she said to herself as she reached the sanctuary of her bedchamber. Roger Trevor might be a hypocrite, a traitor, and a spy, but he would never hurt her, his oldest friend. She wasn't so sure, however, about Francis Lacklin.

She threw herself in bed, overwhelmed by a heavy exhaustion. Just before she sank into sleep, she remembered her lovely ivory-and-gold comb as she had last seen it, lightly held between the lean brown fingers of Roger Trevor's hand.

4

ONE WEEK later, Alexandra stood at the dressing table in Lady Douglas' bedchamber at Westmor trying to arrange her mother's thick silvery-gold hair. The wood-and-glass casements of the onetime monastery had been flung open to let in the light, and the fresh scent of late-summer flowers helped dispel the less pleasant odors of human habitation which were unavoidable around a large household, even one as meticulously clean as Westmor Manor. Lucy Douglas was fanatical about cleanliness, making certain that both her person and her surroundings were subjected to frequent scrubbing. She had just emerged from her daily bath, which her servants considered an oddity.

Alexandra was having difficulty with her task. Each time she secured one of the heavy locks with a hairpin, several stubborn strands would fall loose. Lucy Douglas frowned at her in the polished metal mirror.

"Sometimes you are really quite hopeless, Alexandra," she said, reaching up to assist her daughter.

"You know I'm no good at this, Mother. Where's your maid?"

"Abed with the ague, or so she claims. She's probably got herself with child again, the little slut. If it weren't so difficult to find a competent attendant, I'd be rid of her."

"I'll send mine in if you wish."

"What does she know about hair, that trollop you insisted on employing? She never touches yours, I vow. You always wear it loose or hanging down your back in braids, like a schoolgirl. Really, child, you ought to develop some sense of style."

"Unmarried maidens are supposed to wear their hair loose," said Alexandra in as neutral a tone as she could manage. She was anxious to finish. She had several errands planned for the day, and the sun was already well up.

"You are a grown woman. It's high time you added some feminine accomplishments to your arsenal of Latin, Greek, and, may the Lord bless us, violent physical exercise. Your ability to swim faster than all the village boys is not going to help you find a husband."

"I'm not looking for a husband."

"No, you've never had to look, never had to worry. With Will Trevor alive, your future was assured. But matters are different now that you must go to London seeking a husband. Your lack of skill in the courtly arts is quite appalling."

Alexandra had heard this before. She did not doubt it was true—she could knit the coarse country woolen or stitch herself an everyday gown, but she was hopeless at embroidery and needlepoint, and she couldn't have done a stately dance to save her life. She couldn't sing or play the virginals, and the only thing she knew about current court fashions was that her own gowns were years out-of-date.

"'Tis silly to learn all those things; you've told me that yourself. You wanted me to be able to read and write, Mother. It was you who first sent me to Alan's tutors. You never did a stitch of needlepoint, you said, once you were wed."

"I wanted a literate daughter, certainly; but I never intended you to make a scholar of yourself. If I hadn't been able to read, write, and cipher, we'd have been in a pretty pass with your father never home to manage things. Lord knows I've had my hands fill. That miserable bailiff couldn't add a column of figures if his neck depended upon it . . . There's a bit coming loose on the left side."

Alexandra stabbed in the last hairpin and stepped back. "That's the best I can do."

Lady Douglas turned her head from side to side, critically surveying her reflection. "It will have to do. My looks are fading, I fear." She sighed. "Not that it matters, of course. Be thankful you're not a beauty, child. Better by far a man loves you for your good sense than for your looks."

Her mother had been a famous beauty once, everybody said so. Now she rarely saw her husband, and if what Roger had said about Sir Charles Douglas was true . . . But she could not bear to think about that.

Alexandra glanced at her own reflection. She knew she was no beauty. She didn't possess the blue-gray eyes, the blond hair, or the milky white skin which the poets had declared ideal. Her forehead was too high, and the summer sun had brought out all her freckles. But her features were regular, at least: her eyes big and green, her nose straight, and her mouth generous.

Alan had told her that she had a tolerably nice smile. She grinned at herself, considering. There were herbs she could use to bleach the freckles, and plant dyes that would darken her eyebrows and thicken her lashes. Her friend Merwynna, the witch of Westmor Forest, dispensed such items all the time; next to love potions, beauty enhancers were the most sought-after mixtures the wisewoman prepared. Alexandra had learned the recipes long ago, but she'd never bothered to use them. It seemed foolish to go to all that trouble when she would never be able to do anything about her most lamentable feature, her screaming red hair.

"Your hair is still so lovely," she said, wondering why her mother insisted on pinning the golden tresses up and hiding them beneath a trim linen cap. "Why couldn't I have inherited yours, instead of Father's?"

"Fortune, my dear. At least you'll be noticed in a crowd, which might prove useful at court."

But Alexandra was beginning to wonder if she would ever get to court. At Will's burial her father had announced that he was going to find a place for her there forthwith, but there had been no word from him since. Sir Charles was not known for keeping promises to his family.

"Roger likes my hair. His tastes must be jaded from his life in the East."

"Roger this, Roger that. I'm weary of hearing about that young troublemaker. I suppose that's why you're so eager to be off this morning. You're going to Chilton to admire the fascinating Roger?"

"No. I'm going to visit Merwynna. I imagine you've heard more about Roger from servants' gossip than you have from me. I've seen very little of him."

"He's too busy antagonizing his father to have much time for you. He's already succeeded in driving that nice Francis Lacklin off the estate. He's leaving tomorrow, I understand. I do wish you would be more courteous to Mr. Lacklin, Alexandra. At poor Will's burial you were positively rude."

Alexandra, too, had heard that Lacklin had decided to return to London. She certainly wouldn't be sorry to see the last of him, but Roger's words of that disillusioning first night kept repeating themselves inside her head: *If you really expect any help from me, you will leave Chilton.*

She had told no one what she had overheard. She felt torn: for all her dislike of the policies of Queen Mary, she still found treason shocking, and Roger's casual mention of a plot to murder the queen deeply disturbing. If Francis Lacklin seriously intended such a crime, he deserved to hang. But her mind balked at the idea of hanging Roger.

In retrospect she was unable to determine exactly how deeply Roger was involved. He was not, it seemed, a heretic. He'd expressed nothing but contempt for his friend's religious beliefs. Yet he certainly seemed to have agreed to help Lacklin in some manner. What Alexandra could not fathom was *why.*

If Roger were really indifferent to politics and disenchanted with religion, why have anything to do with Lacklin? What was the attraction? Did he thrive on danger and intrigue . . . or was he the sort of man who committed treason simply for the sport of it?

One thing was certain: Roger Trevor had not dealt honestly with any of them. His years away from home had turned him into a hard and clever man, a consummate actor who used his charm to manipulate and deceive. At least, this is what she kept telling herself, for despite her knowledge, she was finding it very difficult not to like her old friend Roger.

He had returned her comb the morning after his homecoming with a note that read, "Forgive my unmannerly treatment of you last night, if you can. As you saw for yourself, I was vilely drunk. Let's not quarrel, Alix. Please accept my gift with my apologies." There was no signature, just a scrawled R. At breakfast she'd assured him she would gladly accept both, and that day and every day subsequently, he had treated her with grace and good humor.

There had been no further lustful advances. She had tried, without complete success, to put the memory of his touch out of her mind.

There was a knocking at the door just as Lucy Douglas finished adjusting her headdress. "That must be Pris," she told Alexandra. "She's here to do some needlework for me."

"I'll let her in," Alexandra said as she opened the chamber door to the young widow from one of the neighboring farms. Pris Martin had recently borne a son, who had died after only a week of life. Eight or nine months before, she had lost her husband, who had left her with a spate of unpaid debts. Pris was forced to supplement her meager income by means of her skillful needle.

Alexandra welcomed the widow kindly, but Pris responded with her usual reserve. They were close in age, but Pris had persistently rebuffed the amiable overtures Alexandra had made toward her. Alexandra had never understood why.

"'Tis good to see you, Pris," she said now. "How are you? Are things any less difficult at your farm? Have you managed to straighten out the tangle of Mr. Martin's affairs?"

"No," said Pris. She raised her eyes to Alexandra's, and something angry and resentful lingered in the depths of those cool blue eyes. "My husband's debts have not melted away, if that's what you mean."

"No, of course not—how could they?" Alexandra said quickly. She'd been tactless. She always seemed to say the wrong thing to Priscilla. She felt clumsy and awkward around her, too. Pris had soft dark hair, an elegant figure, and a quietly alluring air which never failed to attract the attention of any man she came in contact with. Alexandra felt certain she would escape her debts by marrying again.

"Forgive me if I've offended you, Pris. 'Twas not my intention, honestly."

Pris' eyes seemed to soften and for an instant she looked almost friendly; then a cloud came over her again and she acknowledged Alexandra's words with nothing more than a nod.

Alexandra turned back to her mother, who was still primping in the mirror. "May I go now, Mother?"

"Yes, but kindly don't be gone all day. You could at least return in time for the midday meal. Sit down, Priscilla. You look most fair, as usual; my daughter would benefit if she paid attention to the way you move, dress, and speak. Alexandra . . ."

Alexandra had nearly escaped. She reluctantly turned and looked back.

"I've just remembered: see that you discourage your outlandish friends from loitering around the kitchens. That half-wit boy from the forest has been coming around and bothering the cooks."

"Ned, you mean? Coming here?"

"Looking for you, I presume, while you're out gallivanting around. He frightens the servants. If I see him here again, I'll have him whipped."

"Oh, Mother, have some pity. He's a poor outcast whom everybody hates and fears, but he's not dangerous."

"Isn't he indeed? I wonder." Her mother reached into a cupboard and pulled out something. "Look what I took away from him yesterday . . . look at this and tell me he's not dangerous."

It was a dagger. Her mother held it with some distaste on the flat of her hand. It was small, a narrow-bladed bodkin with a carved handle. Part of the blade was chipped out near the hilt, as if somebody had taken a bite out of it.

"'Tis yours, I suppose? I gathered that the agitated young fool was trying to return it to you. Really, daughter, I'm astonished that you could let such an object come into the hands of that madman. Have you no sense at all? God only knows what he might have done with it had I not taken it away."

Alexandra took the dagger from her mother and turned it over curiously. It looked vaguely familiar. She tried to recall where she had seen something similar. " 'Tisn't mine. What made you think he wanted to give it to me?"

"Not yours? Well, really, I shudder to think . . . a big strong fellow like that with half his wits and Lord knows what unrestrained lusts and murderous intents, and you going blithely around, alone in the forest, never even taking a groom—"

"Did he ask for me specifically?" Alexandra interrupted. Her mother had no true fear of Ned, she knew. Lady Douglas was exaggerating as a means of expatiating on one of her favorite themes: the worthlessness and unreliability of all the members of the male sex.

"How could he—he can't even speak. Oh, he signaled some sort of nonsense. He seemed frightened—Lord knows why. I assumed he was looking for you. I told him I would give you the knife, which was the only way I could rid the kitchens of him. Even after I threatened to whip him, he continued lurking about. As I say, it wasn't the first time." She glanced at Pris Martin, who was listening to this exchange with an inscrutable expression on her exquisite face. "I'm certain *you* don't associate with such riffraff, Pris."

Alexandra ignored the implicit comparison. "How long has this been going on?"

"For a week or so—off and on since your famous Roger returned. Very furtive he is, too, this Ned, appearing and disappearing like a demon."

Alexandra remembered the fear Ned had exhibited in front of Roger near the ditch where Will had fallen. She stared at the dagger. The blade was dull and rusty, but the carving on the handle was very intricate. "Mother, if he comes again today, will you ask him to wait for me? I'll be back by noon, I promise."

"I would prefer that you had nothing further to do with a knife-wielding half-wit," Lady Douglas insisted, but when Alexandra gave her a pleading look, she relented. "Oh, very

well. Though why you make friends with these waifs and
ne'er-do-wells, I'll never understand."

Alexandra stuck the dagger into her girdle and thanked
her mother. Lucy Douglas could be a difficult woman at
times, but Alexandra knew full well that although her tongue
was sharp, there was very little she would not do for her
only child.

Ten minutes later Alexandra was outside, walking briskly
along the flower-lined path that led through the hedgerows
to the freedom of the moors. She had a pack slung over one
shoulder filled with warm bread, fruit, meat pies, and home-
brewed ale—her weekly offering for the ancient wisewoman, Merwynna. It was a cool day, with a breeze rolling
through the heather. The sky was so intensely blue it hurt
her eyes to look at it.

As she slipped through the hedges, she glanced back at
the rectangular buildings that comprised her family home.
Westmor was very different in appearance from the imposing, if crumbling Chilton Hall. A former abbey, it stood in
a grassy valley, and the construction was more modern than
Chilton. The grounds were replete with gardens, once tended
by the monks who had lived there prior to Henry VIII's
deconsecration of the abbey.

Shutting the gate carefully behind her, Alexandra struck
out through the knee-deep moor grasses toward the forest.
The smell of the heather delighted her. She let out a spon-
taneous laugh and pulled her skirts halfway up her legs so
she could feel the sensuous brush of wildflowers against her
bare skin.

She tramped over several hills before coming back to the
track that led into the woods. As the path dipped down into
the trees, the blue sky vanished, completely obscured by
the ancient forest's ceiling of green. Unlike some wood-
lands, Westmor Forest did not begin gradually with a few
scrubby trees; as soon as she crossed its boundaries, she
entered a different world, a land of darkness, secrets, power.
The paths were few and twisted, as if the forest tried to
obliterate them as quickly as they were laid down. Branches

caught at her clothes and long fingers of green brushed at her face.

Few people knew Westmor Forest as well as Alexandra. From childhood she had explored its farthest reaches, aided by an excellent sense of direction and an almost mystical reverence for its gnarled old trees. She felt at peace here, and she believed that the forest knew her and accepted her as one of its own.

After a lengthy trek, she entered an ancient grove of oaks whose trunks were thicker than Alexandra was tall. Beneath their boughs, the air was cool, even chilly. Although the trees were well separated, their leaves were so concentrated that no single ray of sunshine could penetrate to the acorn-scattered ground.

Sometimes Alexandra would sit down on the moss floor to rest and dream, but today she did not intend to linger. She was walking rapidly, singing a merry ballad, and enjoying the vigorous exercise of her hike, when a movement ahead in the gloom caught her attention. A lull in the breeze enabled her to hear the sharp metallic clash of steel striking steel. For a moment she could not identify a sound which was so foreign to the place. Curious, she walked toward the shadows circling one another beneath the vaulting branches. Two men were doing battle there. Each was wielding a sword.

For a second Alexandra thought they must be apparitions playing out some ancient feud. Two men dueling in Westmor Forest? In the heart of the woodland, not far from Merwynna's cottage? It was outrageous. She advanced upon them as if she were a defender of the place.

In the next moment she realized who they were and what they were doing. She stopped, but it was too late: this time they had seen her. She visualized the gloomy hall, the low fire, the voices she had not wanted to hear, although she had listened. She seemed doomed to intrude upon them, whether she liked it or not.

They put up their weapons and Roger waved. There was nothing to do but go on.

"Good day to you," she said brightly when she reached

them. "Don't stop. How often do I get the chance to see two masters fencing? Who's winning?"

Roger and Francis Lacklin exchanged a look. They were both stripped to trunks and hose—naked to the waist—and they were sweating. Each held a slim practice foil, and a supply of blunted rapiers stood leaning against the trunk of the nearest tree. The rest of their things—clothes, a couple of knapsacks, and a flagon of wine—were also piled there beneath the tree.

"He is," Roger answered with a nod at his companion. His hair was plastered down across his forehead; with one hand he reached up and pushed it aside. There were beads of sweat on his throat, too, and on his wide bare chest. Alexandra stared at them, fascinated, while his glance took in the pack on her arm. "What are you doing here? Are you on an errand of mercy to some woodland cot?"

Alexandra looked into his eyes in a futile attempt to take her mind off his smooth, sun-browned skin covered with its mat of silky dark hair. "I'm going to visit Merwynna."

"Merwynna? You mean that old wisewoman, the witch? God's blood, is she still alive? She must be eighty."

Roger had been friendly with Merwynna too, she remembered. Until the day he had gone to Merwynna and demanded that she put a spell on his father, who had beaten him bloody for some childish prank. Merwynna had bound up his wounds but refused him the spell, which angered Roger. He'd insisted afterward that she was no true witch at all.

"She's old, but as spry as ever. I see her often. My way lies through this grove. What are you doing here?"

She asked this even though she already knew the answer. Francis Lacklin was leaving Chilton tomorrow. He and Roger must have wanted to be alone to discuss their treasonous plans.

She expected Roger's glib tongue to answer her, but it was Lacklin who said, more to Roger than to her, "He's been after me for days to prove I could still cut him to ribbons, so I'm finally obliging, even though I'm out of practice, while he's fresh from fighting Saracens in the Middle Sea—"

"Cut me to ribbons! Ha! I felt but one hit, and that only just barely palpable. Come on, Francis, you pompous black-guard, don't think I'm about to let you catch your bloody breath because of Alexandra. Defend yourself!"

She felt a rush of excitement. They were going to continue, in spite of her. And she knew instinctively that it would be a match the like of which she had never seen before.

Lacklin gave her a rare smile and took up his position opposite Roger. "Very well, my reckless friend, I'll give you a lesson or two. And Alexandra too if she pays attention."

She sank down to the forest floor to watch. "I won't miss a moment of this, I promise you."

But in fact she did miss some of it because it went too fast for the eye to see. They fenced in an unfamiliar manner—some European style, no doubt. Instead of using a long sword to attack and a dagger in the other hand to defend, they fought only with the slim and flexible rapier, attacking and defending in an intricate series of beats, feints, and parries.

They were both excellent swordsmen. Being younger, Roger had an edge in physical conditioning and speed, but Lacklin made up for this with the sheer brilliance of his technique. Every movement he made was fluid and precise, every flick of his wrist and arc of his arm as smooth and controlled as a dance. His blade wove silver threads in the air, perfectly, effortlessly. Roger attacked with great energy, but clever though his offensive moves were, he had difficulty penetrating his old friend's guard.

Smiling abstractedly, Lacklin played Roger until the younger man began to tire, then picked up the tempo and attacked more vigorously. Roger parried, faltered, and was hit, the blunted tip of his adversary's weapon touching him lightly on the left shoulder. He yelled in frustration and fought harder. Francis Lacklin laughed, sending Roger into full retreat, pressing him until he stumbled and missed a crucial riposte. Lacklin moved in mercilessly, and within seconds he had cut Roger to ribbons as much as it was possible to do with a blunted foil. Moaning with mock despair, Roger threw down his sword, and then his body, collapsing on his back next to Alexandra, breathing hard, running with sweat.

"You're dead," she laughed. Her excitement in the match faded as her consciousness of his nearness increased. She caught the faint masculine scent of tangy exertion and was surprised that it was so pleasant, attracting, compelling. She envisioned him touching her breasts before the hearth at Chilton, blowing against her lips, kissing them. Jesu! Every hard breath he drew sent tingles through her.

"Aye," he acknowledged when he recovered his breath. "God's blood, Francis, remind me never to have a falling-out with you."

"You did very well," said Lacklin, sitting down on the other side of Alexandra.

"A lot of good it does me—I'm still dead!"

"This time, yes. One of these days it could go the other way. You're edgy about your parries in *quarte*, aren't you?"

"Aye," said Roger, rubbing several places on the left upper quadrant of his body where the blunt tip had struck him. "That's where you penetrated. I always feel vulnerable in that area. I was concentrating on parrying effectively."

"Obviously so. You let me see your weakness, so when you got tired . . ."

"Devil. Exploiting my weaknesses." He rolled over onto his side and leaned up on one elbow. "I said he was good, didn't I, Alix?"

"You said he was the finest you'd ever seen." She was looking at Francis Lacklin with more respect than she'd ever felt for him before. "It was marvelous! I loved it. Thank you for allowing me to watch."

Her enthusiasm must have been catching, for the two men treated her with great good humor as they continued to analyze the bout. Their rapiers were Italian, she learned, and their style of fencing very innovative. In battle, said Roger, he'd prefer to have a heavy broadsword and a long-handled dagger.

"What's in here?" he demanded, pouncing on her knapsack and rolling open the canvas which covered the food-stuffs for Merwynna. "Christ Almighty, this is enough to last a month. Alix, love, I'm starving." He plucked out an apple and bit into it.

"So am I," said Lacklin, helping himself to a pear.

"Merwynna only grows herbs. She depends on me for other things," Alexandra protested. But her knapsack was full today, so she too took a piece of fruit.

"Who is this Merwynna anyway?" asked Lacklin. "I've heard of her, but I don't know much about her."

"She's the local witch," said Roger with his mouth full. "I'm amazed you haven't tried to exorcise her, or whatever one does to witches."

"She's not that sort of witch," Alexandra objected. "She doesn't consort with the devil. Her gods are the Old Ones, the spirits of trees and rocks and hollow places. They're the ones she prays to, they're the ones who assist her in her magic."

Both men stared at her. "Christ, Francis, listen to her. You're worried about the corrupt practices of the papists, but at least they're Christians. This girl is a bloody pagan."

She laughed. "I'm not."

But Roger was serious. "Whatever gods the old woman worships, people are certain to think she's in league with Satan. Power such as hers is considered evil."

"Nonsense. There's nothing evil about Merwynna—she cures the sick and practices midwifery—women's arts, in other words. She rarely casts spells. I know, I've been her protégée for years."

Roger cursed softly. "You're Sir Charles Douglas' daughter; you can't be the next witch of Westmor Forest. Are you mad to mix in such doings?"

She bristled. "There's no danger, no harm at all in what I do. She's my friend."

His handsome face was thunderous. "You fool, Alexandra! I don't believe what I'm hearing. What d'you mean, no harm? Witchcraft is a crime punishable by hanging. Do you want to end your life on the scaffold?"

Her own temper flared. "Who are you to be so judgmental? You're in more danger of ending your life on the scaffold than I!"

Silence greeted this remark. She thought she saw them

exchange a lightning-fast look. Twisting her fingers together, she stared down into her lap. Now I've made them suspicious, she thought nervously. When, oh when, am I ever going to learn to control my too-ready tongue?

"What else have you got to eat in there?" Lacklin asked, pointing to her knapsack. She risked a glance at him. He was, as usual, cool and unruffled. Was there anything, she wondered, that could ever shake his self-possession? Just as no one would ever be able to penetrate his guard in a fencing bout, no one would ever understand the mind or heart of him either.

"Here, take whatever you want."

Lacklin removed a chunk of cheese, saying, "May I share some of this with you?"

"No, thank you. I'm not hungry." She no longer felt easy with either of them. Lacklin was dour and cold, and as for Roger, he was damnably moody. One minute he could be the pleasantest man she had never known, and the next he was an angry, opinionated bully. He had been like that as a boy, too: she suddenly remembered how often they'd argued with each other. She'd adored him, it was true, but she hadn't cared for the way he used to order her about, even then.

She glared at him, but he was looking at the ground, his eyebrows drawn together in concentration or annoyance.

Francis Lacklin said, "Here, Roger, have some cheese. And stop worrying. No doubt Alexandra knows what she's doing."

Roger looked up and Alexandra felt the power of his dynamic brown-eyed stare. His eyes were beautiful. They drew her, lured her, bewitched her. Gazing into them, she felt something leap inside her . . . and once again she was burning with the memory of the way he had touched her on his first night home. Her muscles tightened and her heartbeats thickened as she yearned to feel that delicious touch again.

"Give me a piece," Roger said to Lacklin, not dropping Alexandra's gaze. He spoke her name: "Alix. You're my oldest, dearest friend. It frightens me to think of you tangling with such a crime as witchcraft. I want you to be careful, that's all."

Her color rose. He was smiling at her. She loved his smile. It made him look younger, almost boyish. "I'm always careful, Roger."

They stared at one another until Francis Lacklin cleared his throat rather loudly. "Got a knife? This cheese is like a rock."

"Try one of the foils."

"I've got one," Alexandra offered, pulling out her dagger from her girdle. "Here." She handed it to him without paying attention to what she was doing. She had focused on Roger's lean and tough body, bare to the waist . . . the subtle play of muscles beneath the skin, the dark wires of chest hair that she longed to stroke . . . the scars of other weapons which had snaked inside his guard. She drew an uneven breath, dropping her eyes to his long-fingered hands playing idly with the forest moss. She was his oldest, dearest friend. He was domineering and quick to anger, but he cared about her. She closed her eyes. He's a traitor, she warned herself. He might even be a regicide.

Francis Lacklin was futilely sawing at the hard mound of cheese. "Your blade is dull," he observed, looking down at the rusty old dagger in the palm of his hand. "Where do you keep it, in a puddle?"

As she realized her mistake, Alexandra's fingers flew to the leather girdle at her waist, where her own dagger still lay cradled. It was Ned's chipped and rusty knife she had given him.

She shot a quick look at Lacklin's face, but it was, as usual, impassive. She didn't know where Ned had found it, or what the dagger represented, but her mother's tale of the peasant boy's urgency had alarmed her. "Forgive me, I gave you the wrong one. That old thing probably wouldn't slice butter."

"Let's see," said Roger. Before she could grab it, he reached across her and took the knife from Lacklin's hand. "This isn't yours, is it, Alix?" He was turning it over and staring at the carving. "Where did you find it?"

"Ned gave it to me. You remember him—the half-witted boy whose throat you threatened to cut on your first day home."

Roger looked up, saw her watching him, and frowned. He glanced at Lacklin, who seemed to be ignoring them both. Then his expression turned deliberately bland. He handed the dagger back to her. "Worthless piece of metal."

Alexandra felt a ripple of unease. She sensed that the dagger held some significance for Roger. She recalled that Ned had been frightened of Roger—terrified, in fact.

"Who's Ned?" Francis Lacklin asked.

"Just a harmless peasant boy." She thrust the knife back into her girdle. "Here," she said, giving Lacklin her other one. "I understand you're leaving tomorrow, Mr. Lacklin?" She was eager to change the subject. "Where are you going?"

Lacklin tossed Roger a piece of cheese before answering, but his cold gray eyes were on her. "London. I have friends there."

In sooth, you do, thought Alexandra. Treacherous friends.

"I might be going to London myself shortly," Roger announced.

"Why? You've only just come back."

"He can't abide his father."

"That, yes," Roger confirmed. "But I also thought I'd taste the pleasures of the English court, if there are any to be had among that bunch of Mass-mouthing papists."

If he was going to London, he would be mixing in Lacklin's nefarious doings, of that she had no doubt. "What about your responsibilities here?"

"What about them?" Roger said coldly. "My father hates me; we do nothing but argue, and even Alan's hero worship is wearing thin, just as I knew it would. Once the hero is revealed to be an ordinary human being, the worshiper invariably turns on him."

"Alan's turning on you? After only one week?"

"Come over and see for yourself. It's my own fault, of course. I'm impatient and bad-tempered, not to mention bored. I'm accustomed to more activity."

"It's a comedown after playing sealord of the Mediterranean," said Lacklin sarcastically.

"Well, it is. I'm willing to concede that. My father still rules Chilton, and I have never been good at adopting a subordinate role."

"You'll be under the queen's authority if you go to court. You'll have to simper and fawn and play the hypocrite, going to Mass twice a day whether you like it or not." She paused, fiddling with an acorn cap. "Unless of course you opt for danger, excitement, and freedom of conscience by joining the heretics."

"Thank you," said Lacklin. "I couldn't have put it any better myself. Appeal to his spirit of adventure."

"I'd rather simper and fawn than have anything to do with a pack of raving dissenters. No, Alix. I have no intention of seeing anything of Francis and his fanatical friends in London."

He spoke it very slowly and clearly, as if he wanted to be absolutely certain that she put any such idea out of her mind.

"You might be seeing something of me. As I told you, my father intends to drag me to London to marry me off."

A silence; then Roger said silkily, "Not to me, I trust."

Alexandra rose, collecting her knapsack and her knife. "We've already established that." She gnawed on her bottom lip a moment, then added, "I'll probably be over at Chilton this afternoon." She was determined not to take them by surprise again. "Alan and I plan to study some Greek."

Roger's eyebrows went up. "Greek, is it? Excellent Alexandra, you are indeed a woman of many talents."

She was tempted to stick out her tongue at him, but she rejected the gesture as too childish. The idea of doing so, however, made her smile. "Till later, then."

"Till later, poppy-top," said Roger, employing one of his oldest nicknames for her. It almost made her believe he'd read her mind.

5

ALEXANDRA fingered the dull blade of Ned's dagger as she hiked on toward Merwynna's cottage. She wished she knew why Ned had wanted her to have the rusty old knife. She would swear that Roger and Francis Lacklin had treated her differently after seeing it. Damnation. She cursed herself for a fool. She shouldn't have shown it to them.

If she hadn't had her attention on Roger Trevor's body, she lectured herself, she wouldn't have been so careless. But lecturing herself did no good at all . . . once again she forgot about the dagger as her mind began conjuring up a few special images: Roger's merrily-arching eyebrows, his furry, naked chest, the flash of his smile, the look in his brown eyes when he'd called her his "oldest, dearest friend."

Warming to the theme, her imagination pictured him passing his hands through her hair (*red hair is very rare and much prized in the Middle Sea*), then pulling her close against his sun-browned body and kissing her violently. His fingers would wander a little, gently along her collarbone, softly upon her breasts, seeking out those tender, wayward nipples once again. She would protest as he jerked apart her laces, even though, in sooth, she didn't want him to stop. And he wouldn't stop—he would be too enflamed to listen to her half-hearted pleas for restraint. He would stroke her naked breasts, then slide his hands lower . . . he would

smooth away her skirts, then strip his own virile body bare
... he would press her back in the sweet-smelling grass and
come down atop her, against her, between her naked thighs
... seeking her, finding her, making hot, sweet love to her
until all the stars exploded with light and fell from their
spheres.

She pushed a branch aside so carelessly that it came back
and slapped her in the face. Cursing in an unmaidenly fashion, she muttered, "The devil take Roger Trevor." He cared
about her, yes, but not in the way she'd just envisioned,
despite what had happened between them on his first night
back. He'd had too much to drink that evening.

Stop thinking about it! Even if Roger did feel a lusting
for her again, he'd made his feelings about honorable wedlock very clear. He would never wed her. If she were so
foolish as to develop a passion for him, she would deserve
the heartache which could be its only possible outcome.

The path to Merwynna's wound around a small hidden
lake. One minute all was dark and green; then the woods
opened up like a mouth to reveal the lake's silent waters.
As always, the sight swept Alexandra clean of thoughts and
passions. Her sense of the forest's power was particularly
strong here. Standing on the flower-laden bank, she watched
a crow wheel over the water, then rise and disappear. She
shivered, hoping the dark bird was not an ill omen.

Sometimes, if the weather was hot and she was feeling
adventuresome, Alexandra would swim the lake rather than
go round on foot, but today she did not attempt it. The
ancient wooden boat, kept by Merwynna for emergencies,
was tied up on the far side. It was rarely used. Alexandra
jested with her that like all witches, Merwynna did not care
to cross over water.

She was so heated by the time she reached the thatched
cottage that she wished she'd swum across after all. She
knocked on the oaken door, but received no answer. Leaving
her sack of provisions inside, she went around the back and
found Merwynna bent over in her herb garden, gathering
herbs for her healing brews. The old woman turned at the
sound of Alexandra's approach, her vivid dark eyes ac-

knowledging the girl, but she did not speak. Talking would break the age-old charm.

Silently Alexandra removed her shoes and stepped into the garden to help. Merwynna had taught her to go barefoot as a sign of respect for the earth. Some said it was even more efficacious to remove all clothes and gather the herbs skyclad, but Merwynna wore her usual gown of brown homespun. The dress was a mystery to Alexandra—she had never seen the wisewoman wash or mend it, yet it always looked clean and new.

She knelt beside her friend in the rich earth and gathered herbs carefully in her left hand, transferring them afterward to her right while she continued to pluck. Each herb had to be addressed with an old rhyme, some of these in languages so ancient that Alexandra could only mouth the sounds, having no idea of their meaning. After she plucked each herb, she poured a libation of mead from Merwynna's jug into the earth from which the plant had sprung.

Merwynna collected many of her herbs, barks, and roots from the wilds of the forest, but here in the neatly laid-out garden she cultivated the plants that she used most often. There was yarrow, the blood-stancher for wounds, and the bitter-smelling wormwood, which brings down fevers and keeps the demons away. There was the tall valerian, also bad-smelling, but an excellent cure for insomnia and nervousness. The scrubby thyme, good for preventing infection, grew in the front, where it could garner plenty of sun, near the square-stemmed vervain, a necessary ingredient in Merwynna's much-in-demand love potions.

She also grew mullein, St. John's wort, tanzy, chamomile, cinquefoil, and fennel, all important remedies for various ills; and, in one corner apart from the others, the powerful narcotic poisons: henbane, wolfbane, hellebore, and deadly nightshade. The uses of these plants were unclear to Alexandra and she was not permitted to touch them. Even in small quantities, their distillate could kill, although there were many nonlethal uses for them. "Ye're an apt pupil, but never can ye be an initiate," Merwynna had told her when refusing to explain the rites that depended upon these plants. "Such knowledge is not for ye."

When the herbs were gathered, Alexandra and Merwynna carried them into the cottage to sort them. Some would be mixed into brews, others dried and stored for the winter. Now that the ritual picking was over, they could talk, so Alexandra launched into her story about Ned's dagger, and her meeting with Roger and Francis Lacklin.

Merwynna knew Ned. He was the only other person who made his home in Westmor Forest, although not even she was certain exactly where he lived. "I havna' seen the lad for several days," she informed Alexandra. "The last time we met there was a shadow round about him," she added ominously.

"A shadow? What does that signify?"

Merwynna's gnarled fingers made the sign against evil. "I offered him an amulet to wear about his neck. 'Twould ha' warded off the dark powers, but he didna' seem to understand. He fled, the fool."

"Ned's usually not so timorous. He acted oddly that day when Roger caught him lurking near the road. Even after Roger put his sword away, Ned was still afraid." She looked into Merwynna's black pool eyes. Her friend had an angular face, with a bony nose and narrow lips; her skin was dry and thin as parchment. Her braided hair had long been white, but her eyebrows remained dark and bushy, giving her face an undeniable forcefulness. "Is there any reason why Ned should fear Roger, Merwynna?"

"Bring Roger to visit me and I shall tell ye."

"But surely you remember him?"

"I remember the lad he used to be, but I know not what path he's followed since he left his home. Deeply troubled, he was, growing up torn betwixt two warring parents. He is Scorpio; ye must beware the men of his birth sign."

"He and I ought to be compatible, then. I am Pisces."

Merwynna gave her a sharp-eyed look. "Do ye burn for him?"

Sometimes it could be unnerving, knowing a witch. "It scarcely matters, since he doesn't burn for me."

Merwynna shrugged. "There are ways."

Perhaps there were, but Alexandra didn't think she wanted to bewitch Roger Trevor, or any other man. It would be dishonest, and besides, what would happen if the spell wore off?

"He draws me," she admitted. "But I don't trust him, or understand him. I like to be able to understand people. I like things to make sense."

Merwynna nodded slowly. "Ye strive with yer mind, with yer intellect, analyzing the world and all the people in it. Ye come to me, ye go to the farms to talk with peasants, ye read all those ancient historians and poets, filling yer brain with knowledge."

Believing she was being praised, Alexandra quickly said, "I also waste a good deal of time dreaming."

"Ye waste all yer time," Merwynna said sharply. "No soul may know the hearts of people nor the mysteries of the gods by means of reason. Ye're proud, my daughter. Ye shall suffer for it."

Alexandra was stung by this criticism. "I don't put all my trust in reason," she objected. "I wouldn't be here with you if I did, would I? I have faith in God and in the powers that dwell here in the forest. I've no desire to unravel divine mysteries. I simply wish to solve the human ones around me."

Merwynna simply frowned and repeated, "Ye are proud."

Alexandra sighed. Merwynna was always urging her to rely more upon her intuition. She gathered up the last bunch of herbs and tied them into a bundle while Merwynna swept the table clear. "Forgive me my pride, then, and use your magic to help me solve this mystery." She brought out Ned's dagger and placed it in the center of the table. "Reason certainly hasn't told me much about it so far. I want to know where it came from, whom it belongs to, and why it is important to Ned, and . . . I think, to Roger."

Merwynna looked long into Alexandra's eyes before nodding in agreement. She passed her hand over the blade and repeated a charm in an ancient tongue. Then she lifted the dagger and held it high over her head on the flat of her hands.

Alexandra watched nervously. She did not often ask Merwynna to perform her magic—the part of her that wanted the world to make sense did not know how to deal with

Merwynna's strange powers. There were moments when her old friend frightened her profoundly.

For several minutes there was silence. At last the wise-woman opened her eyes. "I receive nothing. The Goddess is not with me today."

"Nothing at all?"

"I am sorry, child."

Alexandra tried to hide her disappointment. Was it possible that the dagger simply had no tale to tell?

As she reached for it to put it away, Merwynna took her hand and turned it palm-up on the table. "What are you doing?" Alexandra asked. "You never look into my hand."

When her friend didn't reply, an irresistible desire to know her future seized Alexandra. "What am I fated for?" she asked. A question came into her mind, the same one the village girls so frequently asked. "Will I ever marry, Merwynna? When Will was alive, my future was certain, but now I have no idea what to expect."

Merwynna abruptly dropped her hand. "It is not wise to know yer destiny."

"You prophesy for others. Come, what's the use of knowing a witch if she never tells my fortune? Be frank with me, please... will a beautiful stranger love me to distraction?"

Merwynna did not smile. "Ye are dear to me," she said slowly. "'Tis not given to me to see the futures of those who are my friends. 'Tis the Goddess's protection against despair."

"I cannot imagine there could be much to despair over in my future. I'm only asking about love; that's not so serious. Come, you must be able to see something. Try."

Merwynna was silent for so long that Alexandra's nerves began to crawl. Was there some dreadful reason why her friend would not tell her fortune? Was there a shadow round about her as well? She wasn't certain whether to be glad or frightened when Merwynna finally nodded. "Very well, I shall attempt it. But, as I say, the power doesna' seem to be flowing through me today."

She took Alexandra's hands in hers, looking first into the

left, then concentrating on the right palm. She ran her fingertips over the fleshy mounts beneath the roots of the fingers, then traced the lines. "Yer hand is strong. Good deep lines. I see loyalty here, and unswerving love for yer friends. Yer mind and passions are both powerful; at times they will pull ye in opposite directions. At times ye shall not know which to trust. Ye must learn to follow yer heart. Lovers? I see four: one who cannot, one who will not, one who dares not, one who dies."

The last sentence was uttered in a voice much deeper than Merwynna's natural one. Alexandra looked up, startled. The witch's eyes had turned up in their sockets, and she was sinking into a trance. This happened when she was communing with her strange gods—Alexandra had seen it several times before. The powers were present, after all.

Merwynna's eyes flew open, and someone—or something—stared directly into Alexandra's soul. She shuddered. It was not Merwynna looking at her like that. It was a stranger.

"Snakes," said a hoarse voice. "Snakes around his neck."

"What?" Alexandra whispered. Her heartbeats were echoing in her ears and her hands were trembling. "What do you mean?"

"Beware," the Voice said loudly. It was hollow and uninflected, with no discernible accent. "Water is your element. Trust the water, beware the fire, embrace the earth, but let it go." There was a slight pause; then the Voice hissed. "Her brother. Beware her brother. . . ." Suddenly Merwynna's body jerked spasmodically.

"Whose brother?" She wondered if the Voice were truly addressing her. Perhaps it thought she was someone else.

The ensuing silence lasted for such a long time that she thought the prophecy was over. She was about to reach out and shake Merwynna, who sat as if frozen solid, when a single word issued from the wisewoman's mouth. "Celestine," it said, quite clearly. Merwynna drew a long breath; then more words rushed out, harshly: "You have two enemies. I see blood and steel. I see dark water and death."

"You just told me to trust the water," Alexandra objected.

"Trust the water," the Voice agreed. "Look in the cave," it added.

There was a sharp, withdrawing hiss, then Merwynna crumpled in her chair.

"Christ have mercy," Alexandra whispered, crossing herself. Jumping up, she ran around the table and put her arms around the small thin woman, massaging the old bones, the stringy muscles. "Merwynna? Please, Merwynna, are you all right?"

The wisewoman lifted her head. Alexandra pulled her to her feet and helped her over to one of the straw pallets which were always kept ready for the weary or the ill. Gently she rubbed Merwynna's temples. Her friend's eyes slowly returned to normal, but they looked away from Alexandra. Sounding extremely weak, she asked, "What did he say?"

Alexandra repeated the words of the prophecy. "But what does it mean?" she demanded. "It doesn't make the least sense. 'One who cannot, one who will not . . .' It certainly doesn't sound as if I'm to have much luck with lovers. 'Beware her brother'? Whose brother, Celestine's? Who the devil is she? And who are my two enemies?" She sighed, exasperated. "Merwynna, I don't understand."

"The Voice often speaks thus. The future will make all things plain."

Alexandra thought of the various oracles she'd read about, and complained, "Why can't the Voice speak in ordinary language? He's playing games with me deliberately, because he knows I have no liking for mysteries."

The eeriness had lifted and her usual aplomb was returning, although a faint unease remained. She smiled bravely at Merwynna, who had sat up, her back firm and straight once more. "You haven't told me whether or not I shall every marry."

The wisewoman disdained to look into the palm which Alexandra bravely held out again. "Ye shall marry," she said, gazing out through the cottage's small front window into the depths of the black lake. "But ye shall not come a maiden to yer bridal bed."

More than that Merwynna would not say.

6

IN THE AFTERNOON of the same day, Alexandra met Alan in the old schoolroom at Chilton to resume their study of Greek. She had seen little of her friend for several days, and she thought he looked dispirited, hunched over a book, leaning his head on the heel of one hand. Nor did he brighten up when he saw her.

"Well, finally. I thought you weren't coming," he said testily.

"I didn't think I was late."

"It's your turn to translate," he said, giving her the book.

Alexandra had prepared the passage, but her mind kept wandering to Roger, Francis Lacklin, Merwynna, and Ned. On arriving back at Westmor at noon, she had gone directly to the kitchens to inquire after Ned, but he hadn't turned up today. "Perhaps he finally believed me when I swore to have him whipped," said Lady Douglas with obvious satisfaction. Alexandra had left instructions with the servants that she was to be summoned immediately, should the boy appear.

And then there was Merwynna's disquieting prophecy. Alexandra would have been delighted with the prospect of not one, but four lovers, but really: "one who cannot, one who will not, one who dares not, one who dies"! She wondered how she could possibly end up deprived of her virtue before her wedding night with four lovers of so little promise.

She'd been translating for five minutes, making numerous mistakes, when Alan interrupted her. "I don't know where your attention is, but it's certainly not on Euripides."

She pushed the book to him. "You do it."

"What's amiss with you?"

She was sorely tempted to tell him about Ned's mysterious little dagger, but decided that too many people knew about it already, through her own carelessness. Glancing up, she saw that Alan was staring curiously at her. She would have to tell him something. "I cannot focus my mind on this. I must be out of practice. We shouldn't have taken such a long break from our studies, just because Roger was home."

"We've been wasting our time this past week," Alan agreed.

Again she noticed his drawn face. "Why do you say that? Are you having some kind of trouble with Roger?"

"How did you guess?" said Alan glumly. "He seems to be deliberately trying to make enemies of everyone. I'd forgotten how he always used to bully me."

"Perhaps if you stood up to him a little more—"

"I have been. Last night, in fact, we nearly had a fight."

Alexandra cast an anxious eye over his face, his body. "He didn't hurt you, did he?"

Alan smiled ruefully. "You don't ask if I hurt him."

"I don't care if you hurt him, as long as you're all right," she said loyally.

"Well, nobody got hurt. I wanted to strike him, but I didn't have the courage. I was afraid he'd beat the wits out of me. I'm such a coward," he added bitterly.

"No, you're not. You're canny, that's all. Roger's an experienced warrior—'twould be folly to take him on." She paused a moment then added, "What happened, exactly?"

Alan's lips tightened ominously. "I'm only repeating this because you might have to protect yourself. He's not to be trusted, Alix."

She waited. Alan's expression was a curious mix of embarrassment and anger. "He insulted you. In sooth, he's lusting after you, Alix, now that you're a woman grown. He's damned if he'll ever wed you, but he'd be pleased, he says, to have you in his bed."

Alexandra's senses leapt. She remembered that night in the firelight at Chilton, and this morn, in the forest. . . .

"He thinks he can take you, too, without much resistance on your part. Red hair indicates a passionate nature, he says, and he's already had a taste of it with you. That was when I jumped up to hit him, the bloody-minded liar! If I weren't such a coward, I'd have done it."

For once Alexandra was speechless. He'd "had a taste of it"? She felt the color washing through her face and neck.

"So you see, I had to warn you. He's going to try to seduce you. He doesn't care about your honor. He's only interested in appeasing his lusts. And he once studied to be a priest!"

Here Alexandra's sense of the absurd came to the rescue. She drew a deep breath, grinned, then laughed delightedly. "Oh, Alan, why do you suppose the Church is so besieged with reformers? It's full of lecherous priests!"

"It's not funny." Alan glared, obviously miffed at her reaction.

"Oh, Alan, I appreciate your defending me. Truly. But I doubt that Roger meant a word of it. He was teasing you."

"'Tis not a subject for teasing. He's a whoreson bastard, Alix!"

Something in Alan's tone caught her attention. She tried to see his expression, but he was staring down at his hands. "One who dares not"? No, surely Alan could not be one of the ones Merwynna's prophecy included. They were like brother and sister.

"Thank you for taking my part so faithfully."

"I don't think you ought to be alone with him, Alix."

"I hardly ever am, but if I should be, I assure you, red hair or no, I'll defend my honor to the death."

She said this cheerfully, but as she spoke, she remembered Merwynna's words: "Ye shall not come a maiden to yer bridal bed." Frowning, she opened the Euripides again. "I think I'm exactly in the mood for *Medea* now." And, as

Alan looked on approvingly, she proceeded to deliver a perfect translation.

Alan was translating half an hour later when a light tap on the schoolroom door interrupted him. Dorcas Trevor hovered on the threshold.

"Forgive me for disturbing you."

"We were just finishing," Alexandra said, looking up with a smile. "Come in and join us."

But Dorcas remained near the door, her attention scattered. "No, I only wanted to ask you if you have any more of that herbal potion you gave me for Richard's nerves? It's nearly finished. He's been overwrought lately."

"Since Roger came home?" Alexandra noted the dark circles around Dorcas' eyes. She was a small, trim woman, still young; she had been only eighteen ten years ago when she'd married the Baron of Chilton. Through the years she and Alexandra had become close friends.

Dorcas made a face as she nodded. "Damn Roger!"

Alexandra had never heard Dorcas blaspheme. "You're angry, aren't you? You and Alan both—how extraordinary. I would never have dreamed that one man could wreak such havoc."

Dorcas came to sit down beside them. The strain in her face was even more obvious from close up. "Richard is much too ill to be engaging in these arguments with Roger. His heart is not strong. No excitement, the physician said— doesn't Roger realize this? Is he trying to kill him? They're at it again down in the winter parlor—you'll hear them if you go out into the gallery. It never stops. They're like children, the two of them."

"They never got on together. The baron used to beat Roger. Horribly sometimes," Alexandra said.

"You always make excuses for him," Alan complained.

"I'm trying to understand him," she said wearily. God's bones, there was much more bitterness between the two brothers than she'd realized!

"They are both at fault. Neither will give in." Dorcas' large gray eyes were alight with pain. "All I know is that

I have no child and I don't want to lose my husband. One of these hateful tantrums could kill him."

Alexandra jumped to her feet. She put her arms around Dorcas and gave her a hug. "Come, I don't believe in passively awaiting disaster. Let's go and put a stop to their quarreling once and for all." She marched out into the gallery, with Dorcas and Alan hurrying after.

"How? What d'you intend to do?" Alan asked. "You can't stop them—nothing will ever stop them."

"We can't heal the breach between them, but mayhap we can stop Roger from killing his father. Has anyone ever told him how ill the baron is? I can't believe he would deliberately drive his father to the point of a heart seizure."

"He probably wants Father dead so he can be Baron of Chilton himself."

"Stuff and nonsense! He's not Malice Incarnate."

As Dorcas had said, they could hear the quarrel as soon as they stepped out into the gallery. The door to the winter parlor was open and neither man was making any attempt at restraint.

"I'm blasted if I'll sit up here in the country like the proverbial rusty-armored knight, growing weeds and counting cattle," Roger was saying.

"It suited your brother well enough."

"Damn my brother! I'm fed up with hearing about his loyalty to Chilton, his submission to you, and his supposed devotion to Alexandra Douglas and her father's fat purse and conveniently adjoining lands. I don't think you've fully faced it yet—your precious eldest son is dead, Father, and you're not going to turn me into the paragon you seem to think he was."

Alexandra backed away. "They're fighting about that wretched marriage. I don't want to hear it."

But she could hardly help hearing; no doubt the entire household was privy to the baron's battle with his son. "You have responsibilities, whether you like them or not," the baron was shouting. "One is to marry and beget an heir, and Alexandra would make you an excellent wife. Besides the pragmatic considerations of the match, she is a bright and virtuous girl, of good family, well-educated, and much loved by all—"

"I'm well aware of her virtues. She's got too damn many of them. I prefer the ladies of the court, the city, and the docks—whores, in other words."

"You've had ten years of wildness and vice. That ought to be enough for any man."

"Ah, but I've developed nasty habits." Alexandra could imagine Roger's careless shrug, his sardonic smile. "Wildness and vice suit me, I lament to report. And I would hate to expose the fair Alexandra to the darker side of my nature. No, Father. If you care for the girl, you will guard her from me, not nudge her in my direction."

"A good and innocent maiden might cure this heaviness that sits upon your soul."

Roger laughed shortly. "I think not. Dangle no virgins before me unless you want to see them ruined. I'm going to court. There I will find women to match me in vice, whatever their professed religion."

"I forbid you to go to court. I'm damned if I'll have you mixed up with the bloody papists."

"You forbid me?" He laughed again, even more harshly this time. "Perhaps you can intimidate Alan in that manner, but I shall please myself. Still, I wouldn't despair if I were you. I lead a reckless life, and it may well be a short one. With luck I'll meet an early death, and you can mold Alan into a virtuous country squire. I never asked to be your goddamn heir."

"You're not as indifferent as you pretend to be. You vanish for ten years, but no sooner do you learn your brother is dead than you appear at my gates again. There's something damned odd about that, if you ask me."

"Dear precious Chilton," Roger mocked. "Next you'll be saying I murdered Will for the lands and the title. His death is in doubt, as they say. I'm astonished you haven't accused me already."

"If I had a scrap of evidence, I wouldn't hesitate to accuse you. You were always jealous of your older brother."

Alexandra swallowed hard, aghast. Roger had been jealous, yes, but not of Will's rights as heir to Chilton. All Roger had wanted as a child was to be accorded the same amount of love his older brother received from their father.

"What a convenient way to be rid of me," Roger said. "Hang me as a murderer. What a shame it's so difficult to kill a man in the north of England from the quarterdeck of a trading vessel in the Mediterranean. The magistrates would laugh you out of chambers, my lord." There was a taut silence; then he went on, "It is plain enough that the wrong son died. Misfortune dogs us both. As far as I'm concerned, the wrong parent died."

"You wouldn't be so quick to say that if you knew the truth about your mother," the baron was driven to retort.

Roger's voice suddenly rose in pitch. "If you imagine I'll stay here to listen to you blacken her name, you're mistaken, God damn you."

There was a rapid step; then, before anybody could move, Roger stormed out of the winter parlor into the gallery.

"Oh, perfect! What have we here but the sweetly virginal heiress who's supposed to snatch my blackened soul from the devil's pit."

Alexandra was directly in his path. When she did not step aside, he deliberately slid one hand into her hair at the nape of her neck and ran the other over her breasts, fondling them roughly through the bodice of her gown. "My honored father would have me wed you and lawfully beget grand-children for him, Alix. But, lecherous villain that I am, I would prefer to divest you of your virtue and leave you weeping . . . or dead, with a bloodless face and blank, ac-cusing eyes." He shook his dark head as if possessed by demons, then thrust her away. "Get out of my sight." Push-ing her aside, he strode off down the gallery to the stairs that led down and out of the hall.

Alexandra tried to control a barrage of feelings that ranged from fury at his rudeness to a weak-kneed awareness of the burning spot on her breasts where he had touched her. She threw back her shoulders and started after him.

Alan tried to stop her. "Let him go," he begged her, but she hardly heard. She tore down the winding staircase and out into the courtyard. She saw Roger ahead of her, striding over the moors at a killing pace. Breaking into a run, she chased him, catching up with him atop a scrubby hill.

At first he ignored her; then he was moved to snap, "I meant exactly what I said. Follow me and I'll do you a mischief."

She planted herself in his path, saying, "I do not doubt it, but I mean to speak my mind anyhow. Your father nearly died last winter of a heart seizure. His physician has warned that ill temper and excitement could bring on another. Perhaps you're ignorant of that, or perhaps you simply do not care. But keep it up, Roger, if you wish to be lord of Chilton; keep it up if you want vengeance for every wrong that was ever done you. Keep taunting and baiting and battling that old man until you kill him, if you really believe his death will bring you peace!"

She paused, short of breath, her side needling with pain from the chase. When he didn't move or speak, she hazarded a glance at his face. His lips were pressed together; his eyes looked into hers as if he wished to turn her inside out. The silence stretched on like a dream.

At last he stirred, passing the back of his hand over his brow. For an instant he looked unutterably weary. Blindly she reached out to him, offering the same refuge she'd lent him as a child years before. But when her fingers touched his sleeve, his eyebrows winged and his mouth twisted with a humorless smile. There was no warmth in that look, and none of the affection he had briefly shown her earlier in the day.

"Brave Alexandra. You'll face anything, won't you? I can rant and threaten, but it doesn't move you. No matter what I do or say, you continue to appeal to the good in me, with perfect faith that you will find it. After all, you are an excellent judge of character."

She flushed at the sarcasm. One of his hands began to fiddle with a loose lock of her hair, pulling it, wrapping it around his fingers. At his touch, she felt a tightening somewhere in the vicinity of her womb.

"Do you really think I'd shed a tear if the old bastard fell dead at my feet? For the most trifling transgressions, he used to flog me until the blood ran. Do you remember that, Alix?" He tugged on her hair, bringing her closer. His brown eyes were hot with anger and long-buried pain. "If there had been any justice in it, I could have accepted it, but there was none. I've tried to forget, dammit; I've even tried to forgive. But he hasn't changed, and neither, it seems, have I."

"Why did you come home? If you could not forgive him, why come back at all? Your returning at such a time made it seem to everyone that you intended to step into Will's shoes."

"My return had nothing to do with Will's death," he said, frowning. "'Twas pure coincidence that he should have died so soon before I landed in England."

As he spoke, an uneasy feeling swept her, something she could not name. Suspicion played at the edge of her consciousness. She sensed a lie.

She felt him staring narrowly at her. His finger moved over her cheek and he used it to lift her chin, forcing her to meet his dark, shadowed eyes. "Nothing to say, for once, Alix? Don't tell me you also suspect me of Cain's crime?"

"Of course not!" she cried, but something was bothering her, niggling at her brain, some piece of information that she had either missed or forgotten.

"No, you wouldn't, would you?" His other hand was touching her too, moving slowly up her right arm from her elbow to her shoulder, exploring, caressing. His thumb pressed back and forth across her collarbone, then found the pulse at the base of her throat. "You've always trusted me to the point of foolhardiness. Even when we were children and I played vile tricks on you, you used to laugh and forgive me. Would it be like that still, Alexandra sweetling? Can I do anything I wish to you and get away with it?"

One arm fell to her waist and jerked her against his body. He felt tense and hard all over. Innocent though she was, her feminine instincts sensed his sudden lust, and she tried to pull away. His arm like a bar at her waist restrained her, kept her close. He arched against her and she could feel his heart beating against her breasts, his loins seeking hers through the thick layers of her skirts. "No," she whispered as he bent his head to kiss her. His response was a low laugh; then his tongue was in her mouth.

Alexandra's senses leapt as his tongue moved inside her. She tried to close him out, to keep her lips from parting, but it was impossible. He drove against her teeth, pressing their edges first, then the sensitive flesh behind them.

"Open your mouth," he ordered, raising his lips a fraction of an inch from hers. The tip of his tongue stroked her from one corner of her mouth to the other; then his teeth closed over her bottom lip and nipped it gently. She moaned; fire seemed to flash through her veins. "Open to me!" he repeated, then savaged her lips with another devastating kiss.

Unthinkingly Alexandra obeyed, making no protest as he turned his head slightly so his lips slanted over hers while his tongue sought new depths, new angles. One of his hands slid through her thick hair, caressing her scalp rhythmically while his other hand pressed at the back of her waist, guiding her against him, teaching her exactly what male arousal felt like. She shied, but he relentlessly brought her closer, kissing her until the sky above her whirled and the world tilted on its axis.

Sweet Jesu! Her arms had somehow wrapped themselves around his neck. Desire was a fever, softening her body, dampening her skin. Roger's hands weren't particularly gentle, nor was his kiss, but it didn't matter—her own passion was as wild as his. She met his intrusive tongue with her own, eagerly copying his motions, learning from him. She reveled in the sensations that were flooding her body . . . she wanted to feel more, know more. This pounding of the blood, this swelling of the breasts and aching of the loins . . . this strange, irrational light-headedness—she wanted to experience it all to the fullest. Not even in her wildest fantasies had she imagined anything could feel so good.

And then his hands were pushing her back slightly, his fingers were tearing at her bodice. Oh God, he was going to touch her breasts. And she wanted him to. "Here," she whispered, helping him push aside the simple woven fabric of her square-necked gown. His dark eyes shot her a heated glance as he slipped one hand in beneath the dress, beneath the fragile lawn shift to smooth the firm, soft flesh of her breast. His body trembled, his skin was flushed and damp against her own as his palm slid back and forth, up and down over the small mound, exploring her, caressing her.

"Alix," he breathed against her lips. His fingertips drew teasing circles around her areola, deliberately avoiding the hardened tip. Her torment grew as he abandoned that breast and attacked the other, weighing it gently in his hand, stroking it, flirting once again with the nipple, promising relief, but never quite delivering.

"Harder," she choked, unsure what she was asking for, knowing only that everything he had done so far had only heightened the fires inside her. Some way, somehow, she had to quench them.

He touched the peak of her breast, squeezing it carefully between his forefinger and his thumb. She moaned. "You like that?" he asked huskily.

"Oh, yes!"

Was it her imagination, or did his touch roughen slightly? The hand at her waist held her still while he ground his hips against her. She could feel his manhood, hard and shockingly aroused. "How about that, little virgin, you like that, too?"

Lost in him, she gave the only answer that was true. "Yes," she whispered. "I like the way you feel, the way you touch me; I like everything about you."

To her amazement, he tore his hands away from her breasts and thrust her roughly away. "Damn you, Alix!" He shook her. "What's the matter with you? Why don't you fight me? Why don't you slap me, kick me, scream? Shall I throw you to the ground, my sweet *virtuous* maid, and end your innocence forever? Or is this a lesson my brother taught you long ago?"

"Whoreson!" His injustice infuriated her, and she was out of control as she went for him, raising her nails to his face. He captured her wrists before she could scratch him, his lean fingers manacling her hands to her sides.

"Be still, little cat, or I'll hurt you."

"To the devil with your threats! You started this—you

attacked me!" She brought her knee up sharply, aiming for his vitals. "I'll not endure your insults!"

Her blow was on-target and he groaned and let her go. "God's blood, you needn't castrate me, Alix! Jesus!"

She turned as if to flee, but he managed to grab one of her arms just above the elbow. For an instant they stared at one another. He ran his other hand through his dark hair in the despairing, agitated manner she was beginning to recognize. His breath was coming hard; as hard as hers. And his mouth had twisted with the pain of her blow.

"I'm sorry," she said. She was fumbling with her bodice, shivering now, with frustration and distress. "But how could you . . . if you were just amusing yourself with me, it was a very cruel thing to do."

"Oh, Christ! Listen, Alix." He touched her again, one finger lightly stroking her cheek. "Stay away from me. Stop meddling in my affairs. Do you heed me, Mistress Quick Wit? Be warned, and keep clear, for I can give you nothing but angry words and an empty heart." She could read the anguish in his eyes as he added, "I don't want to hurt you, Alix. Don't make me hurt you."

What he said disturbed her, but what he left unsaid disturbed her even more. Why did he have so great a potential to hurt her? There was something between them, something heady, something powerful. She felt it; so did he. "I wish to God you had never returned," she whispered.

"You could not possibly wish it so much as I." Without further words he turned and stalked off through the heather, leaving her standing there staring stupidly after him. Out of the corner of her blurry eyes, she saw Alan approaching—coming to defend her, no doubt—and she knew she could not bear to talk to him with her body still throbbing and her brain as soft as cornmush. Waving him away, she ran in a direction which took her away from both brothers, down through the long grass, toward the comforting shadows of Westmor Forest.

Alexandra stopped at the edge of the forest, weary from running and conscious of an achy feeling in her limbs.

Swallowing hard, she noticed a slight sore throat. She must be coming down with a head cold.

She had reached the point where the Chilton road twisted up behind the rocky hill and collided with the woods—the place where Will's horse had thrown him. Depressed and grim, she flopped down on the edge of the ditch, dangling her legs into it. Two months ago Will Trevor had been alive and Roger no more than a memory. Now Will lay in his grave, and for the week since Roger had been home, she had scarcely given her dead friend a thought. She had not been to the chapel again to pray, nor had she given any further consideration to the odd circumstances of Will's accident. She seemed to hear Roger's words of a few minutes ago: "His death is in doubt."

Oh, Roger. The warmth of his kisses still lingered on her lips. But he would hurt her. He had a "darker side," and he preferred to consort with women who could match him in vice. Good heavens—in comparison, Will had been the soul of courtesy and good humor. I've hardly even mourned him, she thought guiltily. Staring down into the ditch where Will had fallen, she tried to revive his image, so recently dead, so soon forgotten. But all she could see was Roger's comely sarcastic face.

Next you'll be saying that I murdered Will. . . . I'm surprised you haven't accused me already.

If I had a scrap of evidence, I wouldn't hesitate to accuse you.

Uninvited, the distressing thought crept into her mind that Will's death and Roger's homecoming might somehow be linked. Roger had denied it, but his denial had sounded like a lie.

Why had Will Trevor ridden breakneck down the Chilton road at midnight on that dark night in June? Why had he, a nondrinker, been crazy-full of wine? And why had his horse thrown him here, at the only place on the road where the encroaching forest offered shelter to malefactors?

What a perfect place for an ambush, had said the careless voice of the man who had shown no emotion while standing before his brother's tomb. *I trust nobody had a grudge against Will?*

Stolid, even-tempered, cheerful Will—everyone who had known the man had liked him: servants, tenants, his friends. Nobody had borne him a grudge. Nobody had had a reason for wanting him dead. Nobody, except one man, had benefited from his death, though as Roger said, it was difficult to kill a man in the north of England from the quarterdeck of a trading vessel in the Mediterranean.

But what if Roger hadn't been in the Mediterranean on the day of his brother's death? How did anyone know exactly when he'd reentered his homeland? He could have returned secretly to England months ago. He was in league with Francis Lacklin, entangled in a web of treason, intrigue, and espionage. No doubt he had sufficient reason for keeping his movements in and about the country confidential.

Dear God. Suppose he had come home and sent a message to Chilton, claiming to be in some sort of trouble and begging Will's assistance. When Will had rushed to his aid, Roger could have stretched a rope across the road . . . or flung rocks to scare the horse . . . or. . .

Sickened, she tried to stop the breakneck flow of her thoughts. Roger Trevor might be a liar and a traitor, but surely it was impossible that he could have had anything to do with his brother's mysterious death? Surely it could not have been he who had lured the heir of Chilton into a deadly ambush? Surely a man with riches of his own in the exotic East could have no ambition to succeed to an unimportant barony in the northern wilds of England?

No. However much he might have changed, however hard and unprincipled he had become, Roger wasn't capable of such evil.

Resolutely she rose to return to Westmor, determined to think no more disloyal, suspicious thoughts about her oldest, dearest friend. But as she stood, her feet slipped in the damp earth, and she found herself sliding down into the ditch, landing clumsily on her hands and knees. As she pushed herself, cursing, out of the mud, one of her fingers was scraped by something hard. She reached down for the thing that had cut her.

It was a small piece of metal, straight-edged on one side and rounded like a crescent on the other. As she stared at it, trying to recall where she had seen something similar, her heart seemed to contract. With stiff, uncooperative fingers, she yanked Ned's knife out of her girdle and pressed the metal piece into the side of the blade where the chip was. It fit precisely.

Alexandra dragged herself out of the ditch and collapsed on the side of the road. The afternoon sun soaked into her hair and scalp. Looking back into the ditch, she remembered the way Roger had jumped down there his first day back.

It was here that they had encountered Ned, here that Roger had attacked him, here that she had seen the first signs of the terror that had apparently been plaguing the boy ever since. "Aye, he's been actin' real scared," the head cook had confirmed when she'd asked about Ned at noontime. "When he gave the mistress that rusty old dagger, he was shakin' all over. He probably stole it like, and now he's afeared he'll be hanged for a thief."

Anxiety gripped Alexandra, sending cramps ripping through her belly. Something was forcing itself up from deep within her . . . she was on the verge, she felt, of discovering something terrible, something she could not bear to face. A thrush flew over her head, calling to its mate. The wind raked the trees behind her, and from the distance came the tinkle of cow bells. All her senses were sharp and clear, and her brain was working fast, furiously spinning out a wild, incredible chain of events. If she was right, if the ideas flooding her mind were in any way related to the truth, she knew the connection between a chipped and rusty dagger, a mute boy's fear, and her old friend Roger Trevor. Jesu! *She knew.*

The knife had been in the ditch. Ned had found it there, where Will's murderer had dropped it. And the poor half-witted boy had run from the place in terror on the day of Roger's homecoming because he had recognized Roger as the stranger who had been lurking about the spot on the night of Will's fall.

It was impossible, yet it must be true. She knew now why she had sensed Roger's lies. She'd remembered something Roger said, which, because it had come at the same moment as an indictment of her father for adultery, she had avoided reflecting upon until now. *I saw Sir Charles in London on May Day, I think it was, with a wench on each arm*, Roger had said to Francis Lacklin that night in the great hall at Chilton. May Day was the first of May. Will had suffered his fatal accident on the twenty-second of June. Roger Trevor had indeed been back in England at the time of his brother's death.

7

ALEXANDRA lay propped up in her bed at Westmor, sneezing and feeling sorry for herself. For five days she'd been laid up with a feverish cold, which none of Merwynna's remedies had been able to cure. Alan sat on a stool on the far side of her bedchamber, taking frequent sniffs through a scented handkerchief. "You don't mind if I sit over here, do you?" he had asked upon entering her room. "I don't want to take sick."

"I'm surprised you came at all," she'd responded with unusual testiness. Alan's efforts to cheer her up were unsuccessful. The possibility that Roger Trevor had murdered his brother had darkened her soul.

During her fever she'd had nightmares about daggers and bolting horses, and hands which closed around her throat. Once she woke sobbing so hard that her mother had had to comfort her. Until the fever broke on the second day, everyone in the household had been worried about her. It was unlike Alexandra to be so dispiritedly ill.

"Would you like me to read to you?" Alan asked. "No? A game of chess, then? I'll surrender a pawn to you at the start."

She smiled faintly. "You don't defeat me that often."

"Where's the chessboard?"

96

"I'd rather not play, not today."

He pulled his stool nearer her bed. "Your mother said your fever was down. Why are you still abed? You're acting damned odd, Alix. Is it to do with Roger?"

Her eyes jerked open. "Why do you think that?"

Alan's eyes had narrowed and his nostrils flared. "What passed between you out there on the hill the other day?" he demanded. "If he's hurt you . . ."

Alexandra vividly remembered the roughly exciting caresses he'd subjected her to. She felt a tiny pulse in her loins and cursed her rebellious body, which still seemed to desire Roger, no matter what he'd done.

"He didn't come home for hours that day," Alan went on. "He wouldn't have come home at all, I suspect, were it not that Francis Lacklin was leaving the next day. They proved friends, after all, despite their differences."

"So Lacklin's gone?"

"Aye. Father feels the loss of him the most."

"Doubtless. Without him there, Roger will probably have your father in his grave within the month."

Alan looked at her in surprise. "So you've finally stopped defending him?"

Alexandra's fingers worried a long lock of her hair as she avoided Alan's eyes.

"You must have given him a formidable lecture out there," Alan went on slowly. "In spite of Father's best efforts to engage him in verbal combat, Roger hasn't allowed a nasty remark to pass his lips in days."

Alexandra sat up straighter. "I don't believe it."

"'Tis true. He still sharpens his claws on me, but he's been leaving Father strictly alone. You must have frightened him."

"Frightened him? You overestimate my powers. He was extremely hostile. I certainly didn't expect him to pay any heed to my words."

Alan shrugged. "Why not? He's not Malice Incarnate, as you said. He doesn't want to be Baron of Chilton at the expense of anybody's life."

Alexandra responded with a violent fit of coughing. Ever since recalling the words with which Roger had betrayed his presence in England, she'd been trying with all her heart to smother her suspicions. Over and over, she'd assured herself that there was no real evidence against Roger. He had denied owning the dagger. There was no proof that it was his. And as for Ned's excessive fear of Roger—what could one expect? Roger had threatened the lad with a sword.

She still hadn't talked with Ned. Until she did, she told herself, she shouldn't jump to wild conclusions.

The door to her room opened and Alexandra's mother entered, saying, "The two of you are no longer so young that you can visit indiscriminantly in each other's bedchambers. You've been here long enough, Alan. I want her to rest."

"He's doing me good, Mother, and you know full well there's no harm in our being together."

"I know nothing of the sort. Really, Alexandra, your father will be most displeased to learn of your habitual lack of decorum."

Alexandra noticed the paper in her mother's hands. "My father? Is that a letter from him?"

"Yes. He will honor us with a visit. He will arrive within a day or two, he says; my only surprise is that the letter reached us in advance of his own party. He usually employs such incompetent messengers. I certainly hope he doesn't come today. The cooks are ill-prepared for a crowd of travel-starved retainers."

Alexandra clapped her hands in the first gesture of enthusiasm she had shown for days. "Oh, Mother, I'm glad!"

"I thought you might be. Not that Charles deserves your slavish devotion—he never even takes the time to write to you. But perhaps you'll consider rising from your sickbed now and throwing off this unaccountable gloom."

Alexandra reached for the letter and perused it rapidly. "He says nothing about my returning to London with him. I wonder if he's arranged a position at court for me."

Lady Douglas pursed her lips. "I certainly hope he's given some thought to your predicament—a woman grown and still unwed. 'Tis a disgrace."

"She's but eighteen," Alan objected. "No one thinks a

man ought to marry so early. There's been no talk of my marrying."

"I wish there'd been no talk of mine," said Alexandra, blowing her nose. She gave her mother a belligerent look. "You and he ought not to expect me to marry on command. I won't, you know. I intend to have some say in the matter this time."

"Indeed? You're a willful child, Alexandra. Whomever you wed, he'd better have some mettle in him or it will be a most uneven match. Which reminds me, you've just had another visitor, but I sent him away. I refuse to permit you to entertain *that* scapegrace in your bedchamber. Anyway, I didn't suppose you would care to receive him after the way you were raving about him during your fever."

Alexandra's breath caught and she coughed violently. "You mean Roger? He came to see me?"

"Roger, of course. He was very put out that Alan was allowed in and he was not."

Alan looked smug until Lady Douglas added, "I told him Alan was just leaving."

"What did he want?"

"How do I know? To wish you well, I imagine. I told him you would be quite well as soon as you roused yourself from a fit of black vapors. He looked rather guilty, I fancied. Did you and he quarrel? Is it going to be like the days when he was the only child who could ever make you cry?"

"He never made me cry."

"He most certainly did. I well remember the time he knocked you down in the stables because you'd overheated his favorite horse. You hit your head on the stall and ended up with a lump the size of an apple. And he gave you a black eye on another occasion."

"I don't remember that."

"You ought to. The boy was a menace. I never liked him."

"Oh, Mother, of course you liked him," Alexandra insisted. She didn't want to think about anything from the past that confirmed Roger's wildness or bad temper. So what if his games had been a little rough? All children were cruel to each other at times.

"He can be very obliging when he tries, I'll admit that," Lucy went on. "He was willing to make himself useful just now by going after Ned."

Alexandra had begun sliding down in bed to a more comfortable position, but now she jerked upright again. "What do you mean, going after Ned?"

"Your precious half-wit friend. He came round to the kitchens again today, asking for you. Much against my better judgment, I decided to bring him up, since you'd made such a fuss about it the other day. I'd shown him into the hall while I was talking to Roger, but the ridiculous creature took fright again and ran off. I asked Roger to go after him and bring him back, at sword point if necessary, so you could question him about that wretched dagger you've been sleeping with night and day . . . What the devil is the matter with you, girl? Are you ill again?"

Alexandra could feel the blood draining from her face and neck. "You told Roger I wanted to question Ned about the dagger?"

"Yes, of course. I was about to let a half-wit in to see you when I had just refused the heir of Chilton—I had to tell him something. I explained that the entire business had assumed an undue importance in your mind . . . that you were raving about Ned, too, the other night, and his blasted dagger."

"Oh, Mother!"

Lady Douglas frowned. "I see I've committed some sort of indiscretion. My dear child, I wish you wouldn't make such a secret of your affairs. Is it Roger the boy's afraid of? I thought he was running away from me."

Alexandra had bitten off the tip of one of her nails in her agitation. She could hardly think because of the way her heart was pounding.

"What's this all about?" Alan demanded. "What has Ned to do with Roger?"

Alexandra threw back the bedclothes and hopped out of bed, her red hair flowing down her back as she ran to the mullion-paned window. She had a view of the road which led down to the front gates of the manor. "I don't see either of them."

"They'll be in the woods by now. Roger was on horseback. Get back into bed immediately. You're not even decently clad. Alan, please leave us."

But Alan followed Alexandra to the window, where she stood barefoot in her shift. "You're hiding something from me. I want to know what it is. What's this dagger you're talking about? And how does Roger know the village half-wit?"

She turned to him, her green eyes full of supplication. "I'll explain, but not now. The most important thing is to stop him. Alan, 'tis a long tale, and most of what I know, I've only guessed, but it's possible that Roger means harm to Ned. We've got to go after them. You start. I'll dress and catch up with you."

"But, Alix, what do you mean? What sort of harm?"

"Please, Alan!" She ran to her cupboards and began pulling out a gown, but her mother snatched it away from her.

"Alan may do as he pleases, but you're not going anywhere. I've never heard such folly. One minute you're lying there half-dead, and the next you're proposing to plunge into the damp forest in pursuit of a pirate and a half-wit. No, I said. I'm still your mother, and until you're wed, you're bound to obey me."

As she tried to argue, Alexandra was again seized with a fit of coughing. Her mother pushed her back into bed and said to Alan, "Go on, lad, humor her. You see how distressed she is. I've never known her to behave in such a manner. May the good Lord curse that brother of yours!"

Still looking doubtful, Alan went to the door. "I probably won't be able to find them. Which way did they go?"

"Up the main road," Lady Douglas answered.

"Take one of the horses," Alexandra ordered. "And be careful, Alan. If you find Roger, don't tell him anything."

"How can I?" Alan sounded disgruntled. "I don't know anything."

As he hurried out, Lady Douglas pulled the bedclothes up around her daughter. "You're still ill. Lie down."

"I'm not still ill. I wish you'd let me go. I don't have fever and I'm not an invalid."

Lucy sighed. "What's he done, I'd like to know. If he's injured you, your father will have his head. Men! They're all alike. He hasn't attempted you honor, I trust?"

"No, Mother, it's nothing like that."

"Then what is it?"

Alexandra was thinking of the foolish way she'd admitted to Roger and Francis Lacklin that it was Ned who'd given her the knife. Her words on his first day back now haunted her: *If someone did lay an ambush for Will, Ned might have seen it. He's always in the forest, even at night.* If it was true, if Roger had ambushed Will, and Ned had witnessed it, then Ned's life was very much in danger. A man who could cold-bloodedly murder his own brother would have no qualms about dispatching the one person whose evidence could hang him.

"If you refuse to tell me, I shall have your father get it out of you," Lady Douglas threatened.

"Oh, Mother, if you must know, I had an argument with Roger the other day, and now I've taken it into my head that he bears malice toward everyone. It's silly, of course." A sudden idea struck her and she voiced it immediately, knowing it was the only thing her mother would believe. "Perhaps I'm miffed because Will wanted to wed me and Roger doesn't."

"Are you in love with him?"

"No, of course not." But when they were out, the words seemed to hang in the air, heavy as storm clouds. She looked helplessly into her mother's eyes, and, to her very great astonishment, she found herself in tears.

Lucy Douglas put her arms around her while Alexandra sobbed on her shoulder. She gently patted her daughter's head. "It's just as I said. Roger Trevor is the only person I've ever known who could make you cry."

8

LATE THAT afternoon at Westmor, Alexandra was sitting in the library with her feet up on one of Pris Martin's embroidered stool cushions, making notes on the subject of Will Trevor's death. If she wrote it all out, maybe she would be able to make some sense of her suspicions. And if she could make some sense of them, maybe she would be able to dismiss them from her mind.

She hadn't heard a word from Alan since he'd left to follow Roger and Ned. It had been several hours. If she didn't hear something soon, she intended to defy her mother and ride to Chilton to find out what was happening.

Sweet Jesu, she thought, tapping her quill against her chin as she read over what she had written. Laid out in harsh black ink, the case against Roger was formidable. And yet, how could it be true? He was her oldest, dearest friend. How could he be his own brother's murderer?

A loud knocking on the library door interrupted her. She jumped up to open it. There on the threshold stood the object of her ruminations.

"Roger?" She retreated as he strode into the room, still wearing his cloak, his boots, and his sword, and apparently oblivious of the mud he was tracking onto the floor. It was raining, and he must have been out in the thick of the storm.

"I need you," he said without preliminary.

She edged around him, making for the writing table and her notes. Dear God, what if he saw them? "Why?" Her voice wavered. "What's wrong?"

"Alan and I had a row this morning in the forest. He mounted his horse and went tearing off alone. That was hours ago, and his horse has just come home with an empty saddle. I've already got people out searching, but you know the forest better than anybody, and I want you with me."

Her heart kicked and doubled its rate. She was instantly propelled backward in time to the day when Lady Catherine's horse had come home alone. And to the night when Will had been found, his horse groaning beside its master's body, its legs broken from the fall. She drew a deep breath and had a fit of coughing.

"I'm sorry to be dragging you out in this weather. Are you well enough to come? Will your mother prevent you?"

"It's only a cold, and my mother's gone to the village. I'll come, of course. But . . . " She hesitated, her distrust of Roger raising numerous objections. "You mean he hasn't come home since this morning?"

"Aye. I met him in the forest this morning . . . he was following me. We argued."

A cold hand clenched in Alexandra's stomach. If Alan was hurt, it was her fault.

"He's been acting damned odd." He was pacing, looking more wound-up and nervous than usual. "This always happens to me," he went on, more to himself than to her. "Some blind young fool sets me up for an idol and breaks his heart when I prove a man. Or, in this case, his bloody neck."

"I doubt if he's broken his neck. He's been known to fall off his horse before without coming to any serious harm. He's probably just lost. He's hopeless at finding his way around in the forest."

Roger leapt at this reassurance. "You think I'm overly concerned? He's been gone most of the day, and 'twill be dark in a couple of hours. After what happened to Will—"

"Of course. I'll just go up and change my clothes."

"Good. Hurry up." To her dismay, Roger moved past her and sank down on the stool behind her writing table, drumming his fingers on her notes. Alexandra's palms went damp.

Her writing was large and clear—all he would have to do was look down and he would know that she suspected him of murder.

"In the meantime, you know Joseph, our bailiff? You'd better go tell him I said to get the men out to help us search. Why don't I meet you out by the stables?"

"Aye." He made no move to get up. His dark eyes challenged her. "Well? What are you waiting for?"

"You're dripping all over my Greek translation." She leaned over the table and tried to jerk the papers out from under his arms. To her horror, they didn't come.

Roger's eyes had narrowed. "What are you made of, Alexandra . . . Alan's lying out in the woods somewhere and you're worried about your blasted Greek?" He picked the papers up and threw them in her direction. With trembling fingers she gathered them up and held them protectively to her chest. "Go change!" Roger yelled at her, and she ran.

Up in her bedchamber, Alexandra changed into trousers, boots, a warm cloak, and a broad-brimmed hat to repel the rain. Her maid, Molly, the village girl whom Alexandra had employed despite her mother's disapproval, helped her dress.

"Ye're never goin' out in this weather, are ye? Ye'll catch yer death."

"I have to find Alan."

"Yer mother'll skin ye."

"Never mind. Where's my bundle of medicines? I'll need them if Alan's hurt."

"If he's kilt hisself it's no use ye makin' yer cold worse over him. If 'twas the other one, Master Roger, I could see it. That 'un would be worth takin' a risk fer. Be ye goin' off with him, then?"

"With Roger, yes."

"Alone?" Molly was smirking.

"Not alone, no. Some of the men are going with us." If her voice was sharp, it was because the question had aroused all her fears: was it safe to go anywhere with Roger? Under the circumstances it was probably a very foolish thing to do.

Her head whirled with confusion. Seeing him face to face had made her suspicions seem nonsensical. He was clearly worried about Alan. She'd never seen him so distracted.

Still, she stared at the papers she'd written downstairs. It wouldn't hurt to take an elementary precaution. It might be melodramatic, but Will was dead, and now Alan was missing. She folded the papers and sealed them, writing on the outer fold, "To be opened only in the event of my death."

"Here, Molly, take this and put it in my cupboard."

Molly squinted at the direction on the outside of the papers. She could not read. "What's this, then?"

"Nothing that need concern you, unless—and this is highly unlikely, mind you—unless I should fail to return home. If you heard, for example, that anything had happened to me, then I would wish you to deliver those papers to my mother. Do you understand?"

Molly's shrewd eyes were speculative. "Be ye runnin' off with him, then?"

"No, certainly not."

"Mayhap ye are and mayhap ye're not. He's a fine-lookin' man, they all say belowstairs. One o' the servin' maids over to Chilton swears she's been in his bed, but the others say she's just a-braggin'."

"That's enough, Molly," Alexandra said with dignity, gathering up her medicines and leaving the room. "And kindly hang my clothes up properly before you go; this chamber is a disgrace."

When she reached the stables, she found Roger had already ordered a groom to saddle her horse. He was waiting for her in the courtyard, pacing impatiently. There was a flurry of activity as other mounts were being readied to join the search.

Roger took note of her costume with a slight elevation of his eyebrows. "I hardly recognize you, lad," he teased, but his voice was abstracted. He can't be a murderer, she told herself as he helped her mount. His eyes, his every gesture, belied it.

As they rode out the gates she asked, "What did you and Alan argue about?"

Roger scowled and refused to answer.

Roger rode ahead to give orders to the search party, and

Alexandra seized the opportunity to order Jacky, one of the young Westmor grooms, to remain by her side during the search. Roger was sending people off in different directions, and she preferred not to be left alone with him. As they got deeper in the forest, this precaution proved wise, for it was not long before it was only the three of them pursuing one of the trails which Alexandra had identified as a favorite of Alan's. It was still raining intermittently, and the forest was particularly dark and gloomy—silent except for the sound of their passage and the hissing of the rain as it fell through the leaves.

They stopped frequently, looking for tracks, but there was no sign that Alan had come this way. Alexandra called out his name every few yards. The muffled echo of her voice was disconcerting.

"Nothing," said Roger, remounting after checking a sheltered grove she and Alan occasionally visited. "Any other ideas?"

"Have you tried Merwynna's?"

"I ordered several of my men to do so."

"You say he fled from you in a northeasterly direction?"

"Aye. Toward this quarter of the forest."

"There's not much in the way of shelter around here."

"What is there in the way of hazard?"

"Only the bogs, farther to the east. And to the north, Thorncroft Overhang. But he can't have gone there."

Roger's dark eyes met hers. "Why not?"

"I don't know. Why should he? There's nothing there." She spoke uneasily. Thorncroft Overhang was the cliff where Roger's mother had met her death. It was the one part of the forest which Alexandra habitually avoided. She could not look upon the slippery cliff and the rocks which lay like sharpened knives beneath without trembling. She had been with her father, Sir Charles, on the day they had found Lady Catherine's broken body. She still remembered the ashen look on her father's face when he'd discovered the corpse.

Roger turned off onto a path which would lead them to the ascending track which wound along Thorncroft cliffside. "He won't have come this way," Alexandra protested. "No one ever does."

"Maybe not, but I must be certain. I've been obsessed with fear ever since the moment when I saw his riderless horse come trotting into the courtyard."

"Roger, 'tis a waste of time. You said yourself it'll be dark before long. He's not there, I promise you."

"Go on without me, then, for I must see for myself."

Instead she followed him, unwillingly. Jacky was muttering to himself behind her. He was only ten, and scared of the forest. Alexandra had to turn and smile encouragement at him.

The fog was thick around them, and although the air was warm, the drizzle made her shiver. Damn Alan, she thought. But a moment later she was praying to heaven that he was safe and sound.

They came, eventually, to the rocky bottom of the cliff. Thorncroft Overhang brooded above them, misty and still. There was no sign of Alan. "You see?"

Roger was staring toward the summit. He spurred his mount toward the path which led to the top.

"I'm not going up there."

"Then don't."

"He's not the sort of person to go recklessly up to that ledge and jump. Surely you don't think that, Roger?"

He frowned at her. "His final words to me were something on the order of 'You'll be sorry for this when I'm dead.'"

This didn't sound like Alan. He was afraid of death. He wouldn't deliberately court it. On the other hand, he could get very whiny when he was upset about something. . . . "What did you do to him?" she demanded. And what did you do to Ned? she wondered.

"Nothing. He's disillusioned with me, that's all."

"I suppose you bullied him into another of your nasty, mocking battles, taunting him the way you taunt your father."

Roger halted his horse and turned on her. She could see the tension around his eyes and mouth. "You have a right to be outraged after the way I dealt with you last week," he acknowledged, "but I've been bending over backwards lately to control my bloody temper in front of my father."

"Surely not because of what I said to you?"

"Yes. Until you spoke up, nobody had bothered to tell me the truth about his health." He sounded furious. "Not even Francis. They all assumed I knew, as if I were possessed of some sort of supernatural insight."

"You must have noticed his bad color, his loss of vigor."

"I haven't seen the man for ten years. I thought it was age. Oh, no doubt I saw what I wanted to see . . . I'm not claiming to be free of malice. But I didn't know his heart was weak." He paused a moment, then added, "I meant it when I told you I won't grieve when he dies, but I certainly don't wish to be the instrument of his death. As soon as we find Alan, I'm leaving Chilton. I haven't enough self-discipline to control my angry passions around my father."

He had listened to her, she realized with awe. As much as he resented her interference in his affairs, he had nonetheless taken the time to reflect on what she'd said to him, and amend his behavior accordingly.

Staring at her, he added, "I am a harder man, perhaps, than you believe, but I'm not hard enough to add a father's death to the sins that already weigh upon my conscience."

His words lifted her spirits, making her feel more light-hearted than she'd felt in days.

"And I don't wish to add Alan's death either, so let's hurry. I can't get from my mind the image of him hovering up there on the ledge, wishing someone would come and prevent him from leaping."

"Alan's not your mother," she said sensibly. "I've never heard him talk of suicide, not seriously, at least. He's probably safe at home by now."

"I fought with my mother on the day she died. I've always felt guilty, thinking that it might have been the straw that broke the camel's back. If Alan . . ." He paused, twisting his lips together in a way that moved Alexandra's heart. "I'll just take a quick look."

She argued no further. He'd fought with his mother? She'd never known that. Roger and his mother had been very close, but both had had reckless, unruly tempers. Poor Roger. He'd accused his father of killing his mother, but all these years, he had also felt responsible. Death causes so much guilt in the living, she thought miserably, following Roger as he rode as fast as he could travel along the treacherous track.

Thorncroft Overhang was a rocky promontory which rose out of the woods at the northern edge of the Douglas property. Its soft, crumbly stone was particularly dangerous because of frequent rock slides. The track that wound up to the top was blocked by fallen branches and scrub, which forced them to detour through dense undergrowth. About halfway up, they had to dismount and continue on foot. Roger ordered Jacky to stay with the horses.

"What—stay here alone?" the boy objected, looking uneasily around him. "This is the cliff what's haunted, so they say."

"The whole forest is haunted, if it comes to that," said Roger. "'Tis naught but legend, lad."

Jacky appealed to his mistress. "It's worse haunted up here, m'lady. Can't I just go home? I'm wet through to me skin."

Roger clapped Jacky's shoulders, saying, "We're wet through, too, my lad. But you'll be doing your mistress and me a great service by tending the horses for us, cold and wet and gloomy though it is here. What's your name, lad?"

The boy responded with a timid smile, "Jacky, m'lord."

"Well, Jacky, you're right: 'tis a place to try the courage of the best of us, but if your mistress, a young woman of gentle birth and upbringing, is brave enough to face the terrors of Thorncroft Overhang, a sturdy lad like yourself ought to be able to subdue his qualms. You've a fearless heart in you, I warrant."

"Aye, m'lord," said Jacky with more spirit.

"You'll be fine." Roger tipped him a coin. "There'll be another for you when we come back down."

Jacky turned the silver over and over in his grubby hands and vowed to wait.

"That was impressive," Alexandra said as they tramped off together. "A few words, and the lamb turns into a lion. Is that how you manage the sailors on your ship?"

"Something like that," he agreed.

The track became increasingly difficult and narrow. It

was raining hard now and Alexandra could see no sign of any clearing. Slimy branches kept slapping her in the face, but Roger climbed fast, and she had to struggle to keep up.

The trees disappeared as they reached the ledge that led directly to the summit. To their left, the cliff fell away, but the heavy ground fog deadened their footsteps and hid from view the tangled vines and pointed rocks at the bottom. What a deathly place! Alan would never have come up here—he was afraid of heights. "This is madness. I can't imagine what you expect to find."

They crept round an outcrop of rock and came to the uppermost ledge—the one from which Lady Catherine had fallen ... or jumped. Roger stopped and took her by the arm, helping her over the debris of a recent rock slide. Behind them the cliff rose another fifty feet or so, but it was sheer rock, and one couldn't climb much higher without a rope.

The ledge was empty.

"No Alan. Are you satisfied?"

Still gripping her arm, Roger stepped to the edge. His expression changed as he stared out into the fog that swirled around their feet. "No Alan," he repeated, his voice strange. He seemed in a trance.

Alexandra looked down, trying vainly to see the bottom. There was a heavy ache in her head, and she started to cough. Roger thumped her between the shoulders. The feel of his hands on her back with the drop at her feet unnerved her. *Now,* she thought. Now it's over. Like a perfect idiot, I've come up here with a murderer. One push and I die like his mother. He's brought me here to kill me.

She jerked away, backing up until she felt the security of the cliff wall behind her. A cloud opened above them and the rain came down in torrents. She shivered there, watching him warily, feeling trapped.

He grimaced and little lines cut into the furrow between his eyes. "What's ailing you? You look as if you expect me to throw you over."

"I ... I can't bear being so near the edge. There's something evil about this place. Something malevolent." Her nerves tingled as it occurred to her that with his shadowed face, the black of his lashes, and the thin line of his mouth, he looked as if he fully participated in whatever wickedness there was.

He smiled faintly. "Relax. It would be a rather extreme punishment for so venial a sin."

She lost track of her thoughts. "What?"

He moved away from the edge and in against the cliff until he was almost, but not quite, touching her. "You sent Alan out after me this morning, didn't you?"

"I . . . No. What do you mean?"

He had a funny half-smile, but his eyes were cold. He reached out and lifted her chin in his fingers. "My foolish little brother doesn't have the wit to make sense of what he sees directly before him. But you do. How much do you know, Alix?"

Sweet God! Let me be wrong, please *let me be wrong about him. Please don't let this become some ghastly moment of revelation.* "I don't know what you're talking about. And I don't like heights. I'm getting off this ledge."

His other arm came around her, preventing her. She had to look up at his hard-boned face; she could feel the tenseness in his muscles and smell the faint male aromas of musk and leather. Her head spun. "I thought I'd made it clear that you weren't to meddle in my affairs. What do I have to do to stop you?"

"I've sworn off meddling," she insisted. "You convinced me very nicely when you assaulted me out on the moor."

The rain beat against them as they confronted each other. When he didn't speak, Alexandra added, "Is this why you dragged me up here? To point me to the edge of the cliff and threaten me?"

He shook his head slowly. "Not you. Some other woman, perhaps. I'm beginning to learn that threatening you is useless. No, with you it's obviously going to take action, not threats."

Alexandra's stomach was painfully knotting and unknotting itself. *This is the end,* she thought again. *He's going to kill me and it will serve me right. I knew, and yet I came up here with him. How could I have been such a fool?*

"You're drenched, aren't you?" he said. The arm around her tightened, drawing her close against his warm, hard body. She could feel the tension in his arms, his thighs . . . and the strength. There was no way to fight him, she knew. He could break her in pieces if he chose. "And you're still sniffling from your cold, poor lass. I shouldn't have brought you out in this."

Then, to her utter astonishment, he bent his dark head and brushed her lips with his. Once, twice, three times— light kisses, all of them. Despite her fear, a spark leapt in her. Her mouth tingled, her body ran with excitement as she remembered what he had made her feel a few days ago in his arms. His tongue flicked out and rubbed along her bottom lip. She quivered all over. Sweet Jesus, she didn't know from one minute to the next whether she was about to be strangled or caressed! *I'm a madwoman. He's about to kill me, and I'm lusting after him.*

He released her after one more brief kiss and swung himself up onto a massive stone at the far end of the ledge. "We'll sort out our differences later. I think there's a break in the fog. I'm going to climb around the other side and see if I can make out anything in the way of a light. Maybe my idiot little brother has had the wit to kindle a fire."

"Be careful," she said.

"You rest a minute. There's a cave back there, if my memory serves me well. Get in out of the rain. I'll be back presently."

Trying to quell her lustful shivering, Alexandra moved farther in among the rocks, and after a bit of struggling with some scrubby vines, she discovered that, yes, there was a narrow opening behind her, well-concealed behind a boulder at the widest section of the ledge. Bending down, she peered into the low cleft in the cliff wall. He was right—it was a cave.

She hesitated. She had a nightmarish feeling that she'd been here before, although she couldn't remember ever visiting a cave at the top of Thorncroft Overhang. *Look in the cave*, the mysterious Voice had said. Her head felt heavy as threads of anxiety wound themselves around her. Was this the cave he'd meant?

Taking a step into blackness, she pulled a tinderbox from her knapsack and made a light. In the brief flare she saw that the cave went back, high and deep. The rock floor appeared dry. She scurried inside, glad to get away from the downpour. Away from Roger. Away from the edge of the cliff. "I've found the cave," she called to him. "I'll await you within."

Lighting one of the candles she'd brought in her pack, she advanced into the musty-smelling air. To her surprise she saw before her the remnants of a fire, some wooden eating bowls, some rags on a straw pallet that apparently served as a bed. Somebody lived here. Her nerves ran with an increase of the uneasiness she'd felt outside. The stale air closed around her like a glove. Somewhere water dripped.

Alexandra endeavored to dismiss her nervousness: what's the matter—like Jacky, do you think the cliff is haunted? Take heart, Alexandra. It's just a cave, and an inhabited one at that.

"Hello?" she called out. Who on earth would live in a cave at the top of Thorncroft Overhang? A homeless peasant? An outlaw hiding from justice? "Is anybody here?"

Her voice echoed eerily, but there was no reply. She lifted her candle and looked about. Nothing. No one.

Taking off her cap, she shook it out. It was soaking; she was soaking. A puddle was forming on the floor at her feet. If only she could get rid of these wet clothes and warm herself before a good fire. She hugged herself, shivering.

Why had Roger kissed her like that? Such a proprietary embrace—one that asked no leave, made no apology. He touched her, held her, kissed her as if he had a right to do so . . . a right to do anything to her that he wished.

And why had he suggested taking shelter in the cave? Was he planning to come in here and seduce her? Her body grew hot again at the thought. What should she do if he attempted it?

She rubbed the back of her hand across her forehead. Her head was pounding in rhythm with her heart. I should be thinking of a way to defend myself against him, not wondering how it would be to lie in his arms, she castigated herself. But her brain and her body were telling her two opposing things, and she didn't know which to believe.

There was a low whistle as the wind beat against the cliff and a draft was sucked into the cavern. Out of the corner of her eye she thought she saw something move in the blackest end of the cave. She raised the candle high, peering into the darkness. Her breath caught. There was definitely something moving—swaying ominously back and forth.

"A little courage now," she said aloud. As her eyes became adjusted to the deeper darkness, she saw more clearly the outlines of a huge shape floating on the stagnant air a few feet from where she stood. It looked almost like an enormous sack filling with some sort of lumpy material . . . hanging in midair . . . yet there was something vaguely human about it.

Her hands were sticky with sweat, but despite a screaming in her brain that told her to go no closer, she could not shake the urge to know what this unearthly thing was. She raised her candle like a weapon before her and advanced a step or two, slowly, cautiously, squinting her eyes to get a better look. . . .

Oh God! She let out a little cry and dropped the light. Gasping, stumbling back from the horror that hung there, she fell to her knees, scraping herself on the rough stone. There was a boulder near her, and she put her arms around it and hung on with all her strength. *Snakes around his neck,* she heard a hollow voice intone. *Look in the cave.*

A body was hanging there by a twisted rope. Above the coils which had choked away its life, the face was black and unrecognizable, a grotesque caricature of a human face. "You'll be sorry for this when I'm dead." Surely Alan could not look like that, even in death. Surely he could not have meant those words. Dear heaven! Don't let it be Alan!

Gulping for air, she crawled toward the dim light that marked the mouth of the cave. The swollen image of the face crawled with her, following her even when she shut her eyes. Nausea gripped her. She turned her head and was sick.

After several minutes of heaving and coughing, Alexandra lurched to her feet. Clutching the inside wall by the cave's entrance, she breathed in the foggy air from outside until she began to feel better. Then she turned back to look for the candle. She knew she was going to have to go back for a second look, and quickly, before Roger followed her into the cave.

Retrieving her tinderbox and candle, she struck a new light. Forcing one leaden foot in front of the other, she walked back to the place where the dreadful thing was hanging. Of course it's not Alan, she kept telling herself. He's not suicidal. He's not despairing. He's too afraid of death to plunge forward to meet it. Roger, yes, Roger could kill himself—it would be exactly the sort of defiant, melodramatic thing he'd be likely to do. But not Alan. The dead man could not possibly be Alan.

And yet, hadn't Alan told her that he sometimes thought it would be preferable to die than to go through life crippled by his fears? He was dreadfully afraid sometimes. After Will's death Alan had had the shakes for at least a week. He would flush and sweat; his heart would pound while his whole body trembled uncontrollably. Many times she had embraced him to comfort him, only to feel him vibrating helplessly against her. "Don't you ever feel as if you're suspended over an abyss, just barely holding on with the tips of your fingers?" he had asked her. "Don't you ever feel as if the demons of hell are pushing open a door inside your soul? Don't you ever glance at you reflection in a scummy pool and see a stranger staring back?"

The memory of Alan's fears magnified her own, and she nearly dropped the candle and fled. But she forced herself to go on, telling herself that if Alan were dead, she must cut him down and attend to his body. She owed him those final devotions. He was her friend, her brother, and she loved him. Tears blinded her suddenly. She couldn't imagine a life without Alan.

Dear God. Please make it someone—anyone—else!

She raised the light toward the body. I've seen death before, she reminded herself. Courage.

The first thing she noticed was that the corpse was clothed in coarse woolen trousers, not trunks and hose. Surely Alan would not be dressed so. She looked at the hands. Surely these square ringless fingers did not belong to Alan. And the hair—Alan's was short, not so long and tangled. The face—she forced herself to look carefully upon the face. Relief flooded her. Distorted though the features were, there was nothing of Alan in them. She leaned closer. No, no, it wasn't Alan.

It was Ned.

Alexandra turned away, sinking back to the floor of the cave. Her muscles had no strength, and she was trembling. "There's a shadow round about him," Merwynna had said.

Once again she noticed the sweet-stale smell of the cave—the smell of death? Her stomach heaved again. Jesu! Poor Ned.

For what seemed forever, Alexandra huddled there on the cold stone, her body weak but her mind illuminated with a harsh and bitter light. No longer were her thoughts thick and sluggish: no, she knew herself now for a heedless, credulous fool. Her own words had condemned Ned. And now she too was about to die.

She looked back again at the dead man hanging with his feet swaying in the draft, appearing for all the world like a suicide. But he had not hanged himself, of that Alix felt sure. Someone else had looped the rope around his neck and twisted it until he died. Someone who feared him for the knowledge he possessed about the night of Will Trevor's death. Someone who had followed him into Westmor Forest this morning, strangled him, and then come back for her. Someone whose lips were sweet and whose body was the only one she ever wanted to take unto her own. She began to weep silently. Her worst imaginings were true.

And Alan? Perhaps he'd never caught up with Roger this morning . . . perhaps Alan wasn't missing at all. Perhaps it had all been a ruse to get her alone, to lead her into the forest on this dark and gloomy day, to trick her up to Thorncroft Overhang, where nobody ever went, to arrange an accident for her just as he had arranged one for Will. "Don't underestimate Alexandra," he had said to Francis Lacklin that night in Chilton Hall. He didn't. He knew she was a danger to him. He knew that if she were left to herself she would unravel the entire vicious plot.

Unfortunately, nobody had ever reminded her not to underestimate him. He had outwitted her on every point. He had lured her out despite her illness, separated her from the rest of her party, flattered her into trusting him, and effortlessly unloaded Jacky, her groom. He had even calmed her fears out there on the ledge, confusing her with a kiss. Why hadn't he pushed her then and been done with it?

He'd enjoyed the embrace. He was a self-indulgent man. He'd decided to rape her first, and then murder her.

"God help me," she whispered, burying her face in her hands. Roger Trevor was going to kill her.

9

"ALEXANDRA? Where the devil have you disappeared to?"

Courage. Take heart, Alexandra, take heart. What did Merwynna say was the way to still one's terrors? You must empty the mind. You must ignore the inner turmoil that seeks to drive you deeper into panic. You must stop all thinking, all imagining, and let your spirit float.

Sitting there on the cold floor of the cave, listening to the approach of her beloved friend and most deadly enemy, Alexandra tried to relax her muscles and float. She repeated the charm against fear which Merwynna had taught her long ago:

> Avaunt thou, Fear,
> Thou Menacer,
> Thou Shadow, thou Mirage
> I see thee not, I feel thee not,
> I rise up firm and proud.
>
> Avaunt thou, Fear . . .

"Alexandra?" he said again, from just inside the mouth of the cave. His voice echoed in waves around the cavern, destroying her attempt to quiet her mind. How can I escape? became her only thought. Where can I hide?

He cursed. There was a scrape of metal, then a heavy thud. "Sweet Christ, there are snakes in here," he muttered. "Are you mad, sitting on the ground?"

Roger hated snakes. The only way to frighten him as a boy had been to threaten him with one. Once, in petty revenge for some now-forgotten prank, she'd put a small garden snake in his bed. He had shrieked blue murder, and at least a fortnight had passed before he'd even considered forgiving her.

Were there really snakes here? *Snakes around his neck*.

Roger moved cautiously toward her, his eyes on the ground. By the feeble light of her candle, she could see that he was holding something. There was a glint of metal as the flame danced in the draft. It was his rapier.

Alexandra rose numbly to her feet, staring with perverse fascination at the flexible metal blade. Would it hurt? They said it didn't. They said you could be stabbed through and never feel anything but an odd weakness, which grew stronger as you died.

It was impossible to get past him. The cave was too narrow. It was too late to hide, and pointless to scream. Neither could she fall at his feet and plead for her life. Never, never would she die like that—demeaned, disgraced. No, there was only one thing to do: she drew her dagger from her belt and took up the standard defensive posture taught to her long ago by her father's men-at-arms, her knife held flat out, poised and ready.

"It won't be a fair fight, but I'm certainly not about to die passively. I don't suppose you would consider giving me a sword? I've had several years of instruction. Alan's fencing master didn't want to teach a woman, but we insisted. And I know your weakness—you don't parry well in *quarte*. You might find me a more able opponent than you expect."

Roger had stopped a few feet away. He was staring at her with a quizzical expression on his hard-boned face. "No doubt," he finally said. His voice was light, almost playful as he added, "But I don't have another sword."

How could he be so nonchalant? Anger swelled in her, driving out her fear. "I don't believe this! How can you look like that? What about your blasted conscience, Roger? How can you do this to me?"

He took two strides, and the tip of his blade was at her throat. His hand snaked out, twisting the dagger from her fingers with humiliating ease. "I'm damned if I'll trust you with a knife, lass. What—are you angry because I kissed you out there? What do you suppose I intend to do now? Terrorize you into stripping off your ridiculous boy's clothes and opening your legs for me? Do you fear I'll force your compliance with the edge of my sword?" He allowed the rapier point to slide down over her throat until it touched her left breast. He didn't hurt her; the blade barely whispered over her flesh, leaving tingles in its wake. "Dear Christ, but I'm tempted," he added savagely.

Something even stronger than fear pulsed in her. Lust again—that harsh-sounding word—even now it was beating between them. Her face grew hot as she admitted it to herself. There in the darkness, his sexual vitality burned her like a flame. Yet all he need do was lean on his sword, and she would die.

Desperately she sought a distraction. "I've found him," she said. "He's very efficiently dead."

Her adversary's eyes abruptly lost their focus. "What?"

She nodded toward Ned's body in the shadows. Roger's face changed to an expression of such genuine surprise that it sent confusion roaring through her once again, confusion which was magnified as the rapier fell unregarded from his hand and he cried out his brother's name.

"It's not Alan," she said as he ran to tear at the rope which held the body. "You know it's not Alan! It's Ned, Roger, it's Ned. You know it's Ned."

But he acted as if he did not know. He used her dagger to cut the boy down, then threw it aside as he dragged Ned closer to the light, stared into his bloated face for a moment, then bent and pressed his head to Ned's chest. Alexandra felt as if she were going to be sick again. What was he doing? He himself had strangled Ned. He knew perfectly well he was dead. Why was he still playacting?

This is mad, she told herself. She no longer knew what to believe. Her thoughts had stopped making sense. Everything that was logical declared him guilty—everything except his behavior, which was baffling. Still, she had to assume him guilty. He was stronger than she; he had her at his mercy. She dared not trust the instinct that insisted he was no murderer.

Her eyes fixed on his rapier, lying on the stone floor near her feet. He had held it to her throat. Didn't that prove he meant to murder her?

And now—was he unarmed? He'd thrown away the sword and the dagger, but he still had a dagger of his own in his sword belt, and maybe other weapons concealed within his doublet. Still, the rapier was superior to other weapons, and in sooth she did know how to use it.

She was about to bend down to grab it when Roger turned to her, his face contorted with anger. "I thought it was Alan. I could kill you for frightening me like that."

Frightening him. "Take care—there's a snake behind you," she cried, pointing to the cut length of rope which extended from Ned's neck along the dark floor of the cave. It did indeed look like a serpent in the flickering light, and Roger recoiled sharply. Alexandra swept his rapier into her hand and lunged at him. He cursed and ducked aside, but she kept her nerve and moved with him, poised to defend herself against any retort that he, a trained soldier, might venture to make. But after a moment of staring incredulously at her, he relaxed and straightened, his eyes holding hers as she determinedly pressed the edge of his blade against the pulse beating in his throat.

"I understand. You found him hanging there—that would have been enough to unnerve anybody. You'd best get out of here until your head clears, Alexandra. Put down the sword."

It was exactly the tone he had used to Jacky: soothing, reassuring, and authoritative. He was Captain Trevor, master of a ship full of Mediterranean ruffians. He was accustomed to being obeyed, and he showed not the slightest fear of the deadly metal threatening to spill his lifeblood.

"Murderer," she said very clearly and distinctly.

His dark eyes compelled her as he put out his hand. "Give it to me, lassie. You're distracted."

She was seized with a wild temptation to obey him. Breathing hard, she fought it down. "No! I'm not distracted and I'm perfectly capable of ending your miserable existence if you make the slightest hint of an aggressive move."

The soothing tone vanished. "Then what the bloody hell is the matter with you? 'Tis an ugly sight, a hanging corpse, and to you, I know, a particular loss; but what have I to do with it if some foolish half-wit boy decides to end his own life?"

"Stop pretending. I know it was you. You followed him here and wrung his neck, all because I showed you the dagger that you lost in the ditch on the night you murdered Will."

Roger was slowly shaking his head. "You're raving. Your mind's unhinged."

"And don't think you can save yourself by murdering me. I'm not a complete ass. I knew it would be perilous to go anywhere with you. I left papers at Westmor stating the evidence against you. Killing me won't be sufficient to procure my silence."

"You left papers," he repeated slowly, as if he wanted to be absolutely certain he was getting it straight.

"Aye, with orders that they be opened immediately should I fail to return from this nasty little expedition of yours."

"Christ! You think you're clever, don't you, Mistress Quick Wit? I murdered Will, did I? You see the mark of Cain upon my forehead, do you, sweetling? What about Alan? Is he really missing or have I cheerfully dispatched him too? . . . Give me that."

He grasped the blade of the rapier in his bare hand and jerked it away from her. Blood welled up immediately in his palm as he flung the sword into the farthest corner of the cave. For an instant she didn't move, staring in dismay at his injured hand, startled into an unwilling admiration of his strength of will. Then she turned to run.

She got perhaps three yards before he caught her from behind. One strong arm circled her neck, choking her, while the other jerked her back against him, her buttocks colliding with his steel-hard thighs. One of his hands plunged into her hair. She tossed her head despite the pain this caused her, frantic to get free. She raised one booted foot and slammed her heel into his knee. As he stiffened in agony, she tore savagely at his injured hand. He nearly lost his hold on her. "You little bitch!"

Muttering obscenities, he forced her left arm up behind her back and twisted it until a sound escaped her. "Stop squirming or I'll hurt you, Alix. I mean it. I'll snap your bones like kindling if you don't desist."

She went limp, and his roughness instantly ceased. Stumbling, she sank to her knees, as if in a swoon, but she was merely waiting for another chance. As he dropped down beside her, she reached out and snatched the second dagger from his sword belt. Now, she thought, exultant. *Now.* She turned it on him, but, quick as she was, Roger was quicker. Before she could inflict more than a scratch on his shoulder, the side of his hand descended on her wrist in a sharp, numbing blow and the knife clattered to the ground. Cursing more loudly now, he wrestled her to the rock floor, and they rolled over wildly for several seconds before his superior strength prevailed and he pressed her down on her back beside a conical pile of loose stones. Straddling her slender hips, he captured both her wrists and pinned them on either side of her thrashing shoulders.

Panting, she looked up at him, noting with dismay the fury in his dark eyes, the tight lines around his narrow, sensual mouth. The desperate fight had exhausted her, but even so he couldn't completely stop her frantic struggles, not even with the full weight of his body.

"Be still, Alix," he ordered. He brought her wrists together and clasped them in one of his large hands, then entwined the other in her thick red hair. When she continued to squirm, he added, "You're only making me more determined, lassie."

There was an unmistakable lilt to his voice. He was enjoying this. She stole another glance at his face, so close to her own. His eyes, so deep in color, so expressive; his mouth, which had kissed her passionately, arousingly. Like hers, his clothes were wet; through them she could feel his body's heat. He shifted slightly and she became aware of the lean hardness of his thighs pressing against her own. Oh, God. Once again she knew that queer melting excitement deep within her, deep. He shoved a knee between her legs, forcibly parting her thighs. His loins were tightly locked with hers, and she could feel the hard fullness of his sex. They couldn't have been more intimately positioned if they had been making love.

She moaned softly as one of his hands slipped between their bodies and closed possessively over a breast. His fingers caressed her gently. Tears pricked her eyes. The fascinating Roger—she could almost hear her mother's mocking voice. Despite everything that had passed, she was drawn to him still.

"You're something," he murmured. His eyes had gone soft and smoky, and his mouth had a carnal twist to it that could almost be called a smile. "Fierce as an Amazon, I vow. Who taught you how to fight?"

"You're going to rape me first, aren't you?" She swallowed, her throat as dry as ash. "Please, Roger. This much mercy I *will* beg: kill me if you must, but do not put me to shame."

His hands turned rough again as he shook her soundly. "By God, I'll beat the wits back into you if I have to, Alix!"

"There's nothing wrong with my wits!"

"It must be your excellent judgment, then, which has failed you." He cast a wary look around, adding, "If I were going to rape you, the last place I'd choose would be this bloody snake den."

"There's one crawling toward you now."

He laughed, his voice ringing through the cavern. "My dear resourceful Alexandra, you are truly an admirable adversary, but here's a lesson for you: never use the same trick twice."

Then she would have to use some other trick. After a moment's deliberation she allowed her body to go slack beneath him and her voice to waver as she said, "His face was horrible, Roger . . . so grotesque. I've never seen anything like it. When I came into the cave and saw him, the entire world seemed to reel and go crazy." She looked in the direction of the corpse and made no effort to repress her shudders. "I . . . I think I'm going to be sick."

He hesitated, gazing narrowly into her eyes. His hands moved skillfully over her once again. "Art sure? 'Tis no compliment to me for your gorge to rise at a moment like this."

" 'Twill be even less of a compliment if I vomit in your arms!" she retorted. "You're heavy, and your weight upon my stomach . . ."

He rolled over onto his back beside her, freeing her. "Get up, then, and don't tempt me further," he said harshly.

She pushed herself up to a sitting position, keeping both hands clamped over her mouth as if in danger of convulsing. Given all that had happened, it was not difficult to feign. Roger lay unmoving, his mouth tight with some sort of intense concentration. One leg was bent, his fists were clenched, and the pulse at the open throat of his white lawn shirt hammered visibly. Nervously Alexandra noted the taut stretch of fabric in his groin. He wanted her, she knew. It pained him not to take her.

She felt another wave of confusion as it occurred to her that he looked young, and, apart from that rampant maleness, not a threat to her at all. *Oh, Roger, would that I could read your mind at this moment!* More than anything in the world, she wanted to trust him.

Then she saw Ned's body once again. Could someone *else* have killed him? Who but Roger had had reason to fear him? Who but Roger had had reason to want Will Trevor dead?

"I thought you were sick? Go outside, for God's sake, and take some air," he ordered.

Outside. The ledge. Of course he could not strangle her or kill her with his sword. He had to make it look like an accident.

She stared blankly at the odd cairn of stones on the cave floor just to the left of Roger's body. It looked like an altar of sorts, erected to whatever gods the poor half-witted Ned had worshiped.

Forgive me, gods, she said to them in silence. *But you*

didn't help Ned very much, did you? Then she shifted her weight and kicked with all her strength at the bottom on the pile.

The stones came crashing down on Roger, who snarled a multilingual spew of expletives that he'd undoubtedly picked up in some Middle Sea den of iniquity. Alexandra grabbed several loose rocks and threw them at him. One struck him hard in the temple. He bent over double, the dust from the rock collapse rising around him. Alexandra lurched to her feet and fled.

Unbelievably, she found herself out of the cave, stumbling over the dead body of a snake at the entrance. The light of the gloomy afternoon first startled, then uplifted her. She glanced behind her, but saw no sign of pursuit. He must be hurt. She had to fight a perverse desire to return and make sure he wasn't badly hurt. You'd better hope he's badly hurt, she screamed at this weak side of herself. You fool, Alexandra!

Moving cautiously along the treacherous ledge, she flung herself onto the path that would lead her back down to level ground. It had stopped raining and the fog had lifted, making it easier to find her way as she careened down the track. When she reached the spot where Roger had left Jacky with the horses, she was startled to find the boy gone. So much for Roger's clever way with underlings—Jacky's fears had apparently proved stronger than his pride . . . or his greed for another silver coin.

For the next several minutes Alexandra thought of nothing but escape. She knew she would not feel safe until the gates of Westmor Manor closed behind her. When she reached the bottom of Thorncroft Overhang, she avoided the main track and plunged directly into the woody undergrowth. The going would be harder, but the way was more direct.

Her panic eased a little in the thickness of the forest. She was relatively certain that Roger would not follow her this way, particularly if he were hurt. If he had any sense, he would not follow her at all—he would turn and flee the region. He was a murderer. He would never be Baron of Chilton now.

She moved quickly through the undergrowth, checking her progress every now and then by the sight of a familiar tree, but in the near-darkness she found the trek harder than usual. Cold and weary, she moved clumsily, leaving broken branches and trampled bushes in her wake—an easy trail to follow, should he insist upon pursuing her.

Her way ran beside the lake where Merwynna lived. She considered seeking refuge with the wisewoman, but the witch's cottage was on the far side of the lake, and she would lose precious time tramping around. Besides, what protection could Merwynna offer her against Roger? She possessed no weapons and there was no place in the cottage to hide. No, Westmor Manor was the only place where she would be safe.

Alexandra was alongside the lake when she thought she heard a cry. She stopped, panting. The darkness gathered around her, and there were wisps of fog floating along the ground. She recalled all the legends of demons and spirits who dwelt in the forest, and despite her familiarity with the woodland, she felt the skin on the back of her neck prickle.

There it was again—a faint cry. Merciful heavens. It sounded like Alan.

Her mind circled blankly for a moment. Alan was safe at Chilton: Roger's tale about his horse coming back without its rider had been a ruse to get her out alone with him.

But the cry came again, moaning, fainter now, and it definitely sounded like Alan's voice. Alexandra turned toward the sound. She had a sudden vision of Roger leaping at the corpse hanging in the cave, his anguished voice calling out Alan's name. She remembered his anger, his denials, his insistence that her wits were addled. What if she'd been wrong? What if he hadn't meant to harm her after all?

Her head was throbbing. "Where are you?" she screamed to the moaner. She was going out of her way now, nearer to the lake, risking the loss of precious minutes if Roger was chasing her, but she tried to put these considerations out of her mind. Whoever it was in the undergrowth, he was hurt and needed her help.

Five minutes later, Alexandra stumbled over a man's body under a tree, one of his legs twisted under him in an unnatural position. He opened his eyes, grabbing for her hands. "Alix," he whispered, tears of pain and terror running down his cheeks.

It was indeed Alan.

"Oh, dear Lord, what happened to you?" she cried as she dropped to her knees beside him and hugged him close. He was cold and wet and in too much pain to talk very much. He'd been trying to get to Merwynna, he told her. He knew he couldn't make it back to Chilton.

"I thought I was going to die," he managed. "During the last few minutes, I truly believed it. I've never been so glad to see anybody in my life. How did you find me?"

A quick examination revealed that his left leg was broken. "What happened? Did Roger do this to you?"

"Roger?" His voice wounded vague, as if he were just barely conscious. "No, I fell off my horse. Just like Will."

She shivered at the image this evoked. "What passed between you and Roger?" she demanded as she endeavored to make him more comfortable. She would have to get him to Merwynna; there was no doubt about that. The question was, how?

"I had to get away from him. The things he's planning, the things he said—he's so cruel sometimes, Alix. I rode off in a temper, not looking where I was going. I think a branch swept me off my horse's back, and I crawled here."

"What did he say? What did he do? Was it something to do with Ned?"

"Ned?"

"He's dead, Alan. Roger killed him."

There was a short silence; then Alan whispered, "Are you sure? Why would Roger kill Ned—you never explained that to me."

"What happened between you and Roger?" she persisted. "Please tell me. It's important. He may be coming after us this very minute."

But Alan proved unexpectedly stubborn. "No, I'll never tell you. I swore to keep silence. Alix? I think I may faint."

"Alan!" She shook him, but he was too weak to answer her. Damnation! She stripped off her wet jacket and covered him with it. She would have to run to Merwynna for help;

she could not move him alone. "Alan, can you hear me?
I'm going for help to Merwynna. She's not far, just on the
other side of the lake. I'll be back directly, I swear to you.
But, Alan—this is important—don't call out or moan again
if you can help it. Just be silent. Do you understand? I'll
be right back with help."

"No! Don't leave me. I'm afraid. I'm dying."

"You're not dying. I know 'tis difficult, but please try
to keep your nerve up for a few more minutes." She leaned
over and embraced him, kissing his face. "Courage, Alan.
Please!"

He nodded weakly and she kissed him again. His lips
were cold. In sooth there was no time to lose—she had
seen people die of a broken bone or some other relatively
minor injury if they were left out in the damp air for long.
It was not cold—even now the night air remained warm,
but there was a stiff breeze, and Alan's clothes, like her
own, were drenched.

Alexandra coughed violently as she rose to her feet and
ran down to the side of the lake. Alan wasn't the only one
who would suffer from this exposure to the wet night air.
In all likelihood, she would have her fever back again tomorrow.

On the edge of the lake, she hesitated only for a moment
before sitting down and removing her boots, her trunks and
hose, and finally, her wet jerkin. Wearing only her thin lawn
shirt, which hung down around her thighs like a shift, she
dived into the dark water of the lake.

Swimming was by far the quickest way to get to Merwynna's cottage. She would fetch the boat from the other
side and use it to transport Alan to the wisewoman. If Roger
sought her there . . . She forced herself not to consider that
possibility. Alan's welfare was more important.

Alexandra was a strong swimmer, but even so, she would
never have leapt into the lake at night if there had been a
choice. She loved the water, but she was also wary of it.
Even strong swimmers, she knew, could drown.

Besides, there were legends about this lake—legends
that one could laugh at by the light of day. Some said a
demon dwelt within its depths, a huge primitive creature

which poked its ugly head out of the water on moonlit nights. Alexandra had never seen it, and Merwynna merely smiled inscrutably when she asked her if such a creature existed.

She imagined this monster stalking her now as she plowed through its domain on her errand of mercy. Once she thought she felt the water heave beside her, but nothing appeared. She was frightened, but Merwynna's words comforted her: "Water is your element . . . trust the water."

Coughing and exhausted, she finally reached the bank where Merwynna's cottage stood. She found the boat, and left it ready while she ran up to the cottage to summon her friend. But nobody answered her knocking. Flinging open the door, she found the one-room cot empty. Merwynna must be attending a childbed or a deathbed. Alexandra cursed and bit her lip in frustration as she realized she would have to manage alone.

Grabbing a blanket and a bottle of blood-warming cordial, she raced back to the boat. Jumping in, she rowed fast, looking over her shoulder every few strokes to be sure she was headed in the right direction. When she reached the opposite shore, she steered the little boat in beside the rocks and tied it to a low-lying branch. The breeze felt chill on her scantily clad body as she ran to find Alan.

He was still conscious when she reached him, but his breathing was quick and low. There was no time to lose. She wrapped the blanket around him and ordered him to put his arms around her shoulders. "This will not be easy, but we'll manage. You'll have to take some of your weight on your uninjured leg. I'm strong, but I can't carry you."

As they tried to rise, Alan moaned, "I can't. It hurts."

"You can."

He tried once more, then sank back again in despair. "Leave me. I'm going to die. I know it."

"Alan, don't be silly. Lean on me. Come, try again."

She managed to drag him a few steps toward the boat; then he stumbled and they both fell. Alan began whimpering softly. She tried to raise him, but he refused to cooperate. "'Tis impossible," he whispered. "Leave me. I can't make it."

"Then you can lie here and rot, for all I care!" she shouted at him, as all the tensions of the day suddenly erupted. "Dear God, I'm trying to help you—are you such a sniveling coward that you won't move an inch to save your own life? You're not afraid of death, Alan, you're afraid of living! You love death! You court her like a mistress! Go to her, then, and be damned!"

At her wits' end, she stalked several paces away. She had a savage desire to kick Alan's broken leg until he screamed. Recklessly she picked up a piece of dead wood and slammed it against the nearest tree trunk until it disintegrated. "I hate you all, you bloody Trevors!"

"Alix?" Alan had pushed himself up on one knee and was trying to stand. "Please, I need you. Don't leave me."

"Oh, God, Alan..." Her anger drained and shame rushed in to take its place. It wasn't Alan's fault that his brother was a murderer. She went back to him and gently touched his hair. "It's all right, I'm here. Forgive me—I didn't mean it."

"No, you're right—I haven't your courage—I've never had it. But I'd slit my own throat rather than disappoint you. And I don't love death."

"Prove it," she challenged.

He complied, and somehow or other they managed to move the last agonizing steps to the edge of the water. But when she hauled him into the small boat, Alan fainted. Alexandra covered him snugly with the blanket and pushed the boat away from the rocks with one of the oars, then settled down to row. The crossing seemed to take forever this time. Her shoulders ached and her left arm was hurting where Roger had twisted it during their struggle. It struck her suddenly that this was the only thing he had done to hurt her. He had suffered far more at her hands than she had at his.

Why? she wondered. If he'd intended her death, why should he care whether or not she suffered in the process? He'd had her helpless, completely at his mercy. He could easily have stripped off her clothes and raped her. He could have picked her up in his strong arms and thrown her over the cliff.

He was a tough, ruthless sea captain whose physical

strength was far superior to hers. It came to her like a hammer blow that she would never have escaped from the cave if Roger hadn't deliberately set a limit to the amount of force he would use against her. He hadn't wanted to injure her. There could be no other explanation.

Oh, sweet Jesu, what if her rock had killed him? What if *she* was the murderer? What if it had all been a ghastly mistake?

The rowboat struck the rocks in front of Merwynna's cottage. Alexandra jumped out and pulled the little boat up on the stony shore. Alan was still unconscious, although he moaned every once in a while. How the devil am I going to get him inside? she wondered. Damn Merwynna for not being here when I need her!

She was bending over the boat when she felt a prick on the back of her neck. Thinking it was an insect, she reached around to slap it. Her fingers encountered steel. Slowly she turned. Roger was standing there just behind her, his legs braced slightly apart, his graceful, slender body taut and hard as an ancient colossus. Once again he held a blade to her throat.

10

*T*HEY STARED at one another, two quiet shadows in the gathering dark. Roger's face was pale, his forehead dark with blood where the rock had struck him. He lowered the knife, but it still glinted between them, a reminder of what she had just recognized while rowing—he had all the strength, all the weapons on his side.

The clouds parted briefly, allowing moonlight to wash her poised, silent adversary. Alexandra could clearly see the way his eyes were taking in the wet shirt sticking to her breasts, her bare legs and thighs, her long waves of soaking hair. In her concern over Alan, she'd forgotten her near-nakedness. A knot squeezed in the pit of her stomach, while the rest of her sagged in weariness. She knew she could run no farther.

Roger reached out and took her by the shoulder, his fingers melting through her flesh to grip her very bones. With his injured hand he thrust the dagger into his belt, then pulled her roughly against him. "No," she whispered, but it was already too late. His mouth came down and smothered the syllable.

He kissed her with a fierce, single-minded fury that unnerved her just as much as anything he'd done in the cave. When she twisted her face away, he wrapped his fingers in her thick hair and jerked her lips back to his. She struggled against him, her mind numb, her body beginning to burn. Through the flimsy barrier of her shirt she could feel the tense contraction of his sinews, the rapid thud of his heart.

"You expect me to rape you?" he muttered against her mouth. "Aye, then, I'll do it. Far be it from me to shatter your expectations, particularly since I've lain awake night after night imagining this."

This proved to be the slow descent of his palms over her wet breasts. Her nipples buttoned instantly against his fingers and the inside of her head buzzed.

"I'd have wagered my richest cargo that you'd have fled home to Westmor, yet here you are, bare-limbed as a water nymph, swimming or rowing or some bloody thing. Did you guess that I'd come to the witch to have my wounds tended, or are you a witch yourself?"

"Merwynna's not here," she whispered.

One of his hands slid over the curve of her hip and down to the place on her thigh where the skin was bare. "All the better." Her flesh burned where he touched her. "I'll be able to ravish you undisturbed."

He hadn't seen Alan in the rowboat, she realized. Alan was safe. No, no, he wasn't safe. If he were left outside for much longer, he would die.

Alexandra tipped her head back, looking into Roger's eyes, trying to see the essence of the man he really was.

His mouth twisted under her scrutiny. His good hand moved up again to grip her chin between his thumb and two fingers. He stared; his forefinger rubbed the surface of her bottom lip; then he said something unintelligible and bent to kiss her again.

As the heat of his body warmed her, Alexandra dimly recognized that she had stepped into another realm, a place where there were no thoughts, only feelings. For good or ill, there was some fundamental part of her that trusted this man. "Ye cannot know the hearts of people, nor the mysteries of the gods, by means of your reason," Merwynna had told her. You couldn't know another person, nor could you alter your own fate.

And she made the leap beyond reason into faith. "I've found Alan," she said.

He ignored her, thinking, no doubt, that it was another trick. Leaning backward, she fought the hand that was so tightly fastened in her hair. His body was all around her, hard, insistent, overwhelming. In response, she was soft and open to him, unafraid. But despite the excitement running in her veins, she couldn't forget about Alan. "He's in the boat," she added, just at the moment Alan made a low sound.

Roger lifted his head. His face was contorted by passion. He stared blankly at her for a moment before his eyes cleared; then he looked back toward the boat.

"His leg is broken." She was gasping for breath, and the pit of her stomach felt congested and achy. "He needs dry clothes and a hot fire at once. I found him on the other side of the lake. I had to swim across for the boat."

Roger pushed her away and stalked back to the boat, bending over Alan and feeling for his pulse. "What happened to him?"

"A low branch swept him off his horse. He was trying to crawl around the lake, seeking Merwynna's cottage, but he wouldn't have made it. Fortunately I heard him groaning and found him." She spoke calmly, but she was beginning to shake.

Roger's breath hissed out in a low whistle. "Fortunately for him, but not so fortunately for you. You'd be safely out of my clutches if you hadn't stopped for him, would you not?" His eyes ran over her bare limbs again. "You took your clothes off to swim more freely?"

"I certainly didn't do it with you in mind."

He shook his head several times. She could see that his shoulders were shot with tension, his fingers clenched as his eyes devoured her. They alone were enough to make her melt. He didn't even have to touch her.

"Between us we ought to be able to carry him," she said.

"I'm astonished that you expect help from me." Bitter anger flowed from him in waves. "Don't you think 'tis high time I added another brother to my murderous tally?"

"I don't know what to believe! I don't think I care anymore! If you really intend to kill me, I don't know how I can stop you."

"My dear," he said, "you could stop an army."

With some difficulty, they got Alan into the cottage and laid him down on one of the mattresses. Roger turned to build up the fire on the hearth while Alexandra began stripping the wet clothes off Alan's wet body.

"Can you set his leg?" Roger asked.

"Yes, if the bone's not shattered." She vigorously rubbed Alan's skin as she undressed him.

"Here, I'll finish that," said Roger as she got down to Alan's body linen. "Go over there by the fire, and for the love of God, wrap something around you. If you continue to parade about in front of me like that, I won't answer for the consequences. I suppose your clothes are on the other side of the lake?"

She nodded. "I forgot them. Anyhow, they were wet."

"A common complaint. We'll all strip and have an orgy."

But his voice was filled with mockery now, and he seemed to have controlled the impulse that had led him to seize her outside. He had no control, however, over the fire he had kindled in her.

In Merwynna's cupboard she found a simple peasant's tunic, which she pulled on over her damp shirt. Roger bundled Alan up in several blankets and pulled his straw pallet nearer to the hearth. Alan moaned faintly and moved his head. "He's coming around," Roger noted. "Fortune is clearly with you tonight. 'Tis only the necessity of tending him that's preventing me from beating you within an inch of your life."

Alexandra winced as she selected a strong painkiller from the medicine shelves, mixing it with another drug to make Alan sleep. "He may be difficult," she warned. "He doesn't bear up under pain the way you do. He's had a bad fright, thinking he was going to die out there."

"It's fascinating how oddly people behave when they think they're about to die." He took a step back. "You deal with him."

She knelt beside Alan and carefully placed a small pillow beneath his head. His eyes fluttered and his body stirred.

"I suppose I was wrong," she said. "I suppose you really haven't the slightest intention of murdering me."

"I'm suspending judgment on that," Roger snapped.

Alan groaned and opened his eyes. He looked around blankly for a second, then fixed on Roger. His eyelids flicked shut again. "Alexandra?"

"I'm here. You're safe now. We're going to give you something to drink, Alan. Open your mouth."

"But ... Roger ..."

"He won't hurt you," she promised.

"I remind you of our agreement, Alan," Roger said.

"I'd sooner make a pact with the devil," Alan retorted with surprising energy.

"Nevertheless, you made one with me, and I engage you on your honor to abide by it."

What were they talking about? "He's far too weak to be harangued about pacts and bargains, diabolical or otherwise." She raised Alan's head. "I've a medicine that will lessen your pain."

Her patient obediently swallowed the brew. "I feel as if I'm floating," he whispered a few minutes later. He sounded anxious. "Am I dying, Alix?"

"I gave you a drug. You're going to sleep, that's all."

When Alan slipped back into unconsciousness, Alexandra made her preparations for setting his broken leg. Roger strolled over to help. For several minutes they worked in near-silence—she speaking only to give directions and he obeying without comment.

The break was clean, just above the ankle. When the bone was set and splinted and bandaged, and the patient peacefully asleep on his pallet, Roger held out his injured hand, saying, "My respect for your talents increases continually. I expect you can patch me up almost as skillfully as you slashed me. Just don't lace it with poison."

A retort leapt to her lips, but she left it unsaid. There was a persistent pounding in the depths of her stomach, and she felt alive to every nuance about him—the shifting tones of his voice, the light nervous quality of his movements, the slight crinkle of his rain-slicked hair. It struck her that despite all his callousness toward his brother, he had shown nothing but gentleness in helping her set Alan's leg. He had ignored his own injuries—the palm that was still seeping blood, the ugly bruise on his forehead. They must hurt, but he hadn't complained.

I have injured him, she thought, staring at the wound that ran diagonally across his palm. A new line for Merwynna to read. She wondered if it would change his fate.

She numbed the area with a special herbal ointment before stitching it quickly with Merwynna's stout medicinal thread. He bore the operation in tight-lipped silence. "Very nice. Are you always so tender with brother-killers?"

She sank down on Merwynna's stool in front of the fire. "You came upon me with a drawn sword, Roger!"

"I'd been using it to kill a bloody snake."

"You put it to my throat."

There was a silence. The logs on the fire hissed their warmth into the small room, and Roger paced for a moment in front of the hearth, then pulled an empty mattress up beside her and sat down. He had removed his doublet, leaving his shirt and hose to dry on his body.

"I shouldn't have done that," he admitted. "It was not done with any serious intention of harming you."

"Then why—"

"There was a look on your face when I came into the cave . . . I misread it, obviously. Some women like to be taken fiercely—not hurt, but mastered. As a child, you loved it, remember, being tied to trees and such. For a moment I thought you were playing a game with me . . . an adult version of our antics of long ago." He paused, his eyes glowing with the reflected flicker of the flames. "For a moment I wanted to play."

Alexandra was speechless. He was speaking of things far beyond her experience, things that made her realize how much of an innocent she still was. And yet she was not shocked. If anything, his words aroused her. She flushed a little as it occurred to her that the intense excitement he'd engendered in her years ago was not unlike the feelings she had for him now. Her love for Roger had always been tied up with yearning, with passion. In that way it had been very adult.

"But I ought to have known," he continued, "that you of all women would defend your honor with a knife."

"It was my life I was defending, not my honor. At least, that was what I thought at the time."

"Against me?" He was shaking his head. "Because I am lustful, your honor may indeed be in danger from me, as I have warned you several times. But your life, Alexandra? God's bones, until now I thought I could count on having at least one sensible friend, one person who saw me neither as a god nor a fiend. Your faith in me was something I thought I could depend upon."

Ashamed, she countered, "You told me a few days ago not to put any faith in you. You didn't want it, you insisted. You didn't deserve it, you implied."

"I was in a rage that day. I'd have said anything to be left alone. And since when do you take my warnings to heart?"

"Then you deny killing anybody?"

"I deny killing anybody lately. I certainly didn't murder Will or your friend Ned. He hanged himself."

"He couldn't have hanged himself. It's impossible. Don't tell me he hanged himself, Roger."

"Anyone can hang himself. Don't let your affections get the better of your reason."

She laughed at the irony of this. "It is my reason that accuses you. My affections are clearly influenced in your favor."

He put his head in his laced hands. "Let's go through it, Alix. I want to hear exactly what you're accusing me of."

"It began with Will's death."

"You can't seriously believe I murdered Will. My life has been violent and I've done many things I regret, but I draw the line at murdering my own flesh and blood."

"Don't tell me you weren't in the country at the time," she went on, determined to have everything out. "I know you were. If you lied about that, you could have lied about a lot of things. You're a very clever liar, Roger."

"How do you know how long I've been in the country?" He raised his head and she saw the tight little lines around his mouth. "I've been back at Chilton for only a fortnight, and already you've got my entire recent past mapped out and chronicled? Forgive me, but I don't think that's possible, not even for an expert meddler like you."

"You're the only one who's gained by Will's death. You're the heir to the barony now."

"That doesn't make me his killer. By God, Alexandra, if I wanted to murder someone, I'd have chosen a more reliable method. Will died a clumsy, accidental death."

"You sent him a message asking him to meet you secretly that night. He was excited—that's why he got drunk and rode so recklessly. Will would never have acted like that under ordinary circumstances. The proof lies in his character, and in Ned's. An accident happens to a man who rarely drank and never rode wildly out at midnight. Suicide happens to a half-wit who is too simpleminded to conceive of such an act. It smells bad, Roger—that you'll have to admit."

He stared at her. His expression was unreadable. "Go on."

She went on with her analysis of the crime, explaining about the dagger that had been in the ditch, and Ned's fear. "My mother told you that I was worried about the dagger. You didn't know how much Ned may have seen on the night of the murder, but he was obviously a danger to you. You followed him and hanged him. As for me, I'd guessed too much. You had to kill me too."

"Why, then, Mistress Quick Wit, are you still alive?"

She was examining the knuckles on her fingers with great concentration. "There's the rub."

"There indeed. Of course I haven't ravished you yet. I always ravish the women I murder, especially the redheaded ones."

She lifted her head and met his harsh brown eyes. His mouth twisted into a caricature of a smile. "I didn't do it, Alix. I didn't touch either one of them, and that's the solemn truth. Disbelieve me if you choose. If you're determined not to trust me, I can't think of any way to change your mind."

Shame overwhelmed her. She knew he wasn't guilty. Perhaps she'd always known it, deep down where reason didn't reach. In her quest to make sense of the man he had become, she had ignored what he'd always been: a fundamentally decent person. Like everyone, he had passions and flaws; like everyone, he could be insensitive and cruel. Indeed, he was probably more sinful than most people—"I deny killing anyone *lately*," he had said.

But he wasn't heartless, he wasn't depraved. His code of ethics might be unconventional, but it bound him firmly nonetheless. There were some things he simply would not do.

Her mistake had been in failing to listen to the voice that had occasionally whispered, "But this is impossible." In her efforts to see behind his mask, she'd trusted rational analysis instead of instinct. Merwynna had been right: her excellent judgment had failed her. "Ye are proud," she'd warned her. "Ye will suffer for it."

She rose from her stool and fell to her knees before him on the straw pallet where he sat. "I believe you," she whispered, bowing her head against his upthrust knees and mentally castigating herself for her thick-headedness. "Forgive me."

He didn't touch her, but she felt his entire body stiffen.

"I ought to have known better. I've deeply wronged you, Roger. I'll never doubt you again."

She felt his fingers slip under her hair, gently caressing her ears, the sides of her head, the nape of her neck. He leaned forward, pulling her close against his body until she was all but sitting in his lap. "I wouldn't go that far," he said wryly. "Trust me as far as I deserve, and no more, Alexandra. I assure you, I'm very far from being a saint."

"I know." Her voice was muffled against his shoulder.

"Some of this foolishness was my own fault. When I came into that cave and found you frozen there, I ought to have recognized that something was amiss."

His unbandaged hand drifted over her shoulders, smoothing the tension away. "I won't soon forget how you fought me. You've the wit and courage of a champion, you know

that? Would you were a man, and at my side in battle, lass."
He paused, allowing his hand to move lower, then inward,
toward the swell of her breasts. "No, I take it back. I'm
full glad you're not a man."

Alexandra drew a jerky breath and lifted her face to his.
His slightest touch could make her forget that there was
anything else in the world between them besides passion.
Eagerly her lips parted, and her hands trembled as she fixed
them on the thin material of his shirtsleeves. Aching with
desire, she closed her eyes and waited for him to bend his
head and take her mouth.

But he didn't. He pushed her away and rose swiftly to
his feet. By the time she'd opened her eyes, he had already
flung another log on the fire and turned to Merwynna's
shelves. "Is there anything to drink in this hovel?"

"If you mean spirits, no."

He swore and slammed his fist down on the herb table.
Alexandra bit her lip and tucked her knees up, hugging
herself.

"What are you thinking?" she asked, watching him stare
for several minutes into the fire.

He turned abruptly and allowed his eyes to rove her body,
leaving no doubt in her mind what he was thinking. But his
reply denied it: "That there are several points about your
story that disturb me. Will's behavior in particular. You
knew him; you were betrothed to him. If you say he wasn't
likely to do what he did that night, I'm inclined to believe
you."

"And Ned, Roger. Why would he hang himself? It just
doesn't match up with what I know of him. I mean, whoever
heard of a peasant boy hanging himself in a fit of melancholia?"

"You told me yourself that he led a miserable existence—
the butt of everybody's jokes, the village outcast. Peasants
have hearts and souls too. They're just as entitled to be
bitter about life as the rest of us."

"I know, but the timing is exceedingly suspicious—you'll
have to give me that. He'd been trying to find me, trying
to tell me something. He gave me the dagger, and he was

terribly frightened. Now he's been silenced forever. The only people who knew about the dagger were Ned and my mother, Pris Martin, Francis Lacklin, and you."

"Pris Martin? The widow? How did she know about it?"

"She was there when my mother passed the dagger along to me."

"Somehow I can't imagine her murdering anybody."

"No, I can't either." She looked at him. "And Mr. Lacklin?"

Roger was silent for several seconds. She looked curiously at his face, but she couldn't guess what he was thinking. Finally he said, "He's a man of God."

"He's a hypocrite," she said with some trepidation. She didn't want to reveal how much she knew about Roger's interaction with Lacklin. He'd been patient with her so far, but instinct warned her not to push him any further. "It seems to me that he's far more concerned with secular power than he is with God."

"In his eyes, they go together."

"He's nearly as bad as the queen: if people don't agree with him, they must be either converted or destroyed."

"He's not that fanatical."

"He was right here at Chilton when Will died."

Roger was staring down at the bandage on his hand. He was considering the possibility, she would swear it. Her mind leapt. Of course! It could have been Francis Lacklin. Before his accident, Will had become disillusioned with heresy . . . he had been about to recant . . . at the end he had even asked for a priest. Perhaps he had guessed that Lacklin was plotting treason against the queen. Perhaps he had threatened to reveal what he knew to the baron, and Lacklin had felt it necessary to silence him. Alexandra wondered why she hadn't thought of this before.

"Of course he's not at Chilton now," she said unwillingly. "He's left for London. We know Ned was alive this morning."

Roger raised his eyes suddenly. He glanced at Alan, then back to her. His mouth twisted. "I can't believe that Francis would dirty his hands in such an affair. Even if he had a reason for doing away with Will, he would refrain. In honor I'd have to avenge my brother's death. I'd have to challenge him. And since he's more skilled with the rapier than I, he would be forced to kill me—an outcome he could never support. No, Alix, you'll have to do better than Francis if you want to convince me that there's anything more than your fertile imagination to all this. I know him; he's not guilty."

His voice was fully confident. She was shaken. In a few seconds she'd seen Roger accomplish what she herself had been unable to do: acquit a friend of suspicion. His sense of loyalty was stronger than hers. If their positions had been reversed, he would never have doubted her the way she'd doubted him.

She rose to search Merwynna's shelves for a headache powder. "I can't think anymore," she said. "I feel sick."

He pulled her stool closer to the hearth and made her sit on it. "You're still wet. Get closer to the fire." He returned to the shelves and began rummaging. "I hope there's something to eat in here. All this excitement is making me hungry."

"Me too." She grinned at him. "This afternoon in the cave, I was certain I'd never eat again."

"Idiot," he said affectionately, giving her soaking hair a tug. He found bread and cheese and laid them on the table. "This looks tempting. Use your black magic to make me some supper, witch. Then we'll discuss how I'm going to punish you for your vile suspicions of me."

Alexandra laughed to hide her sudden ungovernable yearning.

11

OUTSIDE Merwynna's cottage it was raining again, and the wind had risen to a whistle. Merwynna had not returned. She often stayed out all night if a new mother's labor was protracted. And even if the babe were already born, Alexandra knew of no family who would send the midwife away on a night such as this.

After a supper of hard bread and cheese, Roger moved aimlessly about the tiny cottage, poking into Merwynna's strange jars and packets before finally sitting down to stare at his sleeping brother. "He's resting easily. Will he sleep through the night?"

"Undoubtedly. I gave him a hefty dose of medication."

"You don't need me then. I'd best go."

She surveyed the bandage on his head. "You're in no condition to go anywhere."

"Have you forgotten the searchers? There are three of us missing now."

"I don't care. 'Tis a wild night, and too long a distance to Chilton for you to tramp with that lump on your head."

To emphasize this, she went to the door and opened it, waving a hand at the driving rain. "No one will be out in this. Your men will conclude that we've sought shelter for the night."

He came to her side and stared into the storm. When he

spoke, his voice was quietly tense. "It is far better, Alexandra, that I go."

His deep brown eyes, the arch of his eyebrows, the warm curve of his throat, his clever, long-fingered hands . . . She retreated to the hearth. Am I mad? she asked herself. Of course it was better that he go. Now that her fear of him was gone, there was nothing to restrain all her other feelings. "Your head must ache," she heard herself say.

He shut the door, contemplated it briefly, then sat down again on the empty mattress. "Aye," he admitted. He glanced at her where she was standing in front of the fire, her red hair loose on her shoulders. "I'm a mass of aches and pains, thanks to you. You're something, Alexandra Douglas. You draw a dagger against a sword. You, a schoolgirl, stand there proposing to fight an armed man, a mercenary, a seaman who knows every filthy trick there is. I've never seen anything to match it."

"Oh well, you'd have sliced me up in no time if you'd really been the villain I thought you were," she said in the quick, bright way she spoke when nervous. "It was considerate of you not to use your filthy tricks on me. No doubt I deserved them."

"And swimming that black lake to get the boat for Alan, even though you must have known it would enable me to catch you."

"I couldn't just leave him there, could I?"

"Gallant Alix," he said, not looking at her now, staring instead into the fire.

She sank onto her stool. An image came back to her— Roger's face just above hers in the dark, his body pressing her hard against the floor of the cave. The feel of him, the warmth of him.

She gazed into the red coals before her. The only sounds were Alan's breathing and the crackle and hiss of the burning wood. A translucent orange log stretched and crumbled into ash, consumed by its own propensity to flame.

"As soon as the rain lets up, I'll go."

She couldn't bring herself to speak.

"You can manage here alone, can you not? I'll return in the morning with enough men to carry him home."

She drew a deep breath. "I wish you wouldn't go."

"Think what you're saying, Alix." His voice was harsh.

"It's not as if we're alone," she retreated, nodding at Alan.

Roger raised his eyebrows at his brother's sleeping form, then shook his dark head slightly, frowning. Outside, the rain pelted the trees, thudded into the thatch above their heads. It was violent, short-lasting. It was bound to let up soon, and then he would go. He intended to leave Chilton soon. Who knew when she would see him again?

"You should always wear your hair loose."

She turned to meet his eyes, her face hot from the fire. She felt his glance take in not only her hair but her entire body—the lawn shirt, still damp about her throat and breasts, the simple tunic which ended somewhere in the vicinity of her knees. She felt as if his hands were moving over her. By the time his eyes came back to hers, the heat in her face had nothing to do with the fire.

"The truth is, sweetling, I've no wish to go anywhere."

"Alan warned me that you were going to attempt to seduce me. I didn't think you'd do it in his presence. What if he wakes up?"

"Actually, I have a strict policy of not debauching virgins, particularly when I don't intend to wed them."

"Whatever your policies are, you've never been famous for your self-restraint."

"No. Still, a sailor's life requires some discipline. I can control myself. You needn't pull another knife on me."

And suddenly she couldn't bear his bitterness. She rose and blindly crossed the few steps to him, kneeling down on the mattress beside him. "I made a terrible mistake today because I followed my brain instead of my heart. I don't want to do that again. I don't want to reason, argue, or spar with words. I just want to do what I feel."

He hushed her with his fingers on her lips. His roughness against her softness was a sweet enticement. "Where feelings are strong, action is dangerous, love."

She kissed his fingertips. "I don't care."

"Listen to you." His voice vibrated as if he were trying to speak lightly, but not quite able to manage it. "Your mother would tear her hair out, lassie. Haven't you been warned about lecherous villains like me?"

"Endlessly." She knew she was courting disgrace and dishonor, but she couldn't help it. He wanted her—she could feel it in every fiber of her body. He really wanted her. She took his hand and pressed it into her thick mantle of hair.

His brief smile vanished. His face became as hard and hooded as it had appeared on the cliff when she'd thought he meant to throw her over. His fingers slid up through her hair and tightened convulsively while his other arm came around her and drew her closer. As he slowly bent his head to kiss her, she thought she would faint with desire.

His mouth this time was gentle. She thought of him as a man of fire, not of tenderness, yet he kissed her in a careful, loving fashion, as if nothing were sweeter than their joining. His tongue ran wetly over the surface of her lips, then probed between them in a manner she was beginning to recognize. She knew how to meet the subtle invasion with her own tongue now.

Her arms rose to encircle his shoulders. Her tired limbs melted against his hard frame. He felt wonderful, all muscle and warm flesh and taut sinews beneath supple, fragrant skin. His dark hair curled around her fingers as she fondled the nape of his neck. At her touch, he groaned and deepened the kiss, giving her a startling new awareness of her feminine power.

"Sweet mother of heaven," he breathed against her lips. "If you knew how much I've wanted this, dreamed of it, yearned for it..." His hand dropped to her breasts and hovered. Her breathing grew frantic as she waited for his touch. When it came—a gentle, rhythmic kneading—she threw her head back and moaned her approval. "You arouse me in a way I can't explain, Alix. There's neither rhyme nor reason to it." He dabbed her throat with a series of short nipping kisses, each one seeming to increase in intensity. Then he pushed her roughly down beneath him on the mattress.

Dimly Alexandra thought she should stop this, but the idea dissolved like a specter as Roger lowered his body, supporting part of his weight on his elbows and leaning over her for another sweet, slow kiss. Their tongues swirled together, hers as hungry as his, their heads moving from side to side. He broke the kiss as suddenly as he'd started it, burying his face against her dark red curtain of hair while they both gasped for breath.

"You, my friend, are showing much more promise than you demonstrated that night in front of the hearth at Chilton when I first made improper advances to you."

She laughed. "I learn quickly. You've always known that."

He lifted his head to meet her eyes in the darkness. His were dilated, hard and bright and predatory. But the corners of his mouth were turned up in a smile. "Even as a child you came to me for knowledge. I taught you your first Latin words, do you remember?"

"Yes, you devil. They were obscenities from some scurrilous piece of Roman trash. There I was, six years old, declaiming classical erotica! My tutor was appalled."

His fingers were loosening the laces that secured the neckline of her tunic. "Why, in more than ten years, haven't you learned to put the action to the Latin words? You're a woman grown. Did Will never—"

"No," she interrupted fiercely. "And as soon as you came back I realized I'd been waiting for you."

"Oh, love." His hands trembled as they jerked the tunic down to her waist and rolled up the lawn shirt, baring her breasts. He made a low sound in his throat as he looked at her. "Christ, Alix, this is the one thing I ought not to be teaching you." His fingers touched her tenderly, circling the taut brown nipples until they glistened ruby-hard. His voice was unconvincing as he added, "Help me to stop."

But she was skimming over the earth on a wave of deep, gut-wrenching pleasure. As never before, her body was aglow with the fires of life. "Don't stop. If you stop I'll die."

"Beloved," he murmured. He shifted his knee so it pressed between her thighs. He brought it up, hard, to the place where through the thin material, she could feel herself damply burning. She gasped with combined desire and shyness, twisting beneath him. No man had ever touched her there.

"Shh, let me. I want to pleasure you. Relax, love, relax."

His liquid words had instant effect. One moment she relaxed, the next she was arching to get closer to him as his hand continued to fondle one breast while his mouth moved down to take the other. He drew on her gently; she moaned and writhed as the tender torment escalated. So this is what it's like, Alexandra thought. No wonder people kill and die for love.

She felt him slide a hand down to her waist, her thighs. He pulled at the tunic, raising it enough to caress the soft skin behind her knees. His mouth was still sucking her nipple, teasing it with his tongue, biting it just enough to add a hint of pleasurable pain. Once again she remembered their struggle in the cave—the feel of him taking her down and lying hard between her thighs. It astonished her that an event which had filled her with panic only a little while before could be the source of heightened excitement for her now.

His hand crept around to caress the dewy skin on her inner thighs. She moaned with anticipation as he feathered closer and closer to her most vulnerable spot. He was kneeling over her now, watching her intently while his hand mercilessly closed in. His eyes were hot, his mouth a sensual slash in his dark face. He enjoyed teasing her—it was his revenge, perhaps, for the way she had treated him. God! She was about to scream at him to touch her *there* when he finally did.

Her body convulsed and his mouth captured her cry as his fingertips strummed her. She felt him shudder. She knew a brief moment of anxiety wondering if she was supposed to be as slick down there as she was, but it passed when he whispered, "Look at you, so warm, so ready for me. Sweet Jesu, Alix, 'twould be so easy to take you."

"Take me, then. I want you to."

He groaned and the hand between her legs moved with increasing pressure, seeking out and finding tiny pleasure points and arousing them to a pitch of sensation she had never known before. Once his finger probed her internally, but retreated when she stiffened in sudden, unexpected pain.

"Virgins are a pack of trouble," he whispered in her ear.

"I'll grit my teeth. I'm not afraid."

"You may not be, my Amazon, but I am." His voice sounded strained and breathless. "Afraid of hurting you, afraid of ruining your chances for decent wedlock, afraid of getting a child upon you. None of these things need happen, however, if we're careful. I haven't spent years in the erotic East for nothing."

"What do you mean?"

"Here, I'll show you. Relax against my hand. That's it, love. Now move against me, your hips, your thighs. Yes." He kissed her hard, his tongue driving into her mouth. His breathing was labored; she could feel his heart pounding against her own. "Feel good, sweetling? Just let your body do the work; your body knows what it wants."

Alexandra clutched at him, feeling the world tilt crazily as she responded to his lovemaking. She had no fears or inhibitions, she was lost, fevered, a stranger to herself. When he shoved the shirt up around her waist and slid down to flick his tongue along her thigh, she was surprised, but she made no protest, not even when he nudged his head closer to the thick auburn curls between her legs. He parted her with his fingers and touched her with his tongue. "Roger?" She made a halfhearted effort to squirm away. His strong arms held her; his knees pressed hers wide apart and held them that way.

"Grit your teeth," he suggested as he began to nibble deliciously at her.

Everything turned hazy then as she melted into a panting, moaning creature who possessed neither reason nor shame. She moved to the rough rhythm he created, arching to meet his infinitely clever, darting tongue, helping him find the most exquisite spot and pressing it harder against him. Her body flushed, curvetted, and steamed a soft film of perspiration; her heart galloped, her breathing grew fevered. And still he continued, murmuring dark words against her, words whose breath fanned her pleasure-knotted tissues and sent her higher until at last she lingered briefly on the edge of a peak so soaring that even she, with all her courage, was momentarily appalled. She was about to tumble into a realm she'd never entered.

"No," she gasped, making one last desperate bid for control.

"Yes." It was no more than a whisper against her, but his will was stronger than hers. He nipped her gently until her body jumped and exploded in an incredible series of achingly wonderful tension-releasing spasms. She keened until he abruptly slid up and covered her mouth with his own. "Hush, my love, hush. Under different circumstances I'd love to hear your pleasure sounds, but if Alan wakes, he'll have my head for this."

She cast a glance at Alan, who was breathing deeply and not stirring. She looked back at Roger and burst out laughing, transported for a moment into the past, when as the two most mischievous children on the combined Trevor-Douglas estates, she and Roger had done something for which they feared punishment.

But he didn't join in her laughter. Rolling to her side, she hugged him. "Oh, Roger, that was wonderful! What was it?"

"*La petite mort*. The little death. It's what people steal and kill and barter kingdoms for." His voice was tight, his body stiff, and his dark eyes a little forbidding. He still caressed her, but his fingers were no longer so gentle. "A great deal of folderol for a few moments of bliss, don't you agree?"

"Roger?" Instinct combined with her new knowledge to help her understand what was wrong. "What about you?" She wanted to touch him, explore his firmly muscled flesh, give him the same pleasure he had given her. Shyly she allowed one of her hands to inch down his body.

"Leave it," he said, twisting sharply away. "If I don't stop now, there'll be no stopping me till your virgin blood flows thick beneath my thrusts." He threw one arm over his forehead, fist clenched, knuckles white. "Move away from me."

"I've told you I have no fear of that. My virginity is nothing to me, nothing but a barrier that keeps you from me!"

"And your honor, Alexandra Douglas? What of that?"

"'Tis an empty word, a man's word."

"And if your belly blossomed with my bastard? Then you'd care, I assure you."

Across the tiny room Alexandra saw the shelves with Merwynna's medicines. Potions to make you beautiful, perfumes to attract your lover, drugs to help you bear his child without great pain. And other drugs—potions about which she knew very little, save they were ways to ensure there was no child. These were things Merwynna had not taught her. Deep secrets. If men knew women could control their procreation, with whatever small success, they would call it the work of the devil, Merwynna said. But surely Roger was not so closed-minded; he had lived in the East, where the physician's arts were advanced. Lived there, and loved many women.

"There are ways to prevent that from happening. I wouldn't be surprised if you knew some of them."

He laughed without mirth. "Dear Alix. Passionate, but practical. Aye, I know a way or two, but experience has taught me that such precautions don't always work. Oh Christ!" His face darkened; he blew out a harsh breath, then closed his eyes as if in agony. "We must be mad, both of us!"

"We're not mad." She reached for him again.

He jerked away as if she'd scorched him. Jumping up, he stalked the width of the cottage twice, then squatted down before the fire, running his fingers through his disordered hair. "Don't come near me again, do you understand? Ever."

She sat up. "I love you."

"And don't talk like a half-wit. 'Twas lust, pure and simple—on your part and on mine." He stared at her body in the firelight for a moment, then averted his eyes. "Dress yourself."

It was as if he'd slapped her. Lust, pure and simple? He'd given her the most intensely moving experience she'd ever known, and he could dismiss it as lust?

"Why are you so all-fired intent on giving yourself to me? Do you think 'twill gain you your precious marriage? The alliance between us that everybody except me seems so bloody eager for?"

"No!"

"I'll never wed you, Alexandra Douglas. Not if you successfully seduce me, not even if you grow heavy with my child."

"You think I'm trying to seduce you into marrying me?" she demanded, stung. "Well, you're wrong! I love you!"

He came back to her, seizing her arm in a harsh grip and pulling her around to face him when she would have turned away. "You think so now, in the first flush of passion. 'Twill pass, Alexandra, I promise you. Be grateful when it does, for I'm not your faithful, chivalrous Alan. I take my pleasures where I find them, and then I walk away. I care for nothing and nobody, and I'm not going to change."

She looked into his eyes and saw nothing tender there, nothing that might indicate that he spoke aught but the truth. To her dismay, tears began coursing down her cheeks. Look at me, weeping because the man who frightened me out of my wits this afternoon is not in love with me tonight. He *is* the only person in the world who can make me cry. She pulled away, sinking down on the nearby straw pallet and snatching up a blanket to wrap around herself.

Roger paced the cottage, making no effort to comfort her. Alan stirred restlessly but did not wake. Sitting alone and cold in the middle of her mattress, Alexandra wept until she was empty.

The fire had died down. When at last there was no sound from her except an occasional sniff, Roger took several logs and built it up again. As the new wood caught and the heat blazed up, she raised her head and found that he was watching her, his expression determinedly free of emotion, except for his dark eyes, which somehow seemed to mirror her own agony.

"You're right, of course," she finally said. "My behavior today has been unforgivable. I ought to be thanking you for your restraint. Most men wouldn't have had such scruples."

She tried to say this in an easy, generous manner, but she was more hurt by his rejection than she could bear to admit. She wished she were a child again, solid in the conviction that there was no other girl in the world he loved more than herself, his oldest, dearest friend.

"I'm sorry for tempting you," she added. "Although I

don't suppose it was really all that much of a temptation. I know I can't compare with the sort of women you're used to. I don't say that in bitterness; I'm content with what I am. It's just that sometimes I can't help feeling wretched about being so unpolished and"—she came up with his own expression—"undebauched."

He shook his head slowly, but did not speak. After a moment he sat down with his back to the fire, pulling his stool a little closer to her, though still far enough away to make her feel as if there were a moat between them.

"We used to be the same, even though you were older. But now you've gone so far beyond me. I don't know you anymore. Still, I meant it, and I'll never take it back: I've always loved you, Roger, and I always will."

His eyes closed momentarily, and his shoulders slumped as if he were bending under a heavy burden. "Then you must learn how little I deserve it. I want you to understand why you can never be part of my life."

She stiffened at the word "never."

"Listen, love. My brother Will was a gentleman farmer whose conscience was so clean he probably had to make up sins to confess to the parish priest. A catalog of my sins, on the other hand, would send the average cleric into a reel. You're a sweet, bright, and honorable young woman. I'm a rogue, bound for hell." He hesitated, then continued, "'Twould be an offense against nature to wed you."

"Roger—"

"Don't interrupt. Except for brother-killing, there's no crime I haven't committed. You want to know what happened to the last young gentlewoman whose destiny crossed with mine? I killed her. No, don't be so quick to shake your head in doubt. You thought me capable of killing a few hours ago."

"In battle, perhaps, or in a duel. Not a woman. Not by murder."

"She's dead, whether by murder or not." His voice was heavy with guilt. "Her name was Celestine de Montreau, and she was a French noblewoman, the sister of a friend of mine. At least, he used to be a friend of mine. Now he's after my lifeblood."

Celestine! It was the name mentioned by the Voice. Celestine, and . . . *beware her brother.*

"She ended up a passenger on my ship last summer in the Mediterranean, and I seduced her." Roger's voice hardened. "Actually, the seduction was mutual, but Geoffrey didn't believe that; he thought she was innocent when in fact she was no virgin. Still, she was but eighteen. Your age exactly. And she fell in love with me. But I tired of her, as I always do." He lapsed into silence, staring into the fire. He seemed to be looking into the past, and there was a vulnerability about him that moved her deeply. She didn't believe he'd killed her, but whatever had happened to Celestine, Roger had suffered intensely for it. Was this the reason for his black moods, his world-weariness?

Alexandra clasped herself tightly in her blanket as it occurred to her that he was right to make light of her declaration of love. He was so much more experienced than she. He had lived a life she could barely conceive of. And he was a man who needed more than simple love—he needed tolerance and wisdom and great strength in a woman. He needed forgiveness; he longed for peace.

"How did she die?"

He shook his head slowly. "I don't want to talk about it after all. Suffice it to say that she might have been alive today if I'd been able to give her some of the love she offered me."

"Is giving love so impossible for you, then?"

"Yes. I've looked inside myself and seen a black and heartless void at the center of my being, with nothing wrapped around it that's not composed of selfishness and pride." He shifted uneasily. "Not a pleasant vision, I assure you."

Alexandra stared into the fire. What did she see when she looked into her own soul? she wondered, trying to understand him. She saw a tiny star of light, burning steadily there in the silence.

"I am sorry for you, Roger." To herself she added: But it'll take more than pity to turn me away from you.

12

ALEXANDRA awakened in the morning to the sound of horses' hooves outside. She sat up and saw that Roger had arisen from the blanket he'd spread out on the floor on the other side of Alan.

"Who's that?" she whispered.

"How do I know? I'd get dressed if I were you."

She snatched her clothes from the stool where they'd been drying in front of the hearth and pulled them over her head, smoothing the tunic down just as a loud banging began on Merwynna's cottage door.

She and Roger exchanged a look. His hair was in his eyes; he pushed it back. His face was dark with the overnight growth of his beard. "I fell asleep," he said sheepishly. "What time is it, I wonder."

"Well past dawn," she guessed from the quality of the light. She got to her feet and leaned over Alan. He still slept deeply, but his color was good. "I hope our search party hasn't been out in the storm all night while we've been resting here."

"Open in the queen's name!" somebody shouted.

"That's not our search party," said Roger, frowning. "That's a London accent if I ever heard one."

"Break it down," a calmer voice commanded.

"Oh sweet Jesu," Alexandra said. "It's my father."

Roger buckled on his belt and ran a hand through his untidy hair. "Your father. Lovely, Alix. That's all I need. I don't even have a weapon to defend myself against the inevitable charge of virgin-snatching. I thought he was at court."

"We heard yesterday that he was on his way here. . . . The door's not locked," she called, rushing forward to open it.

"You'd better talk fast, my girl."

She threw him a smile. "At that, I'm an expert."

As she flung open the door, three burly men-at-arms stumbled shoulder-first into the cottage. Sir Charles Douglas was right behind them, a hefty-red-bearded man with the insignias of his court office stitched onto his richly wrought sleeves. He was followed by another three soldiers.

"Hello, Father," Alexandra said with aplomb, stepping into the thick of the pike-armed retainers to greet him. He grabbed her and pulled her into a fierce embrace. "Welcome home," she added from deep in his arms.

"My dear little lassie, we've been afraid for your life!"

"Fiddlesticks, I'm perfectly safe. 'Tis Alan we were worried about. He broke his leg and needed warmth and shelter. he's safe, but the baron must be notified at once."

Sir Charles kept hold of his daughter while he looked from the unconscious boy on the pallet to the scruffy-looking young man who was nonchalantly sitting on a stool before the hearth. Alexandra followed his gaze and wished that Roger would take the trouble to appear a little more respectful. Her father was accustomed to a certain deference.

"You remember Roger, of course?"

Sir Charles made a gesture and his men surrounded Roger, their pikes directed at his body. Alexandra noticed an almost imperceptible stiffening of his arms and legs, a clenching of his unbandaged hand, but he did not move. "This is convivial. 'Tis a pleasure to meet you once again, too."

"You have dishonored my daughter," said Douglas in a tone Alexandra had never heard from him before. He had drawn his rapier; his hand was trembling. "I see no reason not to kill you on the spot."

"Father, please! We were stranded here with Alan. Roger

had a crack on the head and he fell asleep . . . there's been no dishonor, and no harm done."

"Indeed?" Alexandra could feel her father regarding her thin garments, bare feet, and loose long hair. Roger looked no more formal in his open shirt, rumpled trunks, and hose. She blushed. Her father's men were staring openly at her, and giving each other significant looks.

"They don't believe you, love," said Roger. "My reputation for lechery is apparently more convincing than yours for honesty and virtue."

Vaguely guilty over her not-so-virtuous behavior during the night, Alexandra lifted her chin and said, "I demand the respect of being believed." She marched up to the most insolent-looking man-at-arms and jerked the pike from his hands. His mouth dropped in astonishment, but when he belatedly jumped forward to retrieve his weapon, she was directing the point of it at his chest.

"I will defend my honor against anyone who seeks to impugn it," Alexandra declared.

Roger buried his face in his hands and laughed.

Sir Charles, who was apparently well-acquainted with his daughter's mettle, cursed his careless retainer and ordered him outside to take care of the horses. "By your own account, this man is a murderer," he said to Alexandra, drawing papers from the inside of his padded doublet. "Yet after spending a night in his company you defend him with a pike. You impugn your own honor, daughter, by such a contradiction. I demand an explanation."

Alexandra recognized her own handwriting on the notes. Molly must have given her fanciful speculations about Will's death to her parents. She cast a glance at Roger, who was making a noble attempt to control his mirth. "Remember yesterday when I told you I'd left papers detailing my suspicions? Papers to be read in the event of my death?"

"A bluff. No?"

"No." She turned to her father. "I'm not dead, am I? Those papers were sealed, and ought not to have been opened."

"You vanish from a sickbed leaving behind a cryptic note

about your possible demise and don't expect us to read it? Your mother's at her wits' end, Alexandra. When I arrived home last night the entire valley was in an uproar. One brother was dead—murdered, it was now suggested; another brother had disappeared; and you, despite your allegations, had blithely ridden off with the murderer and failed to return. We've all been sick with fear."

"Come on, Douglas," said Roger. "You don't seriously think I murdered my brother."

"It was a mistake," added Alexandra.

Sir Charles glared at both of them. "A mistake. It all sounded damnably plausible to me, particularly after one of the Westmor grooms came tearing home with a wild story about the two of you disappearing into thin air on Thorncroft Overhang."

Jacky, thought Alexandra. Blast the boy!

"We searched the area and found the body of the half-wit, Ned, or whatever his name was. We also found a rapier, later identified as Roger's, stained with what we believed to be your lifeblood—was that a mistake too?"

He addressed Roger, shaking the papers at him. "Your father says you corrupt everything you touch. What have you done to her, to turn her into your ally? I don't care if you've murdered ten brothers, but if you've tainted my daughter, I'll kill you with my own hands!"

Roger leapt to his feet and five pikes immediately prodded him. "I haven't touched your precious daughter. If you believe me guilty of a crime, you'll have to bring me before a duly appointed magistrate. If you're not prepared to do so, I suggest you call off your thugs before I lose my temper."

"I am a duly appointed magistrate," Douglas informed him. "I arrest you in the name of the queen."

"Oh Christ," said Roger softly. The look he gave Alexandra was a mixture of annoyance and forbearance. "Put that thing down and defend me with the truth, my dear Amazon. This is your doing."

"I know." She was miserable. "Forgive me."

"Take him," Douglas ordered his men.

When one of them pulled out wrist irons, Roger grimaced

and said, "That won't be necessary, dammit," but the man closed in on him while another pikeman grabbed Roger's arms from behind and tried to hold him.

"Don't!" cried Alexandra, sensing the coming explosion from the look in Roger's eyes. It was too late. Roger whirled on the man behind him and struck him on the back of the neck. He slumped to the floor unconscious. It happened so fast that the others were paralyzed for an instant; then they all jumped forward. Hands tightening on her pike, Alexandra too would have leapt into the fray, had her father not seized and held her.

"He's hurt! They'll kill him!"

"I doubt it," said Charles as Roger flipped one of the pikemen over his shoulder and snatched up his pike to defend himself against the other three. One gamely tried to engage him while another drew his broadsword. The third began to edge toward the hearth to get in back of the prisoner. Sparring with the others, Roger ignored him until he was out of sight, then unexpectedly whipped the heel of his pike backward into the man's groin. The unfortunate soldier screamed, fell backward upon the smoldering coals of last night's fire, and shrieked again.

The man with the sword rushed Roger, who ducked, twisting out of range of the thrust of the one remaining pike. He grabbed a jar from Merwynna's herb shelves. "This is acid, and somebody is going to get it in his face." He glanced over at Sir Charles. "Are you going to call them off, or does your desire for entertainment extend to watching the disfigurement of one of your men?"

"I'm admiring your ingenuity. One unarmed, battered-looking man with a bandage on his hand efficiently dealing with five soldiers. How often does one get to see such a spectacle? Ten to one there's no acid in that jar."

"Shall I fling it at Alexandra, then?"

"No," said her father, trying to thrust her in back of him. She wouldn't go. He barked an order to his men, who retreated slightly. They were all cursing under their breaths, and Alexandra could tell from their faces that they'd like nothing better than to attack this man who'd made such a fool of them, and batter him to his knees.

"What the devil do you intend to do?" Douglas demanded. "What we want from you is an explanation. If you're really not guilty of any crime, you'll give us one."

"I've no objection to answering Alexandra's ridiculous charges; in fact, there are one or two points about my brother's death that I myself would like to see clarified. But I refuse to be manhandled or clapped into irons. You have my word that I will not attempt to flee."

Douglas seemed to consider. Alexandra noted the way his shrewd eyes assessed his adversary. She thought she recognized a spark of admiration for the man who, as a boy, had been the closest thing he'd had to a son. "Very well," he finally said.

Roger unstoppered the jar and poured some pungent-smelling perfume into his hands, then rubbed a little on his sweating face and neck. Alexandra felt her father's big body relax.

"And I wish to hear no more in the way of insults to Alexandra's honor. I have not relieved her of her maidenhead, much though I might have been tempted." He gave Alexandra a thin smile as he spoke. "You have my solemn word on it."

Charles looked back and forth between them, saying, "I pray God you speak the truth."

Alexandra was a little surprised at his warmth—her father spent so much time away that she sometimes doubted he cared very much about her. But he certainly seemed relieved to hear that she had not been villainously raped.

"We do," she confirmed.

"You'd better," said her father.

Two hours later they were all assembled in the great hall at Chilton—Roger, Alexandra, her father, his father, Dorcas, assorted men-at-arms, the baron's physician, and, sitting quietly near the hearth, Priscilla Martin. "What's she doing here?" Alexandra asked her father. "I thought this was meant to be a private inquiry."

"Richard has insisted upon her presence. I don't know why. Sit down, Alexandra. And don't speak unless you're spoken to . . . if that's possible."

Alexandra collapsed on a bench, feeling weary and depressed. She had slept very little during the night, kept awake by her awareness of Roger's body stretched out on his blanket only a few feet away. He hadn't touched her again, and on the long trek home through the forest this morning, he'd virtually ignored her. She felt like a patient who's just been diagnosed with the plague.

Alan had been put to bed. Master Theobald, the baron's physician, had expressed his doubts over the job she'd done of setting the lad's leg, but he hadn't ventured to reset it, thank God. He was a thin-faced, lugubrious man who drank too much and always seemed surprised when his patients recovered. A Calvinist like his master, he regarded illness as one of the scourges with which the Lord punished the wicked. If you were taken sick, you had probably done something to deserve it. Alexandra knew this wasn't true. She herself had been wicked on numerous occasions, yet she was rarely in need of the physician's dubious arts. Even the cold she'd had yesterday—which by rights ought to be much worse today—seemed mysteriously improved.

Dorcas came to sit beside her. "My poor girl, thank God you're safe and well. I've sent word to your mother. We've all been frantic with worry over you."

"I'm sorry everybody was so concerned. It was all my stupid fault. I was wrong about Roger, and I've gotten him into this intolerable mess. I feel like crawling under the trestle boards with the dogs and staying there until I die."

"Don't fret. Richard knows Roger had nothing to do with William's death."

But when Alexandra looked at the baron, standing stiffly on the dais at the end of the hall, staring without love or pity at his wayward second son, she felt far from convinced.

When the inquiry began, Roger made no effort to smooth the waters between his father and himself. Instead, followed closely by two cautious Douglas men-at-arms, he strolled up to the dais to address the baron: "You've got your wish, after all: here I stand, accused of murdering your eldest son and heir. And you're to hear my case? Surely I'm entitled to a stricter degree of impartiality. You, Father, would hardly hesitate to condemn me."

"If there proves to be a case against you, you will be remanded for trial to the district assizes."

"There to rot in prison, no doubt. Very well, let's get on with this farce. Where are my accusers?"

Everyone looked at Alexandra, who felt herself flush uncomfortably. "As I've already told my father, I have no accusation to make," she said.

The baron held up the papers containing her allegations. "And what of your suspicions regarding Will Trevor's death?"

"A fantasy, my lord, which seemed to require a villain. Because I was angry with Roger, I cast him in that role. Those are my private papers. It appalls me that anyone should have taken that nonsense seriously. I absolutely reject every word."

Sir Charles came forward and looked from the tall dark-haired man to the red-haired girl. "There is the possibility that she is under duress. God only knows how he may have threatened her."

"Alexandra, you need have no fear," said the baron. "Speak freely, please. He cannot harm you."

Roger made a gesture of disgust. "Show them the bruises I left on your body when I tortured you, Alix. Sweet Christ!"

"I am not under duress. If I still believed him guilty of fratricide, my lord, no threat would prevent me from saying so."

"Whether or not my daughter wishes to accuse your son, Richard, there have been two deaths here recently, neither of which has been entirely explained. Although William's death was ruled an accident at the time, the mysteries surrounding it were never cleared up: Where was he going at midnight on the night of June 22? Why was he, a man who rarely tasted spirits, so full of drink? And what was the immediate cause of his violent fall? Whether she likes it or not, Alexandra's speculations on these matters have raised questions which demand answers."

"Very well," the baron said. "Proceed."

Sir Charles read a passage from Alexandra's notes suggesting that Roger's secret arrival at Chilton had been the cause of his brother's odd behavior. Roger denied it. He'd been out of the country at the time of Will's accident. He had papers documenting the arrival date of the *Argo*, his ship. If Alexandra believed him to have returned earlier, she was, quite simply, mistaken.

And so it went on, all her accusations—the broken dagger, the piece of it she'd found in the ditch, Ned's terror—and Roger's calm, slightly mocking dismissal of each point of her elaborate case against him. Alexandra heard the proceedings through a kind of haze. Her eyes saw not the great hall at Chilton, but a tiny witch's hut where Roger had called her his beloved and touched her with passion. Her body flashed with excitement as she relived the feel of his hands between her legs ... the feel of his mouth. She recalled the shivery ecstasy he'd led her to, that incredible sensation of falling off the world. She wanted it again. She wanted him to fall with her.

But he'd made it clear he didn't want her—not for that, not for anything.

They were questioning her now about Ned's death. Her head ached as her father went over and over the events leading up to yesterday. Master Theobald, the physician, had apparently examined the boy's body. He came forward now to say that Ned had died of asphyxiation. The rope burns around the neck were consistent with what would be expected of a hanging. In the opinion of George Dawes, the baron's master-at-arms, the knot which comprised the noose was a clumsy one, hardly the type an experienced seaman would venture to make. In other words, there was nothing to suggest foul play.

Alexandra frowned as all this was revealed. She was still puzzled about Ned. They'll bury you in unconsecrated ground for committing the crime of self-slaughter, she thought to herself. Did you really kill yourself? Why is it that I still can't believe that? Why is it that I still feel there's something very wrong here, something we're not managing to uncover?

It was apparent, when the questioning finally wound down, that despite Roger's calm and rational answers, Sir Charles wasn't entirely satisfied. "The fact remains that two young men, neither of whom should have died for many years, have recently met unusual and sinister ends," he finally said. "At the same time, after years of absence, Roger Trevor has reappeared to take his place as his father's heir. Although we have not been able to prove any connection between his return and these two deaths, I suggest the matter calls for further investigation."

There was a muttering among everybody in the hall. The baron raised his hand for quiet. "Enough," he said loudly. He looked angry. "I have listened patiently so far. And I have heard nothing which convinces me that there is the least substance to any of these ridiculous charges against my son."

Roger looked at him in surprise. Alexandra thought she saw his tan face flush slightly. He clearly hadn't expected his father to speak for him.

The baron went on, "I am well aware that once such allegations are made, they tend to smolder. For this reason, I intend to put an end to the mystery concerning Will's death, even though the information I am about to disclose will bring pain to the hearts of at least two people among you."

The baron had everybody's attention now. There was an almost palpable tension in the hall. Alexandra felt a series of small shivers run over her skin—a kind of premonition. There was complete silence as Roger's father continued, "Will's death was indeed accidental. The reasons for his drinking and his sudden decision to ride out have been known to me since shortly after he died. I have maintained silence on the matter in deference to the wishes of a young woman who did not wish to have her role in the affair disclosed. She has promised to speak out, however, if her evidence becomes necessary. I think she will agree with me that the time for complete honesty has come."

Before he had finished these words, Alexandra's fascinated gaze had swung to Pris Martin. She was the only young woman present to whom he could possibly be referring.

"Mistress Martin, I must ask you to step up here, please."

Pris Martin put down the embroidery she'd been working on and walked slowly up to the dais. As the baron took the widow's trembling hand, Alexandra caught Roger's eye. He shrugged and raised his eyebrows in a gesture of puzzlement.

Dorcas followed Priscilla, putting her arm around the young woman's waist. Dear, kind Dorcas. Pris seemed to welcome her support. The baron gave her a few moments to collect herself, then gently said, "Please tell us the nature of your connection with my eldest son, Pris."

There was a moment of silence during which Alexandra's breath was suspended. She could feel herself leaning forward on the bench; beside her she sensed her father's alertness. The premonition of disaster grew stronger. It occurred to her that if Pris was one of the two people whom this revelation would hurt, she herself must be the other.

Pris Martin pulled herself together and spoke out in a firm voice: "I loved your eldest son and he loved me. Together, we were expecting a child."

"Jesu," Alexandra breathed. Her father took her hand and squeezed it; her fingers clung to his.

"My poor babe was born on the night of his father's accident. I had a difficult labor. I imagine Will was drinking out of concern for me. It was to my side that he was hurrying when he was thrown from his horse into the ditch on the Chilton road." She put her hand over her mouth for a moment, then managed to continue, "They said he lived for three days, and I prayed that he would send for me to say farewell, but he did not. My son died also, leaving me with nothing."

She turned to stare directly at Alexandra. Her beautiful eyes were full of bitterness. For the first time, Alexandra understood why Pris had rebuffed every attempt she had ever made at friendship.

"If Will had lived, he was going to marry me. 'Twas me he wanted, not you."

Alexandra's head felt thick, her throat ached, and her eyes could not seem to see anything around her. She was back in Will's bedchamber, sitting beside his bed. He was dying, the physician had said. He could probably never regain consciousness. But Alexandra continued to talk brightly to him anyway, encouraging him. The physician, after all, was an ass.

At last her efforts were rewarded: Will's eyelids fluttered and his hand moved under hers. He tried to speak, and after much effort, a word came out. "Priest," was what she had heard then. She heard it now as "Pris."

A cry rose in her soul, silent but piercing. She had misjudged Roger, and now once again she knew the folly of believing she could read another person's heart. Once again she had been completely blind. Will had not cared at all about a deathbed reaffirmation of his faith. All he'd wanted was to see Pris Martin again, to have his mistress at his side, to hold her hand and know the peace of dying near the woman he loved. Instead, because of Alexandra's stupidity and blindness, he had been forced to endure the presence of the woman he had dutifully agreed to marry, while poor Pris had waited in solitary grief for a summons.

Alexandra leaned over the trestle table and buried her face in her arms. No wonder Will had never shown any passion for her; he was not cold-natured—he simply loved another. And as for her, no man loved her—not Will, not Roger, and probably not even her father. Who could wonder at it? All there was at the core of her being was a black and heartless void, surrounded by layer upon layer of selfishness and pride. Who was she to pass judgment on Roger Trevor or anybody else? The light in her own soul was nothing but an illusion.

13

*T*HERE WAS a profound sense of unease among the small group of people around the trestle board. Alexandra and Pris Martin avoided each other's eyes, while Roger was silent, absentmindedly rubbing his bandaged hand. Dorcas had gone to check on Alan, and Alexandra longed to find a bed herself. Her cold had begun to bother her again. Perhaps the drenching she'd endured the night before was going to have it effects after all. She sneezed.

"God bless you," said Roger.

She looked at him briefly, then resumed her contemplation of the wood grain in the table. She didn't want to know what Roger thought of her now. If it was pity, she didn't want it, and if it was the scorn she felt she deserved, she would rather not encounter it. She had disgraced him. She had made a laughingstock of herself. She had insulted the baron by suggesting that he had not properly handled his investigation of Will's death, and she had forced her own father to lay out a series of ridiculous charges against Roger. Worst of all, her meddling had brought about a revelation which was a discredit to Will and a misery to poor Pris Martin.

They weren't letting Pris leave, even now. The questioning continued until Alexandra wanted to scream for it to end. Oddly enough, Pris was bearing it better than she was. As always, she seemed to have herself firmly under control.

Pris had loved Will ever since she'd first met him two years before, she reported, but no acknowledgment of love had passed between them until after her husband's death. "I do not seek to justify my conduct," she said calmly. "The misfortune of my pregnancy was in proportion to my sin, but in some ways, God was merciful: people took the child for a posthumous babe of my husband's, so my reputation did not suffer."

Until today, she did not add, but Alexandra was sure she must be thinking it.

"What made you believe my brother would break his contract with Alexandra to marry you?" Roger asked.

"I did not believe it until the end. Indeed, I did not expect it. Will knew his father desired the match and he considered himself bound. But he grew anxious as the time for my confinement approached. Perhaps he had a foreboding. I too was frightened. We had sinned and we both felt that the best way to redeem our sin was through honorable wedlock. Will intended to go to you, my lord, his father, and confess his folly. He was waiting only for the safe delivery of the babe. He trusted you would consent to his marrying the mother of his child."

"And if my father did not consent?" Roger persisted.

Pris Martin shrugged. "It hardly matters now, since nothing turned out the way we had hoped." She smiled faintly at the baron and added, "Your father has been far kinder to me than I deserved. I am grateful."

She was asked to explain exactly what had happened on the night of her travail. "Will had visited me that afternoon. I told him my time was upon me. He wanted to remain at my side, but I insisted it would not be proper. I promised to send him news.

"My labor was difficult. I dared not send for the midwife lest there be gossip—a midwife would know that my baby had not stayed overly long in the womb. No one knew the true father of my child except a single adviser, who finally arrived that evening to be with me."

"Who was that?" Roger asked, but Pris did not answer. As if in a trance, she went on with her story:

"I was in unspeakable pain. Between contractions I would pause in a fearful daze, waiting for the next one with great dread. I suppose it was near midnight when my son was finally born. I was weak, but I wanted to send word to Will immediately. I scribbled a note and sent it to Chilton with a servant." She stopped speaking to look at the baron. "You know better than I what happened next, my lord."

Richard Trevor took up the story. "I was concerned about Will that day; in fact, he had been acting odd for several days. He sat up late in the winter parlor drinking unwatered wine. I asked him several times during the course of the evening if something was bothering him, but he declined to answer.

"Around midnight a note was brought by a frightened servant, who ran off when I attempted to question her." The baron reached into a pocket and withdrew a slip of paper. "I kept the message. Have I your permission, Mistress Martin?"

She seemed startled. "I assumed it had been burned. Will swore to me he always burned my letters."

"He flung it on the hearth after reading it, but he was too agitated to realize that the fire had died down to ash. Later that night, when he didn't return home, I found it, scorched but still legible." He unfolded the paper and read: "'In great travail am I delivered. You have a son. Do nothing rash, I prithee, before we talk. Do not betray me to your family. Come to me, I beg you, tonight. There is a matter I must discuss with you.'"

Finally Pris Martin was showing some emotion, Alexandra noted. Her face was pale and her hands trembled as the fatal note was read. "May I see it?" she asked. For the first time she sounded upset. "I had forgotten exactly what I had written."

The baron handed her the paper. She studied it in silence. How must she feel, Alexandra wondered, reading the message that had sent Will racing out to his death? Without thinking, she found herself addressing Pris for the first time since her revelation had been made, instinctively trying to soften the blow.

"He would have ridden out anyway, note or no note," she said gently. "He would never have passed the entire night without coming to you. Don't blame yourself, Pris."

As usual, it sounded clumsy—she had never been able to say the right thing to Priscilla. But this time the woman didn't even seem to hear her. She continued to stare dumbly at the paper while the baron went on to explain how he'd checked in the village to see what woman had borne a child that night. It had not been difficult to uncover Priscilla's secret. In pity for her, he had done what he could to make her life easier. If the child had lived, he would have been properly cared for, but the boy did not survive his father by more than a few days. It was probably just as well, the baron added. Life would be easier for Pris without a dependent son to worry about.

If the baron expected further acknowledgments of his kindness from Mistress Martin, he was disappointed. She heard him through without expression, then rose, carefully folded the note she'd written to Will, and slipped it into her embroidered girdle. She turned to them, her lovely face pale with emotion. "If you are finished with me, I would like to leave."

No one stopped her as she fled from the hall.

"Poor dear wicked Will," said Roger, breaking the ensuing silence. "He wouldn't really have wed her, of course. She hasn't a farthing to her name. The two of you"—he smiled pleasantly at Sir Charles and the baron—"would never have permitted it." He paused a moment, then went on, "Which reminds me, while we're on the subject, let's not put our heads together and serve up any further family alliances, if you please. I have informed my father, Sir Charles, as well as your daughter, that I am not in the market for a wife. I hope that fact is clearly understood by all?"

"You cocksure bastard," said Charles Douglas. "One of the reasons I hastened to Westmor as soon as I heard you'd returned was to put a stop to any such schemes."

"Indeed? I thought from the way you were proclaiming

me your daughter's seducer this morning that you hoped to force me into offering her my name."

"That's what you thought, is it?" Douglas' volatile temper was aroused; his face had turned almost as red as his beard. "You think I'd turn my only daughter over to a bloody-minded adventurer like yourself? I've heard tales about your doings, Trevor, which, though they be nine parts out of ten a lie, are enough to convince me that you'd be no fit husband for a child of mine. I'd see her in hell first."

Roger affected surprise. "Could it be that my exploits are so well known in London? Good God, I certainly hope there are other such scrupulous fathers at court. The more opposition I encounter from the parents, the quicker the spirited lassie falls into my trap." He winked at Alexandra. "Isn't that true, love?"

She rose wearily. "You're welcome to make sport of me behind my back, but I certainly don't intend to stay here and listen to it. For the trouble I've caused you, I'm sincerely sorry. For the patience you've shown me until now, I'm grateful. I've earned your wrath, I know, but this I promise: never again will I meddle in your life, Roger. I'm going home now. Good-bye."

Roger did not move from his place on the bench, but it did seem to her that the skin over the knuckles on his unbandaged hand turned white with some sort of tension. "I'll wipe the slate clean if you keep that promise," he told her.

"I'll keep it."

Their eyes met. He's trying to tell me something, she thought. Something he can't say before his father and mine . . . something infinitely kinder than the rot he's just produced for their benefit.

He's glad to be rid of you, her new unblinded self retorted. He hopes to God he never has to put up with your foolishness again.

She turned her back on Roger Trevor and followed Pris Martin from the hall.

14

"Merwynna, what am I going to do?"

"Ye will follow yer destiny."

"They're intending to force me to marry, as quickly as possible. I don't know who it will be, but my father has several men in mind. 'You'll wed whomever I choose for you,' he informed me this morning, 'or finish your days in a convent.'"

"A convent is not a possibility," Merwynna assured her.

Three days had passed since the confrontations and disclosures in the great hall at Chilton. Three bitter, busy days. Early tomorrow morning, Alexandra and her father would leave Westmor to travel to London, where she was to take up residence at court. Douglas had kept his promise to secure his daughter a position in the queen's retinue. She was to be a lady-in-waiting, filling the place of a young woman who was leaving her post to be married. Within a year, swore Sir Charles, he would see to it that Alexandra, too, was suitably wed.

In the meantime she was forbidden to have any dealings with Roger Trevor. Both her parents had been adamant on this point. "You're a fool to believe that platonic friendship persists beyond a certain age," her father had said. "If you've escaped with your virtue intact," her mother had added, "no doubt 'tis only because that young devil is accustomed to spending his nights with women whose physical attributes far exceed your own."

Without permission, Alexandra had ridden to Chilton to visit Alan this morning before coming to Merwynna. His leg was mending, but he was still in pain. He refused to tell her what he and Roger had fought about that day in the forest. He'd given his word, he said, and bastard though his brother was, he'd keep it.

Secretly Alexandra had hoped to run into Roger at Chilton, but she had not. According to Dorcas, Roger had been taking long rides on the moors, wearing out one horse after another. Was he getting along better with his father now that the baron had acquitted him of involvement in Will's death? No, Dorcas reported sadly. Roger was subdued, but just as caustic as ever. And rumor had it that like Alexandra, he too had been packing his things.

Would she see him again before she left? she wondered. She looked around the small interior of Merwynna's cottage where they had spent that wild night together. Did he know she was going to London? Did he care?

She stared at the hearth where the fire had glowed, at the bench where she'd sat drying her hair, at the straw mattress where they had lain together. A sharp pang of desire knifed through her, making her shift restlessly on the bench where she sat sorting herbs with Merwynna. Frequently and without warning her mind would flash back to those sweet minutes in his arms. She had not realized before that her physical desires were so very strong.

"The desires of the body are strong but changeable," Merwynna told her now, calmly reading Alexandra's mind. "If ye were somebody else I would advise ye to learn what ye could of lovemaking from this man. Explore the fire in all its heat and golden light. Experience the joy and wonder of yer body with a lover who delights in sensuality. And finally, when yer passion is exhausted, part from him to seek the more enduring love of a man more worthy of yer affection."

"More worthy? I'm the one who's not worthy of him."

"Nonsense. What ye tell me of him confirms what I've always sensed: Roger Trevor is too caught up in the conflicts of his own soul to be able to love another human being."

"He told me that himself. Surely if he recognizes his own evils, he is halfway to dispelling them."

Merwynna shook her head slowly. "Recognition of the evil in one's own soul only makes life burdensome. I have told ye before, knowledge does not save us, not even self-knowledge. Good does not spring from evil, nor does light shoot upward from the depths of hell."

Whenever Merwynna talked like this, Alexandra felt irritated and baffled. "What does save us, then?" she demanded.

"That is something ye must discover for yerself."

She made a face. "You're not very helpful today. What do you mean, if I were somebody else you'd advise me to sleep with Roger? Somebody else like whom?"

"A woman without yer heavy duties and responsibilities. A woman of a lower social order who need not regard her children as the continuance of some vital male bloodline. Even more than poor Pris Martin, ye would be disgraced if ye bore the child of a man who was not yer husband. Ye canna take the risk."

"That reminds me, Merwynna, before I go to London I really think you ought to teach me exactly how one lessens the risk of such a thing."

The wisewoman's black-pool eyes surveyed her. "Am I to give ye license to engage in behavior that could ruin ye? Ye're not listening, Alexandra. Ye are the child of Sir Charles Douglas. Yer rank forbids ye the freedom to indulge in indiscriminate passion." Her lips twisted in speculation. "Ye want Roger Trevor, do ye not? Ye havna' given up the hope of having him."

Alexandra blushed and didn't answer.

Merwynna looked grave. "There's no chance of his wedding ye?"

"I'm afraid not. Ever since he returned to Chilton, he's been quite insistent about that."

"What happened here the other night? Ye say he did not take ye, yet ye are no longer as innocent as ye were before."

"You mean you cannot work a spell to 'see' exactly what happened? I suppose I should be glad of that!"

"Restrain yer playfulness, my child. 'Tis no laughing matter." Merwynna paused to reflect. "It is difficult. I had always intended to prepare ye for yer womanly maturity when the time arrived . . . to teach ye how ye may delight yer lover, and yerself. Ignorance of such is a great sorrow to women."

"And you know how I hate to be ignorant," Alexandra seconded. If she hadn't been so innocent, she was thinking, she would have known what to do to make Roger forget his qualms and take her.

"Yet now, as we speak, I feel a heaviness come over me. I do not know the cause. I feel myself at a turning point, a nexus o' possibilities. I must meditate. I might err if I proceed without great care."

Alexandra leaned forward eagerly. "Merwynna, tell me how I may avoid conceiving a child. That is a thing I fear."

Merwynna drew herself up to her full height and looked forbidding. "Such secrets are not to be imparted lightly. They're dangerous, child, and besides, there is no guarantee."

"I already know which herbs are used to bring on the monthly flux," Alexandra mused. "The most powerful of these you have refused to allow me to toy with."

"With reason—they poison both the mother and the child," Merwynna snapped. Her brow contracted as if in pain. Her voice rose in urgency. "Alexandra, I fear for ye. Ye must take care what use ye make of the secrets I have entrusted ye with, the mysteries I have revealed to ye. Perhaps I have erred already. Perhaps it was wrong of me to open my storehouse to one who could never follow in my footsteps. I fear some unhappy consequence. My mind is filled with darkness."

Alexandra was frightened. Several of Merwynna's recent prophecies had already come true. She touched the old woman's hand. "You made me swear you an oath once. Remember? *Never for evil, but only for good, I entreat you and serve you, O gods.*"

"I remember," Merwynna said, returning the pressure of her fingers. "The trouble is, do ye know the difference?"

She paused and then repeated, "I must meditate." A moment later she looked toward the door. "A stranger comes."

Alexandra had heard nothing, but she knew Merwynna's powers too well to question them. She rose and went to the door. Outside, making his way along the lakeside, was Roger Trevor. "Not a stranger," she breathed as her body instantly responded with a surge of desire.

"A stranger is anyone whose heart ye do not know. He hides his very well. Has he seen ye?"

"I think not."

"Return to yer seat, then, and wait."

Alexandra obeyed, trying to prepare herself for the most painful thing she could imagine: a look on Roger's face that would confirm to her that he had hoped not to meet her.

A few moments later his shadow filled the doorway. Merwynna had risen to greet him. He paused on the threshold, his eyes fixed on the wisewoman he had known in his youth.

"Do you recognize me?" he asked her. "I was a partaker of your hospitality a few nights ago, though you were not at home."

"I recognize ye, Roger Trevor. Ye wish to consult me on a personal matter? Walk in."

"I've come to leave a message," Roger corrected her, entering. He saw Alexandra. He smiled. "For a mutual friend," he went on without missing a beat. "Hello, Alix. I thought you might be here."

Her nervousness receded, but her consciousness of what had passed between them right here in this room did not. She stared at his tall, lean body, comfortably attired in dark trunks and hose and a loose lawn shirt. The material was thin. Through it she could see the dark whorls of his chest hair. Her longing crested like a wave. If Merwynna had not been there, she could have flung herself into his arms. "I'm going away," she said.

"I know. I, too."

"To court?"

"To London. I imagine I'll end up at court sooner or later. You've been forbidden my company, I understand?"

"On the strength of your well-deserved reputation as a defiler of chastity, yes."

He was not smiling now. "Although it is possible that we may see each other in London, you need not fear that I will tempt you to disobey your father. Any meetings we have will be public, polite, and eminently proper."

"Of course," she said joylessly. She looked beyond him. Merwynna had tactfully vanished. "Is that what you came her to tell me?"

"That, and one or two other things." He looked around the room, then back at her. Once again the heat ran between them. His eyes darkened and she sensed that he too was remembering. "Come outside," he said. "This place disturbs me."

They walked down to the edge of the lake. Merwynna was nowhere in sight. The afternoon was hazy and warm and the water lapped gently at their feet. Roger picked up a few pebbles and skipped them on the water's surface with schoolboyish skill. "Pris Martin has disappeared, did you know?"

"What do you mean, disappeared?"

"I went to her farm this morning. Something was bothering me about her story. I wanted her to clarify a few points."

"What points? It all made perfect sense to me."

"It scarcely matters. I found no one but an old servant. The mistress had gone, he informed me. He knew not where, he insisted, but one thing he did know: she would not be back."

"Heavens. She has no relatives that I know of, nor any money."

"Father has given her quite a bit of money recently, it appears. You'd have thought she was *his* mistress."

"Poor woman. I suppose she had no choice but to make do as well as she could. It wouldn't have been easy for her to remain here. She has always been so reserved. How dreadful for her to be exposed in such a manner."

He shot her a glance. "You feel guilty, don't you?"

"Wouldn't you?"

He shrugged. "It is always better to know the truth, Alix,

painful though the truth may be. I, for one, am not sorry for the trouble you caused." He smiled faintly. "It's a relief to know that old Will wasn't as morally upright as he pretended to be."

"Or Pris Martin either," she agreed with a grin.

"It's odd that she should have fled so precipitately," he went on, looking grave again. "It worries me. Even my father, who has been her confidant for months, knew nothing about her leaving. He's considerably annoyed. He wanted to gratify his pride by making a few more beneficent gestures toward her, I expect. She was one of the elect of God, after all, and charity begins at home."

His voice betrayed his continuing hostility toward his father. "He stood up for you," she reminded him.

"Not until the end. He could have spared everyone a good deal of embarrassment if he had spoken out at the beginning of the bloody inquiry instead of waiting for the grand finale. Worse, now he, along with everybody else, expects me to be grateful."

"Which you can't, of course, condescend to be."

"Don't start. No more meddling, remember?"

She nodded. "No more meddling." She watched an egret wheel down over the lake, then rise effortlessly toward the sun. "Was that your message—that Priscilla had gone?"

He reached into his belt and drew out a note. "This was my message."

She unfolded it and read:

> From the Devil to the Queen of Night: Considering the recriminations, it's a pity we didn't go ahead and indulge ourselves, is it not? O Unrewarded Virtue.

"You're the one who was virtuous, Roger, not I."

"Usually, I assure you, it's the other way around."

The note went on:

> No more glum faces, please. I want to remember you laughing, or, better still, defying me with matchless courage in your green eyes and a dagger in your fist.

"That wasn't courage," she interrupted once again. "I was terrified. It's a wonder my legs didn't cave in."

"Courage is not for people who feel no fear. They don't need it, do they? Courage is the determination to look your nemesis in the face, no matter how much you tremble. You're loaded with it, sweetling, and it's a valuable commodity. If you were a man, I wouldn't hesitate to ask you to join me."

"Join you in what?"

There was a fraction of a second's pause before he replied, "Join my ship's company, of course, what else?"

She went back to the note. No more meddling.

> As for how you remember me, no doubt it will be with far more generosity than I deserve. For all your noble sentiments, I sincerely thank you. And now, my oldest dearest friend, farewell. In future, as I trust you'll understand, we shall meet as nothing more than casual acquaintances. I will enforce this. Long and bitter soul-searching convinces me that the break between us must be final.
>
> Forgive me, Alix. God bless you.

At the bottom he had scrawled his name.

She took overly long to read it. She was striving for control. "A curious epistle," she said finally. "The style of the beginning is much at variance with the manner at the end."

He made no answer. She folded up the note and closed it tightly in her palm, then raised her face, trying once again to summon up the quality he had termed courage. It was not needed only for facing daggers and swords.

"You needn't say anything more. I'm not going to argue."

He hesitated for a moment, then did say something more: "This business of Will's—it's upset you. Honest, upright William proved to be false as fog, and now I respond with coldness to your affection for me." He paused. "It must be very hard."

"'One who cannot, one who will not, one who dares

not, one who dies,'" Alexandra recited. "I'm not sure which one you are—the second, I imagine. Never mind—it's my destiny. Unlucky at love, as they say." Her voice was very strained. "Can't we talk about something else? The weather? Does it rain in London at this time of the year?"

He blew out a harsh breath, making her aware that this was no easier for him than it was for her. "There is something else, actually. Something I could not commit to paper."

"My curiosity leaps."

"Your curiosity is precisely the thing I wish to restrain. Listen, Alexandra. I've already been more open with you than I ought to have been, so I'll tell you something more. I have enemies at court. There are people there who would go to drastic lengths to see my poor body broken on some torturer's wheel. The last thing I want is for you to acquire my ill-wishers."

"How could I? If we're to be such unrelenting strangers..."

"Exactly. One of the reasons I intend to create a gulf between us is to ensure that it never occurs to anybody to look from me to you and purse his nasty lips. But even so, there is a danger. Several things about your story the other day suggest to me that you've been nosing about even more than you admit, that for every transgression I've caught you in, there's been at least one I've missed, that you've lied to me now and then. Stop trying to look so innocent. I'm not going to press you.

"My purpose is simple: to warn you that whatever you've seen, or heard, or guessed, you must put it so utterly out of your mind that not even the most subtle scorpion at court will be able to sting it out of you. Do you understand? People's lives—and not just yours and mine—depend upon your silence."

"I knew it. You're a Saracen raider in disguise. The Muslim hordes are about to conquer all of Europe."

One of his hands was still lightly bandaged. The other reached out and gripped her tightly around the wrist. "No jesting, Alexandra. Promise me."

"You're hurting me."

His expression hardened. He did look like a Saracen raider with his dark hair, his sun-brown skin, his carnal mouth. The flare of passion in his eyes reminded her that although he might be master of himself, unruly emotions seethed just below the surface. For an instant she wondered, not without fear, how it would be to have those emotions loosed and directed at her.

"Your promise," he insisted.

"You have it."

His bruising grip did not relax. He was staring at her in the way she was beginning to recognize, the way he could not entirely control. "There's one more thing." He jerked her forward so she stumbled against him. His arms closed around her, and his mouth came down with swift hawklike violence on her own.

It was an embrace devoid of tenderness or love; it was anger, frustration, and despair rolled up into a bristled ball; it was selfish and hurtful and a slap in the face at everyone who had ever injured him, herself included. At least, it began that way.

But the violence faded as she kissed him back, desiring him, accepting him, loving him no matter what he was. In that elemental moment, she was his other half, and his breath was as necessary to her as her own. His cruel little farewell note seemed a futile gesture, a jest, an error. He could not mean it, not when their souls reached for each other even more insistently than their bodies.

He pushed her limp and melting body back. She lifted her eyes and saw to her surprise that his face was calm, even peaceful—free of torment and purged of emotion. He smiled at her and bent to kiss her thrice again, once on each eyelid and once on the top of her head.

"Good-bye my fiery Amazon," he said, running one last lock of red hair through his fingers. Then he turned and walked swiftly into the trees.

"Roger!" she called after him, but he did not look back.

She wandered into Merwynna's cottage and sank down onto a bench. The wisewoman was sitting silently on her stool before the fire. Their eyes met.

"What time do ye have to be home?"

"I know not. Before supper. I still have things to pack."

"We must be quick about it, then."

"You mean you're going to instruct me?"

Merwynna's expression was worried but decided. "It takes no special gift of second sight to foresee trouble between ye and that particular young man," she said grimly. "I will instruct ye."

Alexandra laughed. "Then I defy my fate."

Alexandra rose before dawn the next morning and walked over the moors of her native countryside to the chapel where Will was buried. She lit a candle for his soul, and another for the soul of Catherine, his mother. Then she lit a third for Ned, who lay buried in the forest in an unconsecrated grave.

There in the silence of the church, Alexandra made a vow: "I will turn my face away from death and toward life, but I will not forget you, you whom I have failed to help and failed to love and failed to understand. If wrong has been done you, I swear to God that I will attempt to bring it to light. Farewell, my friends. Rest in peace."

She found her father pacing the courtyard at Westmor, impatient to leave. "I'm ready," she told him, embracing her mother and kissing her good-bye. "Let the journey begin."

II
London, February 1557

Fire is the test of gold; adversity, of human strength.

—Seneca

15

IT WAS a damp and dreary day, but that didn't stop the people from turning out. There were hundreds of them—men, women, and children, shoving and fighting with one another in their attempts to secure a good view. They were mostly the poor, many dressed in rags that barely protected their bodies against the raw winter winds. Around the edge of the crowd some prosperous-looking burghers could be found along with a few spectators of noble blood.

The pickpockets were out, as were the whores. A jongleur plied his trade and various hawkers cried their wares. One in particular drew uneasy laughter with his black jest about the fresh-roasted flesh that had gone into the making of his delicious meat pastries.

Sitting stiffly on his mount on the edge of the crowd, Roger Trevor surveyed the scene with a well-schooled expression that he sincerely hoped was hiding his distress. Why did so many folk regard executions as public spectacles? It was true in every country he had visited. People who in ordinary circumstances were friendly and civilized turned into bloodthirsty savages when some poor scapegoat was led forth among them to be hanged or beheaded or—one of the cruelest deaths of all—burned at the stake. Although there would always be someone who would scream, faint, or run in terror from the scene, the majority of the witnesses would watch with fascination, even pleasure, as their fellow human beings were mutilated and killed.

And yet, distasteful though he found it, Roger couldn't condemn these people. After all, he himself was among them. Once or twice a month he came to Smithfield with the others to see the latest victims of Mary Tudor's relentless cleansing of England's spiritual body. He told himself that he came only to harden his resolution, to convince himself that the double life he was leading was ethical and necessary. But deep in the darker corners of his being he wondered if he did not come for the same reason everybody else did— to give vent to the cruelty and violence that dwelt within his own soul.

A great cheer went up as the priests led forth today's victims. Two middle-aged men and a woman. It was the woman whom everybody watched. She was tall, slender, and very young. The priests were haranguing her, still trying to convince her to recant. She kept shaking her head even as the executioner dragged her atop the pile of faggots and bound her to the stake.

None of the victims recanted. A stir went through the crowd as the torches were lit and the priests droned their final words. Edmund Bonner, the Bishop of London, who had personally supervised the burning of dozens of heretics, lifted his arm and gave the signal. Over the heads of the crowd, Roger could see his face burning with passion and zeal for his calling.

The faggots were lit, and screams were heard above the crowd cheering in appreciation. A heavy, nameless fear came over Roger, making his heart race painfully and sweat break out all over his body. Wheeling his horse, he forced his way through the crowd and fled.

It was the bad beginning of a bad day. At court, where he presented himself for the day's formalities, which included the presentation of credentials of a new cadre of diplomats from France, Roger felt even more of a hypocrite than usual. Because of his wit, his style, and his impeccable command of the Spanish language, Roger had risen to favor quickly at Mary Tudor's court. But he had tactfully let it be known that he had no interest in political power. The life he loved was not here at all, he reminded his new friends, but at sea. His chief concern was building the trading partnerships necessary to keep the country strong and economically sound.

England needed a Levant Company, he frequently reminded his monarch, and an embassy at the Sublime Porte in Stamboul. British ships had traded in the Mediterranean a few years ago, and there was no reason why they should not be there again. Englishmen were hearty sailors who ought to be exploring the world the way the Spanish and the Portuguese were. Only with strong trade ties around the globe could this island kingdom expect to maintain its identity and its independence.

The queen, he knew, was not so obsessed with religion that she didn't recognize the importance of Roger's vision. She had already made moves to explore trade with Russia under Czar Ivan, and the New World beckoned also. She turned a deaf ear to the Council members who reminded her that seamen and mariners were almost always free thinkers who'd turned against the True Church. Roger was careful not to spark rumors about his own religious beliefs. When at court, he attended Mass faithfully.

Today, however, with the memory of the heretic girl's screams resounding in his ears, Roger couldn't face Mass, so he arrived late to court, just in time for the reception of the new suite of diplomats from France. Clad in a formal doublet of deepest blue broadcloth trimmed with satin, he stood among the other courtiers while M. de Noailles, who had recently replaced his brother as the ambassador from the court of Henri II, presented the new members of his train. They were receiving a correct, if strained, welcome from Mary. The two countries were on the verge of war because of Mary's marriage to Henri's enemy, Philip of Spain. Philip was anxious to draw English troops and resources into his feud with the French, and Mary was anxious to please her husband and secure Philip's return to her side— and her bed.

The outbreak of war seemed inevitable. The new French diplomats hadn't a hope of saving the situation, Roger knew, wondering who would even undertake such a mission at this point in time. Their backs were to him, so it came as a substantial shock when the herald read off the name "Monsieur Geoffrey de Montreau" and proceeded with a long list of the attaché's credentials and honors. His last post had been at the Sublime Porte in Stamboul.

As a blond, slender man dressed in sky-blue velvet trimmed with silver fox knelt to kiss the hand of Mary of England, Roger's eyes were irresistibly drawn to meet the gaze of the red-haired lady-in-waiting who stood attentively at her post behind the queen. As always, the lively intelligence of those green eyes warmed him. She had made the connection instantly, he sensed, although her expression did not betray it. In the last six months, she had learned to dissemble.

Alexandra. He said her name quietly to himself, imagining that she could hear him. Take care, Alix, be wary. You'll need every scrap of intelligence you possess to survive among the vipers at this court. Especially now that Geoffrey is here. Geoffrey, the brother of Celestine. Geoffrey, who's sworn vengeance against me. Geoffrey, the cleverest snake of them all. How do I warn you about Geoffrey?

He found an opportunity later that same day. There was dancing that evening to welcome the French, and for once Roger took part in the festivities. The formal pattern allowed little contact with one's partners, but he managed to count off his position at the start so he would end the rond paired with Alexandra. She seemed to have no suspicion of his ploy. She was too busy concentrating on getting the steps right.

Roger nearly laughed when his bedraggled former playmate, now transformed into an elaborately gowned court lady, turned very precisely around three times and stepped forward to meet her final partner. She blinked when she saw who was about to take her hand.

"If you dare make sport of my dancing, I'll kick you," she said with a bright smile.

Any notion he might have had of making sport of her vanished when their fingers met. Body of Christ! Here it was again, the lusting he always felt when in her company.

He wanted to drag her out the door and into some darkened hall, or better yet, into a bedchamber. He wanted to press her down beneath him and bury himself inside her, loving her until they both collapsed in exhaustion. He was so caught up by this fantasy that he hardly noticed the music stop until she drew her hand away. They bowed to one another. He thought her color seemed a little high; he was certain his own was.

Despite his frequent appearances at court, Roger had stuck to his resolve to avoid Alexandra Douglas. They never met alone, and rarely even in company. On the one or two occasions when he'd been tempted to accost her, he'd found his way blocked by the dangerously genial person of her father. Roger was the only man who seemed to merit such a distinction. When she was off-duty, he noted, Alexandra was allowed to converse freely with whatever men she chose, or rather, with whatever men chose her, and to Roger's chagrin, there were quite a few of them.

"You dance very well, my lady."

"My dancing master says I dance with the grace of a hen among swans. You, on the other hand, perform the steps divinely. You're full of accomplishments, are you not? Dancing, Spanish, shipping, diplomacy, flattery, and flirtation. All the ladies here are mad about you, Roger."

"I want to talk to you, Alix. Here, quickly, while we seem to be having a light conversation."

The smile stayed on her face, but he could sense her sudden tension. "Speak then. I shall pretend to be laughing and flirting with you."

"You've changed, poppy-top," he said softly.

"Court life tends to age one quickly."

It was true—she had matured considerably in six months. Somebody had taught her to clothe her slender body in richly fashionable gowns, lightly paint her face with God-only-knew-what to hide the freckles, outline her brows and lashes with something that drew attention to her huge green eyes, and dress her breathtaking hair so it flowed smoothly down her back instead of floating wildly around her face. Wit she had always had, and laughter; now she was growing beautiful as well. Beautiful enough to haunt him, and make him curse himself for the idiotic scruples he seemed to have developed regarding her.

He forced his mind back to the problem at hand. On the far side of the hall, Geoffrey de Montreau, clad like a peacock in pink silk and ruffles, was ingratiating himself with the queen. Roger had managed to avoid him all day, but he doubted if the evening would end without a confrontation of some sort. He knew full well that Geoffrey was aware of him.

"You recall my dread of snakes? There is one now among us. You know to whom I refer?"

"I'm rather good at names. He had a sister?"

"He wants me dead, Alix. And he's a very disconcerting person to have as an enemy. He's deadlier than he looks."

She nodded. "I understand."

Someone ranged within hearing and Alexandra laughed as if he'd made a jest, her green eyes sparkling, her lips so red and soft that he lost his train of thought. Bloody little actress! Who would have thought honest, open-faced Alexandra Douglas could learn the tricks of court life so well in only six months?

"For myself I have no care. 'Tis you I'm worried about," he went on. "Geoffrey is infinitely clever. He can be pleasant, but don't be deceived. He has the instincts of a predator."

"I'll be careful. Thank you for warning me." If she was apprehensive, it did not show.

"He's looking this way. Laugh again, beloved. As you say, all the court ladies are mad about me, and you shouldn't be the only exception."

"I'm hardly that," she said dryly.

He raised her hand to his lips. Her skin was soft and fragrant; he had to fight down the temptation to reverse her palm and nuzzle her with his lips and tongue. "I dare not tarry longer beside you, Alexandra. Another minute and your father's spies will report me. The next thing I know, they'll be hounding me out of the city."

"He has you watched, you know. And not only because of me."

Roger knew this all too well; in addition to his official court duties, Sir Charles Douglas was an intelligence-gatherer, the chief of a large network of agents.

"I hope you're careful," she added.

"Always, lass," he said as he squeezed her hand once more as, reluctantly, he left her.

Geoffrey de Montreau intercepted him as he was about to take his leave. "Ah, Roger, *mon ami,* how pleasant to see you again."

Roger stopped to survey the silk-robed, golden-haired fop in front of him. Geoffrey had the face of an angel—light skin, with blue eyes and long thick lashes. In the shape of his bones, Roger could see another face—also pale-skinned and fair-haired, also guileless and innocent, as if life's experiences had yet to etch their tracings there. The innocence had proved to be artificial, but that didn't excuse his crime. He felt a faint sickness in his gut. He hadn't seen Geoffrey de Montreau since the day he'd informed him of his sister's death. It had been the only time he'd ever seen genuine emotion in the man whom he'd known on and off for several years. Geoffrey had broken down and wept. Later, wildly, he had vowed revenge.

"De Montreau," he said shortly, inclining his head.

"You look a little pale, my friend. Perhaps you miss the fresh air of the Middle Sea? I must confess to a certain surprise. I never thought to see you dancing attendance at court when you could be riding the quarterdeck of a trading vessel."

"And you, Geoffrey? I never thought to see you in the backwaters of an upstart little country like England when you might be brokering power with the Turkish empire. This is hardly your area of expertise."

"But England is fast becoming a power to be reckoned with, is she not? Mary Tudor's alliance with Spain, my country's ancient enemy, forces us to take her seriously. Rumor has it that the queen's advisers have suggested she concentrate on upgrading her naval power. Might this have anything to do with your presence?"

"I am a commercial, not a military sailor."

"You are a mystery, Roger, *mon cher.*" He smiled charmingly. "But I intend to unveil you. I intend to discover what you are really doing at court."

"I have family responsibilities. My elder brother is dead and I am now the heir to my father's title." He paused. "You understand family responsibilities, Geoffrey, surely?"

It was dangerous, but it seemed sensible to keep the animosity between them personal. The last thing Roger wanted was to have Geoffrey nosing around and possibly uncovering his connection with Francis Lacklin and the Protestant heretics.

"I understand them well," de Montreau returned. His golden lashes flicked open, then closed. "I am anticipating your demise, dear Roger, with unparalleled pleasure. It is an event which nothing shall induce me to miss."

"I'll be sure to send you a special invitation," Roger assured him as he quitted the chamber.

That night Roger sat drinking in the library of Chilton House, his father's London town house, where he'd been living since September. His mind wandered from one melancholy subject to another, all inspired by the arrival of Geoffrey de Montreau and the conversation, brief though it had been, with Alexandra. The wine was an indulgence he'd been resorting to more and more often of late. He wasn't certain why, but his nerves seemed to be increasingly on edge. With all his heart he missed standing on the deck of his ship with the ocean heaving beneath his feet. He never needed the sop of alcohol when he was at sea.

And back to sea he would go, he vowed, as soon as he discharged his debt to Francis. He would leave this country with all its treacheries and unpleasant memories. Leave his father, with whom he could not coexist; leave Francis, who wanted far, far more from him than he had ever been able to give; leave Alexandra, the only woman with whom he might have chosen to stay.

Alix. Her image was strong in his mind tonight. There were nights, and this was one of them, when he relived every detail of their abortive lovemaking in the witch's cottage. The memory of her slim-boned body molding tightly to his never failed to excite him. He remembered her eager lips, her soft cries of pleasure, her joyful and uninhibited response to every new sensation he gave her. She was more genuinely sensual than many more experienced women, and no man could be unmoved by such enthusiasm.

But there was more to it than that. There had been an intuitive communication in their loving that he knew to be rare. He would never have expected to be drawn to a tall, coltish red-haired virgin, and yet he was. His need was not feverish, not the intense lusting of a short-lived storm of lecherousness; rather it was strong and steady, like an unwavering flame. And because he avoided her, it was bearable, if only just.

What was not bearable was the knowledge that she was his equal in determination, in courage, in passion, and—rare for a woman—in education. He was tantalized by the chimera of a union of minds, hearts, and bodies that would eclipse any former male-female relationship that he had known. He might almost have believed himself in love with her if he didn't know himself incapable of that exalted emotion. Celestine's death had been the final and most harrowing event that had proved that.

He had long ago decided never to burden another innocent young woman with his particular brand of callous, self-gratifying, short-lasting affection. If he really cared about Alexandra, he told himself, he would continue to protect her from himself, for there was no one else in the world who represented a larger potential threat to her happiness and well-being.

Still, he could not give up his fantasies about her. He was entitled to pleasures of the imagination, at least, if pleasures of the body were forbidden him. Pouring himself another cup of wine, he recalled the exquisite give of her body under his, her lips, her breasts, the pale, soft warmth of her thighs . . . He was debauching Alexandra in his mind when Francis Lacklin quietly let himself into the room. Roger looked up briefly from his wine cup, then dropped his eyes again. Damnation, he thought. But all he said was, "You were careful, I presume? The building is watched."

"No one saw me," Lacklin confirmed. He crossed the

room to Roger's side and removed the cup from his fingers. Then he backhanded Roger across the side of his face, hard.

Roger lunged out of his chair and grabbed Francis around the throat, but he was drunken and unsteady. Francis easily pushed him against the desk. "Tom Comstock can't stop you drinking, he says." Lacklin's voice was furious. "I can, and by God, I'm going to. Are you an animal with no spiritual resources? What the devil are you doing to yourself?"

"What I'm doing to myself is my own affair."

"Not when the lives of my people are at stake."

"Damn you, Francis. I'm not that far gone. I drink too much now and then—so what? There are worse vices."

"I need you sober. If we are to continue to smuggle dissenters safely out of the country, I need your brain working at its maximum efficiency. And I have enough to worry about without your sinking into a pit of self-pitying melancholia."

"Self-pitying? You must have my state of mind mixed up with someone else's. I never pity myself. The people I pity are the poor fools who care enough to fret about me. Like you, Francis. You should have left me in the Mediterranean."

"In the Mediterranean you weren't drunk, irritable, and weighed down with guilt. Not, at least, until your damn French mistress died."

"You hated her, didn't you? Just the way you've always hated any woman I've had a fondness for."

Francis said nothing for a moment. Then slowly and carefully he asked, "Exactly what do you mean by that remark?"

Roger sighed and swallowed more wine. "You know what I mean," he muttered. He was still sober enough to know he was hurting his friend with this baiting, but there was a part of him that wanted to hurt Francis, who had unnerved him for years. Ever since he'd been a lad of fifteen, Francis had been there like a bloody guardian angel, watching over him, extricating him from various scrapes, saving his life on more than one occasion. Like a father, like a brother, like a friend, Francis loved him. And Roger suspected that despite his religious fanaticism, Francis would have loved him like a lover if Roger had ever shown the slightest sign of being drawn to his own sex.

"You really ought to have some outlet for your desires," he continued. "Since you don't seem to have any interest in women, why not a lad? This is London, after all—you can get anything here. It's unhealthy to dam up your vital powers the way you do. I know of a house down by the river where you could go if—"

"Stop it."

Roger held his tongue, aware that Francis seemed on the verge of losing his usual iron control. He was pushing him too far, he knew. This particular subject had always been off-limits between them.

"I came here tonight for a serious talk with you, not to discuss the temptations of the flesh," Lacklin said tightly. "Temptations which, I need scarcely point out, you have always been far more prey to than I. Are you listening? I suppose you know that Geoffrey de Montreau has joined de Noailles' suite at court?"

"Ah, yes, dear Geoffrey."

"You've seen him?"

"Aye. He was perfectly polite and diplomatic. He let it be known, however, that he is looking forward to my expeditious and no doubt inglorious death."

"Will you never take him seriously? He means to destroy you. I warned you months ago, but you refused to believe it. I told you to kill him."

"You're always telling me to kill somebody or other, Francis. It's really not very Christian of you. I'd be elbow-deep in blood by now if I complied."

"Listen, my lily-white angel, he loved that sister of his and he blames you for her death. He's a danger to you, and thus a danger to our work. Helping dissenters escape from England before they're arrested for heresy is a crime he'd love to catch you at. I don't want innocent people to die because you're too squeamish to deal with Geoffrey. If you don't do something about him, I will."

Roger raised his head and gave Francis the lazy smile that had proved over and over to be the one thing capable of shaking the older man's composure. He was marginally more sober now, and ashamed of his behavior. Francis didn't deserve to be the target of his sarcasm, his pettiness. But despite his regret, Roger had no intention of taking orders from him, particularly when they involved his personal affairs. "I know you have my welfare at heart," he said. "And that of the dissenters, as do I. Nevertheless, I want you to leave Geoffrey de Montreau to me. What's between us is his business and mine."

The color rose faintly in Lacklin's face. "He was once your loyal friend. You think that because a man's your friend he can never turn against you. That's where you are a fool. You don't acknowledge that devotion itself can wither and rot."

"Are you speaking of Geoffrey, or of you?"

Silence. Then, "And your tongue, Roger, deadly as an adder. Both. You know it."

"I'm sorry." The edge was gone from Roger's voice as he addressed Francis with complete sincerity. "I've given you all the friendship and good fellowship there is in me to give. I know it's not whole or perfect or enough. If the punishment for my inability to satisfy you is death at your hands, I suppose I'll suffer it someday. Do you think you'll find peace at last, then?"

There was no answer.

"Anyway, you'll have to wait your turn. Geoffrey's got the first shot."

This sparked a reply. "Geoffrey? Or the dear departed Celestine?"

"She haunts me sometimes, still."

"God's wounds! You didn't kill the lass. Why can't you forgive yourself your part in that unhappy affair?"

"I killed her," Roger insisted grimly, swallowing more wine. "And I wouldn't be a bit surprised if she proved someday to be the death of me."

16

THAT NIGHT in Westminster Palace, Alexandra was summoned to the queen's bedchamber. Jane Dormer, the most trusted and beloved of Mary's women, a young woman not much older than herself, was pacing there.

"She's asking for you, Alexandra. She's in a highly nervous and melancholic state," Jane whispered. "Do you think I ought to send for her physician?"

Alexandra looked across the state bedchamber to where the queen, clad in a rich linen nightrobe, knelt at her priedieu with her arms clasped tightly around her barren stomach. Her mistress was moaning; tears were slowly flowing down her haggard cheeks. She looked far older than her forty-one years.

"Is she in pain? The colic, perhaps?"

Jane shook her head sadly, her genuine affection for her mistress clear in her eyes. "Her pain, I fear, is of the soul."

Alexandra felt the twist of pity that had become a daily emotion in the six months since she'd come into the queen's service. In a rigorous apprenticeship that had shaken her forever out of her north-country naiveté, Alexandra had learned many things, not the least of which was that kings and queens were as human as herself. She had come to court awed, and not entirely pleased at the idea of serving the woman who had married the foreign Philip of Spain and taken on the task of cleansing England of heresy. When she had first met the queen, Mary Tudor had seemed to her a formidable woman: learned, tireless, and devout.

Now that she knew her better, Alexandra saw that Mary was indeed all those things, and more. She had all the pride and majesty of a queen, but she was simultaneously a woman. A woman hopelessly enamored of a husband who had abandoned her eighteen months before to take up his princely duties in Flanders—duties which included carousing until the early hours of the morning with lusty barmaids and errant countesses.

"Your Grace?" Alexandra came to kneel beside her mistress. "Jane sent for me. Is there something I can do for you?"

Mary lifted her pale face, smiling thinly. As always, Alexandra was struck with her regal bearing, a certain spine-stiff pride that never deserted her, even in her darkest moments. The queen was a complex woman, difficult to love, even when she was at her best. Alexandra could not love her, but she had come to honor her. Mary had courage, and her analytical yet emotional cast of mind was not dissimilar to Alexandra's own.

"I have heard that you know something of healing, Mistress Douglas, that you can concoct a soothing potion for the nerves. Is this true?"

"My knowledge is of simple country remedies, your Grace. Surely your own physician—"

"Bah! I have no faith in the cossets that charlatan brews. You have proved to be a reliable young woman, Alexandra. Tell me where you learned your simple country remedies."

Alexandra knew such a confession would not be wise. Merwynna, after all, was reputed to be a witch. "In the north, many women still learn the ancient folkways and pass them on to their daughters," she answered vaguely. "I have known the arts of blending certain harmless herbs since I was little more than a child." She put subtle stress on the word "harmless."

"I wish for something that will relax my overtight nerves," the queen stated. She rose from her prie-dieu and stiffened her spine. She was a small woman, thin, but erect in her carriage. There was an energy burning within her even when she was at her most melancholy. Her father, Henry VIII, had had that same kingly energy, people said. Mary's sister, the Lady Elizabeth, was reputed to have it too. "Can you prepare such a potion?"

Alexandra recalled the drink she had concocted for the Baron of Chilton at Dorcas' request. "Yes, your Grace. 'Twill work no miracles, but it might help you."

Mary paced the length of her bedroom and stopped in front of a polished mirror of Venetian glass. Before coming to Westminster, Alexandra had never seen such a mirror. At Westmor, mirrors had been wrought of polished metal, which tended to give back a distorted image. But this one produced a true reflection of face and form—for good or for ill. More than once, Alexandra had stared dumbfounded at her own striking image. If she hadn't been so firmly convinced by her mother's many years of disparaging remarks that she was no beauty, she might have begun to nurse a few sparks of vanity. Instead, she merely laughed at the poised young woman with the eyebrows carefully plucked and darkened with kohl, the bright hair restrained with artful braids, combs, and jewels, the straight healthy body arrayed in stiff brocaded gowns. Even with the help of the royal tiring-women, it took her nearly an hour to get dressed every morning! Anybody ought to look presentable after that much effort.

The queen was clearly displeased by her own reflection. Alexandra waited in discreet silence while Mary regarded herself by the light of the dim night candles. Even in the six months since Alexandra had known her, Mary had aged.

The queen turned her back on the mirror. "Have you a potion, too, for restoring womanly beauty?" she asked, her voice touched with a note of irony. "Not that I was ever in possession of an excess of that."

"The little I know of such arts has been taught me since I came to court," Alexandra said carefully. "Besides"—she drew a deep breath—"there is no such potion, not for you, not for anyone, your Grace."

For an instant, annoyance flashed in Mary's face; then it was replaced by grim amusement. "You are not a flatterer, mistress. Neither are you entirely truthful, I suspect."

Maybe not, Alexandra admitted to herself, but only a fool is entirely truthful at a place such as this. Only necromancers like Merwynna brewed potions to restore lost beauty. Alexandra knew more than one of them—although she was not entirely convinced of their efficacy—but she bore her mentor's warnings close to her heart. *You must take care what use you make of the secrets I have entrusted you with.* Alexandra had no intention of indicting herself for witchcraft.

Mary turned back to the mirror. "My husband comes soon, they say. His suite has returned, his pages, his horses. In his letters, he promises to follow."

Alexandra was tactfully silent. Since her arrival at court, she had heard almost constant talk of Philip's return to England, and yet he had not come. From one month to the next, Mary had awaited him, hiding her longing behind a mask of stoic resignation during the long hours when she worked with her Council, her advisers, the many officers of the court. In private, however, alone with her women, Mary's brave facade sometimes crumbled. She knew, as everyone did, of Philip's infidelities. Several months ago, in a rage, she had kicked his official portrait out of the room. But even so, she pined for him, for the purpose, if no other, of producing from their conjugal union an heir to the throne.

The queen's first pregnancy, of which the nation had had such high hopes, had proved to be a painful and embarrassing error. For eleven months Mary had awaited the outcome, her belly swelling with what was believed to be new life. After hearing Jane Dormer's account of her mistress's symptoms, Alexandra was amazed that the physicians could have deceived themselves—and Mary—for so long. The queen had had a dropsical swelling of the abdomen, not a pregnancy. There had been no telltale movement of a growing child. How could they have made such a mistake?

The false pregnancy had dampened her husband's never-very-feverish ardor. Philip had taken most of his suite and left for the Continent, promising to rejoin his wife soon. But affairs—both public and private—had kept him away for eighteen long months. Was he really about to keep his promise to return? The common belief was that he would, if only to secure England's assistance in the war he was waging with France.

"I should like to look my best for my lord the king," Mary added, her voice rather strained. She turned to Alexandra, her intelligent eyes bright with pain. "A potion for my nerves will do for now. If that works, perhaps you will consider sharing with me some of the other *folkways* you have learned in the north. The beauty-enhancer, for example. Will you help me, Alexandra?" She paused. "In return, I will grant you any boon."

It was a plea, and Alexandra had never been able to refuse a direct appeal from a fellow human being in need. Forgetting her notions of what might or might not be foolish, she took one of her sovereign's limp, dry hands in her own and kissed it. "I will help you, of course, your Grace."

"Thank you, my child."

Back in her own bed that night, Alexandra wished she had the energy to get up and blend a potion for her own nerves. Her head ached, but she tried her best to compose her body for sleep. Her duties began far too early in the morning—Mary rose before dawn and often worked at affairs of state until midnight. Alexandra couldn't remember the last time she'd had more than five hours of sleep.

Today had been particularly exhausting. Today she had danced and talked with Roger for the first time since she'd been at court. To her dismay, her body had thundered to life at his touch, almost frightening her with the force of her passion. Until today she had thought she was finally beginning to quell the unrequited love that had burned in her since last summer. She had almost convinced herself that, unnourished, her attraction for such an unsuitable man would wither and die.

Now, because of the feel of his hands claiming hers, his

lips upon her fingers, his body close to hers, she knew she was no nearer to conquering her love for Roger than she'd been six months ago. The most she could hope was that it wasn't as obvious to everybody else as it was becoming to her. She remembered Roger's warning about Geoffrey de Montreau, and shivered. *Beware her brother.* Merwynna's prophecy was once again coming true.

Before the evening had ended, Roger's enemy had indeed sought her out. From across the room his liquid blue eyes had stared directly into hers, not as a stranger might stare, but with the intimacy of a close acquaintance. With her newly won self-control, Alexandra had allowed her own eyes to slide casually away, but she was startled. Monsieur Geoffrey, it seemed, knew who she was.

A little while later, he came over and bowed, dazzling her with the perfection of his attire and the gracefulness of his address. "Mistress Douglas? You are a woman whom I have long desired to meet."

"Indeed, monsieur? I was not aware that my fame had spread as far as France."

She was prepared to dislike him, and she expected some artificial comment to the effect that her beauty was known all over Europe, since this was the sort of remark she had grown accustomed to hearing—and despising—at court. But Geoffrey surprised her. "It is not on your own account that I seek you out, mademoiselle. You will forgive me? It is because of my concern over our mutual friend, Roger Trevor. Is he ill? He looked far more fit last year in the Middle Sea. He has lost his healthy color."

She had not expected so direct an approach. Forcing an ingenuous smile, she tried not to betray her closeness with Roger by giving Geoffrey any sign that she recognized his hypocrisy. "I do not doubt it, monsieur, without the sun to brown him. We all grow a little peaked in this dreary English weather. Rain does not depress you, I hope? I understand the climate is much more pleasant in Paris."

But Geoffrey was not to be deflected from his purpose by talk of the weather. His thick lashes fluttered as he regarded her smilingly. Sweet Jesu, she thought, he's wearing more paint than I am. "A charming man, is he not, despite his peakedness?" he went on. "'Tis no wonder so many unfortunate young women break their hearts over him."

Alexandra's hands closed on the folds of her expensive brocade kirtle. Surely he could not know about her hopeless love for Roger. Even if he had witnessed their short interchange earlier, she wasn't so obvious, was she? He could only be guessing, and since it was a guess that other people who knew the close connection between herself and her handsome neighbor frequently teased her with, she had her retorts down pat.

"Having known Roger since he was a nasty little wretch who tied me to trees and put spiders down my bodice, I've never been able to understand the attraction."

Geoffrey's eyes were hidden under his lowered eyelids. "So he was cruel to women even then?"

By the Mass! "He was playful, certainly, but no crueler than other children. I repaid his teasing whenever I could. My greatest coup was the time I captured a garden snake and put it in his bed. His brothers and I hid behind an arras to observe the results." She laughed spontaneously, then caught herself. "He doesn't care for snakes," she added. "Human or reptilian."

She instantly chastised herself for that remark, damning her too-ready tongue. Although she'd made great strides in controlling her unfortunate tendency toward plain speaking, she still had a long way to go.

Geoffrey de Montreau seemed more amused than offended. When a dance began shortly thereafter, he solicited her as his partner. It would have been the height of discourtesy to refuse.

He was a far better dancer than she, and she was so busy concentrating on the intricate steps that she was able to ignore the intent way he was studying her. At last, however, he succeeded in irritating her enough to spark comment: "What is it, monsieur? Have I a tear in my gown, or is my dancing really so appallingly bad?"

The fair head bobbed and the blue eyes widened. "Your

pardon, my lady, but I am one of those persons who take inordinate pleasure simply in observing everybody else. One does not learn to dance in the north of England?"

"One learns only when one is forced to. One would rather be climbing trees."

Geoffrey smiled the first natural smile she had seen on his face. "How old are you, mademoiselle?"

"Old enough to stop racing about the forest like a colt, as my mother would say."

"Are you homesick?"

It was a question nobody had ever thought to ask her. Her throat tightened as she had a mental image of cool shady trees and warm heather. Merwynna. Alan—who was now studying at Oxford. Her mother. Dorcas. "I'm relatively new to court," she hedged. "I still have a great deal to learn."

Geoffrey nodded toward the queen. "Your mistress is difficult?"

Homesick she might be, but she was not an idiot. "No. It is not my post that is difficult for me. My mistress is gentle and kind. I miss my family and friends, that is all. No doubt I'll get over it."

"Your father is here at court."

"My father is a busy man. As you will be, I fear, trying to avert a war. What will happen if hostilities do break out? Are you sent home in disgrace for failing at your mission?" She smiled. "For I fear you will fail, monsieur."

She was not speaking of the delicate situation between France and England, and she could tell that Geoffrey de Montreau knew it. The look in his eyes had hardened. "I rarely fail, mademoiselle."

The steps of the dance separated them briefly, but when they came back together, Geoffrey had a new line of attack. "And Monsieur Lacklin? One hears a great deal of the brilliant Roger Trevor here at court, but one hears not a word about his very good friend. You know him too, I presume?"

"One does not admit to knowing heretics, monsieur, if one wishes to keep one's head safely upon one's shoulders."

"Ah, mademoiselle, you are not as frank as everybody says."

"What do you mean?"

"Even though I've been here only a few hours, I've already heard that the queen's latest lady-in-waiting is full of *joi de vivre* and disarmingly frank. She will not last too long at court, the gossip declares: her nature is too warm and her countenance too open for her to survive here. Within the year, they say, she will be either married or disgraced."

As he finished speaking, the dance ended and he bowed and moved away, leaving Alexandra red-faced. They say that, do they? she thought furiously. We'll see about that.

Another partner came to claim her, one of several handsome young men who had been paying her considerable attention for several months. His name was Philip Carington, and he was the son of an earl. Her father, she knew, considered him a worthy match.

"Did that Frenchman say something to insult you?"

"He said I had an open countenance, which is apparently true. Was I blushing?"

"Aye. But not as much as you used to." Philip smiled and swept her off into the dance, and thence into an alcove, where he attempted to embrace her. She resisted goodnaturedly, and they finally compromised on a kiss. She did not mind his kisses, but they were not like Roger's.

17

*T*HE QUEEN was frantic. In a rare state of combined temper, overstrung nerves, and physical illness—she was plagued with a cold and a toothache—Mary had Alexandra and the rest of her gentlewomen reeling as they attempted to get her ready for her reunion with her husband. Philip of Spain had finally arrived on British soil, and his wife was riding out to meet him at Greenwich. He had taken ship from Calais to Dover, and his solid Spanish presence had been confirmed by several of Mary's highly trusted officers, including Sir Charles Douglas.

"He looks ill," her father told Alexandra, after having ridden posthaste from Dover to report the news to her Grace. "It's disturbing how much both have changed in the three years since their wedding. They seem weighted down with the cares of their office. 'Tis natural for her, at her age, but he's only thirty."

"A dissipated thirty, if the gossip is to be believed," Alexandra said.

Her father gently placed a finger under her chin and raised her face. Alexandra winced at the concern that flashed in his eyes. In the flurry of activity of the last several days, she had not applied her cosmetics as cleverly as usual. The dark circles under her eyes, she knew, were huge. "And you look like a dissipated nineteen."

"Eighteen."

He shook his head sadly. "March 20—it's your birthday today, child. Have you forgotten?"

"Good heavens, so it is. I'm afraid the days have been running into one another lately."

"Don't you ever sleep?"

"Sleep?" she repeated as if she'd never heard the word. "Was that something I used to do in my youth?"

"Pack your things, daughter. I have applied for, and been granted, a week's leave for you, beginning immediately."

"But the queen, the king—"

"Will both be here when you get back. You're not going to Greenwich, Alexandra. You're coming home with me."

Alexandra and her father took a barge down the Thames to Charles Douglas' riverside dwelling. The elegantly appointed house had once been the property of a lord who had faithfully served the old King Henry until the intrigue surrounding one of the king's marriages had thrust him out of favor. The queen had presented the estate to Douglas last year, in appreciation for services rendered—services that were, at best, murky.

Alexandra had known for some time that her father was not an ordinary court minister. The memorable conversation she had overheard between Roger and Francis Lacklin in the great hall at Chilton had alerted her to her father's true role in the queen's government, and her own careful inquiries at Westminster had confirmed her suspicions. Sir Charles was quietly acknowledged to be in charge of domestic security for the realm. It was he who made sure that spies, agitators, and insurrectionists were either brought to justice or silenced.

Alexandra would have given almost anything to be certain that her father was ignorant of the mysterious and possibly treasonous activities of Roger Trevor. Unfortunately, however, she knew her father was suspicious. Her suitor Philip Carington was a protégé of her father's and privy to some of the secrets of state security. Through seemingly innocent questioning, Alexandra had gleaned several tidbits of intelligence from him, including the fact that Roger's London town house was being watched.

She felt torn between her loyalty to her mistress and her concern over Roger. Why couldn't he simply be what he seemed—a rising star at court who had no other desire than the furthering of his country's commercial interests? Why did he secretly have to be involved with traitors and heretics whose obvious aim was to undermine the queen's authority?

Every time she saw Roger kissing the beringed fingers of his monarch at court, Alexandra watched nervously for the hint of insincerity that would betray him. She lived in fear that he would be discovered. If her father ever produced evidence against him, Roger would be condemned to a horribly painful death. Traitors were hanged, drawn and quartered. Heretics were burned.

She was thinking so intently about Roger as the barge slid in to dock at her father's landing that for an instant she thought she had conjured him up. A man awaited them on the landing—slim-built, with dark hair and those unmistakably arrogant Trevor features. Alexandra had to look twice before she realized it was Alan, not Roger.

"I neglected to mention a birthday surprise," her father told her as Alexandra called out delightedly to her friend. "He turned up last night."

"But what's he doing here? Isn't he supposed to be hard at his studies at Oxford?"

Before her father could answer, the barge bumped the dock and Alan jumped on board to seize Alexandra around the waist and hug her. "I missed you horribly," he declared. He stared in apparent wonder at her stiff court attire. "Faith, Alexandra, you look different."

"So do you. You're taller." He was straighter, too, and broader in a subtle way that was somewhat disconcerting. He looked much more like a man. Playfully she batted her eyelashes at him. "Heavens, milord, I do believe you're growing up."

Alan gave her his old shy, rueful grin. "Happy birthday, Alix. May I give you a birthday kiss?"

When she nodded, he bent his head and did so, allowing his lips to linger in a manner that was unknown between them. Startled, Alexandra drew back. "What are they teaching you at Oxford? You've never kissed me like that in your life."

Alan looked sheepish. "Actually, I'm not at Oxford anymore."

"What on earth do you mean?"

Alan stared at the river lapping at the wooden landing. He made a show of assisting Alexandra and her several yards of expensive fabric out of the barge. "They've dismissed me."

"What? Not you, Alan, surely. You're such an excellent scholar! I don't believe it. Whatever for?"

Alan shot a guilty look toward Alexandra's father, who was busy paying the riverman and summoning a servant to handle Alexandra's baggage.

"Alan?" she persisted, pulling him a little to the side. "Tell me. What did they dismiss you for?"

"Fornication," was the extraordinary reply.

Later that afternoon, Alexandra lay sprawled on a cushion in front of a roaring fire, drinking small beer and listening to Alan's story. She had changed into one of her oldest gowns, and felt truly comfortable for the first time in months.

"So who was she?" she demanded. She'd been consumed with curiosity ever since they'd arrived. "I hope you haven't ruined some poor tradesman's daughter who didn't know any better."

"Sweet Jesus, no. She was a widow, Alix, ten years older than I. She seduced me. At first I didn't really expect . . . that is, I was what is commonly referred to as a callow youth."

"Oh, Alan." She was trying not to laugh.

He'd met the widow, he explained, during an unsanctioned expedition with several of his friends to a public tavern. She helped her brother-in-law run the pub, and had taken a fancy to the college youths, Alan in particular. "She gave us free ale and encouraged us to sneak out again the following week. It was tricky. We had to climb a high wall to escape the college."

"Good heavens, Alan, I can't imagine you clandestinely scaling walls to meet a lusty widow! It sounds like something out of 'The Miller's Tale.'"

"That's exactly what it was like," he said ruefully. "The second time we went, she lured me upstairs on the pretext of asking me if a certain hand-printed book was valuable, and the next thing I knew, she was attacking me!"

"While you strenuously defended your virtue, I suppose?"

"Well..." He blushed. "She was very pretty. I...uh ...never thought I'd do such a thing. She took me by surprise, and"—he paused—"my body behaved in a manner that was quite foreign to my soul."

"I can imagine," she said dryly.

Alan grinned at her, and once again Alexandra noticed that he had changed. He seemed definitely more self-assured. Male pride, she surmised. "But it was very foolish," he continued. "She was using me to make the pub owner jealous—he turned out not to be her brother-in-law after all, but her extremely bad-tempered lover. The next time I went, he almost caught us together...and she wouldn't have cared, I realized, if he had. I shouldn't have gone back after that, but..." He shrugged expressively.

"You couldn't resist?"

"She was very talented, if you see what I mean."

She saw only too well, although she suspected Alan would be horrified if he ever learned that she, too, had been initiated into some—although not all—of the mysteries of sexual passion. Particularly if he knew the identity of her initiator. "So you went back and fell into the hands of the jealous lover?"

"Not exactly. I fell into the hands of the college authorities. It seems the lady had confessed to her lover, and he, after beating her soundly, had called upon the chancellor to protest. They retorted that the charges must be false—I was such a model scholar, you see—so the publican challenged them to lie in wait for me...and sure enough, like a hawk to a lure, I came."

"Poor hawk. How embarrassing."

"It was grim. It's not exactly uncommon, sneaking out

to drink and wench, but I was the only one stupid enough to get caught. They dismissed me summarily, no hearing, no appeal."

"But, Alan, studying at Oxford was your dream for so many years. Couldn't you have been more circumspect?"

"Perhaps, but in a way, I'm well out of it. Do you know how many Protestants have been burned to date in the town of Oxford? The college is full of royal spies. No one's doing very much studying there these days—the atmosphere is too tense. There are a few radicals who seem to court martyrdom, but everybody else is tiptoeing about endeavoring to avoid the flames."

She did not fail to note the outrage in his voice when he mentioned the royal spies—spies who were very likely paid by her own father. Did that mean that he had become a heretic himself? Six months ago she would have asked him, but with her newfound tact, she'd learned to stop asking personal questions about her friends' religious beliefs. It was far too dangerous a subject.

In silence they both drank deeply of their beer. "Does your father know about this?"

"They've written to him. I didn't go home, obviously. I came straight here. I've always wanted to visit London."

"What are you going to do here?"

"Make my fortune in the city where the streets are paved with gold."

"Alan, that's a fable!"

"Aye, but Roger seems to be doing quite well for himself, I hear. I'll go to him—he's my brother; he'll get some sort of post for me."

"I thought you and Roger weren't on speaking terms. Something to do with some mysterious event that apparently happened in the forest on the day you broke your leg." She spoke a trifle impatiently. She'd never found out what had caused that final breach between Alan and his brother.

"I may have judged him too harshly." He refused to elaborate.

Alexandra took a much-needed rest that afternoon, rising after several hours of delicious, undisturbed sleep full of high spirits and energy. A feeling of freedom blossomed in her soul, and she decided to make the most of her days before she had to return to her restricted life as one of the queen's ladies.

She took Alan on a whirlwind tour of the city, ending up by the Thames River docks, where several trading ships were unloading their cargo. "One of them belongs to your brother," she told Alan. "*Argo,* she's called."

"That's a classical name. Jason's ship."

"Medea sailed on her too, I believe," Alexandra recalled. "She's just returned to port after a voyage to the Middle Sea without him. I think it's that odd-looking narrow one. Some sort of new design, I understand. Faster and more efficient for escaping from Mediterranean corsairs."

Alan squinted out over the water. "My eyesight's not as good as yours. I can hardly see her."

"Would you like to row out for a closer look?"

"Can we?"

Alexandra beckoned a boatman, who rowed his small bark toward them with alacrity. "Why not?" But when she pointed out their destination, the boatman leaned on his oars and looked uneasy.

"'Er master don't like nobody snoopin' around. Took a man out there once, and nearly got an arrow in me back for it."

"Fascinating." Alexandra opened her purse and offered the boatman a gold coin. "I hardly think they would dare shoot at a woman, though. Particularly one of the queen's ladies."

The man eyed the coin with greed and started to reach for it. But he must have thought twice, for he withdrew his hand with obvious reluctance. "Can't do it, milady. Whoever ye be. I've been paid good money not to." He gestured at the other boatmen. "We all been paid."

Alexandra extracted several additional coins. "And if I offer a higher bribe?"

The fellow hesitated, then decided with a sigh, "I took 'is money and gave me word." He turned away as if fleeing temptation.

"Wait." Alexandra extended the man the original coin. "Take this anyway. You are an honest man."

"Thank ye, milady." He flashed her a totally male smile, making Alexandra aware for the first time that the boatman was young, and reasonably handsome. "And ye're a generous woman."

Alexandra had no compunction about using the feminine wiles she had so painfully acquired over the past few months. She stepped closer as the coin changed hands and looked up at the man through her kohl-tinted lashes. "And why is it, do you suppose, that the master of an honest trading vessel should go to such pains to guard against intruders?" She allowed her eyes to widen as if in fright. "He's not one of those dreadful smugglers, I hope?"

"Oh no, milady. 'E wouldn't come brazenly up the river if that's what 'e was. 'E'd hug the coasts, where ships can slip into an unguarded harbor for a few hours at night, and out again afore morning. That's how the smugglers do it."

"Then why?"

The boatman shrugged. "Who knows? But mariners are a free-thinkin' lot. And them that make their life on the water 'ave no wish to die in the flames. These are bad times, milady, for 'eretics."

"So they are," she agreed thoughtfully. "Very bad indeed."

"What was the point of all that?" Alan asked as they walked away from the docks.

"Curiosity. Anybody who goes to the trouble of bribing a dozen river boatmen must have something to hide." Were all Roger's crewmen heretics? Was he trying to keep them safe?

"Do you see my brother often?" There was an odd note in Alan's voice as he asked the question.

"Not often, no. Never alone. He comes to court and I see him there amidst everybody else. We rarely speak. I have been forbidden his company, remember?"

"For your own good."

"What nonsense! Roger represents no threat to me."

Was it her imagination, or did Alan move closer to her?

"I hope you obey your parents with regard to him, Alix. He's dangerous in so many ways. I've often wondered what really happened that night in the witch's cottage."

Alexandra successfully fought down a blush. "I thought from what you said earlier that you'd revised your opinion of your brother's villainy."

"Not with regard to women," he said repressively. "I intend to see with my own eyes that he stays away from you."

"Good heavens, Alan, I don't require your protection."

He gave her a rather charming smile. "You have it, none-theless."

"Very well, then, I shall rely on you to protect me from him when we visit Chilton House together tonight."

Alan paled. "What do you mean?"

"Rumor has it that your brother holds court two evenings a week at your father's town house. Scholars, musicians, mariners, and ladies all gather there for sophisticated debate and conversation. It's the fashionable place to go, and for weeks I've longed to join the fun, but my father's interdict forbade it."

"Your father's interdict still forbids it, Alix."

"My father doesn't have to know. We'll tell him you and I are going out to celebrate my birthday. Knowing my father, he'll be off somewhere tonight anyway."

"And if he finds out you've disobeyed him?"

"He won't. I'll go in disguise."

"Where are you going to get a disguise at this time of day?"

She laughed aloud. "That, you'll discover, is the least of our problems."

18

E VEN BEFORE the arrival of his guests that evening, Roger had already consumed several goblets of the fine Burgundy he'd brought home last summer from France. He'd just parted company with his current mistress, a sultry countess who had been sharing his bed for several weeks. Although she was beautiful, voluptuous, and a wickedly inventive lover, Roger was already growing bored with her, and that afternoon his boredom must have made itself apparent. In the middle of their lovemaking, the lady had rolled off his naked, thrusting body and reached for a cup of wine from the small table beside the bed.

"Your attention is elsewhere, if I am not mistaken," she had calmly observed. "You are cheating me, my friend, and this I will not tolerate."

She drank, then ran the tip of her tongue around her wine-coated lips in a deliberately sensual gesture that left him cold. She was right, of course. He'd found lately that his only enjoyment came in imagining that the countess's legs were slim, and coltish, her voluptuous breasts small and exquisitely sensitive, her silver-blonde hair as red as vibrant flames.

"I do not offer you my mind, countess," he drawled. "My body, I believe, was all that you desired."

She dipped her finger in her wine and ran it over Roger's

hair-sprung chest. "You have been an excellent lover, but body and mind are not as separate as your words suggest. Who is she, Roger? Who is the woman whose name you so gallantly swallow every time you come?"

He stared at her, startled. He had never guessed it was so obvious.

"Do you love her?" the countess persisted.

"No," he snapped. "I am incapable of love."

She laughed, dribbling wine across his belly, and lower. Leaning over, she casually licked it off. "Consider the question more carefully, my dear, before you become incapable of something else as well."

Roger rolled over and pinned her to the bed, removing the winecup from her fingers and thrusting hard between her thighs, swiftly settling any doubts about his capability. He was careful to bring her fully to her pleasure before taking his own. But when the countess got up to go an hour later, she informed him that their affair was over. "It is better so," she said, kissing him lightly as she took her leave. "I always end it before the excitement fades, my friend. That way I preserve my pleasant memories. Farewell."

The worst of it was that her decision left him indifferent. He wasn't drinking that night because he cared; what she'd given him was to be easily had elsewhere. He was drinking because there had been a time when what she'd given him would have been enough. But now, because of a red-haired chit named Alexandra, he wanted far, far more.

Why, he wondered, gulping wine, couldn't he get her off his mind? Why did Alix seem to grow more poised, more lovely, every time they met? Why did his mouth go dry, his body rigid at the very sight of her? Was it simply because she was forbidden to him? If he took her, possessed her, he'd grow bored with her soon enough, too, no doubt.

No, a voice inside him argued. He might grow bored with other women, but not with Alix; never with Alix.

Halfway through a rather dull, uneventful evening when two young men, one dark and one fair, appeared on his doorstep, Roger wondered for an instant if he'd truly overdone the wine this time. His brother Alan was supposed to be at Oxford, and as for the lad beside him with the chin-length golden hair, he'd never seen him before, although there was something familiar about the way he moved. . . . Roger took a closer look into the boy's face, and had to choke back his surprise, and that old familiar rigidity.

He controlled himself enough to approach them. He clapped Alan on the back, saying, "This is a surprise. I thought you'd written me off as the devil incarnate?"

"I'd like to talk to you about that," Alan said.

Alan was looking uncomfortable, as usual, flushing in that boyish way he had. And yet, Roger was not too drunk to notice that his brother was meeting his eyes unflinchingly, and that though unsure of his welcome, he was no longer hostile.

"Had a change of heart? I'm intrigued." His eyes turned to Alan's golden-haired companion. "Who's your friend?"

"Uh, this is Martin. From Oxford. I'm supposed to be looking after him tonight."

"I see." To Alan's companion, Roger bowed gravely and offered deliberately brutal fingers. "Such a delicate grip you have, Martin. And such beautifully-cared for hands. I'd keep them clenched by my sides if I were you."

Keeping his head down, 'Martin' tried to withdraw his hand. Roger refused to release it. "What, shy, lad? Haven't you the grace to greet your host properly?"

"He's from the country," Alan put in quickly. "He's not accustomed to court manners."

"Indeed?" Roger's voice was silky-smooth. "Let me instruct him, then." He raised the graceful hand to his lips. "One bows to a gentleman, but one is allowed to kiss a lady's hand, Martin. Like this." His mouth pressed the sweetly-scented fingers; his tongue flicked out to tease them. "Pray lift the eyelids that are hiding those uncharacteristically diffident green eyes."

The eyelids—and the chin—lifted immediately. As Alix's laughing gaze collided with his, Roger forgot the folly of this in the pleasure of having her here, in his house, in his reach. Christ, but he wanted her!

"Of course you'd know," she said ruefully.

"Instantly."

"Will everyone else, do you think?"

He ran his eyes over the figure she cut in a creamy doublet and hose. Because she was slender and small-breasted, her womanliness was not difficult to disguise. Without the very feminine paint he'd seen her wearing lately, her intelligent face and lively eyes could probably pass for those of a slightly precocious youth. "Not if we tell them you're twelve and your voice hasn't changed yet. Or your beard grown in." He stroked a finger through the golden hair. "Where did you get the wig?"

"From my father's disguise-a-spy wardrobe," she answered readily. "I thought perhaps I could imitate one of those, uh, less masculine men we see at court occasionally. . . ."

"If so I'm glad you have Alan to protect you. 'Tis a pretty boy you are, my dear. You're liable to be taken upstairs and introduced to certain unmentionable acts of sophisticated vice. There are mariners here this evening . . . and you know how *they* behave, deprived so long of the company of women."

Alexandra smiled guilelessly at him, and he wondered if she was too innocent to catch his meaning. Surely not, after all her months at court.

"You're a mariner, too, are you not? Am I to assume that if there didn't happen to be a woman available, you were yourself a party to such vices?"

No, she wasn't innocent. With a flash of jealousy, he wondered just how far her education had progressed. He offered her his arm. "Come upstairs with me now, my lad, and find out."

"For the love of God!" Alan sounded far more appalled than Alexandra. "Must you always find a way to taunt her?"

Roger's good humor abruptly deserted him. "You both deserve more than taunting for attempting such a foolhardy masquerade. If her father hears of this, he'll probably beat her. And challenge me to a duel."

"Your gatherings are famous, Roger. I couldn't resist attending, even at the risk of a beating. Are you going to send me home?"

"Am I your keeper?" Her blithe attitude annoyed him.

It was dangerous for her here. His friends were present, as were some of his ill-wishers. At any court in Europe, there was a fine line between the two. "No doubt you'll do whatever you wish."

"Tonight, yes. It's my birthday and I wanted to enjoy it in the company of my oldest friends."

Roger took in the sight of her green eyes sparkling with excitement as she glanced around at the other guests and knew he couldn't deny her. "How old are you?"

She fluttered her eyelashes at him. "Now where are *your* court manners? One may kiss a lady's hand, but one never asks how old she is. Particularly when she is several years beyond marriageable age, and still unwed."

"You have more than your share of suitors. Why don't you put one of them out of his misery?"

She laughed. "I fear the misery of most men would only be increased if I accepted them! I'm convinced I should make a very poor wife. I'm far more interested in politics than domestic matters; I talk too much, and I don't see how I could ever promise to obey my husband. No, Roger. I've decided to remain a single woman for life. Or rather," she cast a merry look down at her male attire, "a single man for life. Rather like you." She slapped him heartily between the shoulder blades. "We'll be comrades at arms. Lead on, sir, to the wine and the wenches!"

His lips quirked and in a moment he was laughing. "Outrageous baggage," he leaned down to whisper in her ear. "Happy birthday."

While Alexandra grinned at him in pleasure, Roger turned to his brother. "And you, Alan? I know it's not your birthday, and there's no leave for scholars at this time of the year. Don't tell me they've thrown you out?" He looked back and forth between them, puzzled at the amusement in Alexandra's face, and the slightly smug embarrassment in his brother's.

"I was dismissed."

"What for? Studying your lessons in the middle of the night?"

Alan colored, and he answered defiantly: "No. For drunkenness and wenching."

"Good God, you're taking after me." Roger's irritation faded completely. Look at them. They were so damned proud of themselves—Alexandra for her ingenious disguise and Alan for his fledgling manhood. He ought to turn them out into the street before they ended up in trouble, but he hadn't the heart to spoil their fun.

Looping an arm around each, he led his two young friends toward the wine. "Very well—a celebration for you both, then. I only hope we all don't end up regretting it."

After so many months at court, Alexandra was accustomed to conversing with people of wit and intellect, worldliness and sophistication. Alan was not. The gathering clearly awed him, and more than once he pulled her aside to say, "Sweet Jesu, Alix, that fellow's sailed to the New World!" Or "Alexandra, one of those two women has written an erotic sonnet to the other."

There weren't any notorious heretics here, Alexandra was relieved to see. The subject of the burnings did not come up in any conversation she was privy to. Even the prospective war with Henri of France was not widely discussed. Instead the talk centered on the economic aspects of government—specifically, on the subject of ocean-going commerce.

There were several men present who had made the perilous journey across the Atlantic Ocean to the New World. Lurking on the edge of one such discussion, Alexandra was surprised to hear Roger express his desire to trade in the west as well as the east. She envied him the freedom to indulge such a dream. How exciting it would be to walk the decks of a sailing vessel, bound for a life of adventure and discovery in the New World!

"There are riches to be had in the Americas," said a rangy young man named Richard Bennett, who had recently returned from one such voyage. "In the south especially, the Spaniards have made a fortune ransacking the heathen temples of the Aztec and the Inca peoples. I have seen their galleons founder from the weight of the gold and silver stashed in their cargo holds."

"Is that why they founder?" Roger asked, his smile flashing in his dark face. "Are you certain it's not due to the weight of a good English broadside just below the water line?"

"How could that be? We are allied to Spain," Bennett said with a wink at several of his friends.

"At present," Roger said dryly, and it was clear in the face of every mariner there that they were thinking of the day when this might not be so.

Treason, thought Alexandra with a sigh. Yet she could hardly be shocked. She knew full well that treason was uttered daily in every tavern. The English had hated Mary's Spanish husband from the start, and the hostility was all the more powerful now that the Queen had levied taxes to aid her ungrateful husband in his feud with France.

Poor Mary! As Alexandra lingered on the edge of the group watching her handsome, dark-haired host adroitly entertain his guests, she realized she wasn't having a happy birthday, after all. It had been a mistake to come here and torment herself. It only served to remind her of the burden she shared with the Queen of England: both she and Mary Tudor were in love with men who didn't feel a groatsworth of passion for them in return.

Someone offered her a large cup of wine. She drained it and got herself another. She'd heard of people drowning their sorrows, but this was the first time she'd ever tried it herself.

It was not long thereafter that Alexandra set off on her own to search out the privy, which was down a long and badly lit corridor in the rear of Roger's house. She was just finishing up in the surprisingly modern compartment when she heard footsteps pass her and continue on down the corridor. As she stepped back out into the hallway, she recognized the two men who were entering another chamber—Roger and Francis Lacklin.

Alexandra told herself later that there was no excuse for what she subsequently did. On previous occasions when she'd eavesdropped, it had been by accident, but this time she boldly followed the two conspirators down the corridor and put her ear to the door through which they'd passed.

"It's necessary, Roger," Lacklin was saying. "I wouldn't ask you if it weren't."

"I'm not a cold-blooded murderer, dammit."

"For someone who's lived such an eventful life in the Middle Sea, you're cursed with an extraordinary number of scruples."

"For someone who's supposedly a man of God, you're blessed with damned few!"

There was a short silence, then Lacklin said, "I'm warning you—if you don't take action now, you'll regret it later on. We all will. Everything we're doing here could hang in the balance. If anyone should discover what we're hiding in your cellars—"

"Nobody will discover a thing." Roger sounded impatient. "Although I'd be much more confident of that if you didn't persist in appearing at untoward moments, increasing the risk of our being seen together."

"Very well, then, I'll be gone," Lacklin snapped, the volume of his voice rising as if he had turned suddenly toward the door. Alexandra scurried backward, looking for a place to hide. The nearest door was the privy. She turned and fled, forgetting, in her haste, that her head was spinning from an excess of fine French wine. She was just grabbing the privy door when she tripped and fell against it, unaccustomed to the ill-fitting men's boots that rounded out her masculine costume.

Footsteps rang in the corridor behind her as she struggled to her feet. Moments later she felt a heavy hand grasp her arm and haul her upright. She looked up into Francis Lacklin's angry, shadowed face.

Stout-hearted Alexandra felt a wave of pure panic. It was not wisdom, but her dogged instincts for self-preservation that made her accept his grip as if it were solicitous and say in her deepest, gruffest voice, "I thank you, sir. Must have consumed more wine than I thought. Now if I can only get this damnable door open before I heave my guts up—"

"Who are you?" Lacklin demanded, shaking her until she was afraid her wig would fly off. "What are you doing here?"

"I'm looking for the conveniences, a' course. And if I don't find 'em directly, there'll be a mess on the floor!"

There was a tense moment while Francis Lacklin looked her over from head to toe, obviously suspicious of her story. If he recognized her . . . dear God, she silently prayed, don't let him!

"What the devil is going on here?" Roger's voice only made Alexandra's heartrate accelerate. Under the circumstances, she wouldn't be surprised if he gave her away!

"I'm ill, and this gentleman is hindering my entrance to the privy. I was here before you, sir, and I assure you, my needs won't wait!"

"He was lurking in the hallway," Lacklin said to Roger. "There's no telling how long he's been here."

Roger took her other arm and opened the privy door. "It's all right, I can vouch for him. He's nothing but a harmless youth who's tippled a little too much of the wine. My brother's schoolfriend, Martin. You look greener than last week's haddock, my lad. Come on, no vomiting in the hall."

To her relief, Lacklin gave Roger a long look, then left them, moving quietly away, presumably to exit the house as stealthily as he had entered. "Are you really ill?" Roger asked.

"No. That is, I do feel a little queasy, but it was seeing him here, and fearing he'd recognize me that made me say that."

"You're damned fortunate he didn't recognize you. It had crossed his mind that you were spying, and if there's one thing Francis doesn't care for, it's a spy." He left a pause. "Were you spying, sweetling?"

She made her eyes perfectly guileless. "Of course not."

"Come with me." He pulled her down the hallway. "Did anyone see you come out here? Alan, for example?"

"No. He's enthralled with Richard Bennett's tales of the New World. Why? Where are we going?" It occurred to her that his hold on her arm was no gentler than Lacklin's had been.

"Here." He opened a door and she swept through unthinkingly, then looked about in momentary confusion. She was in a small chamber, probably the same one where Roger and Francis Lacklin had just been conferring. It was filled with an assortment of unused furniture, some of which was covered with dust sheets. The only light was a dim oil lamp in one corner. Behind her Roger closed the door. There was a click as he twisted the key. Slowly, she turned to face him.

"What are you doing?"

It was quite evident that he was stalking her. For every step he took toward her, she took one back. "I've been the epitome of self-restraint so far, sweetling, but you should have known better than to put yourself at my mercy like this."

"No, Roger," she protested, not certain why she was retreating, except that it had something to do with the look on his face, which was more angry than lustful. He backed her against a table and took her in his arms. Ungentle fingers at the nape of her neck forced her head back, then his mouth covered hers with something close to violence. She made a small sound, muffled by his lips, and pressed her hands ineffectually against his chest. But the warm caress of his mouth, the silky feel of his tongue stroking over her own, aroused all the aching power of her long-frustrated desire. With a sigh, she melted. Instead of pushing him away, her hands pulled him closer. Shyly, she parted her lips and gave herself up to pleasure.

He broke the kiss off as furiously as he had begun it, nipping her throat, her ears, her hairline instead. His breathing was jagged, and she could taste the lingering flavor of wine from his tongue. "I'm obsessed with you, Alexandra. But not so much that I don't recognize a lie when I hear one."

"Wh-what do you mean?"

His hold on her subtly altered, his hands sliding down to her elbows and forcing her arms back in a grip that didn't quite, but almost hurt. "Francis was right in his suspicion, wasn't he? You were listening outside this door."

"Why do you think that?" Damnation, she muttered to herself. She'd got away with it in the past, but this time it looked as if she'd been caught.

Roger was heavy-headed from all the wine he had consumed, but he wasn't too drunk to feel the tension in the slender body he held so close to his own. "Francis was right, wasn't he? You *are* a spy. Was it your father who gave you those clothes and sent you here tonight?"

She tried to pull away, but he merely tightened his hold. "Of course not!"

"I wouldn't have expected him to send you into my company, but perhaps dear Charles has decided that my raging lust for you is less dangerous to the State than my political beliefs? Or could it be that you no longer have a maidenhead left to guard after six months at court?"

"I wish I *were* a man so I could call you out for that insult!"

"I remember a day when your sex didn't stop you from offering to duel with me. I ought to beat you for the troubles you stir up. What the bloody hell were you doing listening outside this door? And how much did you hear?"

"I heard nothing," she tried, endeavoring to make it sound sincere, but suspecting, with a sinking stomach, that it didn't.

The tiny room spun as he dragged her over to a couch and pressed her down upon it, his body poised just above hers. "The truth, beloved. And don't brandish your stubborn courage at me. I'm certain you don't wish to be roughed up on your birthday."

"I don't require courage. You'd never hurt me, Roger."

"So young and so trusting," he mocked. With a sharp tug, he wrested the blond wig from her scalp. Her red hair was braided and pinned atop her head. "Unpin it."

"What?"

"You heard me. Take down your hair before I rip out the pins myself."

If the command had been given with warmth or passion in his voice, Alexandra might have complied. Here she was, alone with Roger on a couch in a locked room . . . a state of affairs she had devoutly longed for ever since the previous summer. But his eyes were hooded and cold, and his manhandling had induced more rage in her than excitement. "Rip away, if that's how you always treat your guests. I'll never get it hidden again, and the tale of your gallantry toward one of the Queen's ladies will be all over London before morning."

"That is precisely the idea." He pushed her down until she was flat on her back. His hands pinned her wrists as he crouched over her, one knee between her hose-covered thighs. The absence of the usual voluminous yards of skirt fabric made him acutely aware of the sweet softness of her body. Desire clawed in him, making him want to fall upon her and love her until they both expired in fierce deliriums of pleasure.

"My reputation will stand it; in fact, it will probably be enhanced. You have far more to lose than I. And stop looking so innocent and bewildered, sweetling. You're an intelligent woman and I'm certain you understand me perfectly. Talk, or I will expose you."

"You're hurting my wrists," was all she said.

He loosened his grip, but he didn't free her. Her wrists were slim, small-boned, fragile under his larger, harder hands. He wanted to touch his lips to them, his teeth, his tongue . . . "Damn you. Tell me what you overheard, Alix!"

"Oh, very well; it wasn't all that much, anyway. And I've known since last summer that your friend Francis is a Protestant agent. On your first night back at Chilton we argued and I ran up to bed in a temper. Remember? I regretted it and came back downstairs to put things right with you. But you were talking to Lacklin, and I couldn't help but hear what you said."

Roger sucked in his breath. "You've known from the beginning that I was in league with Francis?"

"Yes."

"Christ!" Roger flung himself down on his back, his lust vanquished by his fear for her. He pressed a hand to his forehead. Behind his eyes he felt the beginnings of a headache. "Who else knows about this?"

"No one. And no one ever will. I'd never betray you."

"If Francis were still here, he'd make absolutely certain of that."

"How? By killing me?"

"Of course by killing you! God's blood, Alix! Do you think this is a game?"

"I didn't hear very much," she repeated. "All I learned, in sooth, was that you'd done some favor for Lacklin which had brought you back to England in advance of your ship."

"I came overland from Marseilles, acting as a courier for some of his friends," he admitted for the first time. "The *Argo* was delayed by foul winds near Gibraltar."

"You were back in England in time to have murdered Will, which was all I was concerned about at the time. But since then, of course—"

"—you've thought it over enough to realize that I've been mixed up with Francis Lacklin for years, and that whatever treasonous activities I was engaged in when I returned to England last spring, I'm probably still at them."

"Yes. Tonight I heard that he wants you to kill someone, and that you are reluctant to do it." She reached for his hand, allowing her fingers to mesh with his. "Perhaps there's hope for you yet."

"Alexandra..." He lifted her chin with his other hand, then slid his fingers down until thumb and fingers closed gently around her throat. "You frighten me. You're a loyal Catholic and one of the queen's women. Your father is the chief of state security. You and I are enemies, beloved. I ought to wring your neck."

The juxtaposition of "enemies" and "beloved" rang in her ears. She smiled at him; unthinkingly he responded by shifting her beneath him again. It seemed so natural an action that when the surge of lust took him, he was momentarily nonplussed. How was it possible that he had never taken her? Her body felt so dear to him, so familiar.

"Can I trust you?" he whispered.

"With your life."

"And with the lives of my friends?"

"Of course."

"Francis Lacklin is my friend, Alix."

"I know," she said slowly. "I won't betray either of you."

"If you're ever discovered, and put to the question—"

"Considering the identity of my mistress and my father, I think I can safely say I'll never be tortured, Roger."

"As Queen Nan Boleyn and Queen Cat Howard could never be beheaded? Depend on nothing, Alexandra. Mary

Tudor could turn against you." He shook her shoulders a little. " 'Tis you I worry about, not myself. Remember your vow to me—'no more meddling'?"

Shame took hold of her as she recalled how guilty she had felt at Chilton after falsely accusing Roger of killing Will. She'd sworn off interfering in his affairs, and she hadn't meant to break her promise. "I never intended to meddle tonight. I don't know why I put my ear to the door . . . but it's been so long since I've done anything on impulse. At court I have to be so vigilant. It isn't easy being so bloody perfect all the time!"

His voice gentled. "Is it so difficult, serving the queen?"

She lifted her chin, determined not to complain. "Not difficult, no. Just a little wearing."

His thumbs soothed her cheekbones; then his lips saluted the dark circles under her eyes. "You're exhausted, aren't you? We've got to think of a way to get you safely home."

She grinned with mischief as she wriggled her hips against his. "We can't think very well in this position. Are you going to let me up?"

She knew instantly what his answer would be. There was a slight pause; then his expression changed subtly—his mouth slackened, his eyes dilated to black. It was the face she'd seen in Merwynna's cottage, and so many times since then, in her dreams.

"No," he muttered, sliding his hips more firmly on hers. "I think not." Unable to stop himself, he lowered his face to hers and kissed her hard. Pleasure jolted through him, and from the way her body arched, he knew it was the same for her. He deepened the kiss, thrusting his tongue into her mouth with wildly rhythmic ferocity. A tiny moan escaped her. He felt her tongue tentatively brush his, then, more boldly, imitate his own motions, sending bursts of hot desire along his nerves, and increasing the pressure in his groin until he thought he would explode.

Christ! It was this rush of emotion, this driving tide of sensuality, this irrational desire for a deeper-than-physical union that he didn't feel, couldn't feel, with other women. And yet it wasn't love. Love was unselfish and gentle, and this was neither of those. *I am obsessed with you,* he thought.

That was it—obsession. Mutual obsession, if the look of dazed delight in her eyes was anything to go by.

He slid his hand between their bodies, encountering the padded thickness of her doublet. "You've bound your breasts, haven't you?" At that moment he felt he had every right to touch them, caress them, excite the peaks until they stood in hard pebbles of readiness.

"Yes," she whispered.

He drew back, torturing them both. "Sit up and unbind them for me. I want to see you, touch you."

Dreamily Alexandra obeyed. Holding his eyes, she unfastened her doublet and slipped out of it. She had swathed her naked breasts in a length of cotton to keep them flat; her fingers trembled as she unwrapped the fabric. When it was done, she flushed at the heat of Roger's gaze upon her.

One of his hands reached out lazily and caressed her. His thumb rubbed back and forth over the peak of her breast, causing little darts of sensation to race along her nerves. In the pit of her stomach, her desire pooled and liquefied. He tugged gently on a nipple and she moaned.

"Very nice. Now, come closer, and kiss me, woman."

She pressed against him, feeling the rough texture of his elaborate brocade doublet against her naked breats. "What about you? Surely you have no need of so many garments."

"We'll take care of that all in good time, sweetling. For the moment I'm enjoying having a stubborn wench like you so docile and compliant."

She drew back in mock anger, but he chuckled and held her fast. He lay on his back on the couch and pulled her atop him. "Straddle me . . . that's right; spread your lovely legs and kneel over me. And stop looking so rebellious. I'm your teacher; you're supposed to follow my directions."

"Not if you gloat about it."

"I promise not to gloat anymore." He took both breasts in his hands and excited them so expertly that she threw back her head and unconsciously undulated her lower body against his thighs. "Christ, Alix," he muttered. "You're so sweet and responsive you drive me mad. Can you feel what you do to me?" He captured her hand and pressed it to the spot where his erection was leaping against the restrictive bindings of his clothes. She hesitated for an instant, then closed her fingers around him. He uttered a hoarse, tormented sound.

"Am I hurting you?" She sounded shy, uncertain; she tried to take her hand away.

"God, no. You can't hurt a man like that, not unless you knee him or something... Don't stop."

She continued, watching his face—the high color in his cheeks, the hooded sensuality of his dark, dilated eyes. She could see his pleasure, and it awed her. He'd taken her to the heights of ecstasy that night in Merwynna's cottage, but he hadn't allowed her to return the favor. Perhaps now, tonight, he would.

She experimented further, sliding her hand up and down his aroused length. "That's good," he whispered. He covered her fingers with his own and showed her the motion that pleased him most, then felt his hips arching off the couch as control began to elude him. God's blood, how he ached for her! He groaned again, cursing the clothing that prevented direct contact. "That's easily remedied," she murmured, reaching for the fastenings of his doublet. In seconds, with his help, she had stripped him down to his trunks and hose.

He was beautiful. There was an unconscious grace about his lean, long-limbed body, so strong and subtly muscled, his angular shoulders, his deep chest and taut belly. She was distracted from her more intimate explorations by her need to bury her fingers in the dark wealth of his sleek body hair. "You feel so good," she told him as she gently rubbed his chest. Leaning over, she kissed the flesh over his collarbone, sighing with pleasure, reveling in her desire for this handsome, virile man.

He, too, sighed. "So do you, my lady." He pulled her down until their bare skin was touching from waist to throat. Her soft breasts seemed to nestle quite comfortably against the wall of his chest; her hips molded to his loins as if they belonged there. She was right for him, perfect. And he wanted her so much.

The only impediment now to their union was the hose they were both still wearing, and that, as she had pointed out, was easily remedied. He rolled over, pressing her down beneath him and dragging at the material. "Come, let's get the rest of these things off. If we're going to do it, we might as well do it properly."

"*Are* we going to do it?" She cast a glance down at her strangely clad thighs, wishing she were wearing one of her court gowns and looking her best for him. She hadn't thought, somehow, that it would happen quite this way. She swallowed hard. She remembered the size of him throbbing beneath her fingers and felt a twinge of alarm. She wasn't afraid, she insisted to herself. It was just that she hadn't expected him to be quite so . . . well-endowed.

Roger was glaring at her. "Are you having second thoughts?"

"No," she said quickly, banishing them.

"You ought to be. And I ought to send you away."

Determinedly she slid her hands down his back until they linked around his waist. "I don't want to leave yet. Truly, Roger. I love you. Don't send me away."

He stared down at her. Her face was naked with the love she had never attempted to deny. Wholehearted and trusting love, dedicated to him even though he had done nothing to deserve it, even though he had not solicited it and could not possibly accept or return it. He'd seen that look before, in Celestine's eyes. She too had become entangled in the net which Roger himself always seemed to escape.

But if you *could* return it, a beguiling voice seemed to whisper, the net would dissolve and you could be happy for once in your life. He thrust the temptation away, reminding himself of all the things against it: her innocence, his vice; her gentleness, his cruelty; her religion, his flirtation with heresy; her mistress, her father, and a new complication— his own brother. It had occurred to him tonight as he'd watched them together that Alan was probably in love with Alexandra. He had suspected as much last summer, but he'd doubted that either of them was aware of it. Now, however, in keeping with his recent initiation into manhood, Alan's love would be something to be reckoned with.

The lad would be a better match for her than he could ever be, he insisted to himself. Two good-natured innocents united against a wicked world—why not? If he really cared about her, he would make certain she married Alan.

Resign yourself, he ordered his unruly body, his protesting soul. The decision he had made with such difficulty that night in the witch's cottage at Westmor must stand. She was not his for the taking. She would never be.

And so he rolled away from her, saying, "How's the husband-hunting going? Every time I see you at court, you're attended by one wealthy prospect or another."

Alexandra was stunned. "How can you talk of them, when you and I—"

"—are nothing to each other," he cut in. He sat up, ignoring the angry protests his body was screaming. Jerkily he pulled on his clothes. With forced nonchalance he pulled her also to a sitting position, then helped her into the doublet she'd removed earlier. She sat passively, staring at him in disbelief as he took her wig and placed it carefully upon her still-pinned-and-braided hair. "Nothing has changed, Alexandra. You're far too sweet and virginal for me. I prefer my lovers experienced."

"Liar. You said you were obsessed with me."

He permitted himself a brittle laugh. "Never believe anything a man says when he's got his hands on you in the dark, sweetling."

"You whoreson bastard! How dare you do this to me again? How dare you lie so crudely, trying your best to hurt me? Are you made of ice? I don't understand you, Roger! Truly, I do not!"

He turned away, but not before she saw that his sensual mouth was set in an agonized expression, his eyes regretful, bitter, sad. "No, I am not made of ice. Stop sulking and consider yourself fortunate. If it were not for our long friendship, you would be lying under me even now, naked and writhing while I mastered you."

"So you say! But I'm beginning to doubt it, Roger. Perhaps you're not 'one who will not,' after all. Perhaps you're 'one who cannot.'"

Roger ignored this slur. "Enough, Alexandra." His voice was weary and cold. He rose. "I must get back to my guests."

"Go without me, then. I'll just rest here until Alan's ready to leave. Or perhaps I'll poke around a little in your cellars."

Roger turned on her so fast it made her jump. He seized her upper arms, jerked her to her feet, and shook her so hard her teeth chattered. "Do you know what's down there? Damn you, answer me!"

"No! I heard the subject mentioned between you and Lacklin, that's all!"

"By Christ, Alexandra, I'm tempted to clap you in irons and keep you prisoner in those same cellars until my friends can safely leave the country. 'Twould be no less than you deserve!" He shook her again. "If you ever betray me, do you know what I'll do to you?"

"Rape me?" she hazarded, fascinated by his sudden rage and her own spurt of fear.

He shook his head slowly. "Don't make jests, not about this. There is evil in me, Alix, dark things you've never seen. Tempt them at your peril."

"Don't tempt me either. I've sworn I won't betray you, and I won't. What will it take to gain your trust, Roger? What will it take to stop your lies?" Furious, she insinuated her belly against his, provoking an immediate tangible response. "Virginal I may be, but not so innocent as I was last summer. With you as my teacher, I've learned the significance of this." She rocked her hips wantonly. "You desire me. Why do you persist in tormenting us both?"

"For your own sake, damn you! But noble-minded I'm not. If you push me any further, I will tear every last one of those ridiculous garments from your sweet body and you will learn the full consequences of your recklessness."

Indeed, he was already moving to do it, his discipline blasted by her determination to give herself to him. One of his hands moved slowly, hotly, down over her waist, her hip, her thigh. He felt her shudder. She threw her head back, baring her throat to his lips. But before he could take the silent invitation, she suddenly whirled and jerked herself away. He groaned in frustration, and would have hauled her back into his arms, had she been anyone else but the woman she was.

"I think you love me a little, after all," she said in a barely audible voice. "I don't understand your scruples, but I know you well enough not to tempt you to disregard them. You have enough to fret about without feeling guilty over me."

Then she was gone. By the time he got himself together enough to follow her, she had collected Alan and vanished from his house.

19

TO ALEXANDRA'S dismay, Alan insisted on talking incessantly as they rode their horses back to her father's. He was obviously intrigued by his brother's mariner friends, and his imagination had been stimulated by all the tales of the New World. Alexandra, who wanted nothing more than to pull her cloak over her face and cherish her memory of Roger's abortive lovemaking, instead had to endure Alan's speculation on northwest sea routes to China and the probable worth in pounds sterling of a well-laden treasure ship.

"You're rather quiet," he finally said. "Did something happen this evening to upset you?"

"If it had, you, my protector, ought to have noticed it."

Alan stared at her. "You're not usually so testy. For God's sake, Alix, what happened?"

One who will not, she was thinking. Like a refrain, the words repeated themselves over and over. Roger wanted her, but because of some strange point of honor that she really didn't understand, he would not act. It would be possible, she'd learned tonight, to break him, to force him to take her in the explosion of passion that was always so close to the surface with him. She had always known that a man could force a woman, but now she realized that it was also possible for a woman to take a man against his will. But it would be a violation, and one did not violate where one loved.

"It's Roger, isn't it?" said Alan. "You shouldn't have gone there tonight."

"Oh, Alan—"

"Are you in love with him?"

It had become easy to lie to everyone else, but Alan knew her so well that he leapt on her slight hesitation. Before she could issue her standard denial, he added, "Can you not see that he's exactly the wrong sort of man for you? Alexandra, please don't break your heart over him!"

She would have dearly liked to confide in him, for he had known her secrets since childhood, and her forbidden love seemed almost too much, sometimes, for her heart to hold. But there was something in Alan's voice, in his expression, that stopped her. Her love for Roger, she sensed, was something that to Alan would taste of gall.

"My heart is perfectly safe. I'm tired and testy because the queen never sleeps and we, as her women, are forced to keep the same hours as she. Your flamboyant brother has nothing to do with my moods, I assure you. Truly, Alan, you're as bad as my father."

He looked so relieved that she knew her instincts had been right. Alan was jealous of Roger. He was a man now, a man who had been cast out of Oxford for fornication. He loved her, and it was no longer the love of a brother. And yet he said nothing. *One who dares not?* Oh God, Merwynna—couldn't you be wrong for once? Alan was her dearest friend, but she would never feel passion for him.

Why, she wondered, should this be so? In looks, Roger and Alan were not unalike. Intellectually, she and Alan were suited—they had the identical education, and similar interests. Temperamentally they were different, but this rarely caused conflict. They knew each other's hearts, and accepted each other's foibles as only those who are sincerely affectionate can. Yet Alexandra could no more imagine holding Alan close to her body and saying "I love you" than she could imagine making love to a stranger or to an enemy like Geoffrey de Montreau. Her body did not yearn for his, nor did her soul sense in him its true mate.

But what if his feelings were different? Love, after all, rarely seemed to be reciprocal. It was possible that Alan desired her just as hopelessly as she desired his brother.

"I'm far too reasonable a person to fall in love with Roger. Passion, from what I've seen of it, brings more torment than delight. Look at poor Pris Martin, for example. Loving a Trevor brought nothing but tragedy to her."

Alan knocked his forehead dramatically with his fist. "That reminds me. I knew there was something I'd forgotten to tell you. I ran into Pris Martin in Oxford last month. I thought you'd be interested in hearing about her."

Alexandra silently thanked the impulse that had led her to introduce Priscilla into the conversation. She wanted no more chitchat about love. "You mean she went to Oxford after leaving Chilton? Are you certain?"

"Of course. I recognized her and spoke with her, much to her initial consternation. She was working as a shop girl in a draper's establishment. She'd known the draper years ago—he was some sort of relative, I imagine. Like Pris, he's a Protestant."

A *Protestant*. Not a *heretic*.

"What did she say? Did you ask her why she left Chilton so abruptly, without a word to anyone, not even your father, who'd been so solicitous of her welfare?"

"We spoke very briefly. You recall how quiet and reserved she always was. She became even more so when I turned up. She seemed"—he paused, then added—"frightened."

"Frightened?" The adjective didn't match up with anything that Alexandra remembered of Pris Martin. The woman had always seemed far too in control of herself and her emotions to give way to fear of any sort. Even on that day of revelation at Chilton, she had been straight-shouldered and dignified.

"Yes. I recognize fear in others, being so familiar with it myself," Alan said wryly. "I'd swear she was terrified. But they had just arrested a butcher down the street for heresy, so mayhap she was afraid of the stake. I asked her if she couldn't leave Oxford . . . go north again perhaps, where the ecclesiastical courts are not so avidly seeking dissenters. Or to the Continent. I told her of the folk who are leaving the country to await happier times abroad. I even suggested she come to London, where one can sometimes find people who have the means to assist dissenters in taking ship and leaving England. . . ." His sentence was choked off as he shot Alexandra a guilty look. "I'm talking too much. I forgot that you're no longer simply my oldest friend, but one of the queen's women."

She reached over her horse's neck and touched his arm. "I am your friend first, Alan. Nothing you say to me will go any further." *And I'm accustomed to keeping secrets.* "But you must be wary of all others, believe me. You are speaking treason."

Alan was silent.

"You must be particularly careful in my father's house. As you may or may not know, he's a minister of state who specializes in making everybody's private business his own." She sighed. "Oxford has succeeded where Mr. Lacklin failed, I take it? You, too, wish to reform the Church?"

"Alix, for better or worse, the reform has already begun. The monasteries were dissolved more than twenty years ago—your own Westmor Abbey was one of the first to be secularized. You and I grew up reading Archbishop Cranmer's liturgy and admiring his prose, if not his doctrine. Do you know that Cranmer thrust his right hand into the fire as it was lit around him, because that was the hand which had signed the recantation he later rejected? Have you heard what Latimer said to Ridley as they were about to be martyred? 'We shall this day light such a candle, by God's grace, in England, as I trust shall never be put out.'"

"Brave words, and stirring, certainly. But I do not believe in a God who looks with pleasure on burnt offerings. Nor do I think these hideous fires will cleanse the Church." She spoke vehemently, inspired by her distaste for Francis Lacklin's methods of reformation, which were apparently as bloodthirsty as the queen's. Who was it, she wondered, whom he had asked Roger to kill? A cleric, a government officer, or the queen herself? "The country went mad the day the old king's lust for Nan Boleyn caused him to throw off the authority of the pope, and nothing has been the same since."

"The pope was corrupt. The entire ecclesiastical establishment was full of corruption, and still is. Mary Tudor would pull the cloak of the past over England again. But she will not succeed, for those times are gone. The old must make way for the new."

"But who is to say the new is any more valid than the old? I cannot believe God would be so petty as to care whether the Mass is said in English or Latin, or whether the Body and Blood of Christ are actually present in the Host."

"'Tis you, I think, who are the heretic," said Alan. "You sound like Roger. At Chilton, he expressed similar cynical views, even if he did not truly espouse them."

"My views are not cynical. Cynics do not mourn the failings of humanity—they revile them. And how do you know whether he espouses them or not?"

Alan shrugged and did not answer. "How exactly do you worship, Alix?"

"I go to Mass with everybody else, and while the priests rant and rave about heresy, I turn inward to ignore them, praying in my heart that all this strife may stop and we may live together in peace and tolerance. What do you do? Proclaim your dangerous views in the streets?"

"Of course not. I'm a coward, remember? I admire men like Latimer and Ridley, but I'd never choose their path."

"And what of Pris Martin?" she asked, suddenly remembering how this discussion had begun. "Will she follow your somewhat foolish advice and come to London? Do you really know people who can arrange overseas exile for heretics?" As soon as she asked the question, insight flashed. "Oh, God's blood! You're thinking of Roger, aren't you? The resistance we encountered from the boatman about going out to the *Argo?* You believe he's shipping not only cargo, but refugees."

Alan flushed and turned his eyes away.

But everything was clear now to Alexandra. "You learned at Chilton that your brother was associated with the heretics. At the time you despised him for it, but now, after Oxford, you've changed your views."

His shrug confirmed her suspicions.

"But it's nonsense!" she protested. "Roger's passion is shipping, not religion. You heard him—trade routes to the east, exploration to the west. And he's no true heretic, whatever skulduggery he may be mixed up in. He wouldn't risk his dreams for a sorry bunch of Marian exiles."

"Probably not," Alan was quick to agree. "The idea's probably nothing more than one of my romance-inspired guesses. Seeing him, wrongly, as a hero of sorts. Or as a villain, depending on your political views."

Alexandra frowned and bit her lip, wondering at his disinclination to argue. Could he possibly be right? What exactly was Roger up to with the heretics? And whom had Francis asked him to kill? "I saw you talking civilly with him tonight. You're going to go and live with Roger, aren't you?"

"If he'll have me."

He'll have you, she thought with an uncharacteristic spurt of envy. 'Tis me he won't have.

"Sweet God," she said aloud. "Now I'm going to have to worry about you both."

And worry she did—but not just about Alan and Roger. Her week of freedom passed all too fast, and she was shut up once again with the queen and her courtiers at Westminster, where the atmosphere was one of unrelenting tension. Spring was late that year, and April and May were gloomy with the preparations for war. Alexandra watched with pity as the queen tried so desperately to please her husband both in the council chamber and in the bedchamber. The first involved the twisting of several highly placed arms as one by one Mary demanded that her Council members support her declaration of war against France. The second involved long hours of careful toilette, and, now and then, one of Merwynna's beauty potions. Alexandra tried, for her own sake, to keep the latter a secret, but the word leaked out, as word of such miracles always will, and soon there was a demand for necromancy that would have amused her, had it not seemed so incongruous at a court where prayer was supposed to be more efficacious than magic.

Geoffrey de Montreau continued to plague her. Although

Alexandra did what she could to avoid him, now and then he succeeded in isolating her from her companions. Invariably, at such times, he would maneuver the conversation around to Roger, although this happened so subtly that she sometimes wondered if she were imagining it. She fought back by hiding her consternation, reacting to his remarks with widened eyes and feigned ignorance, as if she were missing his point entirely. But Geoffrey was not deceived.

"I gossip too much—it was ever a flaw in me," he confided to her one evening as they danced. "You are careful to refrain from displaying your wit with me, mademoiselle. Yet with others, I hear, you have a clever tongue."

"Ah, sir, I think I have just been insulted. I strike you as dull?"

"You strike me as better disciplined than I believed when first we met."

"How disappointing for you, monsieur. You are having an unfortunate run of bad luck. Diplomacy has not eased the tensions between your country and mine, has it? There will be war?"

"Any day now, I expect."

"And when it comes, will you return to France?"

His liquid eyes hardened. "I shall return to France when my business here is finished."

She felt a chill in her abdomen. He might just as well have said, "I shall return to France when Roger Trevor is dead."

As still happened sometimes, a demon seemed to take possession of her tongue. "Your sister Celestine died of an illness, I understand." Actually, she had no idea how Celestine had died. "It's not as if she was murdered."

Before her eyes, Geoffrey's carefully constructed mask of diplomacy cracked. Anger blazed in his face, and behind it, just a hint of terrible, unrelieved grief. He whirled her off the floor and into an alcove with less regard than usual for who might be observing them. "An illness?" he scoffed. "Is that the tale he spun you? No, mistress, she suffered no illness. She was basely raped and forced into concubinage by one of the most notorious lechers in the Middle Sea. And then she was murdered."

"Why?" she asked quietly.

"Why?" Geoffrey repeated as if the question were half-witted.

"People don't go about murdering their lovers for no reason. Are you suggesting he killed her because he was bored with her?"

"He killed her because she was carrying a child! Since she was of his own degree in life, he would have been forced to marry her. I would have insisted upon it—that he knew. But he did not wish to wed her, so there were 'complications' of her pregnancy—very convenient complications, I'd say!"

Could any of this be true? Alexandra tried to reconcile it with what little Roger had told her himself that night in Merwynna's cottage. He hadn't mentioned Celestine's pregnancy. But he had reacted full strongly when she had asked if he knew any way to prevent conception. *I know a way or two, but experience has taught me that such precautions don't always work,* had been his words.

What had been the complications? "How far along was she? Did the child survive?"

"Of course the child didn't survive. That's just the point: he didn't want the child. She suffered a miscarriage and bled to death, after being brutally beaten by him. I have a witness, one of his former crew members, who heard his raging and her screaming on the night she died."

I killed her, Roger had said. She shivered. "I do not believe it. I have good reason to know that Roger is no murderer."

"You know nothing," he said derisively. "Roger and I had dealings together some years ago, and I have seen firsthand his way with women. He uses them callously without tenderness or care; if they make the mistake of loving him, so much the worse for them. My sister was a virgin, fresh from a convent education, traveling to Venice to join the man to whom she was betrothed. I had planned to travel with her, but the delicate diplomatic affairs I was negotiating prevented it. Fool that I was, I entrusted her to Roger, little thinking that he would besmirch her honor and mine in so vile a manner."

"Whatever may have happened between them, I cannot believe he killed her," Alexandra insisted.

"What you believe is nothing to me, mademoiselle. I know the truth. She demanded marriage, but as the heir to a barony, Roger apparently had other ideas as to who might be an appropriate mother to his firstborn son. It seems he had another match in mind." He glared at her as if he thought she were it.

"Roger wasn't the heir to the title at the time of your sister's death. And as far as I know, he has no intentions to marry."

"You were once betrothed to the heir of Chilton."

"I was betrothed to a *man,* not to a title. There is nothing between Roger Trevor and me besides friendship."

"I do not believe you, mademoiselle. But it hardly matters, since soon there will be nothing between you but ashes and dust."

Angry and shaken by his threats in spite of her determination not to be, Alexandra turned her back on him and took her leave.

Late in May, amid constant preparations for war, the weather opened up and the queen and her ladies were able to spend an occasional hour in the fresh air and sunshine. Alexandra fervently hoped the fine weather would cheer them all. More than before, she feared for her mistress's physical and emotional well-being. Mary's relations with Philip, her husband, were far from perfect; gossip had it that he would leave her once again as soon as he obtained all the troops and supplies he needed for his war on the Continent. And indeed, at Greenwich, several miles downriver, Philip's ships were in the process of being loaded.

The *Argo,* she had heard, was also at Greenwich, preparing to leave any day now for another trading voyage to the Mediterranean. According to Alan, who visited her whenever he could, Roger was too busy with the preparations for this venture to appear very often at court. It seemed an age since she had seen him. Although she missed him acutely, she was grateful that Roger was temporarily out of reach of Geoffrey de Montreau's malice.

As the warm days drifted by, Alexandra was lulled into a state of false security about Geoffrey. In the four months he had been at court, Geoffrey had made any number of sly remarks and threats, but so far, no harm had come to Roger. Perhaps the Frenchman was more proficient at envisioning revenge than he was at carrying it out. He was such an effeminate fop. Perhaps there was no real harm in him, after all.

Then, early in June, disaster struck. It began innocently during one of the court's summer outings—a barge trip down the river to Hampton Court Palace. The queen's clearly-marked barge, flying the royal standard, had just docked at the landing where she and her attendants would disembark when an obviously drunken boatman lost control of his rowboat and rammed the royal barge. The flustered boatman fumbled with his long oars, accidentally thrusting one of them at the queen, who was about to step from the barge to the dock. The oar did not strike her—fortunately for the boatman's neck—but the queen was forced to jerk backward out of the way, coming perilously close to the edge of the wooden planking. Indeed, if Alexandra hadn't had the presence of mind to grab the royal shoulders and steady her mistress, Mary might have ended up in the river.

The boatman, horrified when he realized whom he had nearly dunked, fell abjectly to his knees and begged her Grace's mercy. It was granted—the queen was always kind and gracious to her subjects—along with a gentle admonition that he give up the evils of strong drink. By the time they all got safely back within the queen's apartments, Mary had sufficiently recovered to shrug the matter off, and Alexandra would have put it from her mind had it not been for Geoffrey de Montreau.

"A word, mademoiselle," he said to her the following morning at yet another court function.

She lifted her chin and turned to walk away, no longer feeling the slightest desire to be courteous to Geoffrey. He was insistent, though, stopping her with a beringed hand on her heavy brocade sleeve. "You distrust and dislike me,

I know, but what I have to say to you this day is something you ought not disregard."

"Very well, monsieur. Speak."

"I will waste no words. Your mistress narrowly escaped injury, even death, yesterday morning, is that not so?"

"There was a small accident. Nothing to be concerned about."

"She does not swim, of course, and there was a stiff current on the river, I understand. Even if she had been safely pulled out, she might have taken cold from the dunking—her health is not the best, they say."

"What are you getting at? It was an accident."

"Perhaps. But accidents happen very frequently around some people. The Trevor family has been plagued with them."

Alexandra tried to pull away from him. His grasp was firmer than she expected, considering the foppish way he dressed. "I thought it might interest you to know that the boatman responsible for nearly drowning the queen was employed until recently as a seaman on Roger Trevor's ship. A coincidence? I have my doubts. Reports say that this supposedly drunken man walked away from the scene of the so-called accident and has not been seen since."

Whatever happened to that clever plan you had to assassinate Mary Tudor and place her Protestant sister on the throne? Jesu! A sick sensation spread through her middle. Could it be the queen whom Francis had been urging Roger to help him murder?

"You are imaginative, as usual, monsieur," she managed, but her palms were beginning to slicken.

"Am I, mistress? We are talking, you remember, about your sovereign, your mistress, the woman you serve so lovingly night and day. Or could it be that your loyalties are divided?"

"My loyalties! Look to your own! You represent a country with whom England will shortly be at war. If something were to happen to our queen, few people would be happier than the French." She gulped breath. "Listen, sir. I'm not a fool—I know you delight in lying to me. You seek Roger

Trevor's death, and because of this I don't intend to believe a single thing you tell me about him. I've had enough of your poison. Kindly do not approach me again."

He bowed, an unpleasant smile on his heavily made-up face.

"And if anything should happen to Roger," she added, "I will personally see to it that you are cast into the deepest dungeon in Christendom, your diplomatic immunity be damned."

She turned to walk away, but Geoffrey had the last word. "If anything should happen to your mistress, mademoiselle, remember I tried to warn you. The man you so stoutly defend is a traitor, a heretic, and a murderer of women."

Try as she might, she could not dismiss the accusation from her mind. She made every effort to carry on with her usual duties, but the worry must have shown on her "open countenance," since her friend and suitor Philip Carington noted it. He had been pursuing her more vigorously lately, hinting that since he might shortly be sent to risk life and limb as an officer in Philip and Mary's army, it was incumbent upon Alexandra to consider accepting his suit. Her father approved of him, she knew. But although Alexandra enjoyed his company, the idea of marrying him had never seriously crossed her mind.

"Is aught amiss with you?" Philip asked her that afternoon after catching her staring vacantly over his shoulder three times during a ten-minute conversation.

"I'm afraid I have a killing headache," she told him, and it was not a lie.

"Slip out and rest, then," he suggested. "I'll tell Jane Dormer to inform her Grace you're ill and have taken to your bed for the rest of the day."

She squeezed his hand gratefully and took his advice. But instead of retiring to bed, she left the court for her father's house, where she was thankful to find him absent. She promptly invaded his wardrobe of disguises, this time choosing the clothing of a somewhat flamboyant burgher woman. Her first stop was the river, where she sought out the young boatman to whom she'd given a coin several weeks before. When she threw back her hood and showed him her face, he remembered her. Aye, he agreed, everybody had heard of the near-accident to her Majesty yesterday at the barge landing. No, the fellow involved did not regularly ply his trade on the river; in fact, nobody had seen him before, or since. Unless, now that she mentioned it, the knave *did* look a little like one of the scowling-faced sailors from that ship in the harbor that everyone had been bribed to stay away from. The *Argo* was gone now, to Greenwich, he believed. He'd heard tell she was due to put out to sea on the dawn tide tomorrow, for a voyage to China.

China! She'd send Roger to China, damn him, if he'd really had anything to do with the queen's near-miss! Heavyhearted, but determined to get to the bottom of this, Alexandra tipped the boatman generously and set out for Chilton House.

20

ROGER and Alan Trevor were sitting around a table in the central hall of Chilton House that afternoon with Richard Bennett and several of his friends, discussing possibilities for exploration in the New World. Alan seemed fascinated with the subject—the boy's dreams were even more adventuresome than Roger's own. Roger himself was finding it difficult to concentrate on trade routes and ship design today. He was too preoccupied with his plans for the night.

Why was he obsessed with the feeling that something was going to go wrong? He kept running the details over in his mind. He and Francis had everything meticulously planned—there was nothing they'd missed, was there? They'd been careful, and nobody in authority suspected a thing. So why was he so damnably jumpy?

He told himself he ought to be grateful that this day was upon them; after tonight, it would all be over. Tomorrow morning when the *Argo* set sail on the dawn tide, he would finally be free of the debt he owed Francis Lacklin, free of the worry that Sir Charles Douglas might order a search of his cellars, free even of Francis himself. After tonight he would be able to forget about the blasted heretics and concentrate all his energies on the things that concerned him most—shipping, trading, and exploration.

A commotion near the front door attracted his attention, and Roger leapt to his feet, startling his guests. Someone had arrived whom his servants were dubious about letting in. "God's teeth," he muttered, fearing the worst. He caught Alan's eye, grimly noting that his brother had picked up on his anxieties. The lad looked pale, his eyes huge in his face. Dammit. Had it been a mistake to take Alan into his confidence? Roger had learned during his years of leadership that giving trust and responsibility to a young, untried man will often bring out the best in him. On the other hand, if the young man was the sort who caved in easily to pressure, it could lead to trouble.

Purposefully Roger tossed a lighthearted grin in Alan's direction, mentally sending the boy encouragement. Then he strode toward the door to see what the fuss was about.

Roger did not recognize the woman who swept into the chamber, chased by two servants; at least, not until she threw back her hood, revealing clouds of red hair and snapping green eyes.

"Body of Christ! Are you mad?" He waved the servants away and slammed the door. "You know full well your father's spies survey this house twenty-four hours a day."

Alexandra pursed her lips, glancing from him to his friends and back. "Perhaps they'll report that you've hired a whore for the afternoon. I'm sure it isn't the first time."

In spite of himself, his mouth twisted up. She always had a comeback, the quick-witted wench. "No. Nor is it likely to be the last." He gave her body a deliberately appraising look. Her court finery was absent today—she was clad in the simple stuff gown of a middle-class Londoner. It was very becoming. Instead of the stiff ruffled bodice and heavy jewels fashionable at Westminster, she wore a laced gown with a soft bodice that curved beguilingly over her small, high breasts and set off the neatness of her trim waist. "You look the part," he added, to goad her. "D'you intend to play it?"

Before she could reply, Alan was at their side. "What are you doing here, Alix?" he demanded.

"You have an excellent answer to that question, I trust," Roger seconded. He took in the distress in her eyes. "What on earth is the matter? Has somebody died?"

"No. It's more a matter of somebody remaining alive, despite your efforts." She flicked her eyes over Alan and the others, then returned to him. "I wish to speak with you alone."

"Ah, but we can't be trusted alone, can we, sweetling? Although which of us would rape the other first is, I should imagine, a matter for dispute."

Alexandra caught her breath. She was feeling uncomfortable enough as it was, pushing past his servants, walking in on what was obviously a conference of some sort. What were these men up to? She recognized one of them, Richard Bennett, as the sailor-explorer she'd met the last time she'd been here. Heretics all, no doubt. What were they talking about? Their plot to murder the queen? Alan looked self-conscious and guilty, and as for Roger, of course he would be nasty. It had ever been his best defense. Very well, she would use his own tactics against him. "If you refuse us privacy, I'll say what I've come to say in front of your friends. After our last discussion, however, I had not thought you would hold your secrets so lightly. Did you honestly expect me to ignore a crime of this magnitude? Or do you fancy I'm so besotted by you that I'll defend the ultimate morality of anything you choose to do?"

The expression on Roger's face turned dangerous. "I bow to your threats," he said, placing his hand on her arm. Through the coarse material of her gown, she could feel the tension in his fingers. "We'll talk in the library. No, stay," he told his friends, who were rising as if to leave. "This won't take long. If you hear screaming, pay no attention, unless it should be *my* voice. She's damnably clever with a knife."

"Just a minute," Alan objected.

"Stay out of this, brother, and take that chivalrous-knight expression off your face. I'll return her to your keeping within ten minutes, pure and unsullied as ever. Come, my Amazon, and explain why you're so hot to have my blood."

He pushed her through into a small book-lined chamber, slammed the heavy wooden door behind them, and locked it. The curtains were drawn and the room was ill-lit. A cavernous hearth on one wall boasted no fire, so the room was cold. Alexandra drew her cloak more tightly around her.

Roger let go of her and backed several paces. "Well? What crime are you accusing me of this time? I haven't assassinated any siblings lately, I'm quite sure of that. Alan, as you can see, is hale and hearty, if slightly more corrupt than he was last summer at Chilton."

"Those men with him, they're heretics, of course?"

"I haven't inquired into their individual sources of ghostly comfort. As long as I worship correctly, which, you'll have noted, I invariably do, I consider my religious obligations to be at an end."

"You hypocrite."

"Introduce me to a man or woman of sense in these troubled times who's not a hypocrite. Have you included Smithfield in your tours around London? Or perhaps you enjoy the pungent odor of roasting human flesh?"

"I thought you simply were helping them, but you're one of them, aren't you? You and Alan both. You're as fanatical as Francis Lacklin!"

"I'm not answerable to you concerning my personal religious beliefs. If there's one thing I would fight for, it would be the individual's freedom of conscience. Which edition of the Bible I choose to read is between myself and God."

"Very rational! Then how, pray, do you justify destroying the lives of those who worship differently?"

"'Tis the queen and her priests who are doing that, not I."

"So that makes your villainy justifiable? She's a murderer herself, so she deserves to die? Even though she is your monarch?"

"What the devil are you talking about?"

"I'm talking about the boatman who rammed the queen's barge on the river yesterday and nearly flung her into the Thames. A careless accident, supposedly, except that the boatman vanished afterward, and looked suspiciously like one of the *Argo*'s seamen."

Roger's eyes narrowed and his whipcord body tautened

further. "I've heard nothing of this. Alexandra?" He took a step toward her, then abruptly stopped. "Tell me exactly what occurred."

She sank into the elaborately carved armchair behind his massive desk and told him. By the time she had finished, he was pacing and his face was grim. "Describe the careless boatman," he ordered. "It sounds like Peters. A vicious little troublemaker whom I personally dismissed a month ago. God's teeth. How very subtle of somebody."

She didn't speak. She noted, dispassionately, that her hands were trembling.

"I take it it really wasn't a very close thing? There would have been an investigation otherwise."

"I suppose not. It did seem an accident. As an attempt on her life, it was rather inept, especially for you."

"I wasn't behind it, Alix."

She looked up, catching her bottom lip between her teeth. "Naturally I want to believe you. The trouble is, at Chilton you and Francis Lacklin discussed killing the queen. And the last time I was here, I clearly heard him proposing a murder."

"A proposition which I declined," he reminded her.

"Yes." She paused in silent thought, wanting desperately to trust him. "There's another suspect for this villainy. I would like to believe him guilty, and you innocent, but the things we want most in this world are not always the ones that are true." She looked up, her green eyes imploring him. "Promise me that whatever you and Lacklin are involved in, it doesn't directly threaten the queen. Helping heretics I can understand, perhaps even condone, but murder is another matter. I can't turn my eyes away from that, Roger, I simply *can't*."

He came and leaned over her, his hands on her shoulders. "My love, this was bound to happen sooner or later. I tried to warn you that your divided loyalties would tear you apart."

"Oh God." She was trembling both from his nearness and her overwrought emotions.

"Calm yourself, please." His voice was strained but gentle. "I wasn't behind this plot, but suppose I had been? You owe your allegiance to Mary Tudor, and to fulfill it you would have had to betray me."

"No." She shook her head vigorously. "That I could never do."

"You could if you felt you were choosing the greater good. Wouldn't you have to place your honor, your integrity, your loyalty to your queen before your fledgling and unrequited love for me?"

"It's not fledgling! And if it were as unrequited as you continue to insist, you'd have found a way to silence me before this. I know too much."

"That's the understatement of the month. Who's your other suspect, as you put it, for yesterday's so-called accident?"

"Geoffrey de Montreau, of course. 'Twas he who called it to my attention, in hopes that I'd blame you." She looked into his troubled eyes. "Which reminds me. How did his sister die?"

He whirled away, pacing. "Oh Christ, Alix, not now."

"Is it true she was expecting your child?"

His face when he turned back to her was controlled and impassive. "As a midwife's assistant, that calls up your sympathy, doesn't it? Aye, it's true. Geoffrey has reason enough to hate me."

"Is that why you're doing nothing to stop him in his campaign to disgrace and destroy you?"

"Now you're beginning to sound like Francis. What do you suggest—that I assassinate an attaché of the embassy of France and start the bloody war single-handedly?"

"What does Francis suggest?"

"Just that. Geoffrey is the man Francis wanted me to kill."

Alexandra was conscious of a great surge of relief. Of course! *That* made sense. It wasn't the queen at all, but the wretched Geoffrey whom Francis Lacklin had urged Roger to murder. "For once I'm tempted to agree with him."

"That's all I need—you and Francis in agreement. If he had any idea that you know as much as you do about my messy affairs, he'd slit your throat. Francis is touchy about security."

"Very touchy," someone said.

At Alexandra's sharp intake of breath, a figure materialized in the fireplace. It stepped into the room, dusting itself off. Alexandra made the sign against evil. It was either Francis Lacklin himself, or the devil assuming his shape.

"The thing that eavesdroppers so frequently fail to remember is that other people also have ears," said Mr. Lacklin's pleasant voice. "Not to mention opportunities."

Roger moved instantly to place himself between Alexandra and the apparition. His hand had gone automatically to the dagger at his belt, a gesture Lacklin saw and grimaced at.

"You needn't say it," Lacklin interjected as Roger drew breath. "I won't touch her. Much as I would like to propose a quick and efficient throat-slitting, I know a sacred object when I see one. Good day to you, Alexandra. It was you in the corridor a couple of months ago, wasn't it? How careless of me not to see through your disguise."

"There's a secret passage to the cellars," Alexandra guessed, staring into the hearth. No wonder there was no fire there. The soot-darkened walls concealed a secret doorway there in the recessed stone of the fireplace. "Will, Roger, and Alan used to play in it as children when their parents brought them to London—I remember their tales about it now." She raised her eyebrows ruefully. "How careless of *me* to forget."

"You said you weren't coming tonight. How long have you been listening?" Roger's voice was cracking with stress.

"Not long. When I heard the sound of a woman's voice, I thought you were entertaining a whore. The library seemed an odd place for it, but knowing your exotic tastes—"

"Kindly restrain yourself in front of Alexandra," Roger snapped. "There's no need to take this out on her."

"I wouldn't dream of taking it out on her. It's you who are responsible. In faith, Roger, taking your brother into your confidence was bad enough, but this! Charles Douglas' daughter, for God's sake. Lady-in-waiting to the queen herself. On the very eve of our largest undertaking, I come in to find our security compromised."

What was their largest undertaking? Alexandra remembered the air of tension in the room when she'd interrupted Roger and Alan and their friends a few minutes ago. Had she stumbled right into the middle of one of their plots?

"I won't betray you," she said.

"No," Lacklin agreed, "you won't." He looked back at Roger. The animation he had briefly shown had melted back into the discipline and control that she had always associated with him. Cold Mr. Lacklin—for an instant he had been hot. She glanced from him to Roger. They were both formidable men.

"Think, Roger," he went on. "Her father's spies are but half a step behind us, and God only knows what purpose Geoffrey's using her for. You trust her, apparently. I'm glad to discover that there's still one corner of your soul that's not given over to total cynicism, but I cannot share your confidence. We dare not allow her to walk out of here, not now, not today. Too many lives are at stake."

Roger heard him out in silence, then slowly turned to look at Alexandra with an expression she didn't recognize. When he finally spoke, his voice was gentle. "I'm sorry, Alix, but he's right. You've disregarded my warnings one too many times."

She felt a thrill of fear that was all the stronger for being completely unexpected. "What on earth are you going to do? Turn me over to him to get my throat slit? I don't believe that, Roger!" She began to walk toward the door, restraining her irrational urge to break into a run.

Neither man moved. "It's locked," Roger said, holding up the key. "And for the love of God, don't scream for Alan; you'll only upset the lad. As it is, he's probably waiting out there with a small cannon, lest I harm a single hair on your head."

"I have no intention of screaming. I never scream. I will certainly argue bitterly, however, if you don't unlock that door and let me leave."

"I'm sorry," he repeated. "You're not going anywhere."

She turned to face him once again, lifting her chin and stiffening her spine. She was blasted if she would give them the satisfaction of knowing she was frightened.

Roger knew, though; she could see it in his eyes. There

was no threat there; she read compassion in those brown depths, and she felt encouragement flow toward her like a wave. It seemed impossible, yet she knew his thoughts, as if their minds were one. "It's for your own safety as much as ours that you must remain here," he told her. "Francis doesn't trust you"—he shot his friend a grimace—"and people whom Francis doesn't trust have an uncanny way of dying young."

"I said I wouldn't touch her," Lacklin retorted. "Do you require me to swear it?"

"No. Let's simply assume that none of us trusts any of the others, shall we? That way everyone is careful and no one is unpleasantly surprised. Anyway, you're not the only danger to her. Geoffrey's behind this, I suspect. I'm sorry now that I didn't take your advice about dear Geoffrey. Can we still have him killed? Now, tonight?"

"I'm not having anybody killed on my account," Alexandra put in. "Not even Geoffrey."

"You're in no position to argue. As you've so cleverly worked out, Francis and I are dangerous criminals, and you, sweetling, are our prisoner."

Her head cocked to one side as she examined their faces. Her heart had stopped beating quite so rapidly. Roger's expression continued to be reassuring, renewing the courage that had momentarily faltered in her. "One of the queen's ladies? Surely that is treason? My father won't like it one bit."

Neither man commented.

"Might I inquire how long my captivity is likely to last?"

"A day or two, that's all."

"And where shall I spend it? Here in your house?"

Roger walked over to the fireplace and tripped the mechanism that revealed the secret passage. He then crossed to her side, took one of her wrists in a hard grip, and led her back to the narrow black oblong. "Here in my dungeons, my love."

21

I NSIDE the hidden passageway, the air was chilly and
damp. Roger's arm slipped around Alexandra's shoulders
as he steered her around a sharp corner. Behind them, Francis Lacklin lit a torch and handed it to Roger, then another,
which he kept for his own use. "I'm going on ahead," he
said. "I've got one more rendezvous before tonight. I'll
return after dusk."

"Be careful," Roger returned as Lacklin moved past them
and disappeared down the steps, his torch throwing his
shadow huge against the mildewed wall. To Alexandra he
added, "Watch the stairs. They're steep and slippery."

"Am I about to find out what you're hiding in your
cellars?"

"Aye, lass."

"I'm no longer certain I wish to know."

"It's too late for regrets now."

She nodded grimly, wondering if caution and restraint
were virtues she would never learn. Her mind ranged over
the possibilities: contraband of some sort? An illegal printing
press where seditious, heretical documents were spawned?
A team of assassins plotting new attempts on the life of
Mary of England? She prepared herself to be outraged.

The reality was somehow less outrageous and far more
disturbing than she'd imagined. The murmur of voices

greeted her as she and Roger passed through an arras in a wide, sconce-lit basement—the high-pitched voices of women and children. They were quiet voices, depressed perhaps, subdued.

There must have been thirty of them, simple folk mostly, clad in worn and tattered garments. Of this number, most were women of various ages, some with small children in their arms. There were only a few men, most of them elderly. In general, the group did not look well—several coughed, some sat or lay listlessly on straw pallets spread out in rows along the stone floor.

"Who are they?" she asked Roger under her breath.

"Religious dissenters. Heretics, as you call them. If they stay in England, they will be burned at the stake."

"Oh God, Roger! Mothers with little children?"

"One of the women already executed was heavy with child when they bound her to the stake. Her labor began while they were lighting the faggots. She gave birth to an innocent child, who perished with his mother in the flames." His fingers had tightened convulsively on her arm. "Was Almighty God pleased with that sacrifice, do you suppose?"

"I've heard that story too. 'Tis fable. Pregnant women cannot be executed until after their babes are born. So reads the law."

Roger scoffed. "Listen more closely to your mistress's doctrines next time, Alexandra. God's law supersedes civil law. God's law as interpreted by Bishop Bonner, that bloody-minded swine. He takes pleasure in having his victims whipped until they recant. Women in particular. Have you ever seen a person flogged, Mistress Innocent? If the torturer is skilled at wielding the lash, there are few torments more exquisitely agonizing."

"So I've heard," she managed.

"But what torments there are, Bonner knows. If the venerable bishop's victims remain firm to their beliefs, horrors follow that even your strong stomach would heave to hear about. Torture is illegal, too, in this land. But I challenge you to find a single prison in England where it is not occasionally practiced."

She made no answer. After a moment she said, "You've been giving these people refuge here? Even though your house is watched? Heavens, Roger, surely there is someplace else where they would be safer?"

"Ah, but that's the beauty of the plan. Not even my enemies will believe I would be so foolish as to shelter heretics right under their noses."

She had to acknowledge the truth of that. "How on earth did you smuggle them in?"

"There is a tunnel leading from these cellars to the river. One of my illustrious ancestors, it seems, engaged in a little smuggling to augment his income. They were brought in that way, and will be removed similarly. In the meantime, your father's watchdogs will attest that no unauthorized persons have entered my house in the past few weeks." His eyes met hers with the faintest suggestions of a leer. "Except an occasional persistent woman of the streets."

She ignored this, looking from one bedraggled heretic to the next. "What will you do with them?"

"How slowly your brain is working tonight. The *Argo* leaves for the Mediterranean on the dawn tide tomorrow. These people will be on it, exiles, going to the German states and Switzerland, where the climate is marginally better for dissenters."

"Sweet Jesu. Alan was right. He guessed what you were up to. I thought he was being his usual overly romantic Malory-inspired self, but he was right about you for once."

"Alan's probably been right about me more often than you have," he pointed out, to her chagrin.

"Does Alan know about this?"

"Of course he does. He's proved to be quite helpful. I'm beginning to see some value in the lad, after all."

Roger introduced her to the piteous group simply as a friend. He then stood back and watched her become exactly that to them. She went from one refugee to the next, speaking gently and encouragingly to them, but without condescension. She played with the children, and checked to ensure that the sick were comfortable. She breathed not a word about politics or religion. But they assumed she was one of them, and when one old man led them all in a familiar prayer in English—not the Popish Latin—Alexandra unhesitatingly spoke it aloud with the others.

At one point, as she moved in front of a torch holding a sleeping child in her arms, the light that was cast upon her face revealed the shadows under her eyes and the faint hollows under her cheekbones. *She is tired,* he realized. There was nothing peaceful or easy about working in the personal suite of Mary of England. Alexandra's days and nights were filled with tensions and worries, like his own.

And yet it occurred to him as she bent over the baby that she was more beautiful than any woman he had ever known. Her splendid hair, the color of fire . . . hair that matched her fiery character . . . warm fire, pure fire. A candle in the dark. And her body, which was straight and stalwart, yet softer, more feminine than it had been last summer at Chilton. She was nineteen. A woman fully grown. Mature in body and in mind; bright in spirit, and generous in heart.

And suddenly he knew that he loved her. The realization struck him where he stood with all the power and force of a squall at sea. He was rent from head to toe—his entire way of looking at himself and his world transformed forever. One minute he believed himself incapable of love, and the next he knew that he would hold Alexandra Douglas in his heart from now until the end of time. That he had always held her there. That she was bone of his bone and flesh of his flesh, and that nothing remained but to acknowledge it.

The feeling was awesome, frightening, and far stronger than anything he had ever known before. Yet his love for her had always been there, ever since they were children at play together. He saw her, wild-haired and imp-eyed, clambering up the highest trees in the forest after him, joining in his most violent games without an ounce of fear, holding him in her skinny arms and trying to comfort him after he'd been beaten by his father. They had been remarkably close for a boy and girl separated by a six-year difference in age. They had been remarkably close by any standards.

He wondered for the first time what might have happened if he had not left Chilton at fourteen. Suppose he'd stayed, growing to manhood beside her, watching her slowly come to maturity herself. Christ! She'd never have reached the age of nineteen with her maidenhead intact if he'd been there when she had begun to feel youthful curiosity and desire for the pleasures of the flesh. He'd been undisciplined then—he'd have taken her without thought for the consequences. There would have been trouble then, for she'd been betrothed to Will. There was going to be trouble now.

As if she sensed his turmoil, Alexandra lifted her head and met his eyes in the gloom, sending him a warm smile. The child reached out in its sleep with one small hand and touched her cheek. She laughed softly and gave it back to its mother, as, watching, Roger felt his heart expand in his chest. He loved her. He wanted to see her thus, holding a different child, a child who'd been conceived from the seed of his own loins. He wanted her for his wife.

Still smiling, Alexandra crossed the cold stone floor to Roger's side. He retreated a step, afraid to let her touch him. There was nothing gentle about his love—it was a love of the spirit, yes, but it was equally a love of the body. And it was unconsummated. The sight and sound and scent of her caused his head to whirl and his flesh to burn with the most intense sexual tension he had ever known. It had been bearable before, but suddenly it was not. If she touched him he did not think he would be able to stop himself from flinging her to the floor, tearing away her clothes, and claiming her as his woman, his mate, his one true love until the end of time. . . .

"Are you all right?" she inquired, tilting her head to one side as she examined his expression.

He nodded.

"You look a trifle strange. You're not ill?"

"No."

"Several of these people are, Roger. One or two of them may not be able to travel unless they have a physician's care."

"That is not your concern."

"But it could be. I have remedies, medicines back in my chamber in Westminster. If I went and fetched them—"

"No," he interrupted.

She pulled him into a more secluded area of the cellar.

Her fingers on his sleeve tormented him. "For heaven's sake, I'm not trying to escape. I'm thinking of them, and you. How are you going to transport the sick? What if more of them take some illness? I can't promise any miracles, but I do have some experience in these matters, and if I left now I could get back before it got too late and—"

"Beloved, believe me, the matter has been attended to."

"By whom?"

"By the surgeon from my ship, if you must know. Tom Comstock, who comes here daily. He was taught in the east and is skillful. You need have no fears for these people's health." He cocked one dark brow at her. "Besides, I have other things for you to think about."

Catching the note in his voice, Alexandra once again studied his face. "What other things?"

Roger hesitated as image after image of glorious love-making rollicked through his brain. She was here; she was his. She loved him, and now that he'd recognized his love for her, why should there be any further need for restraint?

God! He'd held back long enough. Now, today, he would take her up to his bedchamber and tenderly strip away her clothes, leaving a candle alight so he could see her rosy-tipped breasts, her firm, white belly, her long legs, stronger and more muscular than many women's and yet so soft-skinned, so shapely. And her face—how he would love watching every expression as he caressed her body into pleasure . . . how he would treasure each laugh, each sigh, each gasp as the crisis of love approached. He would be careful with her, since she was still a maid. He would make certain her initiation was slow and gentle and entirely free of pain.

"Roger?"

He heard her but he couldn't stop fantasizing. He would marry her, he decided. As soon as it could be arranged and consecrated. Husband and wife, they would stand together in the peace and harmony their souls jointly yearned for. Her contract with the heir to the barony of Chilton would be honored after all.

Her brow was furrowed as she stared at him. "Your mind is teeming with some sort of mischief, isn't it? You're not deciding that since I'm now your prisoner, I deserve to be treated like the proverbial female captive?" When he looked startled, she added, "No. That's not the way it's going to be. You've had ample opportunities and wasted them. Now 'tis I who will reject you."

He grinned. "You think you can read my mind so well, poppy-top?"

She nodded vigorously. "I've seen that look often enough now to recognize it."

"Artful hussy. I don't think you'd reject me if I applied myself with all due persistence to your seduction."

"Well, Alan might have something to say about it, and so, no doubt, would Francis Lacklin."

He frowned. She had a point, unfortunately. Privacy was something they were not likely to be blessed with today. And even if it had been, there was work to be done.

"Besides," she went on severely, "I have more self-respect than you might suppose, Roger. I don't deserve the way you have treated me—warm one minute, harsh and cold the next." She gestured to the cellar full of heretics. "You, for all your noble-minded motives, are a traitor and my enemy. I'm willing to concede now that you've been right all along in insisting that we are gravely mismatched."

She was reminding him, dammit, of facts he could not deny. It was by no means clear that he and Francis would be able to pull off this exodus of a ragtag bunch of religious dissidents without discovery. His contingency plan, in fact, was to leave England himself aboard the *Argo* if anything went wrong. It was a hell of a time to fall in love with Alexandra. Twenty-four hours from now he might be either exiled or dead.

And what would happen to her if his plans went awry? Suppose she were discovered in his cellars? If he were arrested, she would be suspected of collusion.

His thoughts were interrupted by the sound of footsteps descending the stairs. The light of another torch cast a shadow into the cellar as Alan appeared, his expression tight and challenging.

"You said you would keep her ten minutes. And you made no mention of bringing her down here. I demand to know what villainy you intend now. 'Tis growing dark, and Alix will be missed."

"That is true," she confirmed. "If I am not found in my bed tonight, a search will be conducted."

"I thought you said you'd pleaded illness and been excused from the queen's service?" Roger's voice was sharp.

"Only for the afternoon. I had no permission to leave the court. They will expect me to be languishing in bed. And since I share a bedchamber with several other ladies—"

"Oh Christ," Roger muttered.

"—my father will be notified. And where do you suppose is the first place he will look for me?"

"No one knows of these cellars. He will not find you."

"You mean to hold her, then?" Alan cried.

"Until after the refugees are safely out of the country, yes," he said, but not quite as insistently as before.

"They won't get safely out of the country if my father suspects you of virgin-snatching again. You know how violently opposed he is to any intercourse between us—he acts as though death would be a finer fate for me than union with you. At any rate, if I am found to be missing, he'll probably have you immediately detained. Your ship may even be impounded. You must release me." She stared into his eyes. "You'll simply have to trust me."

To hell with Francis' concern about security. The fact was, he trusted her as much as he loved her. She would never betray them. "I think," he said with a trace of a smile, "you may well be right."

Night was falling as Roger covered Alexandra's red hair with her cloak, pulling it well down over her forehead before taking her by the arm and leading her out into the street.

"You're coming too?" she asked.

"Only as far as the carriage Alan has summoned for you." He nodded at Alan waiting by the side of a coach. "You'll be pretending to take him to a place of entertainment; he'll see that you get safely back to Westminster."

"I'm glad you're giving him something responsible to

do. When he went to live with you, I thought you might be patronizing."

He laughed low, his breath near her ear. "'Tis you who are patronizing, Mistress Busybody. Not so graceful—you're a whore, remember? You've just spent a lusty afternoon with one of the most notorious rakes in the kingdom. Swing your hips, please, with a little more abandon."

She giggled, allowing the sound to carry. "You sound like a coarser version of my dancing master. There's our friend. Behind the post."

"I see him. I'll be heading off for an errand in the opposite direction. He'll follow me, as he's paid to do. You shouldn't have any problems getting home."

They had reached the carriage. Roger pulled her against him and inflicted a long, sensuous kiss upon her, then pushed her—rather abruptly, she thought—into Alan's arms, saying loudly, "Amuse the lad for me, wench, and send him back sober in the morning. Here's extra for your pains." He flipped her a gold coin, which she expertly caught, then delivered a vigorous slap to her backside. *"That"* he whispered, "was for the trouble you've caused me tonight." Not to mention the anguish it causes me to have to send you away, he added silently. Then he turned his back on her and resolutely walked away.

Alan handed her into the carriage and jumped up after her. They both looked out the window to see what would happen to the man behind the post. Sure enough, he melted into the shadows in Roger's wake. Alexandra sat back, smiling at Alan. "It worked."

"Aye," he said, letting out what sounded like a relieved sigh. "Thank God we talked him into releasing you. I saw the way he was looking at you. You're lucky he didn't drag you up to his bedchamber and have his way with you."

Alexandra felt a needle of irritation. She'd seen the way Roger had been looking at her too, and found it puzzling. The old excitement that always seemed to beat between them was there, yes; but so was a certain tenderness, an odd limning of affection that was new somehow, she thought. And yet, at the same time, it seemed very familiar. Could it be that his feelings for her were growing? Perhaps there was hope. After all, she was no longer the artless, unsophisticated urchin she'd been last summer. Was he finally coming to see that there were so many ways in which they were perfectly suited to one another?

"It was madness for you to come here tonight," Alan went on, oblivious. "Francis Lacklin will be furious when he finds out that Roger let you go. You won't tell your father, will you? Or the queen?"

"That question doesn't merit an answer. You think I'd turn you, Roger, and thirty helpless refugees over to the courts to be condemned and executed?"

"I . . . No, of course not. It's just that, well, it's astonishing the way he seems to trust you. Francis has told me over and over that Roger trusts very few people. Apparently he was stabbed in the back so many times in the Mediterranean that betrayal's what he's come to expect out of life."

"I'm not surprised, considering the way he grew up, with his father beating him all the time, and his mother committing suicide."

"You still defend him, no matter what." Alan's voice became petulant. "You didn't seem particularly put out at the prospect of being forced to spend a night in his house. Are you still blind to the designs he has upon your person?"

"You're in with him now, Alan—up to your neck, in fact—yet you're still speaking against him. Forgive me if I find that a little odd!"

"I don't speak against him except in this."

"You certainly seemed to dislike him last summer at Chilton. You couldn't find anything good to say about him, as I recall!"

"It's different now. I was wrong about him. When I overheard him planning these rescue missions with Lacklin last summer, I was shocked and angry because I thought it was treasonous and heretical, but now that I've witnessed the evils produced by the queen's policies, I judge things differently."

"It was his character, not his politics, that you seemed to find offensive."

"Well, perhaps I was envious," Alan said with the forthrightness he and she had always shared. "He came along and bedazzled everybody, being kind or cruel as the mood took him, and we all sat back and allowed him to become the center of our world. He's courageous and charismatic and devilishly smart . . . he's all the things I know I'll never be." Alan frowned. "You're right. Sometimes I'm jealous still."

Something he had said a moment ago was niggling at her. "You say you overheard Roger and Francis Lacklin planning to smuggle heretics out of the country last summer? Is that why you suspected it that day we went to the docks to see the *Argo?*"

"Aye. I came upon them together in the forest one day. It was the morning you had me out chasing that poor half-wit fellow who hanged himself—remember? Roger caught me; I thought he'd have my head for it. We had words, and I fled, knocking myself off my horse in my hurry and breaking my leg."

"Good heavens, Alan, are you sure it was *that* day? But . . ." Something was bothering her, and in a flash she knew what it was. "Francis Lacklin had already left for London, hadn't he? I was ill, but I remember being told he'd left several days before."

Alan shrugged. "I was surprised to see him too. He had certainly left Chilton, but he must have stayed in the area, because he was there, I assure you, in the forest with Roger."

"That's strange."

"It hardly matters now, does it? Lacklin had already ridden off when Roger caught me, which is probably the only thing that saved my neck. Lacklin is the very devil with a sword, as you know, and unlike Roger, he doesn't hesitate to use it."

"Very pious," she said sarcastically.

"I know you've never liked him. He terrifies me, to tell you the truth. My brother's a lamb in comparison. Anyway, Roger made me swear up and down never to breathe a word to anyone. That was the promise I'd made him; that was the reason I couldn't explain to you what had caused the argument between us. I've known all this time, you see. Until I went to Oxford and learned to take a different view of the need for reformation in the Church, Roger's heretical activities seemed to me to prove him a villain."

Alexandra was having difficulty taking all this in. Francis Lacklin had not left Chilton when he'd claimed to have left. Which meant, of course, that *he* could have murdered Ned. And Will, for that matter.

Alexandra quickly reminded herself that she had enough problems without dredging up that old mystery again. And she also remembered how incorrect her carefully reasoned conclusions had been. She would not make the same mistake twice.

As for Alan, he had apparently been as indefatigable a meddler as she! He'd known more details about Roger's plottings with Lacklin than she'd ever learned herself. "God's teeth, Alan, if only we'd pooled our knowledge! I thought they were trying to kill the queen! I wouldn't have barged in tonight if I'd realized they were performing an errand of mercy."

"He's a devil with women, though, that's one thing I'm even more sure of since Chilton," Alan went on, back to his old theme. "Especially when he drinks. He uses them so callously, but even so, they come running back for more. Women from the court, women from the alehouses, women—"

"I don't care to hear about his women, thank you."

Alan turned on her, his face white. "You love him, don't you? He trusts you because he knows full well that, like me, you'd die before you'd ever betray him."

She lifted her chin. "Does it matter?"

"Yes," he almost shouted.

"Why?" she demanded, determined to have this out. But though he stared at her in anger, his slender body taut beside hers in a manner that was almost a caricature of Roger's, he didn't speak. A minute passed, two; then he slackened and turned his head away.

"Let's not argue, Alix," he said.

One who will not, one who dares not . . . Damn and blast these Trevors, she thought. But a second later, she was sorry. Poor Alan. How must it be to live always in the shadow of a man like Roger . . . admiring him, copying him, and still half-fearing him? How must it feel to suspect that the girl you'd loved all your life might be turning away from you, and toward him?

She reached for his hand. Alan took it in the darkness, squeezing hard. "We both love him," she said gently. "And one day I fear he's going to leave us very far behind. He'll go back to Turkey, perhaps, or off to America"—her throat tightened convulsively—"or into the ground. Oh, Alan, why does he drink? Or wench coldheartedly, for that matter? And why does he take such risks? He's too flamboyant, he'll trap himself one day. It's the cold, controlled men like Francis Lacklin who never get caught. My father's already suspicious, and Geoffrey de Montreau is openly seeking Roger's death. This refugee plot is madness, Alan! If they catch him, he'll die a traitor's death. Why does he *do* such things?"

The coach came to a stop, presumably at Westminster, but Alexandra and Alan were too involved in their conversation to alight.

"He does it because he promised Francis, who apparently saved his life on some occasion. And because he believes it's right."

She shook her head. "He's not even a sincere dissenter. He's no more enamored of Lacklin's doctrines than he is of the pope's."

"But he *does* hate injustice, Alix. And although he hides it, he has great compassion in his heart. I've learned in the past few weeks that hard though he seems, Roger will always help someone whom he perceives to be weaker than himself." Alan laughed grimly. "Which includes most of humanity."

A voice at the carriage window sniggered. Alexandra gasped as she recognized the face of the man who tore open the door. "Are we talking about the same Roger?" said Geoffrey de Montreau. "Just, compassionate, and a help-meet to his fellow man? Impossible, *mes amis*. The two of you are going to help him, however. You're going to assist him in making a swift end to his miserable life."

22

I T WAS, of course, a trap. Alexandra knew it instantly. Everything that had happened, from the apparent accident yesterday morning, to Geoffrey's voice now in the dark of a London street, had been cleverly, fiendishly calculated: his warning this afternoon that had driven her to Roger; this coach, which must have been waiting near Roger's house for some innocent like Alan to hail it; this house where they had stopped, which was not Westminster, and was probably nowhere near Westminster. Sweet Jesu! She and Alan had been so absorbed in their discussion that they hadn't even paid attention to where they were being driven.

And now? Alexandra's blood curdled at the thought of what was going to happen now. Alan, she realized, didn't understand. When the armed men tore open the carriage doors and ordered them outside, his reaction was confusion.

"Who are these fellows?" he demanded of Alexandra. "They're not dressed as the queen's guard."

She squeezed his hand as they climbed down. They were in a narrow alley between two large houses. It was a district Alexandra didn't recognize, but it seemed a wealthy part of the city. Surrounding them were a half-dozen soldiers, none of whom wore identifying badges. "Don't tell them anything, Alan. I expect they're going to be asking us a few questions."

Alan's hold on her hand tightened and she could sense

his fear, mixing with her own. His fear . . . Oh heavens! She remembered all the times when, as a child, Alan had cravenly broken down because of his two older brothers' threats. What if Geoffrey threatened him with torture and he confessed Roger's plans for the rescue of the heretics?

What if they threaten you with torture, she asked herself impatiently, and you confess? "Whoever they are, they can't do more than harass us," she whispered to Alan. "They'll have my father to reckon with, not to mention the queen."

"Aye," said Alan, looking nervously around. "May God grant that you're right."

"Monsieur," Alexandra greeted Geoffrey coldly. "What is the meaning of this? How dare you detain us? I am on a private mission for the queen."

Geoffrey smiled, mincing into position in front of her, his delicate features triumphant. She could smell his cloying perfume. "I know all about your private mission." He smirked and offered her his arm. "Come. This is not a matter to be discussed in the streets."

She refused to touch him. "You imagine I will yield so easily?" She drew breath to scream but was grabbed by one of the guards, her mouth covered roughly by a glove-mailed hand. Alan heaved himself at her attacker, and was himself seized by two others. They were big, burly fellows, more than capable of restraining the struggles of a woman and a youth. In less than five minutes she and Alan were hauled through the gates of one of the houses, dragged up the path and inside the doors, and half-marched, half-carried down a narrow circular stairway to a cellar that was even darker and dingier than Roger's. The ill-lit chamber to which they were taken was obviously a dungeon. There were no rings or chains or oubliettes, just a well-oiled and rather new-looking rack constructed of light, unvarnished wood that still smelled of the forest.

They were greeted by a beefy middle-aged man with a bald pate and a face as ugly as sin, and his two youthful but husky associates. Alexandra vaguely heard Geoffrey de Montreau dismiss the soldiers at the door to the torture chamber, then the sound of a clanging door and a twisting key. The back of her gown was wet with sweat, and she could hear Alan's frantic breathing beside her. She reached for his hand again.

"The devil, what's this—a pair of children?" said the master of the rack. "Conspiracy begins young now, eh? Well, is it to be ladies first, or is the gentleman chivalrous?"

Alexandra stepped forward. The questioner was English, while the guards, she believed, had been French. She was not certain who held them, but if this fellow was employed by the state, perhaps they had a chance. "I demand to be taken before the queen at once. I am Alexandra Douglas, lady-in-waiting to her Majesty. If you continue to treat me in this despicable and illegal fashion, I assure you, you will be severely punished."

The fellow guffawed, and Geoffrey strolled to Alexandra's side, saying, "Good try, but you're in private hands, *chérie*. He works for me—I heard that he was efficient at his job, so I offered him a good deal more money than the crown was willing to pay. He's very skilled, mademoiselle." Geoffrey glanced at Alan. "Your friend here—Trevor's young brother, is it not?—is looking a trifle pale. Perhaps you would care to answer my questions without any unpleasant exertion?"

It was difficult, even in these circumstances, to take Geoffrey seriously. In the wavering light from a half-dozen torches, she could see that he was clad in pink, with a circlet of pearls around his ruffled collar. "Ignore him, Alan. He wouldn't dare lay a hand on us. You're a diplomat, monsieur. I can't believe you would go to such lengths all because of a young woman who's been at peace in her grave for two years. And I seriously doubt that Celestine would thank you if she could see the evil being wrought on her behalf!"

"Alix, what are you talking about? Who is this man? Who is Celestine?"

"Celestine was my sister," Geoffrey informed Alan. "Your fiend of a brother seduced and murdered her."

"That isn't true!"

"It's not a point I intend to argue, mademoiselle, at this time. Nor is it the crime for which he will be condemned.

Let us forget Celestine, shall we? I am merely assisting the English authorities in apprehending a dangerous traitor and heretic."

"You lie!" Alan cried. "My brother is neither of these."

"No? Your brother threw off his popish views when he left his monastery years ago. And he has never respected the policies of his queen, however much he may pretend to do so at court. No," he gloated, turning his attention back to Alexandra, "I know him well, and I have an excellent idea what he is plotting with Francis Lacklin. All I lack are a few details, which you, mademoiselle, are going to provide. It has not been easy, but his destruction is finally in my hands." He smiled with satisfaction. "And after what he did to Celestine, it seems highly appropriate to me that he will be condemned by a woman's testimony."

"You've chosen the wrong woman, monsieur. The queen herself protects me. You will provoke a diplomatic incident over this. You may even precipitate the beginning of the war!"

"No, *chérie*. My timing is perfect. As you will hear tomorrow—if you survive that long—war between your country and mine is about to be officially declared. I leave London shortly, my peace-keeping mission a failure. But before I go, I will see your lover indicted for treason, that I promise you. Shall we get on with it?" They came forward, each of them taking one of Alexandra's arms. It was then that Alan rushed them.

Roger must have taught him something in the recent weeks at Chilton House, for he managed to floor one of the men with an extremely competent uppercut and send the other reeling against the wall. In the meantime, Alexandra had the presence of mind to deliver a well-aimed kick to Geoffrey de Montreau's right kneecap. Fishing out the small dagger she always carried in her girdle, she lunged for his pearl-adorned throat. The mistake she made was the same as many others had made before her—the failure to see that underneath his peacock's attire, Geoffrey hid the body of a trained athlete. The kick did not fell him after all, and before she could fix the knife at his neck, he applied a wrestling hold which disarmed and rendered her helpless.

The ugly dungeon-master had, in the interim, restrained Alan. He was now allowing the other two thugs to batter him until they recovered their pride.

"Oh, for God's sake," Alexandra whispered. "Make them stop."

"As passionate, if not as effective as his brother," said Geoffrey. He issued an order, and the beating was reluctantly discontinued. "He's fond of you, isn't he? He was terrified when we brought him in here, but it hasn't stopped him from trying to defend you." He was staring speculatively at Alan, who lay curled on his side on the floor, his nose bleeding and his eyes beginning to darken and swell. Alexandra struggled with Geoffrey, trying to go to Alan, but she made no headway whatsoever. He was not much taller than she, but he knew tricks she had not been taught, and restrained her easily.

"It's fortunate we picked him up tonight—it wasn't part of the plan, you see," Geoffrey went on. "But the boy knows even more, I'll wager, about the mysterious goings-on in that house than you do." As he spoke, he forced her over to the rack and down. She fought gamely but uselessly. His strength beneath the pink satin was astonishing. Panting with helpless rage, she felt her body stretched out and fixed into immobility as her enemy quickly and efficiently shackled her wrists and ankles to the hideous machine.

Oh God, she prayed silently. Give me courage.

At Geoffrey's orders, Alan was dragged to her side and held on his knees only a few inches from her trembling body. One of the thugs went to the wheel and took up the slack.

"You're bluffing, monsieur. You wouldn't dare injure me. And I'm not so fainthearted that I'll hysterically offer to tell you anything because of the threat of torture."

"I would never underestimate your spirit so much as to make a threat I did not intend to carry out. Still, there is no need to continue this unpleasantness if you agree to be sensible and tell me willingly now what you will otherwise soon be pleading to confess."

"I will never confess!"

"Alix?" Alan had come to his senses and was beginning to struggle. The other thugs held him motionless, twisting one of his arms up behind him until the bone threatened to snap. "Don't do this to her," he begged Geoffrey. "Let me take her place."

"Such devotion!" Geoffrey laughed. He bent over Alexandra, smiling evilly. "On second thought, you needn't tell us a thing, *chérie*. It's the lovelorn young man who's going to do the talking. But do feel free to scream as much as you like. The walls are thick."

"Don't listen to him, Alan," Alexandra pleaded. "He's bluffing. And don't tell them anything, please, no matter what. Don't look like that! He wouldn't dare hurt me—" Her voice broke as something clicked and something hurt very much indeed. She closed her eyes, unable to face the desperation—and the love—in Alan's eyes. What had Merwynna taught her? *Pain is an illusion. You have a physical body, but you are not your physical body. Your spirit is free. There is no pain.*

Alan mumbled something to Geoffrey. "No, Alan," Alexandra whispered. Somebody screamed. "No!" she cried over and over again.

Alexandra awoke from a short sleep of despair and exhaustion in a comfortable bed with embroidered sheets. The scent of perfume sickened her. She opened her eyes upon the features of Geoffrey de Montreau, clad in an ornately brocaded dressing gown, sitting beside her on the bed.

"I wouldn't try to move if I were you. It'll hurt."

She resisted an urge to lift the sheet and check to see if her legs were still attached to her body. They were, she decided, wriggling her toes. Her arms also, she discovered, were aching, but operative. "In sooth, I thought it would hurt more."

"I've given you a touch of opiates to dull the pain."

"How thoughtful." She considered him. His expression was pleasant, friendly even. But at the top of the dressing gown, where it fell open slightly, she could see the naked skin of his chest. It was white and almost hairless. She took a breath. "I forget. Did you rape me while I was screaming down there or did you decide it would be more aesthetic to do it in comfort?"

"When I rape you, you will remember."

She couldn't restrain a shudder. She felt cold. And she was naked under the sheets. She told herself not to react, and most of all, not to show any fear. "What have you done with Alan?"

"He and his extremely interesting confession are quite safe. You were fortunate. He broke easily. You didn't really need the drug. You'll be a little stiff for a day or two, that is all."

"How dull for you. I could see you were hoping to tear me limb from limb."

"On the contrary, violence sickens me. And I doubt whether a dislocated hip or shoulder would have improved your dancing."

Absurdly, this comment made her laugh—a subdued and bitter laugh, but a laugh nonetheless.

"Do you know that in spite of myself, I am beginning to like you?" said Geoffrey. "What on earth have you got to laugh about?"

"I don't know. The fact that I'm still alive?"

"How ill-suited you and Roger are. I often think that the fact that he's still alive only depresses him."

"Then you'll be doing him a favor, won't you? If you really knew anything about revenge, you'd let him follow his own path to destruction." She shot him a look to see if there was any chance he'd take her advice, and found him raising speculative eyebrows at her.

"There was one thing Alan didn't tell us. I must confess I'm inordinately curious about it. Did he take you to bed this afternoon? Has he ever taken you to bed?"

"Are you referring to Alan or to Roger? Or to Francis Lacklin, for that matter? I'm afraid I get my various bed-partners a trifle confused."

He touched her face with one soft hand, allowing his fingers to trail across her cheek. "You're a virgin, aren't you?" he said, pursing his lips. There was an unaccustomed huskiness to his voice that betrayed his relish of the situation.

"A state I have long considered tiresome. If you're hoping for maidenly squeamishness, monsieur, you'll be disappointed." She yawned elaborately. "I might even sleep through it."

He smiled. "I do like you, Alexandra. You're so determinedly brave and loyal, it almost makes me regret what I've had to do to you. We were very fortunate tonight, I think, to take Alan. His resolution is not as strong as yours. We *would* have had to tear you limb from limb, I suspect, before you'd have told us anything."

Alexandra's bravery suddenly seemed to desert her. Her eyes shuttered out the sight of his face, so close to hers. "Don't do this, monsieur," she whispered.

"Calm yourself, *chérie*." His voice was tender, his breath gentle against her scalp. One of his slender fingers traced the surface of her lips, arousing nothing but disgust inside her. "I do have some sensibilities. I will be gentle with you."

Her eyes snapped open. "I ask mercy for Roger, not myself. Think, monsieur. Vengeance is never as satisfying as one imagines it will be. Besides, he has grieved for your sister, suffered for her. You are a fool if you cannot see this."

"You love him."

"Yes." Her tone was proud.

"So did I once," Geoffrey said dispassionately. "He inspires devotion from both men and women to a ridiculous degree—I've never quite been able to understand why. But sometimes it turns to hatred—I'm not the first this has happened to. Wait until he turns on you, and you will see. He is Scorpio—wait until you feel the lash of the fiery scorpion's tail."

"You're not giving me that opportunity are you? You're killing him!"

Geoffrey began to look impatient. His hand moved down to her shoulder, one thumb lightly caressing the curve of her throat. His eyes were alight now with lust and anticipation. She stiffened as his lips touched her ear, as his teeth tugged gently on the lobe. "Forget about him for now, *cherie*. What's done is done, but not everything that happens this evening need be unpleasant. Relax. There are many arts of pleasing women, and I know them all."

She jerked her head away. "I spit on your arts!" she declared, and did so.

Geoffrey pulled a handkerchief from a pocket in his dressing gown and fastidiously wiped his face. His breathing had accelerated and his blond-lashed eyes had narrowed in anger. "Unlike your precious Roger, I am not usually rough with women, but I will do what's necessary, mademoiselle, to take you."

"You don't want me," she retorted. "There's never been so much as a spark between us. As for your oh-so-gentle escapades with other women, I'm amazed to hear of them since I supposed it was only your own sex you were attracted to. Why is it you really hate Roger? Did he reject your advances?"

For an instant she thought he would strike her, but he did not. Instead he put his hands in her hair and forced her head back upon the pillow. "You will regret that remark, mademoiselle. As Roger took my innocent sister, so shall I take you. And before he dies, I shall be sure to tell him all about it. Every intimate detail."

Dear God! She made one last appeal: "Spare him, and I will be your willing mistress for as long as you desire me. I am inexperienced, it's true, but I have been instructed in these arts you speak of." She paused, then craftily added, "By a witch."

Geoffrey slipped his dressing gown off his slender, unattractive body as he casually made the sign against evil. "A noble offer—one that Roger certainly does not deserve—but I must refuse."

"Persist, and I will use the spells the wisewoman taught me to put a curse on your masculinity that will prevent you from ever threatening a woman again."

Geoffrey laughed and threw back the bedclothes. He slid in beside her and pressed her down with all his disconcerting strength. She felt one of his hands slither between their bodies, seeking her breasts and stroking them. Her stomach twisted with nausea. "Merwynna," she screamed silently. "Help me."

23

IN THE SMALL hours of the night, Alexandra lay shivering in the perfumed sheets where Geoffrey de Montreau had left her. She had ordered herself not to cry, not to waste one tear, one sigh in pointless self-pity, and so far she'd succeeded. She couldn't, wouldn't think about herself. Roger was in danger—nothing mattered but that.

Geoffrey had gone to the riverside to intercept the transfer of the hapless heretics to the *Argo* . . . gone with troops to arrest Roger. For that, she had herself to blame. It never would have happened if she hadn't been so foolish as to tumble into the Frenchman's cleverly baited trap.

Get your wits together, she berated herself. What's done is done. Fears and recriminations will do nobody any good now. Where's all this blasted courage you supposedly possess? All this stoutheartedness and backbone?

To her dismay, she only trembled all the harder, as if her limbs were possessed by some strange nervous palsy. Rolling over onto her stomach, she punched her pillow until its feathers flattened. Furiously she indulged in ugly images of Geoffrey and of the things she'd like to do to him—racking would be only the beginning, she thought viciously. Someday, she swore to herself, she would kill him for this.

Feeling remarkably better, she stepped out of bed and dressed in the clothes that were draped over a stool in the corner—the simple burgher woman's gown she had worn yesterday. She felt a little stiff, but not unbearably so. So this was what it was like to be tortured. She shuddered. She could have held out longer, she believed, if Alan hadn't broken down and told Geoffrey everything he wanted to know. But probably not very much longer.

Poor Alan. He would suffer in his soul for this, she knew. He had been forced to make a monstrous choice, and although Alexandra would have been willing to face anything to save Roger's life, she knew that if Geoffrey had ordered Alan racked in front of her, she probably would have broken too.

Where was Alan now? No doubt he'd been flung into a worse prison than this one, she thought as she walked across the luxurious bedchamber and flung the curtain back from the large diamond-paned window. It was dark outside— somewhere past midnight, she estimated.

Throwing open the window, she looked out over the roofs of London, trying to get her bearings. She didn't know the city well enough to pinpoint her location, but the surrounding buildings were stately and elegant, and she thought she could smell the river. She turned back for another look around the ornate bedchamber, decorated with finely embroidered wall hangings, a silken bed canopy, and several Venetian-glass mirrors mounted at eye level. It was a flamboyant, fussy room, thoroughly in keeping with Geoffrey's character. His room, clearly. She gasped as it sank in that she was probably inside the official residence of the diplomats from France. The gall of the man! Torturing and raping one of the queen's ladies within the confines of the French residence! *Attempting* to rape, she corrected herself.

One who cannot, one who will not, one who dares not, one who dies. Geoffrey de Montreau, to her immense relief, had turned out to be the first. So far, at least. No doubt he'd be back to try to prove that the desperate last-minute witch's spells against his potency were not going to work twice, and that despite his effeminacy, he *was* capable of sexual relations with women.

She shuddered once again at the thought of Geoffrey returning to finish what he'd started. His kisses and caresses had filled her with revulsion. How strange that the same acts which with one man could be so sweetly tender and passionate should with another be the source of nothing but disgust.

"I am going to vomit," she had informed him, and it was no lie, as he must have seen from the expression on her face. Furiously he had left her, frustrated and clearly disconcerted because his enthusiasm was insufficient to carry out his intent.

"I grant you respite then, mademoiselle, but I advise you to learn quickly how to control your stomach, and your manners."

"My manners! In no conduct book I've ever seen is it set down that a woman must be courteous to her rapist!"

Geoffrey had stalked out without troubling to reply, locking the door behind him with a loud scrape of iron keys.

The memory of that sound set her thinking about escape. Although the door was secured, the window was not. She stuck her head out. Her prison was three tall stories off the ground, but there were windows aplenty, and they all had wide ledges.

A heady excitement seized her. Was it possible? It had been a while since she'd attempted any stupendous feats of climbing, but back at Westmor she'd been undaunted by trees, roofs, towers, castle walls. Leaning out farther, she considered the problems. There was a ledge to her left, about six feet down; and just below it, the top of a second-story window. If she could reach that, lower herself down to the sill, then attempt the same maneuver on a first-story window, she could escape. Provided nobody saw what she was doing.

There was a light in one of the second-story windows to her right, but the left side of the house was dark. She took a deep breath, experimentally raising her arms over her head. They hurt, but they had not yet stiffened. Tomorrow she would probably be unable to use them. But that didn't matter—by tomorrow it would all be over, anyway.

There was really no choice. If she wanted to save Roger and his heretics, she had to make it down this wall. She yanked a cord from the bed hangings and used it to bind up her skirts, pantaloon-style. Then, with a breath and a prayer, she stepped out onto the ledge.

The black water flowed over the tops of Roger Trevor's boots, chilling his legs as he helped one after another of the frightened refugees onto the barge that would take them downriver to Greenwich, where the *Argo* awaited them. All was quiet at this hour on the river. There was no moon, which was a mercy. Deeds like this one were meant to be carried out in the dark.

"Hurry," Roger said to Francis, who was accompanying the last batch of fugitives. "There's room for everyone," he told a woman who was hesitating in climbing onto the barge. "Be quick. Your life depends on your speed and silence."

The wind was sharp, so the water was rough; the passengers huddled together against the spray as Roger helped the oarsmen push off from the riverbank. So far everything had gone according to plan. He and Francis had shepherded their little group through the old passage used by his smuggler ancestors and reached the Thames at a spot where the river conveniently curved away from the main buildings of the city. The area was sheltered, frequented by no one except an occasional fisherman by day and a rare drunkard by night. Tonight it had been deserted; no one had witnessed their escape.

Standing well back in the stern, Roger seemed to be surveying his charges, but in fact he was taking stock of himself. His heart was beating strongly and steadily, but overly fast; a bad sign, he thought. In the past when he'd engaged in this sort of dangerous activity, he'd always felt a certain elation combined with his apprehension, a joy at living his life so close to the line that divided security from recklessness. It was a feeling all adventuresome souls could recognize—the thrill of defying fate, of shaking one's fist at the gods. Tonight, however, Roger felt no elation—all he felt was weariness and dread.

He couldn't rid himself of the fear that Alexandra was in some sort of trouble. He had the uncanny sense that his mind was open to hers, that his unease was somehow linked with hers. He had awoken abruptly from the short sleep he'd tried to snatch after her departure, his body sweating, his ears ringing with what he would have sworn was her voice screaming in pain. It was only a nightmare, his rational self assured his emotional self. Alexandra was safe in her bed at Westminster. It was only because he knew now that he loved her that he was suddenly so frightened about her welfare. Alexandra Douglas had proved on numerous occasions that she was perfectly capable of looking after herself.

Still, I shouldn't have let her go, he cursed himself. I should have snatched her away aboard the *Argo*, leaving behind everything I'm supposed to be doing here in England. I should have abducted the vixen, made her mine forever. Damnation—why did I let her go?

"I don't like it," Francis had said when he returned after dark to begin transferring the refugees to the river. "I thought we'd agreed to hold her for the night."

"And risk a search by Sir Charles Douglas? On further consideration, I had no choice but to send her back to her bed at Westminster. She'll not betray us."

"I hope for your sake as much as ours that you can trust her. If you prove wrong on this one, it will break you, my friend."

Roger raised his eyebrows interrogatively.

"There's something between you and that girl. I don't know why you bother to deny it. I think you're in love with her."

"You're imagining things."

"Am I?" There was a pause; then Francis asked the question he never asked about Roger's women: "Have you taken her to bed?"

"That's none of your concern, dammit. God, may we drop the subject, please?"

"You want her, of that I have no doubt. But do you love her? *Can* you love her? And what will become of her if you do?"

Roger was in no mood to have his feelings for Alexandra analyzed by Francis. Neither did he wish his friend to be so certain of the truth. In the most basic and direct terms, he feared Francis' jealousy. So far, the older man had ig-

nored his various women, knowing perhaps that none of
them—except Celestine, briefly—had ever been closer in
spirit to him than Francis was himself. But now that had
changed. Now he would put Alexandra first, before anyone
or anything. And that was a fact that he preferred Francis
not know.

And so he said callously, "Your brain's rotting with all
this talk of love. I'm fond of the chit, but I'm not in love
with her. And as for my wanting her, that too is ludicrous.
I've no yearning for a skinny red-haired harridan in my
bed."

Francis had dropped the matter then, but Roger sensed
he hadn't convinced him. Now, huddling with his charges
in the cold of a June night that felt more like chill October,
Roger wished he had taken Alexandra to bed. Just once.
He wanted to know what it would have been like to lie with
a woman he truly cared for, a woman who loved him too,
a woman with whom he felt at peace. Once, just once, in
his life.

The climb down was easier than it looked. Within ten
minutes Alexandra was on the ground, her legs scratched
and her hands scraped, her heart pounding from the exertion,
but otherwise in fine spirits. Hands on hips, she looked back
up at the wall she had scaled and congratulated herself. "So
there, you scurvy blackguard," she said out loud, with an
accompanying obscene gesture in the direction of Geoffrey's
window.

A bark of laughter greeted her as she turned toward the
cobbled streets. The bright light of a torch blinded her, and
applause sounded in her ears.

"Bravo!" said the scurvy bastard himself. "I thought for
a few minutes that I might have to pick up the pieces."

Alexandra sagged against the stone wall of the house.
Geoffrey and six horsemen surrounded her, all of them
staring insolently at her hiked-up skirts. *I will not cry*, she
reminded herself, only just managing to stop the tears that
threatened to overwhelm her. Fortune was certainly working
against her tonight.

"Come, amazing lady," said her nemesis, bending over,

and with little apparent effort, lifting her up in front of him
against the horse's neck. "Let me assist you, since you're
obviously so determined to be in on the capture. We've just
missed your lover at the quayside, but the wind is against
him, and with swift horses we can ride to Greenwich before
he can make it by water. I've notified the queen's guard.
He hasn't a prayer of getting away."

"He *will* get away," she said, shivering as Geoffrey's
arms came around her body. "Despite you, despite everything! And when her Grace learns what you've done to me,
she'll have you disemboweled!"

"On the contrary, your mistress will reward me for having
saved her from a vicious little witch who's in league with
heretics. I'm not the first person you've tried your diabolical
hexes on, am I? 'Tis common knowledge that you've fed
the queen your evil concoctions, pretending they had the
power to restore her beauty. She'll be most distressed to
learn you were in fact trying to poison her."

Alexandra opened her mouth to protest, then abruptly
shut it again. Despite all that had happened tonight, she
found she was too awed by this further evidence of Geoffrey's malice to be capable of uttering a word.

The *Argo* lay at anchor, a dark shadow against a dark
sky. It had been a slow journey downriver—the stiff wind
had buffeted the overcrowded barge almost to the point of
foundering. But at last they had reached the agreed-upon
meeting place on a stretch of deserted riverbank, where,
Roger was thankful to see, the longboat awaited them. They
couldn't all fit into the longboat, though. He and Francis
quickly divided the passengers into two groups, sending
the mothers with children off first with two sturdy oarsmen
rowing. The remainder huddled on the bank among the cover
of a few shrubs and boulders, staring out across the foggy
river and listening for the sound of the longboat returning.

It was not the first sound they heard.

"Horses!" Francis said in a soft, deceptively calm voice.
"Somebody's onto us."

Roger blasphemed, to the dismay of several of his more

devout charges. "How many?" he asked as they both craned their necks to see.

"Six or seven, maybe more."

There was the splash of an oar. The longboat had returned. "Hurry," Roger ordered. "With the fog, we might just have a chance. Get your people into the boat, Francis. I'll hold them off." He drew his sword from its scabbard. *"Run!"*

There was no time to think, no time even to be afraid. "Keep your heads down and jump into the boat," Francis directed the fourteen or fifteen souls who were left on the riverbank. "The oarsmen will row you to the ship and to freedom." His tone was bracing, his face grim as, with sword drawn, he took up a position a few yards from Roger, poised to fend off their attackers. The dissidents were already running.

"Go with them. They need you," Roger said.

"And leave you? Never."

"Francis, for the love of God—"

"Don't argue. Even you, my friend, might find it difficult to deal with six or seven armed men. But between the two of us, we'll easily manage it."

Roger laughed with the strange elation that sometimes came just before battle. "We will, I think, at that," he said, and then the riders were upon them.

24

THE BATTLE was brief but bloody. The six or seven horsemen proved to be merely a vanguard—a dozen more were soon upon them. A small army, Roger realized, on his knees after being felled by a blow from behind. His head was throbbing; he heard cries coming from the long-boat, which had gone no more than a few yards from the bank before being set upon. "God in heaven, they've brought archers," he heard Francis say, his voice strangely calm as he deflected the swordplay of the three men who had taken him on. Francis forced them back so he could move in closer to Roger. "Get up quickly," he said.

Archers. Roger heard a woman's voice cut off in mid-scream. At least it was a quicker death than the stake. He hoped, as he stumbled to his feet to face the half-circle of men-at-arms who were closing around them, that he and Francis would die as easily.

"Watch your back," he said to Francis as a man with a pike took a swipe at them from behind. A split second later the pikeman was dead on Francis' sword, and the other attackers hesitated briefly before advancing again.

Francis shot Roger a grim but recognizable smile. "I thank you, but we're only staving off the inevitable; it would be unrealistic to think we're going to get out of this. What an ignominious end to our adventures together." He paused, parrying effortlessly. "I have loved you ever."

"And I you." Roger left off the qualifier, *as much as I was able*. He had never really loved Francis as much as the other man had loved him; the only person he loved so wholeheartedly was Alexandra. Oh Christ, Alix. Rebellion kicked violently through his entrails. Yesterday at this time he would have accepted death, but not today. He wanted to see her again. Just once, he pleaded with God, even as his sword arm was violently parrying and thrusting. Let me see her, then you can do whatever you want with me.

Even as the impossible thought crossed his mind, another flashed—an old saying Merwynna the witch had taunted him with one day when he was still a lad. *Be careful what ye pray for, boy, lest the gods see fit to grant yer prayer.*

The soldiers closed. Because Francis seemed to be the more dangerous of the two, they tried to hold him off while directing most of their energy toward Roger. His heart pounded, his weapon slipped in his sweat-sticky fingers, his arms and legs grew leaden. There were too many of them. He was skilled and clever in his own defense, but he couldn't be everywhere at once. It is no dishonor, he told himself, for two men to be defeated by so large a troop.

He felt a monumental wrench and knew they'd succeeded in disarming him; he saw a blade flash in *quarte*, his vulnerable line of defense, the line that guards the heart. Quick. Aim true, you bastard, and my death will be gentle, easy, as effortless as sleep.

All within the space of a moment, he heard Francis yell, and he felt an even stronger wrench than before. There was a groan, and the sensation of a body falling, but strangely enough, it didn't seem to be his own. Then somebody was commanding the swordsmen to put up their weapons, and the attackers reluctantly fell back. When the dust cleared, Roger, though wobbly, was still standing. Francis lay on the ground, bleeding badly from a wound in the right side of his chest.

Roger fell to his knees in the dirt, seizing Francis' shoulders between his two hands. He shook him gently. "You took the thrust that was meant for me, didn't you?" He shook him harder, enraged, although his eyes were moist. "Francis! Don't you dare die, damn you! Lift your eyelids and look at me."

Francis Lacklin obeyed, summoning the strength to gaze around them in what appeared to be amused contempt. "What happened? Why aren't they hacking us to pieces?"

"Someone told them to stop." Roger tried in vain to stanch the alarming flow of blood. Francis' face was graying rapidly, his skin growing cold. "Blast you! Couldn't you let me get killed my own way for once? I'm not bloody fifteen years old any longer!"

Francis coughed, bubbling a pink froth that scared the dickens out of Roger. His attention was directed somewhere over Roger's shoulder. "Forgive me . . . I shouldn't have interfered—your death, I fear, will be crueler than mine. Look, my fair and foolish friend. Behind you. It was your lady who betrayed us."

At first the words made no sense. Then as Francis' eyes drifted shut, Roger raised his head and saw her. She was there, perhaps ten yards away, watching, staring, not moving, not protesting. And beside her, his arm possessively encircling her waist, was Geoffrey de Montreau, who had promised to be present at his death.

"Perhaps there's a certain justice to it after all," said Francis in a considerably weaker voice. "I have wronged her . . . May God forgive me. And you also. Roger? Hear me out . . ."

But Roger could no longer hear him. His head was buzzing, his nerves screaming. He couldn't believe it—not Alix. Dear Lord, it couldn't be Alix. And yet her hair was flaming in the stiff sea breeze—foaming all red and feathery against Geoffrey's throat, and he was smiling, pulling her closer, caressing her. It could not be, and yet it was. Other women, he reminded himself, had proved as false. All his life, the people he'd counted upon had, one by one, betrayed him. This time it was Alexandra—the cruelest betrayal of them all.

Let me see her. Well, there she was. She wasn't an apparition; she was there. She was the only outsider who'd known their plans, the only possible source of a leak in their careful security. She had gone to Geoffrey with the details of tonight's planned escape, Geoffrey the snake who had tempted and corrupted her.

All this flashed through his brain in seconds; then a rage blinded him, a bloody, bloody rage. He turned back to Francis, who was still trying to tell him something. Bending over to put his lips near his friend's, he whispered, "No blasted last words, Francis! You're going to live! You're going to live and help me take my revenge on her. Do you hear me? Live!"

Then, surging to his feet, Roger seized Francis' sword and fell upon the men who had attacked them, the men who had so grievously wounded Francis. The soldiers were driven back as Roger exploded into a frenzy of brilliant, deadly swordplay. One died quickly, two. He'd kill them all, damn them. Alexandra Douglas was the only woman he'd ever ventured to trust, much less to love. Yet in that moment, had she been close enough, he would have driven his blade through her heart.

Alexandra knew nothing but the sight of the man she loved with all her heart and spirit—he was alive, alive! She was drawing breath to call to him when she heard the serpentine hiss of Geoffrey's voice in her ear: "Every word out of your mouth will add a full minute to the time it takes him to die. Do you understand? If you contradict anything I say, I will have him slowly and exquisitely tortured."

"You'll do that anyway." The thin, reedy voice that issued from her lips did not sound like her own.

"No. The mental torture of believing you've betrayed him will be enough."

"He won't believe your lies." But even as she spoke, Roger looked up and saw her, and she understood that he would. For one dreadful instant their eyes met, and his scream of disbelief seemed to echo inside her own head. No, no, she whispered, trying in vain to reach him without words. But somewhere a red tide surged and the gates to his mind slammed shut.

"Restrain him," Geoffrey snapped as Roger began so

ferociously to fight again. He waved more of his men into the fray. "Do what you must, but I want him alive."

And Alexandra, to her own horror, was thinking: No—kill him, kill him. Let him die cleanly, fighting on the strand with the smell of the sea in his lungs. Let him not be tortured, in body or in mind. And yet she feared his death with far more terror than she feared her own, and when she saw that although they had disarmed him and clubbed him to the ground, he was rising again to his knees, still breathing—oh God, still alive!—she cried out in thankfulness and blessed relief.

But the next few minutes were hellish. Geoffrey forced her over to the bloody bank where the abortive battle had been fought. Francis Lacklin lay on his back there, not moving, his eyes rolled back in their sockets. She couldn't tell whether he was dead or alive. A few yards behind his body on the riverbank, a small boat had been drawn back to the shore, loaded with murdered heretics—victims of the archers' arrows. Men, women—all appeared dead. Geoffrey's soldiers were callously pulling them out of the longboat and dumping them on the rocky strand. Alexandra made a sound in her throat as her stomach rose.

Roger was on his knees surrounded by men-at-arms who held their blades to his heart and his throat while brutally twisting his arms behind his back. He was panting from exertion, and a mixture of sweat and blood was running down his face, but, miraculously, he seemed unhurt. In body, at least. His soul, she knew, was in agony.

"One word," Geoffrey warned her while they were still out of earshot, "and I'll have them start with those big brown eyes of his—gouge out the left, and then the right . . ."

She believed him. His voice was high-pitched with excitement and bloodlust, his arm was tight around her waist, his perfume sickened her. She thought for a moment she might faint; she wished she could. But such an escape was not granted her.

"How do you like your Mistress Douglas now?" Geoffrey taunted his helpless enemy. "Not that I need employ so formal an address with her, need I, *chérie?*" One of his hands slipped up to caress her breasts. She scarcely felt it—

her eyes were locked with Roger's and she was pleading with him silently: *Don't believe him, please. I love you. Oh, Roger, don't look at me like that!*

She hardly heard as Geoffrey gleefully told how she had come directly to him after leaving Chilton House to report the success of her spying. "It was really too reckless of you, Trevor. A worthless bunch of heretics. I knew you were up to your neck in something, but I expected treason more dramatic, more colorful than this. 'Tis unworthy of you, truly. I almost doubted your lady when she reported the details of this remarkable venture."

Roger's eyes pierced hers. "Geoffrey de Montreau would lie to the priest on his deathbed. Tell me he's lying now."

Alexandra stared in to those beautiful eyes, soft, brown, mocking; the eyes she had loved all her life. There was a man with a knife just beside Roger; he was watching Geoffrey for a sign. She swayed slightly and said nothing.

Roger's gaze shifted to Geoffrey. "What have you done to her, you son-of-a-bitch bastard?"

Geoffrey smiled. "She's still speechless with wonder, no doubt, from the pleasures I taught her in bed."

Roger laughed. It sounded pathetic. "Have you been in his bed, Alexandra?" When she merely stared, without words, he snarled, "Answer me!"

"Yes," she whispered. It was, of course, the truth.

He moved convulsively; Alexandra gave a faint cry of misery. "Then I shall kill you."

"No! It wasn't what you think," she began, but Geoffrey silenced her with a cruel wrench of her arm.

"Threaten one of the queen's ladies, will you? You're merely adding to your crimes. Her Grace's troops should be arriving anytime now, to take you and throw you in prison. Will they burn you for heresy, or draw and quarter you for treason, I wonder."

Roger ignored this. "Where's Alan, Alix? Was he in on this too, or did you dupe him as cleverly as you duped me?"

Geoffrey had given her no instructions regarding Alan. If he was still alive, poor Alan must be agonizing over the possibility that his brother would find out it was *his* words that had betrayed them. No, she thought. Alan had spoken to stop her torture. The least she could do in return was protect him from Roger's rage. "Alan had nothing to do with it. It was I who revealed your plans to Geoffrey."

"Why, Alexandra? For the love of God, why?"

His voice was like a scream, a cry of rage to a cruel and baffling God. She couldn't think of an answer. A ray of hope darted through her. He would know there was no answer. He would think it over and know there was no inducement in this world that could ever have made her betray him. He would know Geoffrey was lying and that she herself had been most vilely coerced.

But Roger didn't know; he couldn't think. The logical part of his brain had long since ceased to function, and all he was capable of perceiving was a series of overwhelmingly brutal impressions: Francis bleeding, dying; the dissenters set upon and murdered; Alexandra admitting her crime from the shelter of Geoffrey de Montreau's arms.

"Kill me," he said. "You, woman. Give her a sword, Geoff. You hold me responsible for Celestine's death? Let justice be done, then. I took the life of the woman you loved; let the woman I love take mine."

The woman I love. Alexandra gasped as the tension that had been building inside her for hours reached a crescendo and burst. "No!" she screamed. Twisting, scratching, clawing, she fought free of Geoffrey's hated touch. "No! No! No!" She flung herself at Roger despite the swords, the guards, the blood, despite the hands that seized her and fought to restrain her frenzy. Dimly she heard Geoffrey's voice, Roger's, the soldiers' . . . and then another voice, an authoritative voice shouting orders in English from just behind them on the bank. Horsemen, a lot more horsemen. And confusion, as the Frenchmen were set upon by Britishers with weapons drawn and gleaming.

"Unhand my daughter," said the voice, furiously now. "And that young man, too." Sir Charles Douglas waved a drawn rapier at Roger. "You, Monsieur de Montreau, are a diplomat, not a captain of the guard. What is the meaning of this carnage?"

"Father," Alexandra whispered, looking up at him through her sweat-sticky locks of hair. "Oh God, Father!"

"We have prevented an exodus of heretics," Geoffrey declared, sounding a little startled to find himself face to face with Alexandra's father. "This man has proved a heretic and a traitor." He nodded at Roger. "We have detained him for you."

"And murdered English men and women in the process?" Douglas snapped. "It is you, sir, who are under arrest."

The French troops backed off as Sir Charles's men, who far outnumbered them, surrounded them. "You cannot arrest an attaché of the embassy of France," Geoffrey asserted.

"You think not? Our two countries are now at war, and you have committed hostilities against Englishmen, monsieur. To hell with your immunity. Seize him!" Douglas ordered his men. He turned his attention to his daughter. "What the devil are you doing here?"

"Betraying me," Roger answered bitterly before she could speak. "Has there really been valid declaration of war, Douglas?"

"Aye. A pretty mess you've landed yourself in, lad. You'll hang for this, you know."

"You think so?" Roger replied, and Alexandra recognized the strange note in his voice long before it meant a thing to anybody else. Something was about to happen. She felt a flash of fear, followed by a sense of acceptance of the inevitable.

The French soldiers had left a space around them. She was kneeling in the dirt less than a yard from the man she loved. He, surrounded now by English troops, was slowly rising to his feet. Two beefy Englishmen had already grabbed Geoffrey, but Roger was free, and—she saw from her vantage point an instant before anyone else—he had somehow armed himself with a short, bloody dagger.

In that instant she could have tried to run. Instead, she stayed perfectly still and made no sound even at the terrible pain that ripped through her abused arms and shoulders when Roger wrenched her into a brutal caricature of an embrace. Her hair was against his cheek, her head rested against the pulse beating wildly in his neck. And the knife was at her throat.

"This is her doing as much as Geoffrey's," he said in a

strangely exultant tone. "I will kill her, and take pleasure in it, Douglas, if you interfere with me now."

There was a very long pause. Two sets of soldiers looked to Charles and Geoffrey for orders.

"Kill her," Geoffrey urged softly. "Treat her the way you treated my sister, and when you're finished, I'll tell you a tale that will stop your blood."

But Douglas said, "I don't believe you, Trevor. Let her go. I've seen you bluff your way out of trouble before."

Alexandra felt a stinging sensation as blood welled up under the knife.

"Christ have mercy!" her father's voice exploded. "Take care, damn you. Have you lost your head? You're cutting her skin."

"Tell him how she spilled every detail of my plans to you, Geoff," Roger said. "Tell him how hotly she opened her body to you in bed."

"Lies!" Douglas burst out. "Alexandra is a woman of honor and virtue who would never do such a thing."

"Oh, great virtue," Roger said, his voice dripping sarcasm. "You think I don't know whereof I speak? I had her myself that night in the witch's cottage. The more fool you for doubting the evidence in front of your eyes. I took her, I fucked your *virtuous* daughter, Douglas, and a woman who swooned more feverishly beneath my caresses I've never had before or since."

Alexandra moaned in protest as her father's face turned crimson with choler. He cursed a string of violent oaths, looking as if he were about to leap upon Roger, which would undoubtedly result in the death of all of them. Please, God. End this web of half-truths. Dear Christ, forgive us all, Alexandra pleaded silently.

"One step and she dies," warned Roger. He raised his voice at the English soldiers, sounding fully as authoritative as her father. "That man on the ground there, is he dead?" He was referring to Francis.

Someone bent to examine the body. "He breathes."

"Put him into that boat. Gently. And do the same with anyone else of those poor butchered people who's still alive."

Geoffrey raised his voice in protest, but after several moments of hard-eyed contact with Roger, Alexandra saw her father nod to his men. "Do it," he said heavily.

There were only two people left alive besides Francis Lacklin—a woman and a youth. As the three unconscious bodies were being lifted into the longboat, Roger slowly forced his hostage to the water's edge.

She felt no fear. One of his arms was clamped so tightly around her chest that she found it difficult to draw breath; the other held the knife, harshly and steadily, at her throat. Some strands of her hair caught on the fastenings of his cloak as he moved her, but although the pulling stung her scalp, she didn't dare twist free, not with the knife there. Roger's familiar body was hard against her, strong and capable despite all that had passed. With only a slight change in fortune, he might have been bleeding in the dirt like Francis. She felt a tiny rush of hope, born of the fact that they were both still alive.

"You're not taking her with you?" Her father's voice was hoarse with stress.

"Of course I'm taking her—how far will I get without her?"

"Free her. You may take the boat and go. My oath upon it."

Roger told him explicitly what he could do with his oath.

Douglas tried again: "You're lying about that night in the forest," he said reasonably. "I know you. Despite your passions, you are a man of honor. You have not touched her."

Roger barked a laugh but otherwise paid no attention. He'd already stepped into the boat and was dragging Alexandra after him. "You there, sirrah." He addressed one of the English troops. "Push us out."

"*Mon Dieu*, Douglas," Geoffrey shouted, trying to draw his sword. "You think I'll stand here and watch him escape after all I've done to destroy the bastard? My curse on you, Trevor; don't think you're going to slip the net!"

"Silence him," Douglas snapped to his men, and Geoffrey was dragged out of range. "Release her, Roger. You know me for a man of my word. Set her back upon the strand and I swear no one will interfere with your escape."

"No. Sit down, whore. Take up the oars. You can row—very well, as I recall. You're going to row us out to the ship, my sweet. And that's only the first of several services you're going to perform for me."

"Damnation, Trevor! I beg you. She is innocent. To take out your anger upon her would be a heinous crime. Reconsider, damn you!"

Roger laughed, a hollow, horrible sound. The little boat was afloat, and Alexandra was already struggling with the too-long oars. Her shoulders ached from the rack; she bit her lips and groaned as she tried her best to row. In front of her lay the still bodies of Francis Lacklin, the woman, and the young man. Behind her, Roger crouched with his knife still at her throat.

"Trevor!" Sir Charles screamed.

"Save your breath," said Roger. "There's no crime, however heinous, I wouldn't laugh at committing now."

And then they were out of the riverbank surf, in deeper water, where the rowing was marginally easier. From shore, Alexandra could hear Geoffrey de Montreau cursing and swearing at Charles Douglas, calling him every obscenity in the French language. "You should have killed him, you fool," he repeated over and over. "How could you let him go? You're in league with him, I'll wager. I'll denounce you to your queen. You'll suffer for this, I promise you."

"Shut him up, damn him," Douglas snapped. Then he called out once more after Roger, his voice sounding strangely muffled as the distance between the longboat and the riverbank increased.

Out of range of the archers, Roger removed the knife from Alexandra's throat. In relief, she sank back against his knees, only to be thrust forward again. "Keep rowing," Roger said. "I'm not sparing your miserable life. I'm merely extending it long enough to ensure that you are well punished for this night's work."

"Roger, all is not as it appears," she whispered.

"Not a word, or I'll put my knife through your rotten

cheating heart. Shut up and row. Put a little more muscle into it, bitch."

He was too near the edge to be argued with. Later he would calm down; later she would have the chance to explain. Leaning forward, trying her best to ignore the pain, she rowed.

25

ALARMED and worried shouts greeted Roger when the longboat finally arrived at the side of the *Argo* just as dawn was starting to lighten the sky. He himself was at the oars—Alexandra had been so slow and clumsy at the task that he had finally shoved her out of the way. She had crawled to the end of the boat and put her head to the chests of Francis Lacklin, the woman, and the youth. "They're still alive," she'd whispered.

"No thanks to you," he'd snapped, and ignored her for the rest of the trip.

Now with the rowboat banging precariously against the *Argo*'s hull, he called for help, and within seconds several sailors had ropes over the side and were sliding down. A rope ladder came too. "Climb it," he ordered Alexandra, jerking her to her feet.

She stared dully at the ladder, and at the distance up to the deck, then shook her head. "My arms hurt. I can't."

"Climb it, bitch, or I'll slit your throat and fling your body into the sea."

The seamen, who knew him well, seemed startled at the violence in his tone. Roger ignored them. With a spark of her usual spirit Alexandra said, "I don't deserve this."

"No?" Roger felt a sick rage bursting inside him, a rage which would, he suspected, grow even wilder as the full implications of her betrayal sank in. He was not a particularly kind or gentle man—he'd led a rough existence in the Mediterranean, and he was already beginning to feel the freedom from social constraint that was his on the decks of the *Argo*. Here he was master; no one ruled him, no one questioned his decisions or interfered with his pleasures. His crew obeyed his orders without hesitation. If he told them to climb, they climbed.

"So far tonight, I have been tortured on the rack in Geoffrey's apartments, I have scaled the side of a bare stone building in a futile attempt to escape, and I have rowed a heavy boat a goodly distance with oars that were far too long for me. I can barely lift my arms and I won't be able to climb that ladder. But if it will give you pleasure to watch me fall from it and sink into the sea, I will gratify you."

So saying, she reached for the swaying ladder and mounted it, her body crashing against the *Argo*'s hull as the waves tossed the longboat. Her arms were indeed trembling. Tortured on the rack in Geoffrey's apartments? Roger questioned. No. She was a devious little liar, that was all. If she'd been racked, she wouldn't be able to walk, let alone climb.

"Help her, dammit," he ordered one of the seamen as Alexandra faltered and nearly fell. "Hoist her up there and get them to send down some sort of litter for the others."

The sailor obeyed with alacrity.

At first, Alexandra realized, the anxious seamen who hauled her over the rail of the ship, gave her water, and wrapped her in blankets thought she was one of the heretics. Even the dissidents who had made it safely to the ship embraced her, praying over her and asking tremblingly about their comrades who had been left behind. A woman was begging for information about her husband, and a young boy was crying for his mother. Heartstruck, Alexandra tried to tell them as kindly as possible that their friends and relatives were dead. Their sorrow brought forth her own, and she sat among them and grieved until Roger came up behind her and pulled her roughly to her feet.

"Very pretty, Alexandra—mourning for the poor innocents you helped to murder? And to think I never realized what a skillful actress you were, what a mistress of duplicity and deceit. Come, you're a prisoner, not a refugee." He tore the blanket she'd been huddled in away from her drenched and sodden gown. "Like a prisoner you'll be treated. Hold out your hands."

She looked up at him in the light of the dawning day—Roger Trevor, the man she loved and would have died for. His beautiful eyes were cold as they regarded her. Dead. Whatever he had felt for her in the past—whatever passion, good fellowship, youthful affection or love—was gone, vanished as if it had never been. For the first time she began to fear that no explanation would ever be sufficient to undo the evil that had been wrought this night. He obviously didn't believe she'd been tortured. He wouldn't believe anything she told him.

Her eyes dropped from his face to his hands. He was holding a short, ugly length of rope. Jesu. She had a horrific vision of being tied up like a dog in some vile hole deep in the bowels of the ship with the roaches and the rats. "Is that really necessary?" she asked as he wrenched her slender wrists together and wrapped the cord around them, binding them tightly.

"Probably not—we're nearly at the mouth of the river now, and even you won't be able to swim the long distance to shore. Still . . ." His cold eyes moved over her body in an obvious leer that was all the more humiliating because it was so entirely devoid of passion. "I believe I'm going to like you in bondage."

Then he ordered her imprisoned, not in a cell, but in the master's cabin. "When I have time, sweet traitor, I will come to you. You can show me all the lecherous little tricks you learned from Geoffrey. And they'd better be impressive, because the moment you cease to please me with your whoring ways will be the moment you meet your death. Unless I decide to turn you over to the crew first."

Feeling weak and sick and dizzy, Alexandra thought: This isn't Roger and the things he's saying to me aren't real. None of this is real. I am home in my bed at Westmor and when I awake my mother will be there comforting me. Then

I'll get up and go over to Chilton so Alan and I can study our Greek. In the afternoon Merwynna and I will sort herbs while she tells me stories of the Old Ones, and how they keep watch over their own. Why aren't they watching over me now?

"This woman is obviously ill, Roger, or exhausted," a gentle voice rebuked the cruel man she loved. "Whatever she's done, she cannot answer for it now." Alexandra's eyes shifted to look blankly at the gaunt gray-haired man with blood on his shirt who'd come up beside her. She'd seen him bending over Francis Lacklin when they'd hoisted him on board, tearing his clothes away, stanching his blood. He had a kind, infinitely patient face, and eyes that were sad and wise. His features swam, turning sharply familiar. "Merwynna?" she whispered as her legs gave way and the deck heaved up toward her face.

She recovered consciousness on a bed in an exotic cabin that was large by ship's standards and surprisingly pleasant. Above her head was a diamond-paned window through which she could see the red sky of dawn. Across from her a mammoth desk was bolted to the floor in front of a veritable wall of books. There were Turkey rugs on the floor, maps and charts on the walls, and Oriental lamps and braziers, also bolted down, in the corners. And beside her was the sad-eyed man.

"You fainted, mistress. When was the last time you ate?"

"I can't remember. Yesterday sometime." She shook her head slowly. "I never faint. But last night I did not sleep."

"Are you with child?"

She stared at him in astonishment. "That would be a rare miracle, sir, since I'm a maid." With a shudder she remembered Geoffrey. And Roger, that night in Merwynna's cottage. "Just," she added grimly, closing her eyes again.

"Does Roger know this?"

She shook her head. "What he thinks he knows and what is actually the truth are two very different things. Who are you?"

"Thomas Comstock, a physician. I wanted to make certain you were not dangerously ill."

Thomas Comstock. She remembered his name—Roger had mentioned him yesterday afternoon when he'd showed her the cellars. *Yesterday afternoon?* So recently? It seemed as if an age had passed since then.

"You must go to your other charges, then, sir. There are people aboard who need you more than I. I'm stiff and weary and heartsick, but Mr. Lacklin, for one, is at death's door. Unless he has already died?"

"No, he lives. Whether he will survive this day, I am not certain, but I will do my best to save him, for Roger's sake."

She caught the tone in his voice and looked at him more closely. "You love Roger, don't you?"

"Aboard this ship, everybody loves him." He gave her his sad-eyed smile. "If you have injured him, they're not likely to have much love for you."

"No, I imagine not," she said dryly. "This is his cabin?"

"Aye."

"And I'm to be kept here, bound, in his bed?"

"Don't be afraid. For all his moodiness and passion, he is not usually violent toward women."

"He was violent toward Celestine de Montreau."

Comstock's eyes grew, if possible, sadder. "You know of her? It's true she and Roger were in constant conflict toward the end; they argued, but he was never violent, except in his language."

Thank God! She hadn't really believed Geoffrey, but she hadn't seen Roger in a rage either, until last night. "How did she die, then?"

"She died of severe internal bleeding after the child she had conceived took root and grew not within her womb, but within the tiny tube beside the womb. It is a rare condition, and one that few, if any, women survive."

"Oh my God." She knew of the condition—she'd seen it once in a shepherd's wife whom Merwynna had tried to treat. The woman had died bleeding and in great pain. "Celestine's brother told me Roger had murdered her, and Roger didn't deny it."

"Roger holds himself responsible for her death because they fought bitterly on the night she died. But as I repeatedly told him at the time, he did not cause her miscarriage or her death—both were inevitable from the moment the child was conceived. No one was to blame."

Alexandra began to laugh somewhat hysterically. She wished she could cry. All night long she'd held back her tears, but now, when she wanted to cry, she laughed instead. No one was to blame for Celestine's death, and Geoffrey de Montreau had had no reason to demand revenge. All the deaths tonight, all the heartache, had been for naught.

Comstock waited until she had controlled herself marginally, then quietly suggested a certain drug to help her sleep. "Yes, give it to me," she said without hesitation. Temporary oblivion would be preferable to this soul-tearing pain.

She drank the bitter draft he brought her, and within minutes she slept.

It was night again when Roger finally climbed the ladder to the captain's deck and unlocked the door to his cabin. During the day a summer storm had come up, battering the vessel with high winds and crushing waves. For most of the daylight hours Roger had been kept busy shouting the orders that would keep the ship and its crew members safe from the foaming power of the sea. It was a battle he'd fought many times before, a battle that always gave him a strange feeling of exultation as he matched wits with the mighty forces of nature. It was a clean fight, entirely devoid of the malice and pettiness of human strife. On the day the sea won—and he knew that day might come—he would surrender gracefully and accept her victory with none of the bitterness he would have felt toward a human enemy.

The storm had been a mercy. It had given him an excuse to forget about Geoffrey, Francis, Alexandra. But it was over now, and he could no longer escape the thoughts and images that were relentlessly flooding his brain. Francis, taking the blow that had been meant for him, bleeding, dying. Geoffrey, his feral face twisted with satisfaction. And, worst of all, Alexandra. *Let me see her.* How cleverly cruel was fate!

For several hours he had sat beside Francis' bedside in

Tom's makeshift infirmary belowdecks. The physician was not hopeful. Francis' right lung had been grazed, he had bled profusely, and he showed no signs of regaining consciousness. "He's a strong man," Comstock had conceded, "but if infection sets in..."

"Isn't there anything more we can do for him?"

"We can pray."

Roger swore at that. "Aye, God is good, God is just," he sneered. "Where's the sense in this? Innocent, godly people have been slaughtered and Francis is dying after putting his body in the way of a sword intended for me. I'm as sinful as he, but I, as usual, am alive and unscathed. The Lord, in his mercy"—his voice was tinged with bitterness—"never punishes me directly. He just tortures me by massacring everyone around me!"

"Such thinking is the height of arrogance. You are responsible only for your own destiny, not for that of your friends. Besides, the good Lord undoubtedly knows that you're an expert at punishing yourself...for far more sins than you've actually committed."

"Francis lies here dying because of me."

"What better way to die than in defense of somebody you love?" Comstock countered gently.

Roger slammed his fist into the wall. He neither wanted nor felt he deserved that kind of love.

Later he had sat drinking with Daniel Bunty, the old friend and able sailor who had been commanding the *Argo* ever since Roger had left it to return to England. The aqua vitae he'd consumed should have lessened his agony, but it hadn't worked. Bunty had tried in his gruff way to ease his mind, urging Roger to tell him exactly what had happened. But Roger didn't want to talk about what had happened. Talking only increased his grief and fanned his rage.

As the alcohol began to seep into his blood and brain, Roger began to imagine exactly how he would punish Alexandra for her betrayal. The images were confusing. His violence was highly eroticized as he saw himself forcing her into an assortment of sexual acts, many of which were painful and degrading. The fantasies troubled him, but he hadn't the will to stop them. And strangely enough, they all ended with Alexandra crying out in pleasure rather than in pain.

Daniel Bunty must have noticed his preoccupation, for when Roger rose unsteadily but resolutely to his feet, his old friend put a restraining hand on his arm. "You're not going up to that sweet young lassie in your condition, surely?"

Roger was aware by now that everyone on the ship knew of the young woman he had imprisoned in his cabin. Rumors had been flying all day as to who she was and what crime she had committed. Roger had confirmed none of them. He had refused to talk of her. He'd even managed to ignore Tom Comstock's objections to the way he had treated her so far.

"Aye, that's exactly where I'm going," he said now. "She'll be missing me, no doubt."

"She is no light-o'-love, but a gentlewoman, and you're in no fit state tonight for such."

"Enough, Daniel. Don't interfere with something that is no concern of yours."

Bunty backed down, but he didn't look pleased about it. "I only wish to prevent you from doing something you may regret in the morning, my friend."

"My regrets, or lack of them, are no one's affair but my own," Roger retorted as he slammed out of Bunty's quarters and set off on his self-appointed mission of vengeance.

When he entered the cabin, soaked to the skin with rain, and gritty-eyed from lack of sleep, he found Alexandra curled up in the middle of his bed. Her slender body was still clad in the damp gown she'd been wearing on the riverbank, her hair was spread in a fiery mantle over her shoulders, and her sleepy green eyes were apprehensive as they blinked and stared into his.

She looked artless and young lying there. But she was a woman as false and fatal as Eve. He must remember that. No matter what happened tonight, he must make himself remember it.

"Good evening, Alexandra," he drawled. "No, don't get

up. You are exactly where I want you—in my bed, at last. Are you ready to show me all your whore's tricks? I have come, with great eagerness, to learn them."

She slowly sat up, encircling her upraised knees with her arms. Her wrists were still bound together with rope. Roger stared at them, taking pleasure in the sight. "I am no whore. Nor am I guilty of all the crimes you imagine."

"I have not come to argue, but to avenge," he said, drawing out the last word, enjoying the sound of it, and the fear it obviously inspired in her. He crossed in two strides to the bed and sank his fingers into the red flames of her hair. His voice dropped to the low timbre of a caress. "Once, in the cave in Westmor Forest, you expected me to rape you. Tonight, at long last, your imaginings will come to fruition. I wish you joy of it."

"No woman finds joy in rape!"

He pushed her roughly backward until she lay across the bed. "You will, beloved," he said in a parody of his once-gentle and affectionate voice. "I intend to give you great pleasure . . . far more than Geoffrey de Montreau ever gave you . . . far more pleasure, indeed, that you will ever know again. For when it's over, my lovely traitor, I'm going to fulfill the other fear you indulged in that afternoon in the forest. For your crimes, Alexandra Douglas, I intend to end your life."

26

ALEXANDRA made no answer. All the words she'd planned to say to him were sticking in her throat. He looked, she thought, like a scourge sent from hell to punish her. Standing over her in the dim light of the single lamp she had managed to light a little while before, he filled the small cabin with his dark energy. His clothes were shining with seawater and rain, his face was sculpted hard and expressionless. Only his eyes gave his emotions away, and they caused her more disquiet than anything else; she could never remember seeing them so black with anger, pain, and cruel determination.

She closed her own eyes. All evening since she'd woken from a twelve-hour sleep to find herself still alone and imprisoned, she'd tried to plan what she would say to him when this moment arrived. Not even the storm had penetrated the turmoil of her mind, although at times the tossing and plunging of the ship had been so severe that she thought they must surely founder. But the tempest in Roger disturbed her far more deeply than the tempest outside.

And now that the time had come, she knew there was nothing she could say, nothing he would believe. In some sense, she was guilty of all the things Roger believed her guilty of. Through her his plans had become known, through her his friends had died. She would never try to excuse herself by putting the blame on Alan—her loyal friend loved her and would have sold his soul to save her from the rack. The least she could do in return was hold her tongue about his part in the debacle.

As for Roger's belief that she had shared a bed with Geoffrey, that too was true, even though the act had not reached a conclusion. If he wanted a woman whose body had never known the touch of another man, she was no longer that woman. If he could not forgive her for something that had been done to her against her will—and many men would not, she knew—there was nothing there, either, to be said.

She heard Roger throw his cloak to the floor beside the berth, splashing tiny droplets of seawater on her. His doublet was next—she heard the creaking sound of thick material being roughly pulled apart. She knew then that it was true: he was going to rape her. The love she had dreamed of consummating with him was about to be sullied by violence.

"Roger?" She wasn't sure exactly what was behind her impulse to speak his name. To reassure herself, perhaps, that this dark avenging angel was really the man she loved?

"Be still." His boots came off and he bent to work the points of his hose. "I don't wish to hear a single sound out of you. You didn't know how to keep your mouth shut last night; tonight, I promise you, you will learn."

She ignored this; talking was her only defense. "Shall I undress or would you prefer to rip my gown off?"

Roger shot her a glance, noting that the dampness had shrunk the fabric of her dress, pulling it tight across her breasts. He could see her nipples straining against the bodice. There was a surge in the already tight and hardened center of his loins. "You pay no heed to my orders? What, cocky again, Alexandra? And here I'd been thinking you'd lost your spirit when you so gracefully fainted in front of my entire crew up there on deck. That, too, I suppose, was an act?"

"That was a *bona fide* faint, as your physician, I'm certain, will attest."

"Oh, he's been attesting right and left. But he's always been a fool for a pretty woman's wiles. He's been celibate for so long he can't tell the rotten apples from the sound. He's a friar, you see. He once worked with the Hospitalers of St. John."

"I love you," she said, apropos of nothing.

There was a distinct sucking sound as Roger caught his breath. The anger in his eyes shot up and he raised his arm as if to strike her. Alexandra cringed—something she'd never done with him before—and he laughed at her, a cruel, mocking laugh.

"Be still, I said. That's the last one of your lies I want to hear tonight."

"It's not a lie!"

"Everything you say is a lie. *You* are a lie, and I am a fool." His next words were curses as the knots binding his hose stuck. He tore them away and finished stripping in a series of short, impatient motions. "How amusing you must have found my quaint reluctance to dishonor you, Alexandra. All the time you've been a bitch and a whore."

He tossed away the last garment and turned to her, his naked skin gleaming in the light from the lamp. He was hard and lean, well-muscled and virile in all the ways that Geoffrey de Montreau had not been. Broad shoulders, a flat belly, trim buttocks, long, well-shaped legs—he was a man in every sense of the word. Her eyes were irresistibly drawn to the dark, glossy sweep of hair which extended in a narrow ribbon down over his ribs and navel to thicken again between his thighs. Less fearful than fascinated, she stared at the hard spear of flesh and muscle rising out of that thicket of hair. He was highly aroused, she realized. And he was beautiful.

But as he came slowly toward the bed, the light glinted off something metallic in his hand. The dagger from his sword belt. She was afraid then. A pit of dark unreason seemed to open beneath her feet, and just as he had predicted, she was suddenly back in the cave at the top of Thorncroft Overhang and he was coming at her with a naked sword.

"No!" she cried out, sitting up to resist him as he put one knee on the bed and reached for her.

"Defending your *virtue?*" he asked, sneering.

"I have no care for my virtue, and besides, you'll know your mistake soon enough. But I will fight for my life."

His lips curved in an unpleasant smile. "What? . . . Trembling? Where's your famous courage, Alexandra?" He captured her flailing hands and wrenched her closer. The knife blade flashed as he slid it between her wrists. "Restrain your panic—it's to cut your bonds, not your throat." As the hemp fell away, his fingers chafed her flesh, but when he caught himself doing so, he stopped. Although her skin was lightly scored, there were no rope burns; she had not been cruelly tied.

"I would have sworn you'd prefer to have me bound and helpless!"

"On the contrary, I want your hands free. I have plans for your hands, little whore. I'm going to make you show me all the clever tricks you've learned to do with them." While he had the knife in hand, he used it to slice through the laces of her dress. She grabbed at the material as the bodice opened, revealing the curve of her breasts.

"Slip it off your shoulders," he ordered. "Slowly. Artfully. You've had the practice, I'm sure. I want to look at you. I want to see exactly what I'm getting."

She neither answered nor obeyed.

Almost casually he touched the tip of the knife to the hollow of her throat. "There's one small detail about seafaring life you may be ignorant of. I am this ship's master, which means I have complete authority over everyone on board. My orders are obeyed without question or hesitation. Anyone foolish enough to rebel is disciplined swiftly and harshly. Do I make myself clear?"

"I am not a member of your crew and, knife or no knife, I don't recognize your authority."

There was a moment of silence between them, broken only by the creaking of the timbers and the roaring of the sea. Then Roger let the dagger slip through his fingers to the floor. He pushed her roughly down again on her back. "Stubborn as ever, I see. So be it." He took her lips in a punishing kiss, thrusting his tongue into her mouth. She arched in protest, then abruptly slackened beneath him, becoming oddly passive, surprising him. He'd expected her to struggle. Indeed, he'd been looking forward to it.

Her body was soft, warm, and strangely magical in its power over him. Tenderness rushed through him, surprising him still further. The touch of her, the scent of her, overwhelmed him. He wanted to make love to her slowly, gently, with loving consideration. He didn't want to hurt her, no matter what she'd done.

"Witch." He forced himself to remember the horrors of last night. His hands dropped to explore the curve of her throat, the swell of her breasts. Still she didn't protest. Pushing himself up on his knees, he straddled her, his fingers moving down to her open bodice. He was unsteady, clumsy; he snagged the material and cursed savagely. He wished he hadn't dropped the knife; he wanted to cut the cloth from her body and see her naked and helpless beneath him.

Alexandra sensed the confusion of violence and tenderness he was feeling. All her instincts warned her not to fight. She could smell the aqua vitae on his breath, and she knew that it would take very little to drive him over the line into mindless, tragic rage. She could bear whatever he did to her, as long as they survived to forgive one another. Rape would hurt and humiliate her, but it would not break her spirit.

And if she could only make herself relax, perhaps it would not be rape. So far, despite his harsh words, he had not been overly rough. She told herself that this was Roger, the man she'd ached to give herself to for nearly a year; Roger, who could arouse her to passion with a look, a finger-brushing touch. And yet she felt no passion now.

Why? Always before she had warmed to his caresses, but not this time, not on the night he would finally take her. Had Geoffrey's assault done something to cripple her natural desires? The Frenchman's touch had filled her with revulsion, and as Roger duplicated those unwelcome caresses, fondling her breasts, pressing his legs between hers to part them, the nausea and terror she'd experienced last night in Geoffrey's arms began to well up from the place where she'd hidden it, buried it, slammed the door on it.

Quite suddenly she began to squirm, arching her body against his in an effort to free herself. Her struggles brought her pelvis tight against Roger's manhood, exciting him all the more, blasting what remained of his control. He stopped trying to free her breasts from the bodice and simply swept her skirts up over her hips. He tore away the delicate lawn of her shift, leaving nothing but her exquisitely smooth flesh, straining now against him, kicking and writhing as he anchored her firmly with his knees, his thighs, his chest, his arms.

"No!" she cried as he dragged her fists away from his chest. "Do not do this, Roger!"

He closed his heart to her protests. With calculated brutality he pinioned her arms against the pillow, then dragged the dress over her head and off. Breathing hard, nigh to bursting with lust, he stared at her slender naked body. He slid one hand over her soft flesh, between her breasts and down until he found the thatch of burnished curls, and beneath it, the soft petals of her femininity. God, she was sweet. He touched her, parted her. Unlike the last time he had caressed her, there was no moistness, no arousal. It shouldn't matter; he wasn't doing this for her pleasure. But it disturbed him nevertheless. He wasn't accustomed to using force—the women he took to bed were always as ready and eager as he.

He raised himself on one elbow and looked down into her face. Her eyes were wide, wild. "No, damn you," she whispered. She was trembling. "How dare you do this to me?"

For an instant he hesitated. He had never seen her look so hurt, so outraged, not even that afternoon in the cave on Thorncroft Overhang when she'd thought he meant to murder her. The image jogged something in his memory. *I made a terrible mistake today because I followed my brain instead of my heart,* she had told him. Alexandra had been wrong about him. What if he were wrong about her?

But he couldn't be wrong. She was the only outsider who'd known his plans last night, the only possible traitor. And she'd been there watching, caressed by Geoffrey, brazenly admitting her crime. He hardened himself again. "Did you or did you not reveal my plans to Geoffrey?"

"No! It was . . ." She stopped, swallowing the truth.

"It was who? Alan?" His voice lashed her like a whip. "He didn't come back last night. Are you accusing Alan?"

"No," she said miserably. Her voice dropped to a whisper. "It was through me that they found out, but it was not my intention, Roger, I swear. Geoffrey had me tortured on the rack."

"Torture victims don't walk about an hour later as if nothing had happened. Besides, the Alexandra Douglas I thought I knew would have had to be torn apart before she'd have breathed a word in betrayal of me."

"I'm no saint, Roger! I have weaknesses, and pain happens to be one of them!"

"Were you or were you not in Geoffrey's bed last night?"

"Yes, but you don't understand—"

"I understand all I need to know. Silence!" he added as she tried to speak again. He covered her mouth with one rough hand. "If he really had you racked, what I am going to do to you now will be far less disagreeable, I assure you. So stop mewling in protest and accept your punishment."

"I love you!" she cried, truly enraged now. "And I'm determined that our first coming together will not be in punishment!"

So saying, she began to fight in earnest, reminding Roger that she was not as easily subdued as most women. She bit his hand hard, drawing blood, and doubled up her fist to strike a blow at his genitals. She missed—just—and was having another try when he seized her wrists once again and forced them down beside her shoulders. She kicked instead and laughed at him as he struggled to keep her arching body pinned to the bed. Laughed! But her face was twisted in anger.

"You'll have to tie me again," she taunted him. "That's the only way you'll have me. You think I can't stop you, Roger?" Her knee drove upward, with better aim this time. He choked in pain. She wrenched her arms free and raked her nails across his face. "I'll not be treated like this!"

Roger cursed as, slippery as a serpent woman, she escaped his grip and rolled with the sea's motion to the floor. Damn her! He was about to roll after her when he saw the metallic flash of his dagger. Jesus Christ! Alexandra rose to her knees beside the bunk, her red hair tangled wildly on her shoulders and breasts, her green eyes huge and round and dilated with fury.

She held the knife loose and ready in the palm of her hand. "Now," she said softly. "Things are going to be different. I'll use this—you know I am capable of it. You've driven me past all boundaries, Roger."

He could have taken it from her, of course. But to do so, he would have to hurt her. He didn't want to hurt her, he admitted to himself. He didn't want to break her—not her, not Alix. There was something in her eyes—something proud and passionate, something glorious. Look at her, barebreasted as an Amazon, and as heart-stoppingly militant. His love for her swept through him, disregarding all the voices that ordered it to hide its miserable face.

"You've misjudged me," she went on. "You've had reason to do so—that I don't deny. But what's between us ought to be stronger than reason. Were it not for the fact that I once made a similar mistake about you, I'd be tempted to thrust this dagger into your vile mistrustful heart!"

He held out his hand, deliberately pitching his voice low. "Give it to me."

"No." A strange glimmer came into her eyes, making them greener than ever. "'Tis my orders you're obeying, sir. Lie down."

"What the hell—"

"Do it." She rose to her feet, her body undulating with the ship, seeming to have found perfect rhythm with the rough motion of the sea. She had her sea legs already, after so short a time aboard. She took to the ocean as readily as he. "Down, quickly, on your back."

"Why?"

"Why? Did I ask you why when you came at me with your naked dagger, your manhood throbbing with anticipation, lechery written all over your face? Men take much delight in rape, it seems. Can a woman vent her anger in like manner? We shall see." She pressed the flat of the dagger against his hair-covered chest. "Obey me, Roger."

He couldn't credit her words, but the furious determination on her face was impossible to deny. She was in earnest. Once again he debated making the two or three economical movements that would put her at his mercy; once again he dismissed the idea. He could not bear to see her humbled, not by him, not by anyone. For surely nowhere on the face of the earth would he ever find another woman to match his fiercely brave and beautiful Alexandra Douglas.

And so, moving slowly, dreamily, scarcely believing his own actions, he did her bidding, lying full length on his back on the bunk. He waited, holding her gaze while she stared down at him, hesitating. Then he closed his eyes and groaned as she gracefully joined him on the bed, straddling his body and cradling his aching manhood between her thighs.

Alexandra wasn't certain what had possessed her—she didn't think about it; she couldn't. Her head was buzzing with anger, but the secret place between her legs that had been clenched and cold just minutes ago had suddenly become infused with heat. Rape her, would he? After all she had gone through on his account? Damn him! "For a year you have rejected me. Now you would take me in violence, as a punishment." She slid the blade of the knife down over his chest to his hard, flat stomach. She exerted no pressure, but the threat was there. "I do not deserve such treatment. I have not betrayed you, neither with my words nor with my body. But since you don't believe that, 'tis I who will punish you."

"This is punishment?" Roger's voice had lightened to something close to a laugh.

"You find it amusing to be sat upon, threatened, handled . . ." She interrupted herself briefly to brush her fingers over his stiffened member. " . . . intimately, against your will?"

"Not amusing, exactly," he gasped as her fingers continued, rather tentatively, to explore. Dear Christ. He had to close his eyes again because the sight of her naked body riding his set off convulsions in his groin. For a moment he thought he might explode in her hand. Good God, had it been that long since he'd had a woman? He couldn't remember. He didn't want to remember. There was no other woman for him but her. No matter what she'd done. "I don't believe this," he muttered.

She wouldn't have believed it, either, had she been able to think . . . to stand back and observe what she was doing. But she was totally caught up . . . and it was a wonderful, liberating feeling. She traced the swirls of black hair on his flesh with the tip of her knife, enjoying the sight of his lean virile body lying submissive beneath hers. She let his heat penetrate her limbs; she bent her head and nuzzled his chest, intoxicated by his taste, his musky masculine scent. Seductively she rubbed her breasts against his chest. The craving in her belly multiplied a hundredfold.

"Ah, Alix . . . sweet Christ," he moaned as she moved against him. His erection was rampant now, and every motion she made delivered shocks of unbearably sharp sensation. "My love, I want you so much." He molded her buttocks beneath his palms, trying to position her to receive his ready thrust, but she resisted. He felt the prick of the knife once again, on his shoulder.

"Not yet." Her voice was husky. "Curb your impatience. I am a maid, and Merwynna has warned me that I must be soft inside, and yielding, to lessen the pain of penetration. I have had enough of pain. I wish to be further prepared." She moved the knife to the pulse beating in the hollow of his throat. "You are experienced in these matters. Pleasure me."

Roger drew a deep breath, then let it out in a burst of frustrated laughter. He couldn't believe what she'd just said. Everything had run together; nothing made any sense. Surely no virgin would straddle him shamelessly and play sexual games with a knife? "What of Geoffrey de Montreau's bed, sweet maid?"

Her frank green eyes looked directly into his. *"One who cannot.* I put a witch's curse upon him to save myself from his attempted rape."

"Oh, certainly, Alexandra—"

"Be still. Do not say again that you do not believe me or I will put the same curse upon you."

He raised his hands to her breasts and gently kneaded them. Has she gone mad? he wondered. Have I? "Put no curse on me, sweetling. I am at your disposal. If you command me to pleasure you, I will obey."

His thumbs isolated her nipples, passing over and over them until they hardened. He twirled them, tugged them, pinched them gently, noting with satisfaction the slackness that came over her features as he aroused her, the increasing fire in her eyes.

Breathing hard with his own arousal, he swept her entire body with his hands—her shoulders and arms, her breasts, her belly, her hipbones, her thighs. One hand moved slowly to tease the tangled thatch just above the mound of her femininity—it was flame-colored, like the hair on her head. He feathered the curls there, moving his fingers in rhythmic circles that dropped ever lower. She made a sound deep in the back of her throat as he touched the tender, vulnerable flesh between her legs and probed her gently. She was moist now; she was hot. Her eyes closed; she swayed under his expert touch. The dagger slipped out of her fingers and thumped upon the floor.

"Kiss me," he whispered. "Oh, God, love, kiss me." He pulled her down until she was sprawled on top of him. His mouth sought hers, he drank her in. He moved his tongue over hers, teasing, courting; then he caught her bottom lip between his teeth and bore down enough to make her cry with passion and arch her lower body yearningly against his.

"Alix, Alix." This was the woman he loved. Sweet, passionate, responsive. And exciting. Even now she was not granting him total control. She was taunting him with her breasts, the witch, and moving so lithely astride him that his attempts to hold her still and claim her irrecovably were futile.

"Touch me again," he urged her. He captured her hand and moved it down his body. "I want to feel your fingers around me."

Willingly she explored his thick and throbbing shaft,
delighting when he sighed and shuddered beneath her touch.
His response surprised and pleased her. For the first time
in her life she felt truly a woman. She hadn't expected to
be able to elicit so strong a reaction with her inexpert wooing.

"Not too much," he warned hoarsely. He was fighting
to breathe evenly, to restrain himself. "A man who has
desired a woman as long as I have desired you is not likely
to possess much control." With both hands he stilled her,
poising her intimately above him. Dear God, she was fair—
those flashing green eyes, that pale silky flesh, those clouds
of red hair. She was everything he had ever imagined, and
more. Last night was forgotten. He knew nothing but the
present, acknowledged nothing beyond the fact that her
light-boned femininity was the perfect complement to his
dark masculinity, and that he couldn't wait another second
to unify the two. "I'm going to take you now, beloved. Are
you soft inside? Are you ready?"

"Yes, yes."

"Then raise your hips and guide me."

She followed his directions, raising her body enough to
allow his manhood to press against her swollen, moistened
feminine tissues. The intimate sensation made her cry out.
He was breathing hard; they both were. His hands moved
to her waist as he carefully eased her down. He groaned
at the contact and thrust wildly, feeling himself slide
deliciously inside her opening, then lodge there. She was
tense.

"Relax, beloved, relax." He found her breast again and
fondled her encouragingly. He drove harder, his body trembling as he desperately tried to curb the lust raging inside
him. It mustn't be over too fast . . . she needed time . . . he
should have brought her to her pleasure first with his hands
or with his mouth, as he had done that night in the witch's
cottage . . . God, she was so small inside. And she was tense.
She was hanging on to his shoulders with nails that bit into
his flesh, and her body was recoiling from his, refusing him
entrance.

She *was* a virgin, he realized. Of course, *of course* she
was a virgin, and of course Geoffrey de Montreau had lied.

"Alix?" He began to tremble. "Goddammit, Alexandra!" He tried to withdraw from her, knowing with sick self-loathing that he hadn't truly believed her until this moment. Body of Christ! He was debauching a virgin; he was injuring his oldest friend. He was doing the very thing he'd tried for so many months to avoid.

"Don't stop." She slid her fingers into his beloved dark hair. "Please. You must cease being 'one who will not.' The prophecy is fulfilled: *one who cannot, one who will not, one who dares not, one who dies*. Geoffrey, you, Alan, and Will. It is over. I love you."

"Alix, God! What *else* did he lie about? I abducted you, hurt you . . . I came in here tonight fully intending to brutalize you." His voice trailed off as the full implications of Geoffrey's treachery assailed him. "You are innocent!" he added, almost in accusation. "I can't take a virgin, not this way, not with rage and anger between us . . . you'll hate me."

She bent her head and pressed her lips to his. "Enough, my lord. Where's your gallantry? Virgin I may be, but I've sense enough to know that this is no moment to reject a lady." She smiled, her green eyes flashing mischief at him. "If you will not, then I must be the one to finish this." She blinked her eyes shut for an instant, gathering her courage, then pressed down hard, impaling herself upon him. She gasped once as something gave within the soft folds of her femininity. There was pressure and fullness, but very little pain. "There," she laughed. "The wretched deed is done!"

Roger groaned as he felt the exquisite sensation of her warm flesh sheathing the entire length of him. It sent him careening over the edge. Quick as a dream he tumbled her backward so her head was at the foot of the bunk and her body beneath him. He reestablished the intimate joining with a hard, deep thrust. "Witch-woman. Virgin you may be, but you've driven me mad." His thighs pressed hers more widely apart as he took her, possessed her, made her his own, over and over again. Nothing could stop him now. He was incapable of playing the skillful, sophisticated lover. He was full to bursting; he groaned, he cried out against her mouth as again and again he stroked her.

Alexandra began to move with him, watching, feeling, learning. His hands caressed her breasts, her throat, her hair. His lips sucked, his teeth nipped, his long-dammed passion burst in a storm that was as wild and inexorable as the sea. He heard her cry out too, recognizing the sound as one of passion, not protest. Which was just as well, for he was past restraint now, past control, incapable of slowing or waiting or gentling his drive toward release. He was as wild and frenzied as a man possessed.

And she was with him in his frenzy. Caught up in the tender savagery of love, she remembered what she'd felt the night last summer when he'd caressed her into showers of ecstasy, and she knew it was going to be like that again. Sobbing with pleasure, she clasped her legs around him, reveling in the feel of his rough body bearing hers ever higher, ever closer to the light. Then, just when she thought she could no longer endure the strange, delicious tension, the universe expanded and sucked both of them into the void together. Deep inside, her muscles danced—a dance of joy, a dance of fulfillment. He cried out her name and stiffened as he surged one final time inside her; she felt his pulsing warmth, and the gooseflesh that rose on his skin. But most of all, she felt his essence, his spirit, his strong, primal energy—all that made him the man he was. She saw him, felt him, *knew* him in a manner that, for an instant, transcended the physical. It was as if their souls yearned toward each other, and, in a flash of glory, merged and became one.

It was a long time before either of them moved or spoke. Alexandra was profoundly moved. She had looked into the sun and experienced its golden heat, its fury, and paradoxically, its peace. Roger, too, was shaken. This was different from anything he'd ever known before. This was special— a joining not only of bodies but also of hearts and minds. This was a gift.

"Am I heavy, beloved?" he asked finally.

"It is a dear burden, but a burden nonetheless," she confessed, smiling and kissing his mouth, his hair, his chin. He carefully withdrew from her and rolled to the side, pushing himself up on one elbow and continuing to stroke her gently.

"I was too rough with you by far, sweetheart," he said, shaking his head regretfully. The fact that his uncontrolled, ferocious lovemaking had given her pleasure astonished him. She had such passion in her, his Alix, his Amazon, his dearest love. He kissed her again, giving her all the tenderness he'd been unable to offer her before. She was curled against him, quiet now, unresisting.

His fingers touched her lightly between the thighs and came away wet with her blood—the proof, if any could possibly be desired at this point, of her innocence. He cursed softly and rose from the bed to fetch a damp cloth from a copper washbasin. "Here, love, let me take care of you." He sat down beside her and bathed her gently. "Am I hurting you?" he whispered when she shivered slightly and tried to close her legs. "'Tis like this only once, beloved. From now on you will know nothing but pleasure. I promise, Alix. No pain, ever again."

"It doesn't hurt much. Stings a little, that's all. I just felt a little . . . I don't know . . . embarrassed to have you doing that. It seems so intimate."

Smiling, he dropped a kiss on the curly mound of her womanhood. "Such feelings are natural, I daresay, though I do not intend to allow you long to indulge them. There will be no place for embarrassment or shame between us, sweetling. I love you. You're part of me now."

"Roger." She was staring at her own blood on the cloth and beginning to tremble. Her eyes turned dark. "You were going to rape me, kill me. You called me horrible names, you tied my wrists and put a knife to my throat, you—"

"Shh, love, it's over." He raked a hand through his dark hair, then tossed the cloth back in the basin and lay down beside her again. "It's over and we're both still here." He kissed her forehead, her temple, the lobe of her ear. "I love you. I've always loved you. And I would beg you to forgive me, if it did not seem, in sooth, too great a boon to ask."

She turned her face against his throat, tasting the sweet dampness of his skin. "I forgive you freely, for I love you too, more than life itself." But her voice broke, turning the last few words into a sob.

He pulled her fiercely against him. "Oh, Christ, sweetling, don't."

"No, no, I need this, I need it. I wanted to cry before but I couldn't. I thought there was something wrong with me. I feel better now. I . . ." Her voice trailed off as she pressed close against him, grateful for the shelter of his arms, as finally, for the first time since Geoffrey had waylaid her, she was able to give way to her terror and her grief. Roger held her, comforted her throughout, murmuring love words in her ear and allowing his own tears to mingle with hers on the pillow where he had finally consummated the only love he had ever known.

27

As ALEXANDRA watched the sunrise through the diamond-paned Venetian glass of Roger's cabin window the next morning, the brilliant pinks and apricots that sprang out of darkness seemed to be a metaphor for the state of her own soul. And his. He was sleeping beside her, his face peaceful and free of tension for the first time in weeks. Gently Alexandra brushed a lock of dark brown hair off his forehead, loving the silkiness of his hair under her fingers, still feeling, after long hours of loving, the need to touch him, caress him, and have him respond with all his tender violence and passion.

As if he sensed her desire, Roger's thick lashes lifted, revealing his sparkling brown eyes. He gave her a lazy smile. "Good morrow, fair lady. I trust you slept well?" As he spoke, one of his hands moved lightly over her flank while the other sought her breasts.

"I hardly slept at all, as well you know! You kept waking me up for more lecherous debauchery."

He laughed huskily. "I fear you're thoroughly corrupted now, beloved." He blew gently on her ear. "Regrets?"

"One," she replied so promptly that a furrow formed across his brow. She kissed it away. "I regret only that it took me an entire year to seduce you. A more virtuous rake I've seldom met."

She expected him to smile again, but instead, in a swift surge of physical power, he rolled her under him, pinning the arms that playfully came up to push against his shoulders. "Vixen," he said, parting her lips with a rough kiss. "And I was trying to be so noble, protecting you from myself."

"We were meant to be together, Roger. It is our destiny."

"I love you," he told her, as he had told her over and over throughout the night. "We will be wed as soon as possible."

"Our bodies, our spirits are wed already. The rest doesn't matter."

"In the eyes of the world it does. As it will matter to our children."

The thought of children gave her pause. Because of the circumstances of their coming together, she had in her possession none of the herbal ingredients prescribed by Merwynna to forestall such an event. She would welcome Roger's child, it was true; but she had no wish to be quickly pregnant. Particularly aboard a ship sailing for a strange land.

Unwilling to dwell upon the subject, she said lightly, "To think you will wed me after all, when you swore so many times 'twould never happen!"

"Are you gloating, my lady fair?" His legs moved subtly between hers and pressed, spreading her thighs.

"Just a tiny bit, perhaps."

In a long slow stroke he joined their bodies once again, making her gasp with pleasure. His mouth took hers fiercely. "I haven't been so lusty since I was a callow youth who'd just discovered love."

"As I am now," she laughed. "I never thought it would be so perfect—it makes everything bearable, almost."

"Almost," he agreed, turning his mind from the things that weren't bearable—the things he'd succeeded last night in forgetting. She'd given him the first peace he'd known since . . . he couldn't remember since when. Perhaps he had *never* been at peace before. It was like a lovely dream, the sort that usually fades with the morning light. Yet it was morning, and the dream continued.

He felt her catch his rhythm as instinctively as if they'd

been lovers for years. He raised his head and smiled; her eyes were open, she smiled back, her features relaxed and sweet. It was slower this time, more leisurely, gentler. They spun out their pleasure, rising gradually toward a peak, watching each other and communicating both physically and mentally as the fire built and flashed and swept them into its heart and out the other side. When it was over, she giggled with delight, and he, too, found himself joining in her laughter. Then she closed her clear green eyes and fell asleep in his arms.

Roger himself couldn't go back to sleep, although, God knew, he could have used the rest. Yet his wakefulness was reflective, not fitful. As he lay beside her, holding her close and feeling her breath against his throat, his sense of peacefulness persisted.

All was explained, or nearly so. He understood now how cleverly Geoffrey de Montreau had manipulated them all. Rage leapt and burned in Roger as he thought of Alexandra being abducted by Geoffrey, tortured, nearly raped. For this, he swore, he would kill the Frenchman someday. But fantasies of revenge did little to relieve his own guilt at having treated the woman he loved scarcely less brutally himself.

"When I saw you there on the strand, with his arm around your waist, his hand on your breasts, it's as though I went mad," he tried to explain to her. "The dissenters—women and old men, most of them—had been butchered, Francis lay there *in extremis* after taking a sword cut that had been intended for me, the world was falling to pieces, and I prayed, irrationally, to see you one last time before I died. Then suddenly there you were, in the arms of my enemy—"

"Shh," she whispered, holding his tension-slick body tightly against her own. "It's over. Your reaction was natural. I understand."

"I should have known at once that you had been coerced. You're no more capable of betraying me than I was capable of murdering Will."

She smiled weakly up at him. "We haven't done very well at trusting each other, have we?"

He'd kissed her then, slowly, earnestly, determined that she should feel his love, know it, believe in it. "We'll do better, I swear to you. You're my soul, Alix. I adore you."

Later he'd raised his head to gaze into her honest eyes while the sea churned and rolled beneath them. "It was Alan who betrayed us, wasn't it?" He didn't know why he hadn't realized this before. She'd denied it on the beach, but lying to shield Alan was exactly the kind of thing he'd expect her to do.

"No," she said, far too quickly.

"Alexandra, I may have been a credulous idiot, but I haven't lost every bit of sense I possess. Alan is easily frightened—he's been a coward all his life. One threat of torture or death and he'd have buckled like an empty coat of mail. You're protecting him, aren't you?"

She had sighed then and told the truth, insisting that Alan had had no choice, that he had, in fact, acquitted himself quite bravely. "He didn't buckle at all—he defended me stoutly." She explained how Geoffrey de Montreau had ordered her bound to the rack in Alan's presence. "They commenced turning the wheel, making poor Alan watch. It was him they questioned, not me. I begged him to keep silence, but of course he could not."

"No. Nor would I have, sweetling."

"Geoffrey must have realized Alan loved me." Her voice dropped sorrowfully here. "I had only just realized it myself. Poor Alan. Why are things such a tangle? He never told me—he was *one who dares not*."

"I knew," Roger admitted. "I thought he'd be good for you ... it was another reason why I felt I ought to stay away."

"I love Alan as a brother. I assumed he felt precisely the same way about me!"

He had laughed and kissed her fiery hair. "No man with any real blood in his veins could feel brotherly about you for long, love. You've turned into a very exciting woman. It is natural for a man to want to possess you."

"Rot!" she had snorted, obviously—and rather endearingly—not believing him.

It had been harder to ask her what had happened in

Geoffrey's bedchamber, but he needed to make her understand that nothing, however sordid, could alter his love for her one iota. And so he held her close and murmured, "About this attempted rape Geoffrey practiced upon you. When, during all the hectic events of the night, did he find time for that?"

She shivered, convincing him his instinct was right. This was a demon that must be exorcised. Now, at the start. "After the torture session. You're right, I think, that he must have been in a hurry. Mayhap it was that, and not my witch's hex, that prevented him from . . ." Her voice trailed off.

He rubbed her temples lightly with his thumbs. "Tell me. I love you. There's nothing you cannot share with me."

"His body . . . his touch made me so ill I thought I would vomit. 'Twas a defilement. He forced me to touch him, and he was cold, passionless, horrible—like the snake you once told me he was. He couldn't . . . His manly parts were not so vital as yours . . ." She stopped again. "It makes me sick to remember."

"Then forget," he said swiftly, cursing Geoffrey under his breath.

"I was afraid you wouldn't want me anymore, after that monster had so debased me."

"The crime was his, not yours, and it does not debase you, beloved. Do you understand? Nothing could ever debase you, Alexandra. Your spirit is pure as fire, and it's that I love, although your sweet body is very dear to me also."

She smiled.

"I love you, Alix. Whatever harm he did, I will erase. I promise, my sweetling," he said as he reverently renewed his courtship of her. "I promise."

Roger must have slept again after all, for it was full daylight when a loud pounding on his cabin door made him jerk upright in his bunk. Beside him, Alexandra rolled over and groaned. "Christ, lass," he whispered to her. "'Tis well into a new day and we're both still abed. 'Tis not my usual habit, I assure you. My men probably think you've murdered me in here."

"I murdered you! If anyone's life was in danger last night, 'twas mine, not yours."

"Ha. Who brandished a dagger during the act of love? Who ravished whom?"

"You were about to ravish me! I was merely defending myself. Leave it to a man to twist the truth," she added in feigned outrage. "I believe I shall put a hex on you."

He dropped a kiss on the top of her head. "You're a terror, poppy-top, you know that?" Laughing, he rose and strode stark naked to the door, opening it a crack. Tom Comstock, his surgeon, was standing there, with Daniel Bunty just behind him. Daniel looked belligerent, but Tom's sad eyes met his own serenely, as always.

"Francis?" Roger asked in sudden dread. While he'd been romping with the woman he loved, had Francis slipped into a solitary death?

"He's hanging on," Tom replied. "That's not why we've come."

Roger untensed slightly and offered up a silent prayer of thanks. "Well then?"

"The young woman you're holding prisoner is a patient of mine," Comstock said slowly. "I wish to see her."

"Indeed?" Roger's eyebrows went up. "Well, I doubt very sincerely that she'll receive you at the moment, gentlemen."

"You were stinking drunk last night," Daniel said. "What have you done to the lassie?"

"'Tis a little late for the two of you to be leaping to her defense," Roger returned with some amusement. "If you'd really been concerned for her welfare, you'd have found some way to restrain me last night."

At these words, both men looked alarmed, and Roger took pity on them. He looked back over his shoulder to where Alexandra was sitting up in bed with the bedclothes up to her chin and her long hair cascading wildly over the dark wool of his blankets. "There're two rather tardy knights of chivalry asking after your health, sweetling. What shall I tell them?"

Alexandra's voice came sweet and clear. "I am very well, gentlemen, thank you."

"You mean you're there in that bed with him willingly?" Bunty asked, as Roger opened the door more widely.

"Oh yes. And I was beginning to think I'd never get here—it's taken me a whole year to seduce him."

Bunty opened his mouth, then shut it again.

"But I thank you kindly for your concern," she added politely.

Mumbling to himself, Daniel Bunty left. Comstock stayed for another few minutes, long enough for Alexandra to smile at him and say, "You see, sir, I am better."

The physician's eyes moved silently from her radiant face to Roger's naked body. Roger frowned and reached for his clothes from the floor. "Don't go all priestly on me, for God's sake, Tom. I haven't beguiled her with honeyed promises if that's what you think." He sat down, pulled on a shirt and slung an arm around her shoulders, drawing her head against his throat. "The lady is no longer my prisoner. She is my betrothed wife."

Comstock nodded solemnly. "And when do you expect to marry?"

"As soon as possible." Tom Comstock was one of the few men who could make him feel uncomfortable. "Don't glare at me like that, Tom; you're worse than her father!"

"I'm not glaring. You look infinitely better than you looked yesterday, both physically and spiritually. So does your lady. For that I am exceedingly thankful."

"How are your other patients?" Alexandra asked.

"Alive. The boy is better and will live. The woman has a struggle on her hands—the next few hours will determine her fate. As for Francis, there's no change. No sign, yet, of infection, but he hasn't regained consciousness. The longer he drifts in the nether world, the worse his chances are."

"Roger should sit beside him and talk to him," Alexandra suggested. "It may help."

Comstock regarded her curiously. "It may indeed. How do you know that, mistress?"

"I have training in the healing arts. Perhaps I can be of assistance to you in your infirmary."

"I would welcome your help."

"I'll dress and come at once."

"No," said Comstock with a smile. "This day is for you and your lover. The world will crowd in soon enough." He nodded to his captain. "You see? You were wrong—God is more just than you supposed."

"I like him," Alexandra said decidedly as the physician left.

Roger uttered a soft curse. Paradoxically, Tom's words had reminded him that apart from the private world of their love, there was little to be joyful for. "You ought to like him—he's a good man. Me, on the other hand . . . I don't deserve a woman like you. Christ, Alexandra, there's so much you don't know about me. So much in my past that would hurt and sicken you."

"If you're referring to Celestine, your physician told me the truth of that yesterday morning. I know how she died— I probably understand her condition far better than you do, in fact. Malplaced pregnancies are invariably fatal, Roger."

"She wouldn't have *been* pregnant if I hadn't insisted on taking her. I was responsible for her, you see. Her brother had placed her in my care. She was fresh out of a convent, for God's sake."

"You told me once she was no virgin."

"It's true. Convent education or not, she was experienced and quite adept." He envisioned Celestine's lush, wanton body, heard her husky, liquid voice inviting him to love her. "She was young, but she had come early to her womanhood. I cannot even say with absolute certitude that the child she lost was mine. Tom told me later that she may well have been pregnant for several weeks longer than she had been with me."

"Did you tell any of this to Geoffrey?"

"I tried. It only made him angrier. What brother believes his sweet young sister to be of easy virtue? Besides, the condition of her maidenhead is not the point. Virgin or whore, I should not have touched her. I used her without love. When she expected more than that, we fought. We argued bitterly on the night she died, and I feared, I still fear, that the anguish I caused her must have brought on her miscarriage."

"Did you beat her, strike her, hurt her in any way?"

"No, of course not. Why would you think I—" He stopped, remembering last night.

She touched his arm reassuringly. "I don't think it. 'Tis what her brother told me. He had a witness, he said, someone on your ship who'd reported to him that you had physically abused Celestine. I didn't believe it, but Geoffrey, apparently, did."

"Our arguments were probably overheard—there is little that remains a secret in the close quarters of a ship. His witness, no doubt, was Peters, that scum whom we believe to have been involved in the queen's 'accident' on the quayside. But he is wrong if he believes I ever raised a hand in violence to Celestine. Still—"

"Still, nothing," she interrupted. "She did not die of a miscarriage, Roger, not precisely. She died because the child had taken root in the wrong part of her body. It is an error of nature. The babe had no chance, and neither did she. Do you understand? You did not bring on her death."

"Except in placing the child within her in the first place."

"No, my love. Listen: the act of love is life-giving, not death-dealing. You yourself have taught me that. Anyway, the past is dead and your former lover is gone forever. Your present lover would be obliged if you applied yourself to the task of forgetting her!"

He smiled and touched her lips with his. "She is forgotten already, I promise you." They kissed sweetly, but just as Alexandra was beginning to melt against him once again, he turned his face away, still troubled. "Consider the present, then, if not the past. Look at my crimes against you—in front of witnesses, I abducted one of the queen's ladies at knife-point! The story will be all over London by now. The evil was mine, but 'twill be you who suffers. Your honor is blasted forever. Even our marriage will not erase the blot upon your name. You will never again, for instance, be received at court."

"I wasn't brought up to be a fine court lady. I had no

joy in my months there, and I shall not miss that kind of life."

"But what kind of life can I offer you? Between them, your father and Geoffrey will make sure I'm branded heretic and traitor. I cannot return to England, Alix—have you considered that?"

She had a moment's pain as she thought of her mother, her father, Merwynna, Alan. Quickly she put it aside. *"Whither thou goest, I shall go,"* she quoted softly. *"Thy country shall be my country, thy god shall be my god."*

Roger stared at her; his brown eyes were shining with unshed tears. "I don't deserve you," he repeated. "I fear some unforeseen circumstance will arise to drive us apart."

"Must you always look at the dark side?" Seizing his hands, she placed them on her breasts. "Come," she whispered. "Show me again the fire and the light."

He needed no further urging. Moments later she knew the pleasure of his fierce yet tender loving. "Tell me you're mine," he demanded roughly, his carnal mouth poised just above hers while his strong body pinned her deliciously to the bed. "I want to hear you swear it."

"Forever, beloved," she promised as he joined his flesh to hers.

28

L ATER that same day, Alexandra sat beside Francis Lacklin's sickbed in Tom Comstock's tiny infirmary. She was bathing his face and talking to him, determined to bring him back to consciousness. Francis, she had decided, was going to live.

She was determined to pull him through, by willpower alone, if necessary. It was the least she could do to make amends for the massacre on the riverbank. This man was Roger's friend and she was not going to let him die.

Lacklin's face was still and quiet, his breathing barely perceptible, his bones sunken in the manner that often precedes death. Alexandra could not help but remember sitting beside Will Trevor in similar circumstances, trying to talk him back to life despite everyone's insistence that it was hopeless. Francis Lacklin, she recalled, had been the only person who'd consistently watched with her, the only person besides herself who seemed to believe in the possibility of Will's regaining consciousness. How ironic, she thought, that he should be lying in a similar kind of coma now.

Although she'd never liked Lacklin, Alexandra experienced a distinct change of heart as she sat beside him now. She had Francis to thank for Roger's continued existence. His big body had absorbed the sword blow that would have killed her lover. That was enough to make her forgive the man for all the danger he'd led Roger into.

Had Roger and Francis been wrong to do what they had done? she wondered now. She was no longer certain. Perhaps the dissidents were correct in wanting to purify the Church, to cast off hundreds of years of institutionalized abuse. Should they be burned simply because they wanted to restore something closer to the simple forms of worship that Christ himself had practiced when he'd walked upon this earth?

As a lady of Queen Mary's court, she had avoided facing these questions for months. Of necessity, she had closed her eyes and ears to the screams of the martyrs at Smithfield—she would not have been able to maintain her loyalty to her mistress otherwise. But now she felt the queen had been wrong to force her religion down the throats of her people. It was the height of arrogance to declare that by burning their bodies, she would save their souls.

Arrogance . . . pride . . . the certainty that one was right and someone else was wrong: how often this all-too-human fault caused tragedy! It had led her to believe Roger was his brother's murderer, and him to believe she was Geoffrey's whore. To Mary Tudor all earthly evil took the form of heresy; to Geoffrey de Montreau the devil was personified in Roger. Was there no one who was free of this lamentable tendency to see the evil in everyone else's heart except one's own?

Even those who recognized their own faults didn't seem to be able to stop sinning. She had promised herself last summer at Chilton that she would not meddle. She'd failed miserably to keep that vow. And despite Roger's agony over the death of Celestine, he had come within a breath of violating—perhaps even killing—another young woman last night.

Sorrowfully she remembered Merwynna's words: *Knowledge does not save us, not even self-knowledge.*

What does save us, then?

That is something ye must discover for yerself.

She was no closer now to knowing the answer to that riddle than she'd been last summer.

Her head was throbbing slightly when she heard familiar footsteps approaching the infirmary. The door opened, and she lifted her eyes to Roger's.

He came in and sat down beside her. He stared at Francis, his lips pursed with worry. "You're very solemn. Is he worse?"

"No. He's going to pull through, I'm sure of it." It seemed important to say it, to believe it, if she wanted to make it true.

"Then what were you thinking about, love?"

She shrugged and smiled. "Weighty questions of ethics and religion, I warrant."

"That's a sure way to exhaust yourself."

"What do *you* believe?" she asked curiously. "Truly? You're so quick to feign cynicism that I cannot tell."

"'Tisn't feigned. The good Lord and I," he said dryly, "have never exactly been on the best of terms."

"You studied in a monastery; now you shelter heretics. Which are you, Roger, a Papist or a Puritan?"

"I am neither. Don't forget, I've also lived in the Turkish empire, with the infidel, as we so condescendingly call them. I learned something of Islam, a religion which is far more respectful of Christianity than most of us realize. The Koran writes of Jesus and considers him a prophet—did you know that?"

She shook her head, fascinated.

"Once I met a strange and wonderful holy man from the far reaches of Asia who taught me some of the meditation practices of the Hindus. I have met Buddhists, too, who seem to know far more of peace and brotherhood than we Europeans. There are many ways of worshiping God on this earth, Alexandra. I have yet to be convinced that any one of them is better than the others."

She stared at him round-eyed. "Papists and Puritans alike at least are Christians."

"Aye, but what does that signify? The followers of Islam sincerely believe that it is they who will enter Paradise while the Christians are cast into the pit. Who, I wonder, is right?"

"You don't believe in Jesus?"

He made a face. "I didn't say that. I consider myself a

Christian, yes, because the tenets of that faith are very deeply rooted in me. But I recognize that my religion is an accident of my birth. Had I been born in China, I might have been raised in Buddhism, perhaps, and grown up believing it was the ideal religion."

"But such a belief would have been wrong," she insisted. "Surely there can be only one God, one truth. We must send Christian missionaries to the countries in the world where they hold such erroneous beliefs and teach them, thereby saving their immortal souls."

"That is the usual answer," he said sharply. "Your mind is capable of better."

Chastened, she realized she had just parroted the sentiments of Mary Tudor. Arrogance, again. "Is there no truth to be found, then? How does one decide what to believe?"

"I'm not certain. There's a great deal I can't accept about the new Protestant doctrine, but one notion I'm drawn to is the belief that we can each commune directly with God, without the intercession of a hierarchy of clerics and saints. Prayer and meditation seem to be beneficial for the soul. I'm not sure it matters which deity you pray to, as long as you spend a few minutes a day at peace with yourself and try, of course, to lead a moral life."

Merciful heavens. She was in love with a man who didn't know which deity to pray to? "'Tis a good thing you're out of England," she said lightly. "If the bishops knew your extraordinary views, they'd have you tied to a stake in less time than it takes to blink."

"And you too, witch," he reminded her. "Did you not once tell Francis and me that your mentor in Westmor Forest worshiped the Old Gods of rocks and springs and trees? You're a pagan at heart, sweetling, despite your orthodox horror over my views."

"Aye," she laughed, chastened once again. "'Twas Merwynna and her gods I called upon for help when I was most sorely beset," she admitted. "You're right—in England they'd burn us both! 'Tis a lucky thing we've escaped the nasty country."

Frowning slightly, Roger got up from his bench and took a turn around the small infirmary, glancing at Tom's other patients in their beds as he passed. Comstock himself was not present; he'd gone to attend a sailor who'd slipped on the rigging and cracked his ankle.

Gently Alexandra massaged Francis Lacklin's temples. So much had changed since that morning last summer at Chilton when the three of them had accidentally met in Westmor Forest. These men had frightened her then, both of them. Who would have thought that in less than a twelve-month she would come around to loving one and tolerating the other?

Roger came near again, stopping his pacing by the head of his friend's bed. "Why don't you speak to him," she suggested. "'Tis possible that he may hear you. Merwynna says we must always talk to the sick if we wish to restore them to full consciousness. We must give him something in this world to grasp on to, so that he can pull himself back from the borders of death."

Roger reluctantly met her eyes. "I don't know what to say."

"You could thank him for saving your life. I've been doing that all afternoon. And you could tell him you love him—that worked wonders, you'll recall, with me."

To her amazement, Roger's expression changed to one of anguish and despair. "But I don't love him—not the way he wants. And there's a dark corner of my soul that would like nothing better than to be free of him forever."

Not the way he wants? Alexandra's mouth went dry. Good heavens, how did Francis Lacklin expect to be loved? She had another image of that morning in Westmor Forest when she'd come upon them practice-dueling—two powerful men panting, sweating, and naked to the waist. Alone, by choice, deep in the forest.

Sweet Jesu. She was not so innocent now as she had been then. "What on earth do you mean?"

Roger looked away. "Wise as you are, sweetling, I don't think you could possibly understand."

She rose to her feet, the deck heaving beneath her as the ship rolled through the still-choppy seas. She felt a little queasy. Was it possible that he and Francis . . .? Her mind veered away from completing the thought. "You really ought to talk to him. Would it be easier if I left you alone?"

He pushed a hand through his unruly hair. "Aye, perhaps it would. Go to my cabin. I'll join you there presently."

But it was several hours before he came to her. Alexandra spent them worrying, remembering his words about the things from his past that would horrify her. Snatches of conversation came back: *You're liable to be taken upstairs and introduced to certain unmentionable acts of sophisticated vice,* he had taunted her on the night she'd showed up at Chilton House clad as a boy. *There are mariners here this evening . . . and you know how they behave, deprived so long of the company of women.* He was himself a mariner. As was Francis. And it occurred to her now that she had never seen Francis Lacklin with a woman.

Except for brother-killing, he'd said to her in Merwynna's cottage, *there's no crime I haven't committed.* Christ have mercy. She'd always known that Lacklin had some sort of powerful hold on Roger, but it had never occurred to her before that it might be an unnatural one.

Her lover looked weary and discouraged when he slammed into the cabin at nightfall, pulling off his jerkin and sinking down in apparent exhaustion on his bunk.

"Is he dead?" Her mouth could hardly form the question.

Roger shook his head. "No. But he hasn't shown a single sign of life either, although I talked till I was dry."

"There's no infection yet?"

"According to Tom, no. But I get the impression—it's only my imagination, I suppose—that he no longer has much will to live. I think he knows that I love you, that we're together now. Which hardly provides him with much of an incentive."

Jesu! Alexandra waited, not daring to speak. She was afraid of what he might confess, afraid, yet simultaneously curious. Roger seemed unfocused in some way, too tired to monitor his own words. He hadn't slept very much last night. She ought to have insisted he sleep.

"He was wary of you, right from the beginning. He knew I loved you before I knew it myself. In his own way, he's as dangerous to you as Geoffrey was. If you had any sense, Alix, you'd pray for his death."

"I would never pray for any man's death . . ." She paused, took a deep breath, then added softly, " . . . be he lover of yours or no."

Roger raised his eyes to hers, obviously knocked speechless. "What did you say?" he managed.

Sitting down beside him, she stopped his words with light fingers against his lips. "Don't look like that," she whispered. "You don't have to explain anything to me. The months I spent at court were hardly conducive to innocence."

"Alexandra—"

"I can guess how you must feel about his injury," she plowed on doggedly. "Naturally you will grieve more intensely over a lover than a friend."

"You think Francis and I are lovers?"

"Well . . ." Her voice trailed off helplessly.

"And you're not gnashing your teeth in horror?"

"I don't think I've ever been much of a teeth-gnasher," she said sensibly. "What did you expect me to do—revile you for all time? I'm a classical scholar, remember? The Greek philosophers were always falling in love with some handsome young man."

"Alexandra, I am not a Greek philosopher."

She thought she saw the beginnings of a smile quirking the corners of his lips. Confused, she said, "No, of course not, but you might well have similar inclinations. I can understand that . . . I think."

"Christ, woman," he growled, "I assure you, when it comes to loving, all my inclinations are directed toward the female of the species. Francis and I are not—nor have we ever been—lovers."

"Oh." She blushed, feeling like an idiot.

"You have the right idea," he admitted, "but you've got one crucial element wrong. To put it simply—I like women. Francis is apparently drawn to men; that is, to one man in particular: me. But it isn't really physical—'tis deeper than that by far."

"He loves you but you cannot return his love?"

"Aye, lassie." He spoke heavily. "And it's slowly breaking him. Listen—from the time I was a lad of fifteen Francis has given what love he had to me. I don't know why. I never asked for it; nor have I deserved it." He paused briefly, then continued: "You remember, no doubt, that I served my first summer as a seaman on the same ship where Francis was a young officer."

"He was the only one who was kind to you."

"Yes. He saved me from attack, from rape, in fact." He went on to explain that Francis had protected him from the brutality of those coarse Mediterranean sailors. He'd been an idealistic youth with overly sensitive emotions, a slender, still-boyish body, and a face that was too perfect for his own good. He'd known the gentlemanly arts of fencing and horseback riding, but he'd had no experience with the dirty, body-to-body combat that went on in the dark alleys of every Mediterranean port. Francis had taken him in hand and taught him to defend himself, with his fists and his knife. He'd also given him books and taught him to play chess. He'd delighted in Roger's keen, insightful intellect. Despite the ten year difference in their ages, they had quickly become friends.

"When first I suspected it was something more than friendship he desired of me," he continued, "I gnashed *my* teeth. I was frightened; I felt betrayed. For all his fine brains and his gentle manners, he was no better than the perverse villains he'd saved me from, I concluded."

"What did he do to you?" she asked, wide-eyed.

"Nothing. He didn't touch me. He just got a little too full of wine one night and expressed the opinion that a male lover could be just as pleasant as a female lover. I got the impression that he was speaking from experience, and that this was the next thing he intended to teach me."

"So you ran away to the monastery?"

"Yes. I knew little then, of women. I was afraid that if Francis desired me, perhaps there was something wrong with me, too. Perhaps I shared the same vice. In which case, I'd better renounce the world and dedicate myself to the spirit rather than engage in acts I, rather melodramatically, considered foul perversions."

"I always wondered what on earth drove you into a monastery. You didn't seem the saintly, contemplative type."

"No," he agreed, grinning.

"And afterward? You met Francis again? When you returned to Chilton, you and he pretended you hadn't seen each other since those days on his ship. But it wasn't true, was it?"

"No. We ran into each other often in the Mediterranean, and we became friends, sharing battle, adventure, good sport, intellectual diversions. I suspected his feelings hadn't changed, but since he never mentioned the subject again, I didn't feel threatened.

"Over the years," he went on, "Francis saved my life several times with his deadly sword-arm. On the last such occasion, I was so grateful I promised him anything he wanted in return—a rash vow, I realized afterwards. There was one thing, of course, that I couldn't have given him. Thank God he didn't ask it of me."

"But what he *did* ask was that you help him smuggle heretics out of England?"

He nodded. "When I met the poor wretches, I was glad I'd agreed. This present group isn't the first, as you may or may not have realized. We've been at it for several months, using other ships besides my own. Francis was planning it in London last spring before Will died, and when I got home, he insisted I help him. He was nearly arrested then, which is why he went north to Chilton in the first place. London was, briefly, too dangerous for him."

She nodded, pleased at the way the pieces were finally fitting together—old doubts being resolved, old questions being answered. Which reminded her: "Roger, remember the day Ned died in the cave at Thorncroft Overhang?"

"How could I possibly forget?" he said wryly.

"You and Alan argued because he had overheard you plotting strategy with Francis."

"Aye. So what?"

"So Francis was still at Chilton."

"He was camping out in the forest for a few days. There were plans we still had to finalize, and it was always so difficult to talk privately at Chilton."

"The point is, he hadn't left for London after all. If he was in the forest that day, he could have been the person who strangled Ned. Which means . . . " She hesitated, then said it: "He could also have been the person who murdered Will."

Roger groaned loudly. "Lord have mercy. If you start that again, I will personally thrash your lovely little backside. Will died accidentally—we know that for a fact. Poor Mad Ned hanged himself, and Francis hadn't the slightest interest in either of them. There's an end to it, Mistress Never-Give-Up. Now, come here." He got up and divested himself of the rest of his clothing. "We've chatted long enough."

He then began to undress her, encountering no resistance. In sooth, her own fingers flew to unfasten her dress and slip it off her shoulders. Roger's breath caught as he brushed his fingers across one brownish-pink nipple. "Oh my lovely lady. Do you have any idea how often in the past few months I'd betake myself alone to my dreary bed and think of you, imagining how I'd touch you, kiss you, taste you . . . what I'd demand of you, and how willingly you'd comply?"

"I had a few such fantasies myself," she confessed.

"Mmm." He was kissing her. "Did you ever touch yourself, pretending it was me?"

"Well . . ." She blushed.

"Show me how."

"Roger!"

He took her hand and put it to her own breast. "Do it."

"I cannot. I'm ashamed."

"You needn't be. Your body is beautiful, sweetling. There's nothing about my desires or yours that we should ever be ashamed of." He smiled and replaced her fingers with his own, massaging her gently until her nipple hardened and tweaked in his palm. "After so many months of frustration, I'm taking great delight in imagining you similarly desperate, driven to fondling your own body and wishing your hands were mine."

"I thought such feelings were horribly sinful and that I should certainly go to hell."

He laughed and pulled her body down across his, gripping her firmly around the waist and sliding her up until his mouth could reach her breast. He took the nipple carefully between his teeth and drew upon it, then laved it with his tongue. Waves of pure liquid sensation gathered in her belly and flowed outward to the farthest reaches of her body. She moaned and rubbed herself against him.

"If I order you to caress yourself for my pleasure, Alix, you will not deny me."

"Because I've yielded up my virginity to you, you think I shall hereafter obey your every order? I fear you have a good deal to learn about me still."

One of his hands slipped between her legs, parting the sensitive folds of flesh there. His fingers moved, teasing her with devastating skill. She quickened against him, and his sensual onslaught escalated until he was rewarded with the soft sounds of her gasping and pleading for release. Quickly he rolled over and slid between her thighs, his knees parting her, making certain she was securely positioned for his entry. "Rebellious little baggage. I love you."

"Then obey *my* orders, sir, and come to me."

"So I shall," he vowed, and did her bidding.

A day later, with Alexandra sitting at his bedside, Francis Lacklin groaned, stirred, and spoke. Alexandra dropped the cool cloth with which she had been soothing his brow and stared at him in dismay. Was he delirious? Merciful God, had he meant what he had just said? And did he realize she was here beside him, that she had heard it?

His return to consciousness was sudden; Roger was not present, although he'd spent many long hours by his old friend's side. As had Alexandra. Despite what she'd learned about Lacklin's feelings for Roger, she bore him no ill will. On the contrary, she was delighted to find out that he was human, after all, with passions and weaknesses. And she was more determined than ever to make him live.

She'd been talking nonstop for an hour or so, craftily informing Francis that she was in the process of rethinking her position on the question of heresy. Perhaps he could instruct her about the theological positions of such dissidents as Martin Luther and John Calvin. If the possibility of converting her didn't rouse him, she thought secretly, nothing would.

Without warning, just as she was gamely trying to discuss the problem of good deeds versus divine grace, Lacklin had started to speak, saying with perfect clarity: "Priscilla Martin . . . must be found and silenced . . . she has guessed . . ." He tossed restlessly. His eyes were still closed; he appeared to be dreaming. He spoke again, his voice raised in agony this time: "Roger must never know."

Sweet Christ in heaven! Found and silenced—did he mean killed? The beautiful, elegant Pris—what had she guessed? And what was it that "Roger must never know"?

Pris Martin had disappeared from Chilton on the day after the inquiry into Ned and Will's deaths. Fled without a word, as if devils were after her. And when Alan had accidentally come upon her in Oxford, she had been frightened to see him. Why? What did Pris Martin know?

Had it been Francis who murdered Will?

As Alexandra sat there, stunned, Lacklin stirred once more and opened his eyes. They looked into hers with full and complete recognition. "Alexandra?"

"Hello, Francis. So you're back. Your wound is doing nicely—you're going to live. Roger will be so relieved." She knew she was speaking overly fast—babbling—but couldn't stop herself. "He ordered you not to die, you know, but we weren't sure you were going to follow instructions."

Francis took several deep breaths, coughed, then stated, "I do not intend to die. There is too much work to be done." He rested a moment, then asked, "Where are we?"

He seemed to be unaware of the startling words he had spoken. Thank God! If he knew she had overheard him, he might decide that she too should be silenced! "We're off the coast of Flanders, I understand. We're going to land and set ashore your heretics . . . those who survived to escape."

"You seem to have survived nicely, I see." His voice was reedy from disuse. "Has Roger forgiven you? He must love you far more than I thought."

"I didn't betray you." How dare you accuse me of anything! she was thinking. You're lying there talking about searching out a poor frightened widow and *silencing* her! "But that is a long story. 'Twill keep until you're stronger."

There was a brief silence. Then: "It was you nursing me and urging me to live?"

"Yes. Roger too—both of us."

"You called me back. I owe you my life."

"Nonsense." She thrust her hands into her lap, afraid he might notice their trembling. "You're a strong man, and, as you say, you did not intend to die."

"Nevertheless, I thank you, Alexandra." She thought she saw the glimmering of a sardonic smile cross his lips. "Was I dreaming or were you actually expressing interest in the reformed beliefs some minutes ago?"

"Ah, that brought you back, did it? I thought it might."

"And did we talk at all, then? My memory is fuzzy. I seem to recall speaking to someone—was that you?"

Jesu! "You must have been dreaming. You've been unconscious for two days. You did not speak until just now when you opened your eyes."

"Indeed?" He was gazing up at her in a most disconcerting fashion. He closed his eyes, obviously exhausted from the effort he had made. Very softly he added something that sent ghostly fingers scurrying up and down her spine: "I fear you'll rue the day you brought me back, Alexandra. You and Roger both. God help us all."

III
The Argo, July 1557

The joy of love is too short, and the sorrow thereof, and what cometh thereof, dureth overlong.

—Sir Thomas Malory

29

ON A HOT, sunny day in the middle of July 1557, Alan Trevor sat in the stern of a rowboat in the port of the city of Antwerp, northern Europe's busiest commercial center. He was staring at his brother's ship, the *Argo*, which stood at anchor in the harbor. She was leaving in a day or two for the Middle Sea, one of her seamen had reported, after several weeks' stay here in port, taking on cargo. Thank God she was still here. Alan had been afraid he would not arrive in time.

Was there a woman on board? Alan had nervously inquired of one of the *Argo*'s seamen, whom he had met on the docks. Aye, a' course there was. The master's flame-haired lady. Soft on the eyes, she was, too, and a cheerful soul, with a smile for everybody she met. "She's not a proud, haughty one, for all that she's a highborn lady," the sailor reported. "She wanders about the ship questioning us about our duties as if she truly has an interest in our work."

"Then she's free—she's not with Captain Trevor as a . . . a captive?" Alan had asked.

"Such she seemed when first he brought her aboard. He was looking murderous then, and we were all afeared for her, the sweet young lassie. Bound her wrists, he did, and locked her in his cabin," the seaman recounted with obvious relish. "But after a night in bed with the lady, everything

355

changed." The sailor gave Alan a broad wink. "He's a tamed tiger now, the captain is. At her side all the time, caressing her, looking into her eyes. No, young sir. If anybody's the captive now, 'tis Cap'n Trevor. Is aught amiss?" the seaman added, apparently noting the sick look on Alan's face. "Who're you, anyway, the lady's brother?"

"God have mercy," Alan had muttered, and turned away to hide his emotion. She was alive, at least. But apart from that, all Alan's worst fears had come to pass. They were lovers. He should be happy, he told himself, that his wayward older brother was not physically mistreating the woman whose reputation he had so thoroughly ruined. But what future would there be for Alix, intimately involved with a man now infamously known in England as a murderer, a rapist, a heretic, and a traitor? And how was he going to free her from his clutches?

He had a lever to use, thank God, but it was a lever he took no joy in, for if it failed, as it well might, the price would be intolerable.

In London Alexandra's father had come to him, finding him locked in the dreary darkness of a prison cell, three days after the dreadful events in Geoffrey de Montreau's cellar. Alan had been tossing on the rough measure of straw that served as a bed, dreaming that somebody was torturing Alexandra. Her body was stretched out and bound by her wrists and her ankles, her screams were shattering his eardrums. Only he could save her; only he could stop the brutal turning of the wheel. His confession would be a betrayal, but if he did not confess, the woman he'd loved since childhood would quite literally be torn apart.

Groaning, Alan had twisted as violently as if his own body were being tortured. Then he seemed to hear a loud clanging sound, the sound of cruel metal—chains, implements of pain. Bolting upright, he clutched his throat, eyes open and heart pounding. The same dream. Hour after hour, since the morning when the queen's soldiers had freed him from his captivity in Geoffrey de Montreau's residence, only to throw him into an even darker jail, Alan had dreamt the same dream.

He heard the clanging again and realized it was coming

from the door to his cell. A torch flashed in the darkness and the iron door was pulled open. Sir Charles Douglas stood there on the threshold—Alan recognized him immediately by the vibrant red of his beard and hair.

"Alan Trevor?" Douglas' voice gruffly challenged. He held the torch high. "I can scarcely see you, lad. It's taken me all night to track you down. Those blasted idiots who took you thought you were a French spy."

"No, sir, I'm not," Alan whispered.

"No, just an English heretic and traitor," Douglas said. Strangely enough, there was no condemnation in his tone, only a heavy sadness. "Come with me. I want to talk to you, but I've no mind to do it in this hole."

Alan rose unsteadily to his feet and followed Douglas out into a dark corridor, up a flight of stairs, and into a sparsely furnished room. He was weak from fear and lack of nourishment. He'd eaten nothing for three days. "Alexandra, sir? Is she safe?"

Sir Charles spat a vicious curse. "Your brother's got her on his ship."

"Then they escaped?"

"If you can call it escape when a man has rape and murder foremost in his mind. He and his paltry band of heretics were ambushed at the riverside. At least half were killed. De Montreau, that snake, had Alexandra there, and Roger dragged her off at knife-point, as mad with grief and rage as I've ever seen a man. That wretched French fop had him convinced that she had most vilely betrayed him."

"Sweet Jesu. But it was I who—"

"Never mind; I've heard the tale," Douglas interrupted. "It all gets blacker and blacker, like a bloody Greek tragedy." He sighed heavily. "Catherine's son. For her sake, I've left the blackguard alone, even though 'twas no secret to me he was up to some devilry. But I should have clapped him in prison long ago."

Alan swallowed hard as the implications sank in. Alexandra abducted by Roger and a prisoner on his ship. Roger believing her guilty of betraying him when it had been he, Alan, who had given their plans away. Hadn't she enlightened him, explained the true situation? He groaned. Know‑

ing Alix, he realized she probably had not. "Surely he will not harm her."

Sir Charles Douglas just looked at him.

"He will not kill her," Alan said, more to reassure himself than Douglas. "Not even he would go so far."

"He's gone far enough. Her abduction is common knowledge—de Montreau has made sure of that. One of the queen's ladies taken by a daring criminal—the tale is all over London already."

"Mayhap it will blow over and he will wed her," Alan sugested feebly.

"Not likely. I know his type—he ruins women, he doesn't marry them. Don't you know the reason for de Montreau's hatred? Roger seduced his virgin sister, got his bastard upon her, then beat her till she miscarried and died."

"That can't be true." But even as he spoke, Alan remembered Geoffrey's accusation in the torture chamber. It had been the first he had ever heard of the unfortunate Celestine. "Roger wouldn't do such a thing."

"Ha! If you'd seen him the other night on the riverbank, pressing his knife against Alexandra's throat until her blood welled up, you'd sing a different tune, lad." His voice broke in anguish as he added, "In truth, I don't know whether she's alive or dead."

Sick, Alan stared at the red-haired man. Usually Douglas was a hearty, vibrant man, possessed of the same energy for life that his daughter had, but tonight he looked old and drained of vitality. "What can we do?" he asked.

Douglas' expression hardened. "We'll not sit by and do nothing, that is certain." His eyes gleamed ruthlessly. "He's pushed my face in it, and now I'm going to return the favor. I don't like to do it, but by God, he's gone too far this time." His blue gaze shifted and burned into Alan. "That's why I need you, lad. You know where they were headed with their cargo of heretics, do you not? I'll be sending you after them. You're the only person who can save her. If it's not already too late."

But it was too late, Alan knew now, as his boat approached the *Argo* and banged up against the sleek ship's side. Not to save her life; that, thank God, wasn't necessary.

But his brother and his dearest friend had come together finally, just as he'd been dreading they would for the past year. For his own heart and soul and peace of mind, it was far too late indeed.

Alexandra was up on the quarterdeck enjoying the sun and the sea breeze and supervising the first outing on the part of her patient, Francis Lacklin. After several weeks of bed rest, his chest wound had made rapid progress toward healing. The fresh air, she'd decided, would do him good.

"Are you tired?" she asked as they took a turn around the small high deck. She put one arm around his waist. "Lean some of your weight on me."

Lacklin gave her an indulgent smile. "It's really not necessary that you support me, Alexandra. I'm thirty-six years old, not seventy."

"If you ever wish to reach seventy, you'll do as I say."

"Nag, nag. How Roger puts up with you, I can't imagine."

Alexandra laughed. "I only nag people who are too weak to defend themselves. I'm not a fool, you know."

"I know that very well," he said more seriously.

Alexandra ignored the flicker of unease his words created in her. Amazingly, she and Francis had begun to lay down the foundation for a friendship of sorts. Since she expected to spend the next several months in close quarters with him, she was determined not to do—or think—anything to jeopardize this fragile sense of trust.

During his slow convalescence Alexandra had spent several hours a day sitting beside his bed, trying to repress the suspicions that had been aroused by his strange remark about Pris Martin. She begrudged him neither her service nor her time. There were only so many hours a day she could spend lolling about in bed with Roger; and when they'd reached the busy port of Antwerp, her lover had become preoccupied with other matters. There were the heretics to be smuggled ashore—they would travel overland to the German states, where Calvinism was well-established and they would be safe. And when this was done, there were his commercial ventures to attend to. He had a good deal of business ashore. "Because of the thriving cloth trade, Antwerp has become the Venice of the north," Roger explained to her. "England may be a commercial power to reckon with one day, but at present we're no rivals for the Dutch."

Because the Netherlands were controlled by Spain and thus allied to Mary of England, Roger categorically refused to take Alexandra ashore. "'Tis too much of a risk," he told her. So she had no choice but to spend her spare hours with Francis Lacklin, who was also languishing with boredom.

He no longer preached to her as he had done last summer at Chilton. He prayed sometimes and read the Holy Scriptures, but he was easily distracted; often he would frown over a passage, then toss it aside, his face pale, his eyes troubled. Sometimes Alexandra would look up from her own book—Roger's cabin was a veritable library of wonderful volumes—to find Francis staring speculatively at her, and she would feel a little chill as she wondered if he knew what she suspected.

At other moments, when Francis made an unexpected joke, or when she saw him arguing philosophy or playing chess with Roger, Alexandra found herself wondering if the incriminating words he had uttered had not merely been the wanderings of a fevered brain. Fantasies, no more. She knew of no reason why Francis should have murdered Will. It made no sense at all.

She had not spoken of her latest suspicions to Roger. Like the boy who cried wolf, Alexandra knew she would not be believed if she made another accusation in this matter, at least not unless she had amassed a mountain of proof.

Besides, on that night at Greenwich, Francis Lacklin had freely made the greatest sacrifice of all—offering up his own life to save Roger's. On top of that, how could she accuse him? It would bring nothing but pain to all of them if she did.

She and Francis were making one more turn around the quarterdeck when a young sailor shouted up to her that there was a young man asking to speak with her. She helped Francis sit down, then leaned over the wooden balustrade, searching the main deck for someone whom she assumed to be a messenger from Roger, who had gone ashore early that morning. She saw a tall, slender man dressed in the English style . . . then he looked in her direction, shading his eyes in a gesture she recognized. And then she was running, practically sliding down the steep ladder that led to the main deck. "Alan!" she cried, flinging herself into her old friend's arms. "Thank God you're alive!"

Despite his heavy heart, Alan was cheered by the joyful intensity of her greeting. He hugged her hard. "I was afraid *you* might not be. Flung as you were into the lion's den."

"In sooth, I've tamed the lion," she said lightly. "Now, what news, what news? You look gaunt and tired. Come inside; I'll have wine sent up. Are you hungry? Oh, Alan, it gladdens my heart to see you!"

A few minutes later they were sitting in what was obviously the master's cabin—and just as obviously Alexandra's primary abode. There were two gowns—both looked new—hanging on a hook upon one wall, a silver comb and brush on a small table beside the neatly made bunk, and a book of Greek poetry open on the massive desk that, together with the bunk, took up most of the space in the small room. Roger's things were there also: his maps and charts, the sea chests where he kept his clothes, a pair of leather boots, a clean lawn shirt flung over the end of the bed.

Alan shuddered at the thought of what his brother and Alexandra must be doing together nightly in that bed. She, however, seemed unembarrassed by her fall from virtue. She was clad in a simple summer gown made of some silky blue material; her hair was braided and coiled atop her head to keep her neck cool in the sultry heat. Her face was well-scrubbed and free of the fine cosmetics he had grown accustomed to seeing her wear lately; if anything, she looked younger than she had appeared at the court of Mary of England, less worldly, more innocent.

"Alix, I have to ask: are you all right?"

She smiled and nodded. "Don't I look it?"

She did, he admitted grudgingly. She looked relaxed and free of the cares that had weighed her down at court. "Your father sent me after you. But I would have come anyway, to see . . . to make certain . . ." His voice trailed off.

"I'm fine," she repeated. "Now, tell me all the news."

Alan grimly supplied her with the details of all that had happened since she and Roger left the country. He explained that Roger had been formally accused of treason and heresy. "There's a price on his head. He can't go back to England, ever."

"And me? What are they saying about me? Is there a price on my head too?"

"No, Alix. Your father has made certain of that. He tried to put it about that you were ill, that you had retired to Westmor, but the tale quickly got about, as such tales will, that Roger had abducted you. That much Sir Charles finally admitted. You are seen as the victim, the innocent martyr to a ruthless man's machinations. No blame has been attached to you. But of course there is a scandal all the same."

"The queen? What does she say about all this?"

There was no reason not to be fully honest. Alexandra would have guessed the truth anyway, knowing her mistress as she did. "In public she mourns your loss and reviles your kidnapper. In private, to your father, she questions what you did to 'attract the blackguard's lust.'"

Alexandra frowned, then made a rueful face. "So much for my virtuous reputation. Never mind," she added, reaching out to pat Alan's hand. "After all, 'tis true. I did do everything I could to attract the blackguard's lust. And I'm hardly living the life of a debauched martyr now, am I? He may have seized me by force, but I've remained with him willingly."

Alan didn't want to hear it. The topic made him ill. "Where is he?"

"Ashore, haggling one final time with his agent, I believe. Something about a shipment of Flemish lace that hasn't yet been deposited in the *Argo*'s holds. He has an order direct from Süleyman's Kizlar Aga—the keeper of the harem—for lace for the concubines, and he insists that he will not sail without it."

"When will he return?"

Alexandra regarded him steadily with her clear green eyes, then slowly said, "Alan, he knows what happened in Geoffrey's cellar. Please have no fears about that."

Alan could feel the color rise in his neck and cheeks. "You told him it was me who betrayed his plans?"

"Not until he guessed the truth. I also told him how bravely you defended me. When he understood the details, he was proud of both of us."

"And before he understood the details?"

Alexandra shrugged and looked away. "That phase didn't last very long, thank God."

Alan swallowed hard, wondering if he dared ask the question that was burning in his heart. Had his brother raped Alexandra? Despite what the sailor reported about their cordial relations, such a crime would be difficult to forgive. Was she truly content? Might she not welcome an excuse to leave?

Alexandra continued to regard him with wide, owlish eyes. She seemed to be considering something, weighing her words. At last she said, "Alan, I love him. That's something you should know. I've loved him for a long time, and it's finally penetrated his thick skull that he loves me too. We intend to marry."

"You cannot marry him, Alix; he's a criminal, an outlaw!"

She took his fingers in hers and pressed them hard. "I'm sorry," she said.

She knew his secret, Alan realized. He expected pity but found only compassion, affection, and that other familiar, sisterly sort of love. Silently he cursed her, cursed Roger. He wanted her as a woman, not a sister. Wanted her body writhing beneath his in bed, as his brother had her. And hated Roger for taking her away from him.

Tearing his hands from hers, Alan rose and paced the room. "So, what now? Does he intend to take you with him on this voyage to the Middle Sea?"

"Yes, he does."

"And is that not a dangerous . . . indeed, a foolhardy thing to do? Suppose you are captured by corsairs? D'you wish to end your life as a slave in some Eastern infidel's harem?"

Alexandra shrugged. She and Roger had had this identical argument several times. He did not want to take her on his voyage—there *was* danger, a good deal of danger. But neither did he want to be separated from her, and the truth was, she had nowhere else to go.

Seeing her hesitate, Alan quickly pressed his advantage. "Come back to England with me, Alix. Your place is there, with your home, your family. Do not give yourself over to a life of shame!"

"There is no shame in our love." She spoke softly but with great conviction. "And my place is here, with him."

"Your father thinks differently. He wants you back, and he's determined to have you back."

"My father succeeded in keeping us apart for months. There's no longer anything he can do."

"Oh, but that's where you're wrong, Alix. There *is* something he can do; indeed, he's doing it. And he's sent me here to tell you and your lover all about it."

Frightened by his tone, Alexandra jumped to her feet. "What do you mean? Tell me."

Alan tried to control his anger and his jealousy. "I'll wait until Roger returns."

Alexandra grabbed him by the forearms, her green eyes spitting determination. "You won't. Roger has had enough to fret about lately. You'll tell me now, whatever it is."

Silently Alan reached into his doublet and withdrew a scroll of paper. He handed it to her. "This is a copy. The original is in your father's hands. If you do not return to England within the next month, he's going to turn it over to the ecclesiastical authorities."

Alexandra began unrolling the paper. "Whatever this is, it will not work. I love Roger. We *will* be wed!"

"Read it."

Grimacing, she did. The document was a warrant for the arrest of Richard Trevor, Baron of Chilton, on charges of heresy. "Oh sweet Jesu," Alexandra whispered, looking up. She managed to focus on Alan, who was hovering over her.

"The reasoning behind it is simple. You are Roger's hostage. My father is Sir Charles's hostage. He offers a trade. If Roger refuses, Sir Charles will see to it that my father— and Roger's—is tried for heresy and burned at the stake."

30

"HE CAN'T be serious," Alexandra said.

"I'm afraid he is."

"Oh God . . ." She remembered her father's face that awful dawn at Greenwich. Never, never had she seen him look like that. "You say the baron is his hostage; do you mean he has already arrested him?"

"No. My father knows nothing of this as yet. He is old and sick—before I left England I heard from Dorcas that he had suffered another heart seizure. He could not endure the hardship of imprisonment, the anxiety of a trial. Not to mention the dishonor. He has suffered enough already at Roger's hands."

"Damn my father! How can he do this? He's bluffing. Your father is his neighbor, his old friend . . ."

"I fear that will not stop him. Roger has pushed him too far. Anyway, the entire debacle has done immeasurable damage to Sir Charles's credibility at court. He has enemies. Geoffrey de Montreau is one of them, and he has been doing his best to make your father look like an incompetent ass. Douglas has been made to play the fool, and somehow he must recoup. There is no doubt in my mind that he is completely serious."

"Geoffrey is still in London?"

"Yes. He has turned coat on his employers and is now

comfortably installed at Westminster, advising our English generals on French fortifications."

"Sweet Jesu! You mean he has thrown over his many years as a career diplomat? But why?"

"Your father's opinion is that Monsieur de Montreau is still obsessed over his revenge."

"He must be mad!"

Alan shrugged. "He is being well paid, I understand, for his services. But never mind Geoffrey. The question is, what are you going to do?" When Alexandra simply paced, her brow furrowed, her father's document clenched tightly in her fist, he added, "I have a ship ready in the harbor; we can set sail as early as dawn tomorrow. If you return with me, nothing will happen. As your father explained to me, he's not being unreasonable. He doesn't demand that Roger himself surrender. All he wants is you, safe at home again."

"It's not that simple, Alan! Don't you see—it's not as if I were really a hostage whom Roger would just as soon be rid of. My father is forcing Roger to make a choice between his father, whom he hates, and me, whom he loves! Whom do you imagine he will choose?"

"Are you suggesting he would let his own father die just to keep you here in his bed?"

"Oh heavens, think, Alan. Have you forgotten the way they fought with each other last summer? There's no love between them. Do you honestly think Roger would lift a finger to save him?"

"Yes, I think he would. When it came right down to it, I think something inside him would flinch at the thought of his father burning at the stake on his account."

"You may be right; in sooth, for the sake of his peace of mind, I hope you are, for I don't think he could face the rest of his life knowing he was the cause, however indirectly, of the baron's death. Certainly I couldn't face it." She shuddered. "'Tis a diabolical choice."

Alan said nothing. His brother was a man of honor, surely, whatever his feelings toward his father. However difficult it might be for him to renounce his liaison with Alix, he would do it, Alan suspected, to save their father's life.

* * *

It was late in the evening before Roger returned to the *Argo*. Alexandra had sent Alan, who was exhausted from his rushed journey, to bed; Francis also, still weak from his chest wound, had retired earlier. "I want to be alone when I tell him," she'd explained to Alan.

Roger was in a jubilant mood when he strolled into his cabin at ten o'clock that night. He was also, for the first time in weeks, a little drunk. "We've finally secured that shipment of lace," he announced, coming over to the desk, where his lover was nervously pretending to read Sophocles, and looping his arms around her shoulders. His lips nuzzled her ear. "But best of all—look, poppy-top." He unfolded a legal document not unlike the one Alexandra had hidden under her book. "See what I've got for us? 'Tis a special license to wed. I saw the priest. He'll marry us tomorrow. Since we're not from his parish, I had to bribe him with a little wine, which quickly turned him into a most agreeable fellow."

"Evidently he shared his bribe with you." *Tomorrow!* She and Roger were to be married on the morrow!

He laughed softly. "Don't start, woman—you're not my wife yet. Complain too much about my vile habits and I might change my mind and decide not to have you after all."

She knew he was teasing her, but no laughter would come. She dreaded what she must tell him. Now she wished she'd allowed Alan to do it.

"Why aren't you abed?" He caressed her throat with his clever fingers. "I imagined you waiting for me beneath the sheets, your body bare and open, your blood feverish for me . . ." The hand dipped to her breasts and stroked more insistently. Alexandra's eyes closed as a liquid knot of desire formed deep in her vitals, spreading its demanding heat all up and down and through. She couldn't bear the thought of a separation from him.

"Roger." With an effort she removed his hand and looked into his hot brown eyes. "Wait, we must talk. We have had a visitor aboard the *Argo* today."

He still caressed her, uncaring. Then he caught the pained expression in her huge green eyes. "Who?"

"Alan. He's alive and well, thank heaven. And he's followed us from England with news."

"What news? Where is he?"

"Asleep. Tom gave him a berth for the night—he was deathly weary. In the morning you can talk."

He cupped her chin with his hand. "Something's wrong, is it not, sweetling? I can see it in your eyes."

She closed them for an instant. In the weeks they had been together the bonds between them had grown almost psychic in intensity. There were moments when they could truly read each other's minds. He knew when she was worried, angry, sad; he empathized. And when she was joyful, as she nearly always was in his company, he laughed with her, enjoying life as he had not done for years.

"Alix?" His hands were still, his voice gentle. "Tell me Alan's news."

"He wants me to return to London with him, and—oh God, Roger—and I think I'm going to have to go."

Roger stared at her dumbfounded for a moment; then slowly his expression changed. Alexandra could feel the seed of rage that shivered and exploded inside him. "What the devil are you talking about?" He shook her. "I'll eviscerate Alan! What game is he about, damn him to hell?"

"It's not Alan—"

"It's never Alan! You protect him like a lion does its cub! He loves you, you little fool. He wants you even as I do myself."

"No, Roger, truly he is just a messenger."

"'Tis your father, then. He sent Alan, no doubt—the lad wouldn't have got out of England otherwise. Your father will stop at nothing to prevent our finding happiness and peace together."

Wishing she did not have to confirm this, she lifted her book and handed him the document that lay beneath it. "If I do not return, my father will carry out the threat implicit there," she explained. "He is proposing an exchange of hostages."

Wishing he had not consumed quite so much *vin ordi-*

naire with the good priest, Roger read and reread the warrant, then muttered a curse. "What the hell is this? My father's life for yours? But you are not my prisoner. I don't have to surrender you; you're going to be my wife."

"If you'll think back upon the way you took me, you'll see that it probably hasn't occurred to him that happiness and peace could be possible between us. He thinks to extricate me from your evil clutches."

"He'd better think again! I don't believe it. 'Tis ludicrous. He'd never touch my father."

"Alan thinks he will. They have been uneasy friends, at best, over the years. And since your escape, my father's position at court has become untenable. He needs to take strong action of some sort, or be judged a bungler."

Roger tossed the document down on the table beside the matrimonial license. "No. This is a bluff if I've ever seen one. I am not so easily drawn. We shall pay it no heed."

But Alexandra had had several hours to think, and despite her own initial skepticism, she now agreed with Alan that Sir Charles was serious. "You don't know my father when he's in a temper. He's very stubborn. Even if it began as a bluff, 'twill end as a tragedy, for if I do not return, he will, in anger, carry out the threat!"

"Let him." He seized her around the waist and lifted her effortlessly. He carried her to the bed and laid her down. "My father's heretical leanings are his own affair, not mine. I warned him last summer that he was being indiscreet, and he paid no attention. Am I his keeper?"

"Those are Cain's words!"

"Yes, I know." He knelt on the mattress beside her, his sensual mouth hardening with the old cynical, world-weary expression she remembered so well from those days of deep conflict between father and son at Chilton. "Appropriate, are they not, coming from me? Even though it's patricide, not fratricide, you would accuse me of now?"

He was angry and not a little drunk, a combination she had learned to be wary of. "I'm not accusing you, Roger, I'm simply—"

"You're simply passing judgment, the way you always leap to do. Well, hear this, my wise moral arbiter: the Baron of Chilton has washed his hands of me often enough; now I wash my hands of him. His fate is his own. Charles Douglas has miscalculated—I will not peal out like a bell at the slightest pull of my ropes. Particularly this rope. For it is attached to nothing, Alix. To nothing at all."

"Roger, we are speaking of the man who gave you life. 'Tis a simple thing, my going back to placate my father in this matter. It need not separate us for long. If I can save a life by doing so, how can I refuse? Don't you understand that if you allow your father to be sacrificed, you will feel the weight of it on your soul forever?"

"I understand nothing, sweetling, except this." Pressing her back on the mattress, he lowered his mouth and kissed her hard, with all the savagery and force of which he was more than capable. His tongue ravaged her mouth, arousing all the dizzy, heated cravings that she experienced nightly in his arms. Weakness stole through her limbs, and the familiar burning in her loins flashed toward the point of sensual conflagration.

He lifted his lips to whisper, "I'm not allowing you to leave me. I do not think I could bear a life without you— your loss would weigh far heavier upon me than his, I assure you. He has never been a father to me, and his welfare is none of my concern."

"One day, I fear, you may regret your decision."

"Never." His hands swept over her breasts, forcing the material of her gown down around her waist, baring her flesh to his hot eyes. "He is nothing to me. You, on the other hand, you are my life. You I love with all my heart."

Oh God, she thought, torn apart by her passion for him. She did not resist his lovemaking; she could not. He was her other half. God forgive her, but his unwavering decision thrilled her. He would not give her up for anyone, for anything.

She quivered in his arms while he sucked her nipples into his mouth, teased them, tormented them. He slid her out of the remainder of her clothing and touched her intimately with hands that knew exactly how to arouse her to the point where desire roughens into fierce demand. She watched him tear his garments from his virile body; shame-

lessly she opened her thighs for him as he lowered himself
to the mattress and thrust inside her without further ado.
Despite his haste, she was ready for him; so ready that it
took him only a few seconds to hurl her into incandescent
light. He captured her cries inside his mouth as he kissed
her violently, over and over again. Then he caressed her
breasts and began to stroke her slowly, deeply, guiding her
slender hips with his hands until he felt her quicken again.

There was something more intense than usual about their
loving; a quicksilver desperation, a poignant ferocity that
compelled them to touch, murmur and kiss in ways that
they had never touched, murmured and kissed before. "Roger,
I can't," she whispered a few minutes later when he still
showed no signs of stopping or slowing or finding his own
release. "It's too soon, it's not possible, I—"

"Shh, you can. I'll help you. Here." His control seemingly absolute, he withdrew for a moment and reared up on
his knees. Before she knew what he was about, he had lifted
her from the waist and slid the pillows beneath her. "Now
put your legs over my shoulders," he ordered, pulling her
into position and smiling wolfishly as he stilled her long
enough to drive himself inside her.

She gave a little cry as he penetrated far more deeply
than ever before. "Am I hurting you? You're so small inside,
my love. If it hurts I'll stop."

"No, don't stop. Please don't stop."

He chuckled and accelerated his rhythm, simultaneously
caressing her secret places with tender, knowing fingers.
"You see?" he gasped, as his control began to evaporate.
"You're entirely open to me this way; I can pleasure you
with my hands as well as with my body . . . and watch your
sweet expression, too."

"I love you," she murmured, over and over as he stroked
her, worshiped her, spun her into mindless delight. When
the convulsions that finally shook her body died away, she
added, "Until death and beyond, you are my only love."

"Before God, you are my soul, Alix," Roger replied.

But when the dazzling love passages were over and they
slept, her dreams were troubled by images of fire and death.
She tossed restlessly, torn by guilt. And sometime in the

dark of the middle of the night she made her decision: soon, well before dawn, while he was still asleep, she would waken Alan and they would slip away. Whatever his own thoughts on the matter, Alexandra knew she could not allow Roger to sacrifice his father for her. There would be no peace to be found in happiness that was purchased at such a price. She made her decision, and then she wept and held him close until it was time for her to go.

"I will kill her," said Roger.

He was in a towering rage. Alexandra and Alan had slipped away before dawn; no one was quite certain how, but it was apparent she was gone. Alan's ship had already set sail for England. By the time Roger had realized his lover had left him, the departing vessel was no more than a speck on the horizon.

"I will follow her and kill her."

"Don't be so melodramatic," Francis Lacklin said. "We both know you'd never harm so much as a single red lock of her hair."

"She's left me for *Alan!*"

"She left in his company, not in his arms."

"But why, Francis, why?" He was in agony—his face was rough and unshaven, his eyes hollow and dark. In his hand he held a scroll of paper signed and sealed with various official flourishes. He held it up for Francis to see. "This is a special license for us to marry. It's what I thought she wanted from the day I returned last year to Chilton. I would have stood beside her in church today and made her my legal wife. Alexandra Trevor, the future Baroness of Chilton." He took the document and ripped it down the middle. "I've never offered marriage to any woman before." He tore the paper again, more violently, faster, reducing it to shreds. "I will not be so quick to do so again. When I find her, Alexandra Douglas will not be my wife but my whore."

"For Christ's sake. You know full well why she's left." Francis picked up the other document and perused it once more. "She's softhearted; you've always known that. And she lacked the nerve to call Charles Douglas' bluff."

"It's not nerve she lacks, damn her! She has nerve to spare. And she's probably right that Douglas isn't bluffing."

"Then she's done you a favor. You don't want your father's death on your conscience—I know you far too well for that."

Roger ran both his hands through his hair and cursed violently. It was true he understood the line of thinking that had prompted her to leave. She didn't want to be the means of his holding himself responsible in later years for his father's death. *One day, I fear, you may regret your decision.*

And he *had* regretted it, far sooner than she'd expected. He'd lain awake regretting it, knowing, even before she left him, that he could not allow Charles Douglas to try and execute his father.

What he resented—what, indeed, he could not forgive—was Alexandra's lack of trust in him. Why did she always expect the worst? Killing his brother, killing the Queen of England, killing his father . . . If she loved him as much as she claimed to, why did she continue to think so ill of him? Why the hell had she slipped off in the middle of the night, assuming that his drunken proclamation in the heat of the moment had represented his final thoughts on the subject? Damn her! 'Twas certain there was no love lost between himself and the Baron of Chilton, but he couldn't stand by and allow Douglas to arrest his father any more than he could have remained at Chilton last fall and risked arguing his father into another heart attack. He wasn't a murderer. How many times did that fact have to be drummed into Alexandra's stubborn skull?

"She's a rash and reckless woman, forever taking too much upon herself. I've had enough, Francis. When I find her, I swear I'm going to give her a thrashing she'll never forget."

"When you *find* her? What the hell do you intend to do?"

Roger covered his face with tense, white-knuckled fingers. He heard the understated note of alarm in Francis' voice and recognized the emotion from which it sprang. Francis loved him; Alexandra loved him. Between them they had the ability to cut his heart from his body. He'd been wise to protect himself for so many years from love. He was lost now. He was a tortured man. "You know full well what I intend to do."

"Like your headstrong mistress, you will return to England."

"Aye. That I shall."

Francis sighed. "The stake awaits *you* there," he felt obliged to point out. "Or rather, since you're not exactly a dissenter, the traitor's gibbet."

Roger shrugged off the reminder. Without Alexandra, he was dying anyway. Now that he *had* given himself over to love, there was nothing else for him. A life without Alexandra by his side, in his arms, in his bed, was inconceivable now. If he could not have her, he would gladly surrender his body to death.

31

*I*T WAS EARLY September when Alexandra arrived home
at Westmor Manor. Her mother was there to greet her, and
Alexandra couldn't believe how good it felt to be enfolded
in Lucy Douglas' arms, smelling the clean herbal scents she
had always associated with her mother. It had been a full
year since they had seen one another. It seemed even
longer.

Alexandra had half-expected Lucy to scold or reject her,
but it didn't happen. In fact, her mother was gentler with
her than she'd been for years. Asking no questions, she fed
Alexandra and Alan a hearty meal, then sent Alan home to
Chilton while she put her daughter to bed. Bone-weary,
Alexandra slept almost immediately.

The next day, when she had occasion to think about it,
Alexandra couldn't decide exactly how much her mother
knew. That she had been snatched by Roger, yes; *everybody*
knew that. Alan had told her mother that Roger had released
Alexandra into his care rather than risk her life in the stews
of the Mediterranean. Roger had even gone so far as to
offer marriage to the woman he had ruined, he'd explained.
But Alexandra had declined.

"In any other circumstances, I would have called you a
fool for that," her mother told her frankly. "But marriage
to a heretic and traitor would have been worse than the

scandal you face now. What about Alan? He seems fond of you. Why don't you marry Alan?"

It hadn't occurred to Lucy, apparently, that Alexandra had been Roger's willing bedmate, that she loved him, that she longed for him and missed him so much that the days were long and heavy and the nights intolerable. And Lucy appeared to have no knowledge of the threat her husband had held over the Trevors.

The reunion between Sir Charles Douglas and his daughter had been painful for both of them. It had taken place in Douglas' town house, where she had been secretly brought by Alan. Great care was taken to keep the news of her reentry into England from the queen; nobody knew exactly what Mary would have to say about her former lady-in-waiting's adventures, and nobody particularly wanted to find out. Courtiers had been thrown into the Tower for less.

"Oh, Father, how could you have done this thing?" Alexandra had demanded when they met. "I love Roger. I love him!"

Her father obviously had no compassion for such feelings, at least not when they were directed toward Roger Trevor. "I should have married you off to the first eligible man as soon as I got you to court. Who will have you now, I'd like to know?"

"I will have no one but Roger."

"As long as there's breath in my body, you'll not wed that hellbound young devil."

"Would you really have arrested his father?"

Douglas merely scowled.

"Destroy the warrant, please, now that your diabolical scheming has had the hoped-for results. I want your assurance that the Baron of Chilton is safe."

"He's safe," Douglas said tightly as he ripped the document to shreds. "But if I ever get my hands upon his son, I swear I'll take him apart piece by piece."

"I know about your long years of adultery," she retorted. "Your rank betrayal of my mother ever since you've been at court. You have no right to condemn Roger for the same sins you have indulged in all your life."

"Be silent, girl! I am your father, and I'll not listen to such disrespect!"

"You are not my father, sir. From this day forward you are nothing to me!"

But later that same day, she had sobbed on his shoulder and asked his forgiveness. And Charles had held her close and told her of his fears for her, his helplessness on the riverbank at Greenwich, his belly-turning dread that Roger Trevor would slash her throat with his knife. "He's a rough man, without gentleness or softness. How can you, who have always been a sensible, practical young lassie, possibly have developed a passion for such a knave as he? Have you no pride, woman? Art the sort who finds danger in a man exciting? Wouldst end up battered and dying, like that poor French girl, Geoffrey de Montreau's sister?"

"That wasn't what happened. Geoffrey's sister's death was one of the accidents of childbearing. I've talked to the physician who attended her, and he confirmed that Roger had nothing to do with it."

"De Montreau apparently loved his sister with a love that borders on the perverse," Douglas sneered. "No physician's report will satisfy him now. Anyway, your precious Roger was responsible for the pregnancy that killed her, was he not?"

Charles insisted that they must hurry Alexandra out of London. The queen's mood was dangerous now that Philip had left her once again. Besides, Geoffrey de Montreau was still in England. As Alan had reported, he had betrayed his own side and successfully curried favor by providing the queen with military information useful for fighting the war against France, the war that had become a popular success on St. Lawrence's Day when the British had killed twelve thousand troops, including many from the nobility, in a battle at Saint-Quentin.

And so Alexandra and her father had parted. Having discharged one painful duty, Alexandra was free to look to another; for in sooth, she had had a second reason for returning to England. It occurred to her that final night on Roger's ship that in one way at least, she could make a virtue out of necessity. She could go to Oxford and speak with Pris Martin, if the elegant young woman who had been Will's mistress had not already been "found and silenced." She could return to Chilton and reopen the investigation into Will's death. She could spend the time until she saw Roger again amassing evidence against Francis, if indeed he was the guilty party. And, in that way, she could fulfill the vow she had made to her dead friends on the day she had left Westmor last September.

Traveling north with Alan, she insisted that they break journey on the first day at Oxford. She wanted to see the college where he had studied, she told him. And she also wanted to find her old friend Pris Martin and ask if there was anything she needed.

Alan was skeptical. "Since when are you and Pris Martin old friends?"

"I'm curious about her. And I think we have a sort of responsibility to her, don't you? After all, she was the mother of Will's child."

But they could not locate Pris Martin. When they tried the draper's establishment where she had been working the previous winter, they were greeted by a suspicious fellow who either knew nothing or pretended not to. Even the hefty bribe that Alexandra offered produced no results.

"People here in Oxford are wary of strangers," Alan tried to explain. "There've been too many burnings. They probably think you're a spy for the ecclesiastical courts."

Undaunted, Alexandra pressed Alan for information about the dissident congregation Pris had belonged to. They managed to find her pastor, who was slightly more forthcoming. Pris was alive and well, or had been the last time he had seen her. But unfortunately, she had left Oxford for parts unknown only a couple of weeks before.

Discouraged, Alexandra allowed Alan to make arrangements for the remainder of her journey north to Chilton. They made the trip in easy stages because she was uncharacteristically weary. The weather was sultry, the going slow, and her separation from Roger weighed more heavily on her every day. For some reason her thoughts kept returning to Geoffrey de Montreau and his sister, Celestine. Sometimes in dreams she fancied that she knew Celestine, that the dead girl hovered over her bed by night, that she and this woman she had never met were strangely linked. But when she woke, she would deny it vehemently: "I'm not like her," she insisted to herself. "And I'm not going to end up like her!"

But in one way, she feared she was like Celestine. It was a fear that grew with each week that passed. By the time she arrived at Westmor, she knew it must be true; she'd missed her monthly flux for the second time. Like Celestine, Alexandra was pregnant with Roger's child.

Merwynna's cottage looked just the same. And Merwynna. The old wisewoman was waiting in front of the door as Alexandra tramped around the lake on the day after her arrival back at Westmor. "I expected ye, my child," she said with a broad smile as Alexandra rushed into her arms.

"I've missed you so much," Alexandra whispered as she clung to her old friend. "And I've got myself into a fine predicament, I fear."

"I know, my lass, I know. Come inside now, and we'll see what we can do."

The witch gave her a cup of hot herbal brew and then, gently and carefully, examined her. "April, I expect," she told her. "Ye're two months gone."

"Is everything all right? There's no indication of . . . of malplaced pregnancy or anything like that?"

Merwynna gave her a sharp look. "Women who know about midwifery are the worst patients. They worry too much. All is well, Alexandra. Yer womb is expanding nicely; as far as the babe is concerned, ye have nothing to fret about. As far as ye yerself are concerned . . . where is yer husband?"

"Oh God, Merwynna, he's not my husband. And I don't know when I'm going to see him again!"

Merwynna asked no questions; she simply stared at her protégée out of her ageless black-pool eyes. "There is a drug I can give ye. 'Tis risky, but ye're strong. If it is done soon, the womb will contract and the child should abort without complications."

"No." Her voice was agonized.

"Think, Alexandra. Ye're alone, unwed. Shame and disgrace shall be yer constant companions."

"They are already! There's not a soul in London who doesn't know that Alexandra Douglas, lady-in-waiting to the queen, was most vilely abducted and raped by an infamous heretic and traitor. 'Tis the summer's most entertaining gossip. They will not be surprised to find me breeding as a consequence."

" 'Tis no easy task to care for a child alone, lass, without the protection of a man. I advise ye to drink the brew I'll make for ye, and end this folly now."

Alexandra's hands moved to cover her belly protectively. "I love Roger, Merwynna. I love our child. I'll take no drug. I will give birth to this babe, with your help or without it."

Merwynna sighed. "Ye'll have my help, of course, stubborn and headstrong though ye are. But how did this happen, child? I taught ye the means to prevent it."

"Herbs don't grow on ships," Alexandra said ruefully.

"Why not insist that he withdraw himself from ye before his crisis? I explained, did I not, that—"

"I wanted him within me, his body, his seed! I love him, Merwynna!" She grabbed the witch's hands and stared into her disturbing eyes. "Will we be together someday?"

Merwynna's eyes dilated and went blank. Alexandra stiffened, her heart leaping to her throat. Would the witch's Voice have an answer for her?

But, within seconds, Merwynna's eyes refocused. The Voice had not spoken. "I do not know."

Alexandra bit her lip. The Voice, she knew, came only when it was so inclined.

They spoke of other things. Alexandra told Merwynna all that had happened to her at court, and the wisewoman in turn filled her in on all the local births, deaths, marriages, and village scandals. And finally Alexandra said, "There's something else I would ask. Do you remember the widow Priscilla Martin?"

Merwynna's eyes became inscrutable. "What would ye know of her?"

"First of all, whether or not she's still alive."

"She is, of that ye can be sure."

"How do you know?"

Merwynna smiled. "I have something to show ye."

She went to a cupboard and withdrew something that looked like a small piece of cloth. Unfolding it carefully, she handed it to Alexandra.

Puzzled, Alexandra stared at a lovely square of embroidery done in vividly colored thread. It was beautiful, but there was something very strange about it. With deft and careful stitches, the embroiderer had recreated three scenes. In the first, a man was riding a wild stallion around the curve of a woodland road. In the second, the horse, obviously out of control, was rearing, throwing the rider to the ground. And in the third, the most gruesome of all, a second man had emerged from the trees and was beating the head of the fallen horseman against a rock.

"Jesu," Alexandra breathed. The embroidery was so skillful that the men were almost recognizable. The horseman looked like Will Trevor. And the other—tall, dark hair, dressed not as a peasant, but as a gentleman. His face was not clear, but..."Where did you get this?" Alexandra demanded.

"Do ye not recognize the work? Who is the only person you know who possesses such skill with a needle?"

"Pris?"

The wisewoman nodded. "Wait here."

Merwynna went out the cottage door and disappeared around the back. A few moments later she returned, followed by another woman, whose head and face were hidden beneath the folds of a thick hood. As they entered the cottage together, the woman threw back her hood. It was Pris Martin herself.

"Merciful heavens," Alexandra cried. "I certainly didn't expect ... I had no idea ... What are you doing here?"

Pris sent her one of her cool, gracious smiles. She was no less well-groomed and beautiful than ever, Alexandra noted with a twinge of the old envy. Not even a year at court and the love of Roger Trevor had convinced Alexandra that she possessed any great amount of beauty herself.

"Alexandra?" Pris was staring in some confusion at Alexandra's rich gown and neatly plaited hair.

"Hello, Pris."

"Merwynna just told me you were here. I didn't know. When she said someone was coming to consult her, I had no idea it was you. I thought . . . that is, I'd heard . . ."

" . . . that I'd been abducted at knife-point and raped? Don't be embarrassed—everybody's heard that."

But Pris Martin was the first person Alexandra had met who didn't either ask or pointedly avoid asking whether the rumors were true. Her eyes were on the piece of embroidery still clutched in Alexandra's hand. "I'd also heard that Francis Lacklin was dead." Her clear voice was trembling slightly; she looked frightened. "Were it not for that, I wouldn't be here. But Merwynna tells me she's seen him in a vision, alive and well."

Alexandra felt a curious sinking inside her. She realized that she didn't want Francis to have been Will's murderer. "Merwynna is right, as usual. Francis was wounded during our escape from London. He nearly died, but we managed to pull him through."

"You? You saved his life?"

"I didn't have all that much to do with it. Roger has an excellent physician aboard his ship."

"You should have left him to die."

"Why?" She held up the embroidery. "Who is this man with the rock?"

"It is Francis Lacklin," said Pris. "He murdered Will."

32

ALEXANDRA sank down once again on her stool. "Tell me how you know. And why, if what you say is true, have you come back, a year after all our questions about Will's death were supposedly resolved, to accuse him now?"

"I realized at the inquest that murder had been done, and that Francis Lacklin must be guilty. I realized also that he was still nearby, since he'd obviously strangled the half-wit, Ned. I was afraid he would kill me too. That's why I fled. When he'd heard what happened at the inquest, he would know that I knew, that I had finally understood, and—"

"Wait a minute," Alexandra interrupted. "Back up a bit. What do you mean, you realized *at the inquest* that murder had been done? The rest of us were busy realizing that it hadn't! It was your testimony that convinced us."

Pris Martin also took a seat. Merwynna moved to the back of the cottage, humming softly to herself. "This is complicated and I'm a bit unnerved," Pris confessed. "I was so certain he was dead, and it was such a weight off my mind. There was a prophecy once, you see, when I was a little girl. I was told that a gray-eyed man would strike me to the heart."

"Maybe it was a metaphor. Maybe it meant you would fall in love with a gray-eyed man."

Pris ignored this reassurance. "I came back because I owe it to Will's father, who was kind to me. For a year my conscience has troubled me deeply."

"Did you lie at the inquest?"

Pris Martin shook her head. "No. I went into the great hall that day thinking Will had died accidentally. I listened to your reconstruction of the events with incredulity. I thought you were highly imaginative. But my attitude changed when the baron showed me the note I'd supposedly written to Will. Do you remember?" Reaching into her girdle, Priscilla drew out a small scorched piece of paper. She unfolded it and handed it to Alexandra.

> In great travail am I delivered. You have a son. Do nothing rash, I prithee, before we talk. Do not betray me to your family. Come to me, I beg you, tonight. There is a matter I must discuss with you.

"Yes, I remember. You felt guilty because it was your words that had lured him out that night, when he should have been sleeping off his drunkenness in bed."

"No, Alexandra." Priscilla leaned forward; her voice was intent. "There's the rub. *I did not write that note*. I knew it, of course, as soon as I saw it. The hand is very like mine—a deliberate forgery. I did scribble a note to Will informing him of the babe's birth, but I did not ask him to come to me. Indeed, I urged him to stay away! I was weak and in pain, and I did not wish him to see me in such a state. Somewhere between my farm and Chilton Hall, my note was destroyed and this one substituted."

So that was it. With perfect clarity Alexandra remembered how numbly Pris had stared at this note when the baron had put it in her hands, how upset she had seemed. And how rapidly she'd turned and disappeared from Chilton Hall.

"Why Francis?"

"He was the only person who knew about Will and me. After Will became a Protestant, we confessed our sin to Mr. Lacklin, hoping for guidance. He was kind, understanding. I thought of him as a friend. 'Twas Francis Lacklin who was with me that night when I went into labor. I dared have no midwife, remember? Only a servant girl and Francis. When the child was born, I wrote the note to Will and requested Francis convey it to my servant. He must have switched notes before he did so. He had no fear of being caught, I suppose, because he knew full well that Will always burned my messages. As, indeed, he tried to burn this one."

Alexandra's head was swimming. "He lured Will out, then, with the intention of killing him? But why? Roger had a motive, perhaps, for killing his brother. Francis had none."

"I don't understand that either. But you were right that Will was not entirely happy with his conversion to Calvinism. He did it mostly on my account, and he had begun to feel, at the time of his death, that he might have made a mistake. He was going to discuss it with his father."

"I hardly think Francis would kill him for that!"

Priscilla shrugged. "I know of no other reason."

Alexandra jumped up again, pacing in frustration. "What about Ned? I never believed he was a suicide."

"No. I didn't know the boy very well, but my impression was that he wouldn't have had the wits to hang himself. And the dagger you said he found in the ditch—I think it belonged to Francis. I cannot be certain, but I have a vague recollection of seeing him use such a knife to sharpen my pen for me that night as I wrote my note to Will. The handle was ivory, was it not? And distinctively carved?"

"Yes. If you could swear to that, Pris . . ."

"I would not like to swear. I was exhausted and in great pain from the travails of childbirth."

"Still, taken along with everything else we know, it leaves us with little doubt. Francis had the dagger and dropped it in the ditch. Ned found it and died for his mistake. My mistake, actually. I'm the one who told Francis that Ned had given me the knife. Oh God, poor Ned. He trusted me to help him, not to get him killed!"

"Don't blame yourself. You had no reason to suspect treachery."

"Francis was in the forest on the day Ned died. He had not gone down to London after all. Alan saw him there. He could have done it, you see. He could have killed them both."

"He did so, Alexandra; I have no doubt."

Oh, Francis! Alexandra's head was throbbing. She'd actually grown fond of the man, she realized. He loved Roger. Natural or unnatural, Francis' love was a powerful force, the central force, Alexandra suspected, of his life. She put her face in her hands, absently rubbing her fingers over her aching temples. What would Roger do when he knew his closest friend had murdered his brother? *In honor I'd have to avenge my brother's death, would I not? I'd have to challenge him.*

But if he challenged the master swordsman, Roger would die.

"So what are we going to do?" she asked, more of herself than of Pris. "Lacklin is a criminal already, accused of crimes even more serious than murder. He's in exile. It's possible he may never return to England."

"I know not. I only came because I thought Will's family had a right to the truth."

"Are you going to the baron?"

"I had intended to, but he is ill. I came first to Merwynna, for advice."

Alexandra glanced over at her mentor. "I haven't seen the baron yet. Alan told me he'd had another heart seizure. Exactly how ill is he?"

The wisewoman shrugged. "His remaining time is short. He is in no condition to seek justice for his son's murderer."

"I wish to return to Oxford," said Pris. "As quickly as possible. I don't want to stay here, especially now that you tell me Lacklin is still alive. There's not much in this world I fear, Alexandra, but I fear that man."

"He and Roger are halfway to the Mediterranean by now," Alexandra assured her, hoping it was true. "There's nothing he can do to you, or me, or anybody now."

"Nevertheless, I wish to leave. Tonight. You've heard my story now; you can tell it to his father when he recovers."

"Come with me to Chilton. You can tell Alan and Dorcas, at least."

Pris looked uncertain. At last she said, "I have uneasy

feelings . . . morbid dreams. But I will stay, if Merwynna says it is safe."

They both turned to the wisewoman, who nodded. "I make inquiry of the Goddess for both of you."

They sat in a circle at the herb table, clasping hands. Merwynna fell easily into a trance, and for several minutes nothing happened. Then she raised her head and spoke in the harsh voice that Alexandra had heard several times before. She raised a gnarled finger, stabbed it at Priscilla, and said, "Your destiny awaits you. Tarry no longer, but ride out to meet it! In truth, you must be wary . . ." The Voice paused here and laughed unpleasantly, as if at some sort of private jest " . . . of gray-eyed men."

I don't like your Voice, Merwynna, Alexandra was thinking, just as the empty dark eyes turned their attention to her.

"Your likes and dislikes are of no consequence," the Voice declared. "I find you most amusing."

"That much is obvious. Someone is certainly having a merry old time creating disaster after disaster in my life!"

"You accept no responsibility for the consequences of your own actions? You would blame them all on the machinations of a higher power?"

"Or a lower one," she snapped.

Once again the Voice laughed. Its volume and intensity increased. "You have much to bear, but you are strong, Alexandra Douglas. You will need your strength in the months to come. You will need your wits, if you would survive. Trust the water and beware the fire. Embrace the earth, but let it go."

"You said that before, or something similar, and it still makes no sense to me at all."

"No? Then consider your stars, young woman, and do not be so great a fool."

Alexandra swallowed. Her stars? "What of my lover? What have you to tell me of him?"

"The same thing I told you the first time." The Voice cackled. "One who cannot, one who will not, one who dares not, one who dies."

"That prophecy is fulfilled!" she cried.

"Not all of it," the Voice said ominously. "In sooth, two will die. In a hail of arrows shall they fall."

There was a pause. Alexandra couldn't bring herself to comment. She'd always thought "one who dies" had referred to Will.

"You yourself will help one to his death," the Voice added almost conversationally. "As to your own fate, we shall see how well you guard this body." The fathomless eyes seemed to be gazing down over Merwynna's gaunt form. "She will need your protection soon. Take care to preserve her, for I need her, and it is tiresome training someone new." The Voice laughed once again. "If you fail me and she dies, I might be forced to turn to *you.*"

Alexandra broke the circle of hands, too angry to be terrified. Pris Martin cried out softly, in obvious dismay, and made the sign against evil.

"You are a demon!" Alexandra whispered. "Merwynna is possessed. Get out! And do not threaten me—I am not the prey of such as you!"

The Voice continued to laugh, less maliciously now, sounding genuinely amused. "What I am is beyond your understanding. But I mean neither of you any harm. We are linked—I, you, the wisewoman, and the child in your womb. She is female. If you survive to birth her, she will have the potential to live a full life and long. But put one foot wrong, and you will die."

"What good is prophecy if anything can happen?"

"I tell you what is probable. There are no guarantees."

Merwynna shifted spasmodically in her seat and moaned. "We have had excellent contact today," the Voice said cheerfully, "but it is too intense for her. Fare thee well, my friends. Persevere." There was a quiet hiss, as of a spirit leaving a body, then Merwynna's head fell forward onto her chest.

Alexandra jumped up and threw her arms around the old woman. For a moment she feared Merwynna was dead, for she was still and cold; she seemed to have no heartbeat. Alexandra quickly put her fingers to the large artery in the witch's throat, and was relieved to feel the light, rapid flutter of her blood. "Blessed God. She lives."

Pris had backed away to the cottage door. "She's possessed by the devil."

"Well, whoever he was, he's gone now," Alexandra said sensibly. "Help me get her over to that mattress."

Pris helped, but she didn't look very happy about it. "I'd heard she was a witch, but I never believed . . . I never knew she was capable of such. Aren't you frightened, Alexandra?"

"Not of Merwynna. But she has some odd friends, I'll admit."

"Did you understand everything he said?"

"No. But the Voice has been right before."

"What he said about your stars—perhaps he was referring to your birth sign. 'Beware the fire,' he told you. Francis Lacklin once told me that he was born under the sign of Sagittarius. It is a fire sign."

"And Roger was born under Scorpio, a water sign."

"'Trust the water.'"

"I trust him now. When first the Voice spoke to me, I did not."

"And the earth? Who is that?"

"Alan," Alexandra realized. "He is a Taurus—an earth sign. 'One who dares not. Embrace him, and let him go.' I think, Pris, that you are right."

Pris gave her a sympathetic look. "And the child in your womb? You are pregnant?"

Alexandra made a face. "'Tis a mixed blessing, to be sure."

"Then we are sisters," said Pris, and for the first time since they'd known one another, the two women embraced.

Pris insisted upon leaving. She would not go to Chilton Hall, she said; she didn't wish to see the place again. Particularly considering the Voice's urgings that she was to tarry no longer, she wanted to return to the only place where she felt safe. "I've made some friends in Oxford."

"A man?" Alexandra couldn't resist asking.

Pris shook her head, a little sadly, Alexandra imagined. She hoped Priscilla would find a man, a good man, one who would marry her and give her children.

"And you?" Pris asked her. "You love Roger—I've known that since last summer. Why did you leave him?"

Absurdly pleased to have the young woman as her confidante after all that had happened in the past to keep them apart, Alexandra told her. When she'd finished, Pris took her hand and clasped it tightly. "You will be together again. I feel confident of that."

"In sooth, I hope so."

"Guard yourself and your child, Alexandra. Forget about this latest problem. Justice will come to Francis Lacklin sooner or later."

"He's not a bad man," Alexandra said slowly. "Ruthless, yes. He will kill if he has to, of that I am sure. But I can't help thinking that if he killed Will, it must have been an accident . . . it's something he would have been wary of doing, you see, because of Roger, whom he loves."

"Maybe Roger is why he did it. So Roger would be Baron of Chilton someday."

"But Roger has never wanted to be Baron of Chilton."

"The Catholic lords are strong in the north," Pris reminded her. "Whether Roger wanted it or not, Francis may have needed a leader he could count upon here in this part of the country."

"You are right. My brain is working very slowly today. I don't think it wants to hear any of this. It certainly doesn't want to face up to the truth."

"What happened was no accident. He lured Will out, remember? And he murdered the half-wit, Ned, because of his suspicion—it can't have been more than suspicion— that Ned had seen something that night. He's not a bad man, you say. Yet he sat by Will's bed, pretending to be praying for him, for three entire days! You've realized why, I trust?"

Alexandra swallowed hard. "So he could silence him if Will showed any signs of coming out of it alive?"

"He must have been terrified that Will would open his eyes and accuse him."

Dear Christ, so he must. Alexandra had a vision of herself sitting faithfully beside Francis' sickbed on the *Argo*. *I fear you'll rue the day you brought me back.* Curse you, Francis! I should have let you die.

Alexandra and Merwynna put together some food and water for Priscilla, who insisted on setting out for the London road immediately. But before she left, Alexandra sat down with her and copied out her account of everything she knew and suspected about the circumstances of Will's death. It was a formal deposition, signed by Pris and witnessed by Alexandra and Merwynna. And when it was done, Alexandra dutifully made a second copy, which they also signed.

"One copy is for you to keep," she told Pris, "and one for me. We will be widely separated, and it is unlikely that Francis Lacklin can come back and kill both of us. Now, which of us shall keep the note you sent to Will—or rather, the note you *didn't* send to Will?"

Pris handed the note to Alexandra. "I am a heretic, remember. I dare not take this matter before a magistrate. You must take that responsibility, Alix. I've done all I can do."

"I know. And I thank you for it."

"Good-bye. Take care of yourself." Pris touched Alexandra's girdle gently. "And the child. I will pray for you."

"Thank you." Alexandra smiled and added, "I'm glad we were finally able to become friends. Even for so short a time."

"I always liked you, Alix. 'Twould have been difficult not to. You were unfailingly kind to me. But I was jealous because of Will."

"I never loved him. In truth, I was never your rival."

"I know that now. Farewell."

As Pris walked resolutely off into the forest alone, Merwynna squinted after her and said, "If I were ye, I'd send a man-at-arms after her, to keep guard upon her for a while."

"Why?" Alexandra looked sharply into her old friend's eyes. "What can you see, Merwynna? Francis Lacklin *is* in the Mediterranean with Roger, isn't he?"

"Francis Lacklin is with Roger. Whether or not they are in the Mediterranean, I cannot say."

Alexandra shivered slightly. "I'll send Alan. If his father's not too ill, that is, for him to leave."

"'Tis an excellent idea. Alan has gray eyes."

33

*T*HE COCK'S FEATHER INN was a day's ride from Chilton, and respectable, as such places go. But Roger agreed to stop there for only one reason—it was raining hard and Francis Lacklin had a persistent head cold. He didn't complain about it, but Roger could hear him coughing. Although three months had passed since Francis had been wounded in the chest on the riverbank at Greenwich, but Roger wasn't convinced that his friend had entirely recovered his strength. He felt guilty about dragging Francis into such danger as this when the man was still recuperating from the sword thrust he'd taken on Roger's behalf.

On the other hand, Francis needn't have come. In fact, Roger had done his damnedest to convince him not to. "'Tis folly for both of us to risk our necks in England. Alix is my headache, not yours."

But Francis had insisted. His own work was in England, not in the Mediterranean. And he had proved to be helpful in getting Roger from one part of the country to another—the Calvinist dissidents had established a network of refuges and safe houses throughout England. With the help of some of Francis' associates they had been able to travel securely through the countryside to Yorkshire, where Alexandra was.

The journey had been uneventful. They had tarried near London only long enough to learn that their quarry had returned to her father's house a few weeks ago in Alan Trevor's company, only to leave shortly thereafter, headed north. Roger had felt an almost irresistible desire to confront Sir Charles Douglas—the cause of all this trouble—right then and there, but good sense had prevailed and he had refrained. To announce to Douglas his presence in the country would be suicide. Alexandra's father would have no choice but to arrest him.

So northward they had wended, disguised as a pair of traveling friars, a part which Roger, having spent time in a monastery, was highly adept at enacting. Francis, the Protestant, considered the role demeaning, and played it out with lesser grace.

It was a chilly night for September, and the warmth of the fire in the great hearth was welcome to them both. Roger stretched out lazily on a bench with a tankard of ale in one hand, contemplating the red-sparkling flames, which reminded him of Alexandra's hair. Tomorrow. Tomorrow he would see her. Tomorrow he would hold her in his arms. Tomorrow he would press the headstrong baggage down beneath his body and spread her silken thighs. Tomorrow he would make her his again—his woman, his mistress, his whore, damn her. His fingers tightened on the tankard. Alexandra Douglas was going to learn once and for all who her master was.

His anger with her had faded since that bitter morning on the *Argo* when he'd discovered her gone, but he hadn't totally forgiven her. He had been too soft with her, he'd decided, too indulgent. Ever since that hellish night when he'd nearly taken her in violence, he'd bent over backward to be gentle, solicitous, a true courtly lover in the manner of several centuries ago. It had been a mistake. She obviously considered herself to be just as independent a woman as she'd been before she'd committed herself to his bed.

Deep in his heart Roger knew that Alexandra's independence, her quick mind, and her free spirit were the things he most loved about her. But tonight he chose to imagine her as a more conventional woman, a woman who knew the virtues of submission. Aye, the time for chivalry was over. *His* time had come. He would storm Westmor Manor if necessary, he thought, swallowing more ale as he enjoyed his fantasies. In the manner of a ruthless border lord, he would invade the fortress and steal the woman he wanted. If she resisted, so much the worse for her. This time he *would* ravish her, if he couldn't have her any other way.

Francis, seated next to him, sneezed. "Why don't you go to bed?" Roger suggested.

"I believe I shall." He clapped Roger on the shoulders lightly, saying, "Try not to wake me if you're going to be up late."

"I'm not. I'll just finish my ale."

Francis was just rising to head up to the chamber they were to share with several other men when Roger saw him stop and stare at the front entrance to the inn. The door had just opened to admit a fellow traveler, a woman. Roger gave the woman a quick once-over, then dismissed her. She wasn't Alix, and other women no longer held any interest for him.

That she held some interest for Francis, however, seemed obvious. He was staring at the slender, dark-haired, somewhat bedraggled-looking woman as if he were besotted. Odd. Francis rarely gave any woman a second glance.

But what was even more odd was that the woman advanced a few steps into the common room, her eyes searching for the innkeeper or, preferably, his wife. It was unusual for a woman to be seeking accommodations alone. Her husband, perhaps, was seeing to their horses? Roger hoped she had a husband. Several of the men in the inn were drunk and rowdy, and others besides Francis were looking the woman over.

Her eyes briefly met his own. They moved past, then returned, and something changed in them. Christ! Roger casually looked away. In his friar's habit and hood, he didn't think he was particularly recognizable, but they were near Chilton, and he knew several women in the area. She looked familiar, although the light was bad and he couldn't place her face. She wasn't a former bedmate, was she? Someone he'd tossed for a night or two and then forgotten? He sincerely hoped not. He and Francis had come this far safely, and he'd begun, at last, to feel relatively secure. Yorkshire was reasonably distant from London, and the long arm of the queen's justice would not easily seize him here. Still, as long as he remained in England, he was at risk.

The woman looked once more in his direction, then turned and left the inn.

"Do you know her?" Roger asked Francis, who was still rooted to the floor by his side.

There was a pause, and Roger glanced up at him. His expression was strange—Roger couldn't quite place the emotions at play there. Anger? Dread? "Do you?" Francis countered.

"I don't think so. She seemed to know me, though."

"'Twas me she was staring at." Francis drew a tense breath, then added, "She's a dissenter. She and her husband came once or twice to prayer meetings I was holding in the area. She was startled, no doubt, to see me in the habit of a friar."

"She recognized you?"

"She gave that impression, wouldn't you agree?"

"She behaved oddly, that's certain. Still, if she's one of your hapless heretics, she won't betray us."

"I think I may just have a word with her all the same."

"Be careful of the husband," Roger said, losing interest. "He'll probably think you're a lecherous friar."

Francis nodded grimly as he followed the woman out into the night.

As he hurried out to the stables behind the inn, Francis Lacklin's guts were cramping so badly he thought he was going to be sick. He'd recognized the woman instantly . . . but then, he knew her far better than Roger did. The last he had heard, Priscilla Martin been living in Oxford, where, although he'd ordered her watched, he'd left her alone. At one time he had considered taking more stringent action, but in the end he'd decided not to have her killed. Like himself, she was a Protestant, and it went against the grain to harm the elect of God. Besides, although her disappearance from Chilton confirmed that she'd guessed the truth, he was reasonably certain she had no proof.

Why, then, had she returned to Yorkshire? What was she doing here, only a day's ride from Chilton? Had she already met with Alexandra Douglas, or was she on her way to Westmor now? How long would it be before Roger heard what she had to say?

There was only one thing in life Francis Lacklin feared: the look that would transform his old friend's face when Roger learned the truth about his brother's death. He would go to any lengths to ensure that Roger never found out. He would silence Pris Martin. If necessary, he would even silence Alexandra.

"Have you seen a woman?" he demanded of the sleepy-eyed ostler at the entrance to the stables. "Dark hair, young, and—" He broke off as a horse erupted from the stableyard, the woman in question clinging to its back. She came right at him; both Francis and the ostler, cursing, were driven back against the wall. Her face was a pale blur of ill-concealed terror as she thundered by, racing her mount toward the London road.

"A fresh horse, quickly," Francis demanded, tipping the ostler overgenerously, which brought rapid results. "If I don't return, tell the other friar, my fellow traveler, that I'm off to the south on an errand of mercy. Can you remember that?"

"An errand o' mercy, aye, Father," the boy repeated, his broad peasant face displaying neither irony nor curiosity.

"And tell him to go on without me. I shall meet him in a couple of days at our destination."

"Aye, sir. 'E'll 'ave yer message, I promise ye."

"Good." Within minutes Francis was hard in pursuit, riding down the rough road in the rain, chasing the young woman who rode so foolishly without an escort, without protection of any kind. Neither her horse nor her riding skill were any match for his. Less than two miles of roadway were eaten up before he was alongside her, reaching for her reins, fighting to bring her desperate flight under control.

"No!" she screamed, striking at him with her riding whip. The leather caught him across the eyes, blinding him momentarily, streaking his nerves with pain. Francis lunged at her in fury; there was a jarring impact as their two horses collided. Francis' mount reared as Priscilla's crop struck again and again. Her own horse wheeled to get out of the way, but not quite in time. A flying hoof caught Pris on the shoulder and knocked her to the muddy ground. Francis had to fight to restrain his panicked horse, to keep the animal from trampling the woman who lay crumpled and still beneath him. At last he calmed his mount, slid from its back, and knelt beside his prey.

She was unconscious but alive. The rain poured down upon her, washing away the blood on her shoulder. Francis' hand closed over his dagger, drawing it from the sheath in his friar's belt. He hesitated. They were not two miles from the inn, and both Roger and the ostler had seen him go after Pris Martin. If her body were found here, throat slashed, it would take little in the way of wits to come up with the prime suspect.

He resheathed his knife and dragged Priscilla off into the high grasses at the side of the road. He need not kill her. It was chilly and wet and she was hurt; without attention she would very likely die before dawn. His bowels griped again and he set his teeth against the pain. *You'd leave this woman to die on the side of the road?* the voice of his conscience assaulted him. He silenced it. *Be thankful I'm not driving six inches of steel through her heart.*

Methodically he searched her, having no clear idea of what he expected to find. What he did find held him transfixed, truly sickened now. He had to strike flint to read the papers she'd folded so carefully and hidden in her bodice. He read every incriminating line, saw the two signatures at the bottom. He recognized the bold and fluid handwriting even before he saw her name. Alexandra Douglas. Damn her! She knew.

Francis buried his face in his hands. He did not pray; he could not. God would not listen, he knew, to the empty pleadings of a damned soul.

Ten minutes later, Francis Lacklin stealthily passed the Cock's Feather Inn again, riding northwest, toward Westmor. He would ride through the dark and stormy night. He would reach Alexandra many hours before Roger. Reach her and confront her. And it was a sad fact of life that when his good friend Roger arrived at Westmor, his red-haired sweetheart would be dead.

* * *

Roger went to bed soon after Francis left, falling asleep with his head full of erotic images. It wasn't until dawn that he discovered Francis hadn't returned to their room during the night. He'd ridden out after a woman, the ostler in the stableyard informed him. South, back in the direction from which they'd come. Neither he nor the woman had yet returned. "'E said 'e 'ad an errand o' mercy to perform. If 'e didn't come back, 'e said to tell ye 'e'd meet ye at yer destination, Friar," the boy told Roger. "Shall I saddle up yer 'orse?"

If Francis had been some other man, Roger might have shrugged understandingly at the urges that will drive a man out into the rain in pursuit of a pretty woman. As it was, he concluded that the meeting with the heretic woman had drawn Francis into some business concerning the Calvinists and their problems up here in the north. "An errand of mercy," was code for heretics to succor, or pray with, or scheme with, or whatever the devil Francis did with these people. Still, it was too bad; there always seemed to be an inordinate number of people making demands on Francis, and he really did have a hell of a cold. It was a shame he'd had to backtrack to the south on such a wet and dismal night.

Roger mounted his horse and began the final leg of his journey alone. For some reason the anticipation of the night had decayed into a strange feeling of heaviness around his heart. He would see his lover again, yes, but he was also going to have to face his father, a prospect that never failed to fill him with uneasiness. The nearer he got to the home of his youth, the more the ghosts rose up to assault him— that cold, stern giant who'd stood so often over him with a strap of leather in his hand; his Gypsy-eyed, laughing mother, who'd defended him, as he had tried to defend her; his older brother, always more loved, always more favored; his younger brother, the baby of the family, so much younger and weaker and never a very amusing companion.

And Alix. Half his age and a girl, but closer in spirit to him than any of them. It came to him with a jolt that even Catherine, his mother, hadn't been as dear to him as Alix.

He would see her, touch her, make love to her. So why was he uneasy? Why did his blood pound and his palms slicken with sweat? She would not reject him, of that he was certain. She loved him. So why was he as nervous as a boy on his way to his first woman?

With increasing dismay he remembered the last time he had experienced this degree of dread. He had been smuggling heretics out of England while Geoffrey de Montreau was torturing Alix on the rack. Body of Christ! Digging his heels into his horse's flank, he set a furious pace.

34

THAT AFTERNOON in Westmor Forest, Alexandra was tramping through the woods on her way to Merwynna's when she thought she heard a voice calling her. She stopped and clutched at a tree, feeling dizzy and slightly queasy. Her condition. She was tired all the time and out of sorts. She listened, but heard nothing more.

Puzzled, she walked on. A few moments later she heard it again. A hoarse masculine voice muttered something that sounded like, "Go home."

"Merwynna?" She looked around, but the wood was silent. The weather was cool and foggy, reminiscent of the day a year ago when she had found Ned's body in the cave. She heard a whispering again that seemed to come from inside her own head. Goosebumps rose on the nape of her neck, then spread down her arms. After the threat made by Merwynna's familiar spirit during the witch spell day before yesterday, the last thing Alexandra wanted to hear was voices in her head!

"Go home!" it said again, more emphatically. "There is danger here."

Danger to Merwynna? Instead of obeying, Alexandra began to run toward the wisewoman's cottage. Within minutes she had stopped beside the lake, her nerves crawling with the strong belief that all was far from well. The fog was thicker here, and everything seemed unnaturally still. A thin wreath of smoke was rising from the chimney on the wisewoman's tiny cottage, but otherwise there was no sign of life.

She will need your protection soon. Sweet Jesu, what was wrong? Don't let any harm come to Merwynna, she silently pleaded with God. Not her. *I love her.*

She walked to the door of the cottage and pushed it open. For a moment she thought it was empty, for there was no Merwynna seated at her usual place at the herb table. Then she saw the man standing in front of the fire, stirring the coals with the tip of his rapier. His head turned as she stiffened on the threshold. "Come in, Alexandra," he said.

It was Francis.

Alexandra had to clutch the doorjamb to keep herself erect. "Francis?" Her voice didn't sound like her own. "What are you doing here?"

Her words hung in the air between them. He stared at her. *He knows I know.* Alexandra's knees went weaker still. Merwynna wasn't here; the Voice had tried to warn Alexandra away, but she, stubborn as usual, had not listened.

"What are you doing here at this time of day?" He sounded angry. His face was drawn and pale. He coughed once, then continued, "I expected to have to come to Westmor. I certainly didn't expect you to come to me."

Sweet Jesu! Alexandra whirled as if to run. She heard him move and felt the touch of metal on the side of her throat. His rapier. "No. Shut the door, Alexandra. You're not going anywhere."

Numbly she obeyed. She couldn't seem to think of anything else to do. Her wits had turned to smoke.

Francis lowered his sword and gestured with it to the stool at the herb table. "Sit down. You're paler than an unbaked pudding."

She sat. "You frightened me." *Think, Alexandra. How would he expect you to act?* Deliberately she widened her eyes, trying to practice the guilelessness she'd cultivated at court. "I thought I was seeing a specter. You're supposed to be in the Middle Sea with Roger. Where is he? He's not in England, surely? He hasn't risked his neck to come chasing after me?"

"I'm afraid so. I left him last night at an inn a few hours' journey from here." He paused. "'Twas the same inn where I fortuitously met up with Priscilla Martin."

Alexandra made a soft, agonized sound. *Your destiny awaits you. Tarry no longer, but ride out to meet it!* She closed her eyes, but for only an instant. Keep your wits about you, fool! "Pris Martin? But I thought she'd left the north a year ago."

Francis shook his head slightly. "My friend, you needn't playact for me." He looked stricken—more full of raw emotion than she had ever seen him. "I have read the documents she was carrying on her person. I know your handwriting, and I have seen your signature."

She put her face in her hands. Oh God. *Pris.* Further pretense seemed pointless. "Is Priscilla dead?"

Francis looked into the fire and didn't answer.

Alexandra had an image of the elegant dark-haired beauty whose blue eyes had been filled with determination . . . and fear. The female friend she had never been able to make. Finally a bond had been forged between them—affection, confidence, mutual respect. Forgiveness for past injuries. Reconciliation. A new beginning.

Now she was dead. Francis had killed her. And Will. And helpless, harmless Ned.

A great red rage took her. "You bastard! You scurvy, blackhearted *swine!*"

"I've destroyed her copy," he went on as if she'd hadn't spoken. He reached into his doublet and drew out a scrolled paper. "This is your copy, along with the note I substituted that night, the note I thought had been burned long ago. It wasn't very intelligent of you, Alix, to hide it here." He nodded at Merwynna's shelves, which, she could now see, had been thoroughly rummaged through. "I will destroy your copy now."

Without hesitation she leapt up and snatched at the papers, but he whipped them out of her reach. Then he stepped over to the hearth and flung her precious evidence—Priscilla's testimony and the note Francis himself had forged—onto the fire. Alexandra dived toward the hearth, but it was too late. The dry old paper caught immediately, flaring orange, then bright yellow as it burned.

Speechless with anger and grief, Alexandra watched her case against Francis crinkle away to ash. "There's yet another copy." Because she was trembling too much to stand, she resumed her seat at the herb table. "'Tis safely hidden where you'll never find it. If anything happens to me, it will be given directly to Roger."

"Dear clever Alexandra. For your own sake I almost wish that were true." He pulled out a kerchief and wiped hot ashes off the end of his sword, then absently polished the blade. She envisioned him fighting, his smooth fluid movements, the dance that almost invariably brought death to his opponents.

For an instant, as he turned it, the shiny metal blade reflected the red of the fire—fire-red, blood-red. She had seen him kill with that sword. That night on the riverbank at Greenwich, just before he'd been wounded. *A gray-eyed man will strike me to the heart.* No such prophecy had ever been made for her.

"Why did you do it? Why did you murder an unarmed drunken man, a half-wit, and a terrified woman? You're a man of God, Francis!"

"I am damned," he replied, his voice dull and heavy.

"Deny it! Tell me 'tis all a bizarre mistake."

"I cannot." He turned to her, his gray eyes alight with all the passions that he usually kept so well hidden. "You've found me out, just as you were so determined to do. Damn you, Alexandra Douglas! Why the *hell* couldn't you just leave it alone?"

"They were my friends! They didn't deserve to die. What reason could you have possibly had? How do you justify it to yourself? Roger might have had some motive to kill his brother . . . if he were greedy and ambitious, that is. But you . . ."

"Will's death was an accident. That first death, at least, happened by mischance."

She waited, curious, in spite of herself.

"It was my doing, that I don't deny, but I did not intend his death."

"How can you claim that? You lured him out that night into an ambush!"

"No. I lured him out, it's true, but I meant him no harm. What I intended was to talk some sense into him. I knew his plans, you see. If the child was a boy—an heir—he intended to renounce his betrothal contract with you and marry his mistress instead." His mouth twisted into a sardonic smile. "I was doing you a favor. I meant to lecture Will on the legal difficulties involved in breaking a formal marriage contract. I intended to convince him—before he could announce his son's birth to his family—that he was morally obligated to wed you."

"Why should you bother about my betrothal? You never cared for me—from the day we met, we disliked each other!"

"That is true. Until recently on the *Argo* I thought you were nothing but an unmitigated troublemaker. Now, unfortunately for us both, I've grown rather fond of you. No, keep your seat," he added as she half-rose. The flat of his rapier blade touched her shoulder and pressed her back down. "I wanted you married to Will because I knew Roger was coming home and I was afraid of what would happen when you and he met. And I was right to be afraid, wasn't I?"

She was dumbfounded. "How could you have known? I'm not beautiful or witty or seductive—nobody was more surprised than I when he grew to love me. How could you have foreseen such an unlikely event?"

"You underestimate yourself, my friend. Your beauty is not conventional, but it is vivid and alluring—even I, who have no interest in women, can perceive that. You are highly intelligent, also, a quality Roger admires. You are honest, loyal, and determined, and you stand up to him in a way that few people dare to do." He paused. "Your courage too is remarkable. It will be there to support you at the moment when you need it most."

She knew then that he was going to kill her. The breath rushed out of her, leaving her empty and ill. For an instant she thought she would be sick. The room seemed to glide around in slow, surging circles. *He was going to kill her.* And her brains might have been cooked and mashed for all the help they were giving her; she couldn't think of any way to stop him.

He moved a little closer to her; she shrank into herself on her stool. "What happened that night with Will?" she demanded, desperate to keep him talking, desperate to stay alive. Courage? What courage? She'd borne too much already; she didn't have the strength to deal with this.

"I sent the message and went up the road to wait for Will. He came directly, riding like a madman. Despite your speculation, I did not leap out and frighten his horse— nothing like that; I gave him plenty of warning. He saw me and stopped.

"He dismounted and we talked. As gently as possible, I told him that he had a son, but that the child was illegitimate and would remain so. He was legally bound to you. I went on to insist—and this was my mistake, I realize now—that a debt-ridden farmer's widow like Pris Martin was no fit wife for the next Baron of Chilton."

"Oh heavens!"

"Aye. Like all the Trevors, Will was proud. He was also drunk and, because of it, easily aroused to anger. He drew on me and ordered me out of his way. I was unarmed, except for my infamous carved dagger, but he set upon me nonetheless. In short, he lost his temper, and I, who am usually more controlled, responded by losing mine. I kicked the bloody sword out of his hand and hit him as hard as I could. He went over backward into the ditch and struck his head on a rock." Francis stopped a moment, his voice vibrating with tension. "I thought he was dead, Alexandra. I was sure of it."

"But he was still alive; he lived for three days, while you sat faithfully beside his bed, praying, no doubt, for his breath to stop!"

"No. In sooth I have never prayed so sincerely for a man

to live. I was sick with fear that he would die and Roger would discover that I was responsible. Roger's loyalty to his family is far stronger than he lets on. Our friendship has survived many crises, but this it would not survive."

"So, after the episode in the forest, when I so carelessly put your own lost dagger into your hands, you killed Ned, to keep Roger from learning the truth."

"Yes." He thrust his sword back into its scabbard, then sat down upon the herb table, so close to her that she could feel the heat generated by his body. "I was sorry for it, but there seemed no other way."

"No other way! Why didn't you go to Roger and explain? It was an accident, after all. Such tragedies happen, Francis. It wasn't a crime until you hid it and compounded it with other murders. A half-wit boy, Francis. A woman!"

"Pris Martin may still be alive. She fled from me and was thrown from her horse. I found the papers in her bodice. I saw no point in running her through—it was pouring rain last night, and there was nobody about. She was unconscious, and by morning she'd have been dead of exposure. I don't like to put a sword in someone unless it's absolutely necessary."

"Heaven forbid that you should do anything so unchristian!"

He reached out and caught her chin between his fingers. His eyes were as metallic as his sword. "I hate this, Alexandra. I hate every moment of it, I assure you. I should have confessed to Roger in the beginning; you're right about that. But I did not, and now it's too late. He must never know."

She drew a deep breath and jerked her chin out of his hand. "So, what now?" She was ready to grasp at straws. He hadn't been able to run Pris through. Alan had set out after her—perhaps, with luck, he would find her. Perhaps Pris would survive. Perhaps Francis, who had refrained from putting his sword through one woman, would falter again, now, with her. "The evidence has been destroyed and there's no one to speak against you."

He rose to rummage in Merwynna's shelves. "There's you." He turned back to her with something in his hands—

a length of Merwynna's heavy homemade twine.

"No, Francis." She jerked to her feet and backed away, wondering if he were going to strangle her as he had strangled Ned. Again her wits seemed to be operating with all the speed and incisiveness of honeyed candy. Was this how you felt when you knew death was imminent and that this time there was no escape—paralyzed, impotent, helpless?

She put the table between them. "Despite my suspicions, I've said nothing to Roger. Now that there's no evidence to prove my case, there's no point in my ever saying anything. I've cried wolf once too often. Besides, he trusts you."

He kicked the table aside. It crashed to the floor with a violence that shocked her. She made an involuntary little sound in the back of her throat.

"I'm sick about this, Alix. I may not show it, but I feel . . . " He stopped. His hands shook slightly; he wound the twine around his own wrists, then absently pulled it free. "Never mind. It doesn't matter."

She backed again, but there was nowhere to go. She felt the herb shelves hard against her shoulders as he closed upon her. The fire cast his shadow before him, like a demon. "I saved your life, Francis."

"And I told you you'd regret it."

Oh God! He was going to do it! "I am carrying Roger's child."

"Liar!" Cursing, he spun her around, seizing her wrists and jerking them together behind her back. She struggled, crying out at his sudden roughness. He restrained her effortlessly and bound her, winding the twine several times around her wrists before pulling it tight. "I should have killed you last summer. 'Twould have been far less painful for all of us."

"My babe will be born in April. Roger's child." She was babbling now. "He's lost one child already, and one woman—Celestine. You saw how deeply that hurt him. Imagine how this will affect him, Francis. He loves me."

"Yes. And there's a part of me that has wanted to kill you ever since the day I first saw you together."

"Do you think he'll turn to you in his grief? Don't deceive yourself! He doesn't feel what you feel. As much as he cares about you, he will never give you what you want."

"You think I don't know that? I've known it since he was a boy of fifteen. And I've accepted it. I've tolerated his love affairs, his women. I even tolerated you. I made no attempt to stop your marriage, did I? But there's one thing I cannot, *will not* tolerate. I cannot allow you the power to destroy the trust, the friendship between him and me. *That* is something I will not give up, though my soul is damned for all eternity to hell!"

She swallowed. She felt tears crowded behind her eyes, whether for Francis or herself she wasn't entirely sure. "I'll never tell him," she heard herself say. "'Twould hurt him too much. Spare me and I'll keep your secret forever."

"No."

She set her jaw. "You don't trust me? Will's dead! You've already been accused of enough crimes to hang you several times over. Do you think I want vengeance?"

"I think you want justice, Alix. And your loyalty to your dead friends will demand that you reveal the truth. No, don't deny it," he added as she opened her mouth to argue. "I've watched you chase that truth for over a year. Watched you and feared you as I have never feared a woman in my life. I am sorry. Child or no child, you're going to die."

"My child is innocent of any of this! Is that the price of your soul, Francis—a half-witted boy, two women, and an unborn child? Even condemned prisoners are spared execution until after their babes are born!"

Francis was breathing hard, almost as hard as she. He turned his face away from her and coughed. "I see no sign of pregnancy," he said when he could speak. "You are very likely lying."

"I am but two months gone!"

"Then the babe has not yet quickened within you," he countered. His voice rose ominously. "I am damned already, so cease your arguments." He shoved her toward the door. "Enough. I had no more than a few hours' start on Roger. This must be finished now." He took one of her arms just above the elbow. "Outside, quickly, before the witch comes back and I have to do her too."

Her legs felt like sticks. She was afraid. Terrified. She stumbled, and without her hands to save herself, nearly fell. Francis caught her and held her, his hands strong but gentle. When she stumbled again, he lifted her and carried her out of the cottage in his arms.

"Please don't harm Merwynna. I . . . I love her. She's an old woman. Don't hurt her, Francis."

"Your evidence, flimsy though it was, has been destroyed," he said gruffly. "Who'd believe the ranting of a mad old witch?"

"Promise me."

He dragged breath and coughed again. "I won't touch her. You have my word."

"There's coltsfoot in the cottage. A spoonful of the tonic will help your cough."

"Christ, Alexandra! I'm going to kill you and you're worried about my cough?"

No less stunned than he at the absurdity of this, she began to cry.

"So you're a woman at heart, after all. And I expected you to die proudly, stalwart as a man."

Shamed into silence, she fought back her sobs as he carried her down to the lakeside. It was a wild afternoon, dark, and so foggy she couldn't see more than six feet ahead of her. She couldn't imagine what he intended. He couldn't use his rapier, and she had no horse to conveniently fall from. "How am I going to die?"

The old wooden boat she had used to rescue Alan was pulled up on the shore. He set her down in the stern and pushed it into the water. "You're going to drown," he said, taking the oars and striking out for deeper water.

"Drown?" she repeated stupidly. "How would I—?"

"You took this boat out on the lake—who knows why? I doubt anybody will be surprised, though. 'Tis the kind of thing you'd do. A storm came up, the water got rough, as it is getting now. The boat is old and rotten—the bottom seams began to separate, as they will before I'm through. The boat capsized; you could not swim; you drowned."

You could not swim. She stared at him as if she hadn't

heard right. What did he mean, she could not swim? Of course she could swim. She'd been swimming all her life.

But he didn't know that. It occurred to her she knew very few people who could swim. Most of the seamen on Roger's ship, she'd been astonished to learn, hadn't the least idea how to keep their bodies afloat. Merciful heavens! Hope surged in her again. "Then what? You go back to Westmor dripping wet and tell them all you've just tried and failed to save my life?"

"No, that would be far too risky. No one but you knows I'm here. Roger thinks I'm behind, not ahead of him on the road. I won't arrive at Westmor until well after he does, a couple of days, perhaps, from now. By then they will have found your body and Roger will need my comfort and consolation."

She said nothing. He had it all figured out. Except one thing.

He sent her a sharp look, as if he read her mind. "You cannot swim, can you, Alexandra?"

If she had ever needed the skill to dissemble, she needed it now. She raised large round eyes to his, eyes she knew must be dilated with fear and shock and grief. She thought about Priscilla. She remembered Ned's pitiful dying in the dark. She imagined Will lying on that stony bier beneath the altar in the Chilton chapel. "No," she said, her voice shaking convincingly. "In sooth, I'm terrified of drowning. There was a prophecy, once, that spoke of dark water and death. Please, Francis. I'm sorry to disillusion you with my lack of . . . stalwartness, but I don't want to die, particularly in this manner! I will never tell a soul what you have done if you will spare my life."

"They say drowning is the least painful way to die," he told her, not ungently. They were well into the middle of the lake now. The water heaved in waves with the rising wind, and the fog was so thick they could not see the shore. Francis pulled in the oars. "'Twill be easier if you don't struggle. When the water enters your lungs, 'tis said to feel euphoric. Surrender to it, and it will soon be over."

"Many thanks for the advice!"

He moved toward her and she shied back against the side

of the boat. Her wrists were bound, her clothes were heavy; her boots themselves must weigh several pounds. Being able to swim would not save her if he threw her in in this condition.

"Courage, Alexandra," he said.

"My hands. I wish to fold my hands and pray."

The boat rocked as he pulled her away from the side and against his big body. Something flashed—a knife—and then her hands were free. Of course. A drowned body with its wrists bound could only be the victim of a murderer. "Pray, then, but quickly. Your soul will fly to heaven, of that I have no doubt."

She bowed her head, pressing her trembling hands together. God give me strength, she prayed silently. Preserve me, for I do not intend to die. Not while Roger lives. Not while I carry his child beneath my breast. Please, God. Spare my life!

Aloud she said, "Forgive me my sins *in nomine patris, et filii, et spiritus sancti*. And forgive Francis, Father, as I do. Help him do penance so that one day his soul may be free of this fearful sin."

Francis groaned; against her, she felt his body tremble. She knew then that her words were not a lie. She did forgive him, this man whose tragedy was loving a man too much, loving the same man she also loved. In that they were united. She had not realized until this moment that love itself could be a sin. Francis Lacklin's fear of losing Roger's friendship had led to the destruction of his immortal soul.

She raised her head. "It's over for you, Francis. I think you know that. Whatever happens today. You're not killing me, you're killing yourself. Indeed, if you can do this, your soul must already be lost."

"Be still! I will not miss your tongue."

"My tongue called you back from the bourns of death once. Remember that when you pretend to mourn with Roger over my poor drowned body."

He stared at her, his shoulders slumped. For a moment she thought she had broken him . . . and saved herself. For a moment she thought he would not be able to go through with it after all. Then he pursed his lips, and the hard,

controlled expression she'd always associated with him came
down over his features. She remembered his self-discipline—
the quality he possessed in greater measure than either Roger
or herself.

Without another word he picked her up and heaved her
over the side. She caught her breath and held it just as the
cold black water closed over her head.

35

ALEXANDRA surfaced once near the boat, arms deliberately flailing. If he suspected she could swim, he would come after her. The water was choppy, the fog thicker than ever, almost hiding him from sight. The fog, she realized, was a blessing.

Her boots and heavy broadcloth gown combined with the roughness of the water to make staying afloat difficult. As she swallowed water and choked, fear stole through her again. She was a goodly distance from the nearest bank and weakened from her pregnancy. What if she couldn't make it?

"Alexandra!"

Francis was shouting at her. The fog cloaked him, but she could see him reaching out toward her. His limbs seemed to have elongated in a bizarre fashion—a long, ghostly arm was thrusting at her...No. No, it was an oar. Was he having second thoughts, or simply getting ready to bash her with it, to make certain she sank? He yelled again, but the wind tore his words away. Alexandra flailed her arms once more, then took a deep breath and slid beneath the surface. She dived deep and began to swim underwater as fast as possible, away from the boat, away from the man who wanted her dead.

She stayed under until her lungs were screaming for air,

then surfaced, trying not to gasp as she breathed. Fog was all around her. She couldn't see Francis, but once again she thought she heard him frantically shouting her name.

Treading water, she reached down and pulled at her boots. The wind was tossing her and the fog was so thick she couldn't see the shore. She was momentarily disoriented. Perhaps the weather was no blessing after all. Perhaps it was a curse.

As she finally jerked free of the boots and struck out again, swimming on the surface this time, it occurred to her that she could be moving in the wrong direction. Or in a circle. Or back toward the boat. She stopped and listened, hearing nothing now. No more shouts. Did he believe her dead? Shivering, she swam on.

Exactly how long she swam, she didn't know, but when she paused again, arms aching, legs numb, and her breath coming much too hard, she was forced to face the possibility that she might die here. The fog was swirling around her and she no longer had any idea where the bank of the lake was. The water seemed very cold and her body piteously weak.

Trust the water. Once again she seemed to hear a voice inside her head. *Trust the water.* Yes, yes. She'd swum here many times—since her childhood, in fact. She'd challenged these dark waters on the night when Alan had lain injured in the woods and Roger had pursued her, caught her, made sweet love to her in the same cottage where Francis had just revealed the truth about Will's death. Roger, Roger. He was nearby. He was not in the Middle Sea, after all. If she could only manage to survive, she would see him. She would hold him in her arms. She would kiss him and touch his strong, slender body; she would inhale his musky, seductive man-smell; she would feel once again his clever hands, his hot, insistent mouth . . . The image energized her, sending new power through her aching muscles. She swam harder. But still she seemed no closer to the bank.

Treading water, she stopped again and looked around. Nothing. Nothing but cold, rough water and gray mist. What if she was swimming parallel to the shoreline? She altered her direction slightly and struck out again, arm over arm, legs scissoring, over and over. Again. Again.

It doesn't hurt. I'm strong. Anyway, there's the baby. Have to get to shore because of the baby. Wouldn't mind if it were just me . . . but I have a child to think about, to protect. Makes a difference. The baby's life is dependent on mine.

Time drifted; her body grew increasingly weak. Gradually her thoughts began to change: *The water's not cold anymore . . . feels nice. Pleasant. Trust the water. Is there truly a primitive sea serpent in these waters? Perhaps I'll see him. We'll talk, make friends. He'll teach me the secrets of his abode, and I'll tell him what it's like on land, on earth, with my friends, my family, the people I love. . . . Oh God, Roger. The baby! Swim, move, keep afloat. . . . There. Farther. Good, good. Again. No. No. Can't—too tired. Arms won't work. Rest a little, the water'll buoy me up. Trust the water. Lovely water. Soft, like a pillow. Warm.*

From somewhere a warning flitted through her brain that the water was not warm at all; that if she thought it was, something was drastically wrong with her. What could be wrong? she wondered. She felt peaceful, safe. Nothing was wrong. *Fool!* said the Voice. *You are dying.*

It was true. Her body was already beginning to feel like a thing apart. She could look down upon herself from somewhere above the lake; she could see a gasping, flailing woman with sodden red hair clawing at the water as it inexorably dragged her down. She watched the woman's struggles, marveling at her tenacity, her refusal to accept that this was the end. Why was she fighting? It was peaceful here. There was a light around her spirit, warm and bright and beckoning. There was a feeling of freedom and ecstasy more powerful than anything she had ever known. Yet even so, she felt strangely reluctant to leave her body, particularly while it was still struggling. She drifted downward again, watching, listening. Too close—her body grabbed her. She cried out as once again she felt the cold, once again fear arrowed through her. And suddenly she sensed the presence of another being, another person struggling, a smaller, younger being who was even more desirous of life than she.

Heavy with guilt, she tried to explain: *Oh, my babe, I'm sorry, so sorry. We're not going to make it after all. Forgive me. I love you, I love your father. I tried, I really tried to stay alive.*

What had Francis said? "When the water enters your lungs, 'tis said to feel euphoric. Surrender to it." Mmm. Euphoric. Surrender.

She was sinking beneath the surface when something hard scraped her bare feet. She jolted up, gasping for air, and dimly saw, through eyes that had spots dancing before them, bushes, trees, rocks, and solid ground. To die when safety was so close? Impossible! With one last surge of strength she fought her way through the last few feet of water and crawled up onto the rocky shore. Shivering and sobbing, she collapsed upon her belly, her mind and body numb. Can't pass out, she warned herself. Too cold—you'll die if you pass out. But her eyes fluttered shut anyway. You fool, Alexandra, it's cold and raining, thunder crashing— you'll die! Go to hell, she told the Voice. I've done enough; it's not in my hands anymore.

Besides, she did not think she would die. She was in her body. In it. With her babe. The light, the vision of unearthly peace, was gone. Her time had not yet come.

Closing her eyes, she let seductive unconsciousness take her.

On the far side of the lake, Francis Lacklin jammed the bottom of the rowboat against a rock until the bottom seams split. His strength was superhuman, born of anger, born of grief. He wedged the half-sunken boat in between two rocks, where it would appear to have been flung up by the storm that was now spitting lightning and emptying a flood from the black clouds above his head. The entire force of the storm seemed to be directed at him. Nature enraged; God's judgment. Or Alexandra's spirit taunting him.

He sagged against a boulder and let a sob tear at him, then another and another. She was dead. He'd tried to save her—no sooner had he thrown her in than he knew he couldn't do it after all. Not to her. She'd saved his own life. She'd known his feelings for Roger yet had never once condemned him. She was intelligent and brave and bright— a candle in the dark, as Roger called her. She was the only woman for whom he had ever felt a flicker of affection.

He'd held out the oar and shouted at her to grab it, but she must have thought he was trying to strike her with it. He'd seen the expression of fear and horror on her face. She'd believed he was trying to make certain of her death. Of course she believed it. He'd just tried to drown her, hadn't he?

Sick at heart, he'd dived in after her, but she was already going down. He couldn't find her. Over and over he dived. Deeper and deeper, until he'd barely had the strength to pull himself back to the surface. He called for her, screamed her name, but there had been no answer. Silence. Mist and rain, condemning him. No red hair, no intelligent green eyes... never again, except in his dreams. She was dead, and he was damned.

Francis lay against the boulder in the driving rain and fog, expecting each moment that a lightning bolt would send him sizzling to hell. Surely a just God would not let him live after the foul crime he had committed. *Forgive him, Father*. She had prayed for him. She had even offered him a remedy for his cough!

He sobbed again, his big shoulders heaving against the rock. He couldn't remember the last time he had cried. Not even the tragic error of Will's death had made him cry. It had made him desperate, aye, but he had shed no tears.

Father, forgive him. But there was no forgiveness. There was no justice. Indeed, it occurred to him for the first time in his life that perhaps there was no God.

He stayed there until the storm was spent, never noticing the rain or the cold, hardly feeling alive. *You're not killing me, you're killing yourself.*

Killing himself. Francis sat up and slowly drew the dagger from his sword belt. He stared at its blade, turning it over and over in his hands. Killing himself. He remembered the serenity he had felt on the bank at Greenwich when he had believed—indeed, been convinced—that he was about to die. Why hadn't he died then, dammit? Roger would have remembered him with love; Alexandra would have survived. And her child. Was there really a child? Alexandra and Roger would have lived together in love and joy, producing children of charm and wit, bright, laughing children, red-haired, dark-haired, with expressive brown eyes, dancing green eyes. . . .

His mind was wandering inanely, he realized.

He stared at the dagger again, debating. Could he continue to live with this sin upon his conscience, or was it better to end his miserable life now? He thought back briefly to that unpleasant scene in the cave at Thorncroft Overhang when he stalked the half-wit, Ned, to his lair and strangled him. The boy had died pathetically, in terror, struggling futilely against Francis' superior strength. He'd killed men before, but cleanly, with his sword. That first murder had sickened him, and after it was done he'd considered suicide. He'd even walked to the edge of the cliff where Roger's mother had ended her life, and debated the merits of throwing himself over. He'd thought then that he would not be able to live with the guilt.

But he had lived with it. He'd even succeeded in forgetting about it, for days, weeks at a time. He stared out over the fog-misted lake. No doubt he'd forget about this too.

Francis thrust his dagger back into his belt. He was about to leave the bank of the lake when he heard a woman's voice cry out weirdly nearby. For an instant his heart raced with hope: she was not dead after all. Then he heard the cry as "Alexandra, Alexandra?" and knew it was Merwynna the witch, searching for her young protégée. He could not see her through the fog, but he could hear her coming closer and closer. She sounded alarmed, and Francis wondered if the old woman had been hiding nearby . . . if she had seen . . . if she had heard.

He ought to kill her too. For several seconds he considered it, then he remembered his promise to Alexandra. A great relief went through him. He was thankful for the excuse to avoid committing yet another murder.

He melted into the trees as the witch came toward him,

searching the bank of the lake as if she knew exactly what had happened. Canny old besom! Francis unconsciously made the sign against evil as he stealthily quit the scene of his vilest crime.

36

ROGER TREVOR arrived at Westmor Manor feeling cold, wet, and bad-tempered. He was shown into the library by an awed-looking servant who obviously recognized him. Lucy Douglas, Alexandra's mother, looked up from the table where she was adding a column of figures and glared at him with unconcealed dislike. "You! I ought to have expected it. Like a crooked shilling, you keep returning to the purse."

"I want your daughter," he said without preamble.

"You've had her, apparently," she retorted, adding several scathing epithets detailing her opinion of the male sex in general and her daughter's seducer in particular. "Her honor is destroyed beyond repair, her body bruised, her heart broken—"

"Where is she?"

"That's naught to do with you, Roger Trevor! You've treated her full badly. But she's left you and there's an end to the matter. You'll never see her again, that I vow!"

"Lady, I warn you, I've just arrived, I've had a long and tiring journey, and I'm not in the mood to be trifled with. Send for your daughter at once or I'll search the place chamber by chamber until I find her."

"You'll need an army at your back for that. And you haven't got one, have you? Not even a retainer, as far as I can see. How the mighty are fallen! You're an outlaw, Trevor, with no more authority than a mongrel dog. Get out of my home before I have my men-at-arms arrest you for treason and send you to the queen!"

Frustrated beyond words, Roger drew his sword upon his hostess. "You set any men-at-arms at me, madam, and they will die."

Uncowed, she stared directly into his eyes. "Better them— or me—than my daughter," she said calmly.

"I mean her no harm." So this was where Alix got her courage—from her mother. Not to mention her stubbornness. He slowly lowered his weapon. "I love her."

"You raped her!"

"Did she tell you that?"

For the first time Lady Douglas looked uncertain. "No," she admitted with the same honesty he prized so highly in Alexandra. "She said you didn't, as a matter of fact, but she's always defended you from the time you were children—why, I'll never know. You were a hellion then and you're a hellion now. Why didn't you wed her if you love her so much? The way things are, you've ruined her! Your actions are the scandal of London!"

"Our marriage was to have taken place on the day she fled."

"Why, then, did she leave you?"

He stared at her. "You mean you do not know?"

"I know only that you used her as a plaything for several weeks upon your ship. I assumed that for you, at least, the novelty must have worn off. What could she offer a rake of your experience? She is untutored in the arts of pleasing men."

"By God, you think worse of me than I deserve! She was pressured into leaving by none other than your husband. He sent Alan after us with a warrant for my father's arrest. If I did not surrender Alexandra, the Baron of Chilton would be tried for heresy before the ecclesiastical courts and burned at the stake."

"Your father has not been arrested." Lucy was obviously surprised. "Indeed, 'twould be cruel if he were, since he has had another heart seizure. He is bedridden, and far too ill to be prattling on about the virtues of the Protestant reformation."

"Nonetheless, that was your husband's threat. I doubted it myself, but Alexandra believed it. That is why she left. She could not stomach the idea of buying joy at the expense of my father's life."

"Such qualms, I take it, did not trouble you?"

It was true—they all did think worse of him than he deserved. Christ! What had he done to make himself hated so? Never mind. Alix was all that mattered. "Where is she, Lady Douglas? I'm thirsting for the sight of her, and that's the truth."

Lucy Douglas pursed her lips and stared at him for several silent, appraising seconds. At last she said, "She's out in the forest—where else would she be? Running just as wild as if she'd never been at court. She's with that witch again, no doubt. Since it's storming, she'll very likely take shelter with her and not return till the weather clears."

She spoke the truth, he sensed. He shoved his rapier back into its sheath. "Then I'll be going out there after her."

He half-expected her to protest, but she said only: "'Tis dreary outside and you are tired. Will you take a cup of wine or something first?"

But Roger shook his head and wasted not a moment before stalking back out into the rain.

It was nearly dark by the time he reached Merwynna's cottage. The worst of the rain was over, but a chilly drizzle still fell, and Roger was wet through. He dismounted from his horse and rapped sharply on the door to the hut where he had first caressed Alix's sweet body. Receiving no answer, he went in and looked around. The cottage was empty.

He swore. Had Lucy Douglas lied? Or were Alexandra and the witch together at the bedside of some pregnant peasant's wife?

"The Goddess be praised," said a brittle voice from in back of him. He whirled, hand on his rapier, and found himself facing the old witch herself. She was breathing hard, as if she had been running. "I have need o' ye," she told him, pushing past him into the cottage. She seized a blanket from the mattress on the floor and pressed it into his arms, then took up a flask of some noxious liquid. "Come with me, quickly."

Roger was about to argue that he hadn't come here to help the witch with her doctoring, but something in the old woman's face stopped him. She was frightened. And he caught her fear like a burning case of plague. "Alexandra?"

The wisewoman nodded. "We must hurry."

Merwynna led him a quarter of the way around the lake that stretched out in front of her cottage. The going was rough—there were rocks and brambles waiting there in the gloom, threatening to trip them with every step—but Roger hardly noticed. He would have ripped out bushes and up-rooted trees if they had prevented him from getting to Alexandra.

And then he saw her. Facedown on the bank, her sodden hair flaming less brightly than usual. She was covered with a heavy black cloak with pentangles embroidered upon it— the witch's cape, clearly. And she was cold, he discovered as he fell to his knees beside her and touched her. She was so very cold.

Terrified that she was dead, he caught up her wet body and cradled her against his chest. Her eyes were closed, her face waxen-still. He put his mouth to her throat, seeking the big artery there. He felt its pulse, faintly, beneath his lips.

"She needs warmth at once, or she will die," said the witch. "Wrap the blanket around her. Ye must carry her back to the cottage. The Goddess surely sent ye. I could not have managed alone."

"What happened to her?" he demanded as he bundled her in the thick blanket. "Is she ill . . . did she fall . . . was she attacked . . . what?"

"I do not know. I found the boat, battered and broken, thrown up on the rocks on the other side of the lake. She must ha' been out in it. I thought she'd drowned, but I kept seeing an image in my mind's eye, of her body lying upon dry land. I searched until I found her." She paused, then added, "I was attending childbed this day when a fear came heavy upon me. I sensed her danger. I left the birthing in my haste to find and succor her."

"Thank God for that!" He rose with Alexandra in his arms, her cold cheek against his shoulder. Merwynna touched her hair in a fleeting gesture that made his throat ache. The old witch turned to lead the way back to the cottage. "So many people love you, poppy-top," Roger whispered. "Please don't die."

Back at the cottage, Merwynna asked Roger to build up the fire while she stripped Alexandra of her wet clothes. He did so, then dragged a mattress in front of the blaze he had kindled. Together they toweled Alix's bare body and laid her on the straw pallet, one woolen blanket beneath her and another on top.

"Take off all yer clothes and get in with her," the witch ordered.

When Roger raised surprised eyes to hers, Merwynna snorted, "Well? 'Tis hardly the first time. Body heat is the best way to raise the temperature of one who is so cold. Besides, ye look chilled to the bone yerself."

And so he had the pleasure of lying flesh to flesh with his love again, but in far different circumstances than he had anticipated. With infinite tenderness he covered her, warming her breasts against his chest, her belly and her thighs with his own. He pressed kisses against her throat, her cheeks, her forehead, her lips. But he felt not the slightest trace of desire—there wasn't room for it beside his fear. For the first time in his life he had no carnal thoughts about the woman he lay with; he cared for nothing but her heartbeat and her continued breath.

Soon he was hot from the fire and the woolen blankets, and Alix's body no longer seemed so chill. Merwynna was sitting beside them with a bowl of some aromatic brew, stroking her protégée's forehead with one long craggy finger.

"What happened out there, Merwynna, do you know?"

The witch shrugged. "When she wakes, she will tell us."

"I love her. I love her as I have never loved before, never dreamed of loving. She is my life."

"Then ye must be strong, for there are more trials ahead for ye both, I fear."

"And the outcome? Can you prophesy happiness for us in the end?"

Merwynna shrugged. "I cannot see the end," she admitted. "So I do not know."

Alexandra moaned and stirred slightly in his arms. His heart rate quickened. "She wakes."

"The Goddess be praised."

Alexandra was dreaming. Once again she was in her lover's arms; once again she felt his hard-muscled body against her own. She touched her fingers to the smooth skin on his chest, ruffling the curly tendrils there. She snuggled closer, feeling his pulse beat steadily beneath her cheek, his humid, sweet-smelling breath fanning her hair. His long legs were tangled with hers, his hips, his loins taut and hard against her softer curves. She shifted contentedly. She loved his body. She loved him.

She'd had this dream before . . . so many times in the weeks since she'd left Roger. It was more vivid than usual this time. She resisted waking; she didn't want to find herself alone in a cold bed. She wanted the dream to go on forever.

"Sweetling," he was whispering in her ear. She loved the way he called her that. Nobody except Roger had ever called her sweetling. Nobody except Roger had ever held her so close, made her feel so safe and protected. Roger would keep her from harm. Roger would protect her from Francis Lacklin, who wanted her dead.

She came awake with a cry that tore the heart out of Roger. One moment she was nestling in his arms, the next she was struggling to free herself from demons.

"No!" she shrieked. "Oh, please. Not me, not my baby."

Roger swore and shifted his weight to free her straining limbs. *Not my baby?* The words drove through him like a lance. Was she with child? His hand fell to her flat belly and hovered protectively. Had his seed taken root in her body?

"I'll keep your secret. Oh God, not you, not you . . . I saved your life; doesn't that make any difference at all?"

"Hush, lassie, shh." He was trying to keep his voice gentle despite the tension that was ripping through his gut. What the hell was she going on about? Keep whose secret? Had someone tried to kill her? Who, for God's sake? He'd tear the blackguard apart. "You're safe now, Alix, safe. It's me, Roger. Lie still."

"Roger?" Her eyes had opened, but she was looking at him as if she didn't trust them.

"We're in Merwynna's cottage. She's here too, see?" He gestured toward the wisewoman. Alexandra's gaze shifted to Merwynna for a moment, then back to him. She still seemed dazed. She drew a long, shuddering breath, then closed her eyes again. A tear slowly formed at the corner of each.

Gently he caressed her hair. "Alix?"

Her response was slow, labored. "I remember now. I nearly drowned. I saw my own body below me, struggling to keep afloat." Her breath shuddered, racking her slender frame. "How did you find me?"

"Merwynna discovered you unconscious on the bank of the lake, and I carried you back here. What happened, love? Did someone try to kill you?"

Instead of answering, she looked to Merwynna once again. "The babe? Is she still . . . ?"

The witch tenderly brushed a lock of red hair off her patient's forehead. "Aye, lass. She's well-protected inside ye; don't be worrying about the babe."

"Sweetling, are you with child?" Roger was at the mercy of a confused rush of emotions—joy at her recovery of her senses, towering rage at whoever had tried to kill her, and a strong desire to be alone with her, away from Merwynna the witch, who could hear every word they exchanged. He didn't know how he felt about the child. Since Celestine's death, pregnancy had frightened him.

"Yes. You're not angry, are you? Our babe will be born in April." She couldn't help remembering the Voice's qualification: *If you survive*.

"I'm not angry, no, but I will be if we are not quickly

wed, Mistress Independent. I hope you plan to stay by my side long enough, this time, to make your vows."

Her tears began to flow more rapidly now. When she pressed her face against his neck, he could feel them hot against his bare skin. "I'm sorry," she choked as tears turned into sobs. "I missed you so, and 'twas all for naught. My father wouldn't admit it, but I suspect his threat was all bluster and bluff!"

"Hush, love, don't fret about it now."

"You shouldn't be here, Roger. It's dangerous. I'm afraid for you. Geoffrey's still in England, you know, and if he hears you have returned, he'll come after you and you will be tried for treason!"

"Alexandra, you haven't answered my question. Who tried to kill you?"

She burrowed her face against his throat, perfectly well aware that she had given him no answer. In sooth, she didn't know what to say. No longer was she concerned about the consequences to Francis. From the moment he'd thrown her out of the boat, whatever sympathy she might have had for him had died. But it would hurt Roger deeply to know the truth; she was as sure of that as she was that the constellations whirled nightly in the sky. Apart from herself, Francis Lacklin was the one constant friend Roger had, and he trusted him with his life. How could she tell him? And yet, he would have to know.

"She must rest," Merwynna put in before Alexandra could determine what to say. "I want her to drink this broth."

"And I want to know who the devil tried to kill her!"

Alexandra made a small sound in the back of her throat. "I'll tell you, love, I promise. But not now. The tale is long and you won't want to believe it. . . . I'll tell you, but let me rest a little first."

Roger curled his fists in frustration. He had already begun to have some thoughts on the matter, thoughts he didn't like at all. "Very well," he said slowly. "But the next time you wake, I expect some answers from you. Do you hear me, woman? You've tried my patience sorely these last few weeks."

"I hear you." She tried to smile. Obediently she drank

Merwynna's brew, then settled down once again in her lover's arms. Almost instantly she began to drift. Peacefully, wrapped in a cocoon of security and love, she closed her eyes and slept.

Roger dozed on and off throughout the night, but the half-dreams he kept falling into were ominous, and the constant presence of Merwynna with her strange eyes and her foul-smelling potions put him on edge. Rising finally just before the dawn, he dressed in his now-dry clothes and paced the small cottage, firing questions at Merwynna, who was bent over her herb table silently sorting scratchy little plants, roots, and berries, ignoring him. Finally, wound up enough to break things, he left the cottage to pace instead along the shore of the lake. If someone had indeed tried to kill Alix, he intended to find out who, how, and why. Even if the knowledge shattered his peace of mind.

Roger was not a blind or imperceptive man. But his heart was shying away from examining the evidence that his brain insisted he consider. Alix's hysterical, half-conscious words had been haunting him all night. *I'll keep your secret. Oh God, not you, not you . . . I saved your life.*

Roger could think of only one person whose life Alix had saved recently. *The tale is long and you won't want to believe it.* Roger smashed his fist against a tree, hardly noticing the bloody scrape the rough bark delivered. Where the hell was Francis? Had he really gone south, as he had claimed? Or had he traveled northwest, to Westmor? Had it been he who'd attacked Alexandra?

Why was he thinking these things? Was it because the gloomy forest reminded him all too clearly of another night, one year before? A peasant boy who'd killed himself against all expectation and sense. A proud-eyed woman who violated her Madonna image one afternoon by confessing an affair with his dead brother. An ornamental dagger that had lain in the ditch where Will had cracked his head . . . or had it cracked. And a red-haired girl who'd never stopped insisting that murder had been done.

How many times did these facts have to sift through his brain before he was willing to acknowledge the pattern they were forming? Francis Lacklin had been present at Chilton on the night of Will Trevor's accident. He had been in the forest at the time of Ned's death. And he could have been here, at the lakeside with Alexandra, yesterday afternoon.

Roger picked up a handful of stones and flung them one by one into the water. What had Francis said as he lay bleeding on the riverbank at Greenwich, believing himself about to die? Something about having wronged Alexandra. *And you also, Roger,* he had added. Had he wronged Alexandra by murdering Will, the man she was to marry? Had he wronged Roger by taking the life of his brother? But why? *Why?*

God's blood! Roger's head was aching, but the thoughts, now whirling like a top, wouldn't stop.

He flung one more rock into the water. The splash it made seemed to echo around the lake. He turned and stalked back toward Merwynna's cottage. He had to talk to her; he could bear the suspense no longer. If Francis was a murderer, he wanted to hear the truth of it from Alexandra's lips.

FIRES OF DESTINY

37

WHEN Alexandra awoke that morning, she was groggy, but not out of her senses this time. Her sleep had been peaceful, and she had felt safe, knowing Roger was nearby.

Merwynna came to lean over her; she smiled and reached for the old wisewoman's hand. Looking past her, she saw a man entering the cottage. The rising sun was just behind him, and its light dazzled her eyes, making him seem larger, broader, obscuring his face. The welcoming grin she was sending his way died on her lips as, for an instant, this tall dark-haired man seemed to change into the figure from her nightmares, the killer with the deadly sword at his side.

Roger saw the fear come into her eyes. He saw the way she cringed backward on her mattress, and he read the word her lips formed in the second before she recognized him and her terror dissipated. "Francis?" she mouthed.

"Alix, it's me," he said, moving slowly toward her. But inside him the demons were gathering, for he knew now that he had guessed correctly.

"The sun was in my eyes." She managed the smile after all.

He did not smile back. He wasn't seeing her; he was seeing himself, a grief-stricken boy leaping from the dark family pew in a sweet-smelling, ornately decorated chapel ... rushing past the coffin that bore the last earthly remains of his beloved mother . . . standing up in front of an entire village of shocked retainers to accuse his own father of murder. His father, whom he had looked up to and imitated. His father, who, inexplicably, had turned against him, tormented him, beaten him. He had never understood why, how he had offended, what he had done wrong. He had turned to his mother for comfort, his beautiful, laughing mother, who was dead.

Christ! Screaming in rage, rending his clothes in grief . . . then burying those feelings for years. Burying them deep. Fleeing from Chilton and the father he hated, and finding another man to look up to. Another man to imitate. And, very slowly, very tentatively, another man to love.

And now, after years of trust, another betrayal.

His father was not a murderer after all. But Francis Lacklin was.

"Roger?" Alexandra had pushed herself up to a sitting position, cursing her own jumpiness and wondering what had brought that tortured look to Roger's face. Had Merwynna told him about Francis? She glanced at the wisewoman, whose expression gave no help, no hints. "Is aught amiss?"

Roger's sensual lower lip curled with irony. *Is aught amiss?* Nothing much. Nothing but the world blasted to smithereens. Nothing but every truth there is destroyed . . . except one. Alexandra. He focused on her green eyes, her sweet, worried face. Her bright hair. Alix. His candle in the dark.

"Are you feeling better?" he asked.

"Oh, yes. Much better."

He snatched up her clothes and thrust them at her. "Dress yourself, then. I have a horse outside. We're going back to Chilton."

"But surely—"

"Now."

And so within a very few minutes she was sitting astride a big gray gelding dressed in her old gown and wrapped up warmly in a blanket. Her bare feet were hanging down on either side—they had not been able to recover her boots from the lake—and Roger's chest was jammed against her back, his thighs feeling hard and lithely masculine on either side of her own, his breath fanning the tendrils of hair on the back of her neck. The early morning sun cast a subtle rosy light through the stark trees. Unlike yesterday, the new day was fair. And there was a sultriness in the air that promised unseasonable warmth.

They did not speak. Alexandra waited in vain for questions that did not come. She sensed powerful passions burning inside him; she felt them in the rigidity of his body. This, she remembered, was the man she'd fled from, the man who'd stalked her for two months and several hundred miles, abandoning his ships, his men, his planned voyage to the Middle Sea to pursue her into the country where he was now considered an outlaw. He had been gentle and forbearing with her last night, yes, but the arm that encircled her waist was not particularly gentle now. He held her possessively, implacably, as if to warn her she would not escape from him again.

Not that she wished to escape. In fact, as she cast her eyes down and saw the tan flesh of his forearm around her, the strong sinews, the well-shaped bones of his wrist, Alexandra felt a quicksilver flash of excitement. She remembered the deft and tender movements of those hands upon her flesh . . . hands that had not touched her in far, far too long.

Sensing her thought, Roger altered the position of his hand slightly, enough to allow his fingers to slip inside the opening of her blanket and brush across her breasts. An earthquake of desire rumbled inside her. She leaned more completely against him, instinctively seeking the pleasures his body could provide. His hand came up, covering one of her breasts, kneading it, then moving to take the other. As his thumb flicked over her nipple, a sigh escaped her.

His horse slowed and stopped under the thick branches of an oak. Both Roger's hands were on her breasts now, and his lips were nuzzling the back of her neck. He threaded kisses up under her hair and around the side of her jaw. His teeth took her earlobe, bore down, pulled slightly. As he released her, his tongue insinuated itself inside the shell of her ear, darting like a snake.

Alexandra made a sound deep in the back of her throat. Desire, yearning. Roger echoed her with a groan. Quickly he dismounted and held out his arms for her. They were deep in the ancient oak grove where she had once relaxed and laughed with Roger and Francis Lacklin. The huge trees were thick around them, mysterious, silent, and wise. They offered shelter; impassive, they judged not, they knew no sin.

"Come to me, sweetling."

She stared at him, his dark hair, his eyes burning with silken command. His body, tall and lean and beautiful. His hands, which reached for her. His fingers were long and autocratic, beautiful. She remembered the sensual magic they could weave.

She brought her leg over the horse's neck with little of the grace she'd struggled so hard at court to acquire. He didn't seem to mind her clumsiness. He was smiling as she slid into his arms.

Roger carried her into the shade of a giant oak and set her down. With gentle hands he unwrapped the blanket from her body and spread it upon the ground. Then he swiftly unfastened her gown. His fingers had begun to shake, and he couldn't stop kissing her—her eyes, her mouth, her fingers, her throat, and every inch of bare flesh he revealed as he stripped the fabric from her. He jerked the bodice down to her waist and pulled her close, rubbing her breasts against his chest. His eyes were glazed, his breath impossibly fast.

"Christ, love, I'm out of my head with wanting you. Two months of celibacy is enough to drive me to the edge of madness."

"You've taken no other women to warm your bed?"

"God, no. The thought sickens me. It's you I want, only you." He smiled slightly. "Curious, isn't it? I've never felt this way before."

"I've always felt this way. You're the only man I've *ever* wanted."

His hands tightened in her hair. "After you left me, I imagined you with Alan ... you've always loved him—"

"As a brother."

"—and he has a passion for you. Oh, I trusted you. I trusted you, but sometimes, even so, my mind conjured up images that made me wild with jealousy and rage. Wild," he repeated, dropping his head to take her mouth. He kissed her deep and hard, taking fierce possession. "God's blood, how I want you! I could die of it."

"Yes, I know. I feel the same." And she did. She wasn't sure if it was the two months of celibacy, or the need for an affirmation of life in the face of death, but she was drunk with desire. Her wits were fuzzy and there was a conflagration throughout her body, centered deep and radiating outward. His kisses burned her, set her aflame.

He pressed her down on the blanket, careful not to hurt her, yet possessed of a ferocious passion that could barely be controlled. In a few rapid, economical movements, he finished stripping her, then attended to his own clothing. While he tore at his points and hose, her hands brushed over him, teasing the tense sinews bunched beneath his smooth skin, luxuriating in his strength, his ardor, his slightly threatening masculinity. And then he was naked, his body as lithe and beautiful in her eyes as a pagan god's. Her eyes admired his strong yet slender frame—the wide, angular shoulders, the expanse of golden-tan flesh on his chest, all dusted with wiry black curls, the trim waist and taut hips, the tight buttocks, and long, graceful legs. And most glorious of all, the hard proof of his desire, full and swollen and yearning for its haven inside her body.

Grinning, Roger dropped to his knees beside her. "Wide-eyed, are you, lassie?" He pressed kisses all over her face and neck. "One would think you'd never seen it before."

Her brows arched mischievously. "The light in our cabin on the *Argo* was poor."

"True, more's the pity." He guided her hand to him. "Touch me, love, the way I taught you. Aye, that's it." He threw his head back, the tendons in his neck full prominent. After a moment he cursed softly and pushed her hand away. "On second thought, you'd better stop before I disgrace myself, leaving you unfilled, unsatisfied. Give me a minute." He lay down beside her, fighting for control. She curled against him, her fingers dancing over his naked flesh, her lips finding the sweet hollow at the base of his throat and kissing him tenderly.

At length Roger pushed himself up on one elbow and slid one hand between their bodies. He caressed her, taking his time now. Although he could hardly wait to sheathe himself inside her soft, hot flesh, he wanted it to be good for her. Perfect. "Your breasts are bigger, heavier," he murmured. "I can feel the difference, my love."

"Aye, and soon my entire body will be large and ungainly! Will you still want me then?"

"Oh, yes. I'll always want you. I'll always love you. But for own your sake 'tis a jolly good thing you're with child and in need of tenderness. For I was of a mind to thrash you when I caught you, little rabbit." His hand came up and gripped her chin, forcing her to meet his eyes. "You ought to have trusted me, sweetling. I was drunk that last evening when we talked. Were it not for that, I wouldn't have been so callous. I have no great liking for my father, but blood is blood. I wouldn't have sat back and allowed your father to carry out his threat."

"You mean you'd have given in? Sent me home yourself?"

"I'd have done something. Married you, for a start. Offered to meet your father somewhere neutral, so I could have proved to him that what he saw at Greenwich was a temporary madness, a mistake, an aberration. I can't blame the man for fearing for your life, given the way I acted that night."

"I tried to explain to him. He still doesn't believe me, you know. He seems to think you've cast a spell over me."

"Then somehow I will have to convince him that I am not the rogue I'm painted to be." He frowned at her. "I sometimes think I still have to convince you of that."

"What do you mean?"

"Simply that I'm weary of people thinking me such a monster. Plotting to murder the queen, fratricide, patricide, rape—my colorful reputation bears little resemblance to the actual facts."

She turned her face away, heart-stricken by his words. "Forgive me, Roger."

His lips brushed her cheek; his teeth found an earlobe and nipped. "Not until you beg."

She sinuously arched against him, bringing their intimate parts in close conjunction, writhing and seeking him in a way she knew he would not be able to resist. "Like this?"

He groaned; his body tensed in feigned reluctance. "You've remembered very well all that I taught you, I see."

"'Tis hardly something one forgets!"

For one more second he held back. "The babe, Alix? Will we hurt the baby?"

"No, no," she assured him.

"'Twill not cause you to miscarry?"

She laughed gently. "If loving could bring on miscarriage, there would be very few children born into this world!"

The words were scarcely out of her mouth when his hands were on her, caressing her breasts, her belly, her thighs. Gently he parted the soft folds of her womanhood, murmuring love words, sex words, words of praise. Deliciously he stroked and courted her until his fingers were bathed in heat, in moisture. Then, shifting quickly, he brought back his hips and thrust, filling her deeply, then again, more deeply still.

"Oh, my love," she whispered. "'Tis very, *very* good!"

He raised his head, not answering. For several seconds he did not move; he simply held her pinned to the ground by the force of his hips while he stared deep into her eyes with an indescribable expression in his brown eyes—fierce, possessive, angry even, cruel and tender, loving and demanding—all emotions rolled into one.

The pressure inside her was intolerable. She moved fretfully against him, but he was inexorable. He kept her still, impaled upon his bone-hard flesh, his dark eyes all glittery and savage. Then, slowly, so slowly she thought she would die, he began to move, watching her eyes, her face, her breathing with all the instincts of a predator. For a moment she thought that this was her punishment for leaving him. To be controlled, dominated by his sheer physical power. To be tortured slowly until she screamed for release. To be held at the very threshold of ecstasy but denied the relief of falling through that golden doorway. His revenge. He was capable of such, she knew.

But then he lowered his head and kissed her sweetly, and she knew she'd been mistaken. Something was driving him, yes, but it was not directed against her. Something was hurting him, numbing his mind. And she was his only refuge, his only sanctuary.

Forgetting her own fears, desires, and needs, she held him tightly and told him of a love that was unchanging and eternal, enduring till death, and beyond. And in selflessness, she found a release more intense than any she had known before. Without striving, her body found its pleasure, just moments before he also stiffened and cried out. Together they flew above the earth, their joint physical pleasure a triviality compared to the indescribable glory of their united souls.

When it was over, he did not withdraw; he stayed clasped in her arms, his skin slick, his heart hammering, his breathing convulsive. More convulsive than hers—in fact, as he continued to shudder against her, it finally penetrated that he was crying. Roger Trevor, strong and confident leader of men, was quietly sobbing in her arms.

Alexandra stiffened, shocked beyond words. Then, abruptly, she recalled the expression on his face this morning when she'd awakened. He knew, she realized. She did not have to tell him; *he knew.*

With love and pity she caressed and kissed him, giving him what comfort she could. When at last he controlled himself, rolled off her, and pulled her fiercely to his side, she leaned over him and read the confirmation in his eyes. "You know about Francis, don't you?"

His voice was very ragged. "Aye, lassie."

"Did Merwynna tell you?"

"No. I puzzled it out for myself, as I should have done long ago." He brushed away what remained of the moisture on his cheeks. "On some deep level of awareness, I must have known for ages. He said something on the riverbank at Greenwich, but I couldn't face it then. I suppose I deliberately put it out of my mind."

"He said something on the *Argo*, too. Just as he was coming out of his coma. I couldn't tell you. I thought it would hurt you too much. And besides, I had no proof."

"He nearly succeeded in killing you." Roger's voice broke again. "My blindness nearly cost you your life!"

"Shh, don't blame yourself. He did not succeed."

"The peasant boy I could have forgiven him. Even—God save me—my brother. But not you, Alix, never you." His voice hardened ominously. "What, exactly, did he do to you?"

"He tried to drown me. He didn't know I could swim. Or perhaps he did know, and forgot. I don't think he really wanted to kill me. He may even have tried to save me at the end. He held out an oar; perhaps he leapt in after me ... I'm not sure. It was foggy, and I couldn't see the shore. I lost my sense of direction. I swam and swam ... it was cold and I was sick with pregnancy and my own terror. I was drowning when I stumbled into shallow water. If Merwynna hadn't found me, and if you hadn't been there to carry me to warmth, I surely would have died."

"Oh Christ!" There was a silence; then: "Where is he now?"

"I don't know. He meant to dally somewhere, I think, then arrive at Chilton after my ... my body had been found." She paused. "He killed Priscilla Martin too. Do you want to hear the whole tale?"

He sat up and reached for their clothes. "Not now. Not until we get safely back to Chilton." He looked around them, his gaze going from tree to tree. "'Twas folly to stop here in the forest like this. Why do you think I removed you from Merwynna's? I can't protect you here."

"Protect me? What need is there to protect me now? He tried to kill me to prevent you from finding out the truth. He failed. What's left for him now?"

"Nothing, perhaps. But there is none more dangerous than a desperate man. Particularly when he's one of the finest swordsmen in Europe."

"Roger?" Her fingers touched his chest in sudden fear. "You're not going to call him out, are you? He'll kill you."

"Oh, I don't know. I've been practicing, and his sword arm isn't the same since his injury."

"For God's sake, Roger! Please. Promise me."

"I cannot make such a promise. There's a part of me that relishes the idea of taking my naked blade to his throat." His voice was rough, violent. He rose to his feet and helped her into her clothes. "Still, the next move's his, isn't it? Perhaps he's fled and we shall never see him again."

"Perhaps." But as they dressed and mounted the horse again for the rest of the journey to Chilton, both of them silently acknowledged that the final conflict was inevitable . . . and probably very soon to come.

38

A LAN TREVOR sat at the bedside of Pris Martin at the Cock's Feather Inn and worried. She'd been sleeping for hours. Wasn't she ever going to wake up? He had some questions to ask her. She'd been incoherent when he'd found her wandering aimlessly by the side of the London road. She'd been feverish, in fact, which was hardly surprising. Apparently she'd spent all night outside in the rain. There was a nasty gash on her shoulder, but Alan still didn't know whether she had been attacked or if she'd simply fallen from her horse. All he knew was that Alexandra had sent him after her to protect her, and, as usual, he had failed.

On the day Alix had sent him after Ned, the boy had turned up dead. On that dreadful night when he and Alix had been captured by Geoffrey de Montreau and his men, his attempts to defend her had resulted in her being tortured, abducted, and raped. He was not very effective as a protector, it seemed. He was not very effective at *anything*.

He comforted himself with the thought that at least Mistress Martin was not dead. Perhaps if he had been with her from the beginning of her journey he could have kept her from whatever had befallen her. As it was, he had taken swift action in carrying her back to the inn, securing a room, and paying the innkeeper's wife—a gruff soul, but gentle—

to bathe her wounds and make her comfortable. Then Alan had settled down to do vigil at her side.

While she slept, Alan had occasion to think upon many things. He wondered how Alexandra had known that Pris might be in need of a protector. Had Merwynna the witch predicted as much? Unconsciously, he made the sign against evil. Merwynna had always unnerved him; he didn't like to think that there were cunning-folk who could so unfailingly foretell the future. No, surely it was coincidence that Alexandra's fears of an attack on Pris had proved to be justified. Coincidence, coupled with the fact that so young and comely a woman should have had more sense than to travel alone.

Comely. During the long hours of his watch, Alan had had ample opportunity to study the exquisite features of the woman who had been his eldest brother's mistress. Her hair was black silk. Her sooty lashes were dense against her creamy skin. The innkeeper's wife had stripped her of her wet clothes and put her naked under the blankets. Sleep had disarranged her position, and several times Alan had had to tuck blankets around her that had come loose and slipped down to reveal her bare arms, her throat, the pearly flesh of her breasts.

Guiltily he had tried to repress his surprisingly strong physical reaction to this stimulation, but the few brief encounters he'd had with women since his initiation at the randy hands of the innkeeper's mistress in Oxford had left him hungry. Of course it was Alexandra whom he loved and desired above all others, but, as if it had accepted that there was no hope for him with her, his body was beginning to respond to other women. The long weeks of traveling with Alix had been purgatory. She had been as warm and affectionate with him as ever, but it was plain that she yearned for Roger and regarded Alan as nothing more than a brother.

Staring at Pris Martin, Alan found himself imagining what it would be like to kiss those luscious lips and stroke that soft ivory skin. He had always thought of her as a woman much older than himself, but in truth she was

Alexandra's age—only one year his senior. Naked and de-
fenseless, she seemed even younger.

Gingerly he placed a hand on Pris's forehead. She was
cool—no longer feverish. She stirred slightly under his
hand; he jerked it away. Her eyelashes fluttered and her lips
curled faintly, a smile of sorts. Alan was astonished at the
tender, protective feelings that surged up inside him. He
hadn't been there for her the other night, but he was with
her now, and he was damned if anybody was going to hurt
her again.

He had no sooner come to this decision than there was
a loud rapping on the chamber door. He rose and opened
it, exclaiming as he came face to face with another guest—
a man he recognized. It was Sir Charles Douglas, and tramping up the stairs behind him was a troop of the queen's
guard.

"Ah, 'tis you, Alan," the red-haired courtier said. "The
innkeeper's wife was gossiping . . . she mentioned the name
Trevor, and said you had an injured woman with you . . ."
He looked past Alan into the room. "Is it my daughter?"

"Alix? No, sir, she's home at Westmor. But what are you
doing here? I thought you were staying in London."

"I was, but something came up." As he spoke, Douglas
jerked a thumb over his shoulder. Alan looked beyond him,
and nearly swallowed his tongue. He was gazing into the
malicious blue eyes of the pretty-faced, elegant man whose
occasional appearance in his dreams invariably caused Alan
to awaken in a sweat. God's blood—Geoffrey de Montreau!
He was here in Yorkshire. Only a day's journey from
Alexandra, whom he had tortured on the rack.

Douglas cleared his throat loudly. "Our French friend
here, who always has his ear to the ground, claims to have
heard a rumor that the remarkable Roger Trevor may be in
England. I don't believe it, myself, since my own spies
have got no wind of him, but Geoffrey went direct to the
queen with his rumor, and she ordered me up here to in-
vestigate. She heard of Alix's return, you see." He shot a
nasty glance at Geoffrey. "And she's waxing romantic. If
Alix is home, then her lover must be following her. Nonsense, I warrant—your devil of a brother has never chased

a woman in his life. Why should he? They all throw themselves at his feet. When he's done with 'em, he throws 'em over for the next one in the queue. My daughter is nothing more than discarded goods for him now."

Alan couldn't speak. The sight of Geoffrey de Montreau had filled him with revulsion.

His adversary stepped forward, batting his golden lashes. "Have you seen your brother lately, Alan? The crown is naturally interested in the whereabouts of so notorious a heretic and traitor. Indeed, the crown intends to try him for his crimes and put him to death."

"You dare to call Roger a traitor?" Alan sputtered. "You, who have betrayed your own country by turning coat and taking England's part in this war?"

Geoffrey paid no heed to this indictment. He spoke again, his tone steel under silk. "Where is he, Alan?"

"He's in the Mediterranean, with his ship." It was no lie. As far as he knew, that's exactly where Roger was. Unless . . . Christ Almighty. *Had* he followed Alix to England?

"And Francis Lacklin? Does anyone know where *he* is?"

"I do," said a quiet voice from just behind Alan. He whirled. Pris Martin was sitting up in bed, the bedclothes pulled up to her neck for modesty.

Alan rushed back to her side. "Pris! Lie down, you're ill."

Although she seemed a little confused, it did not alter her composure. "It was you who found me, Alan? You who brought me here . . . you who have taken such good care of me?"

"Aye," said Alan, blushing. "Alexandra feared for your safety and sent me to watch over you."

She smiled so sweetly that he momentarily forgot Geoffrey de Montreau.

"Mistress Martin?" Charles Douglas was addressing her. He had thrust one strong arm across the doorway, preventing a frustrated-looking Geoffrey from entering the room. "I'm Alexandra's father—d'you remember me? Forgive me for intruding, but I've a question or two for you. You have something to report about Francis Lacklin's whereabouts?"

"He's in England," Pris answered. "Indeed, he tried to murder me. And I very much fear, Sir Charles, that he is at Westmor, attempting the life of your daughter, even now."

Several voices spoke at once, Alan's included, demanding an explanation. Her voice dry with anxiety for the girl who had so belatedly become her friend, Pris Martin gave them one.

Roger's arrival at Chilton Hall with Alexandra was the occasion for much amazement and delight on the part of the baron's retainers. He was popular with them, Alexandra noted; he always had been. The reports that he was an exiled criminal had apparently been the cause of much groaning here at his Yorkshire home.

Dorcas extended a warm welcome to Alexandra, but seemed uneasy around Roger. When he asked to see his father, she quickly made an excuse. "He's abed, resting. His heart is very weak." She paused. "And I fear what may happen if you and he begin squabbling again."

"I promise not to squabble," Roger tried to reassure her. When still she hesitated, he added, "I'm afraid this is a matter of some urgency." Briefly he explained about Francis Lacklin. "If he comes here, as he is almost certain to do, there will be trouble. My father must be informed."

"I don't know—"

"Listen, Dorcas, if it were I with a weak heart, possibly dying, I would still want to know what the devil was transpiring in my own household. I wouldn't wish to be kept ignorant, treated like a babe in arms. My father, I am certain, will agree."

Dorcas looked anxiously to Alexandra, who nodded encouragement. "Very well. If you think it best. But please try not to upset him too much. He's very ill."

Shortly thereafter, Roger was in the antechamber outside the baron's room, holding Alexandra beside him, his fingers clamped like a manacle around her wrist. "Get out," he ordered Master Theobald, the physician, who was furtively trying to hide a bottle of aqua vitae under his robes.

"You!" Theobald cried. "You can't come in here!"

"Out," Roger repeated, his hand hovering near the dagger in his belt.

The physician fled.

Richard Trevor was awake. His head and shoulders were elevated on two bolsters and he was covered with a blanket that did not succeed in disguising the gauntness of his body. Alexandra was dismayed at his appearance. The baron had changed drastically in the year since she had last seen him, and it was evident that the final dissolution would soon be upon him.

Roger, too, was dismayed, though he did not wish to admit it to himself. His father was dying—God's wounds, he looked all but dead already. He realized for the first time how empty Charles Douglas' threat had been. His father could not possibly have stood trial for heresy. He would be going to his reward—or punishment—long before the Church would have the leisure to deal with him.

The baron gazed upon Roger with an expression of dry cynicism, taking in every detail of his somewhat bedraggled appearance. He was perfectly lucid. "So you're back, along with the young woman you kidnapped and raped. I suppose we should all be thankful she isn't dead. What was that commotion outside the door?"

"Your physician tried to deny me entrance. Perhaps he thought the sight of me would give you another heart seizure."

"My physician is a drunken ass. How are you, Alexandra, after what may be politely termed your *ordeal?* You don't look particularly downtrodden and defeated, I must say."

"Neither do you," she told him with a smile. It was true—despite the wreck of his body, his eyes were as vibrant and energetic as ever. She sat down on the stool beside the bed and touched her lips to his thin, frail hand. "There was no rape. I love your son and we wish to marry."

The baron's thin lips—lips that were so like Roger's—curled slightly. "So you want my blessing, is that it?"

"No," said Roger, coming up behind her and placing his hands on her shoulders. *Men die. It changes nothing between us.* "We don't need your blessing, nor that of Alexandra's father, who has put nothing but obstacles in our way. We've come to speak with you about something else entirely."

"Indeed? Well, since you've never cared about my opinion in the past, I don't suppose I can expect you to care now. I was always in favor of the match, you will recall. Or perhaps you'd rather not recall any matter in which you and I might be in agreement."

Trying to take his father's bitterness with good grace, Roger simply shrugged. "Our news concerns Francis Lacklin. And the manner of my brother's death."

The baron closed his eyes. "There is some connection between the two?"

"Aye, I am sorry to report." And succinctly, in a tone almost entirely devoid of expression, Roger told his father everything they knew.

The baron interrupted him once or twice with questions, but for the most part he listened without comment, his control rivaling Roger's. At the end there was a long silence. Alexandra remembered, with compassion for both men, the fond esteem in which the baron had always held Francis. She had a mental picture of the way he had greeted Francis last year on the day of Roger's homecoming—with more warmth and affection than he had shown his own son.

Francis had converted Richard Trevor to Calvinism. But he had also killed the baron's firstborn son, the son he had loved and favored all his life.

"I'm sorry, Father," Roger said. "I know this must be a blow to you. But in truth, 'twas even more of a blow to me."

There was a long silence before the baron said, "You and he knew each other far better than you let on, did you not? You were friends?"

"Aye." Roger clipped off the syllable.

"I realized it after hearing what had happened in London. You were working for our side all along. Why, then, did you take so violently against me?" For the first time, the baron displayed signs of genuine emotion. "Why was there such strife between us when you came home last summer? Could you not trust me? I would have been proud to know that you were one of us, that you were endeavoring to save Protestants from the stake."

Roger ran a rough hand through his hair. "I am not one of you. You're quite mistaken if you believe I think myself one of the elect of God. Francis had a hold over me, that's all. I worked with him in payment of a debt. My disgust with fanatical religious opinion has not changed one whit."

Alexandra saw the pained look that came over his father's face and wished Roger, for once, might be more tactful. Here was a possible means of rapprochement between the two men. *Please, Roger, don't toss it away.*

Roger shifted uneasily and sent her a rueful glance. "But that's neither here nor there. I didn't tell you because Francis himself had sworn me to silence. Also, we did not want to endanger you. Given what happened in the end, of course, it was just as well that you were not implicated."

Richard Trevor closed his eyes. He looked much more tired all of a sudden. His cheeks were sunken and his skin was an unhealthy gray. "You say Will died accidentally?" he asked.

"So Francis told Alix. I believe him, for what it's worth. But it makes no difference—the outcome will be the same."

"There is no point trying to arrest Francis Lacklin for murder," the baron said. "He is already a fugitive."

"I have no intention of trying to arrest him." Roger's voice was grim. "This is a private matter, which must be settled privately."

"What do you mean?" Alexandra demanded.

The two men stared at one another, ignoring her. "He killed your brother. You wish to satisfy our family honor?"

"He killed my brother and he attempted to kill my betrothed wife. Where honor is concerned, I have no choice."

The baron hesitated slightly before his next comment. "You told us once that he was one of the finest swordsmen you had ever seen."

"He is. But I have no paltry amount of skill with the rapier myself."

"Roger, no!"

They continued to avoid her eyes. "I will do what has

to be done," Roger said quietly, and his father nodded. In this, at least, there was no dispute between them.

Francis Lacklin came to Chilton the next morning. Notified of his approach by the watch he'd posted on the road, Roger decided to meet him in front of the hearth in the great hall. He set several men-at-arms nearby and gave them explicit orders. Dorcas he sent to the baron's bedchamber. Alexandra he stationed on the other side of the archway that led to the stairs—out of sight but within hearing. Then he waited, feeling sick.

Alexandra waited too, behind the stone archway where she had once eavesdropped on these same two men. She saw Francis Lacklin enter, pause a moment, then advance toward Roger, who was seated in his father's armchair by the fire, a cup of wine in his clenched fist. She saw Roger raise his head and meet the older man's eyes, his face carefully expressionless, revealing nothing of what she knew he was feeling. And she heard him say, cheerfully enough, "So here you are at last, Francis. Where the devil have you been doing—making converts again? Or seeing to your former flock?"

Lacklin didn't answer. He came up to Roger, glanced into his cup, and said, "You're not too drunk, I hope? I've never seen such a bunch of gloomy servants. Is aught amiss?"

They had anticipated the question. Roger was supposed to reply that his father was gravely ill and Alexandra missing, but instead he said nothing at all. *Is aught amiss?* The muscles in his jaw clenched and he stared blankly into the wine. He imagined he could see his reflection there, his ravaged face looking out from a sea of red. His eyes closed for an instant; then he flung the silver goblet against the wall. Claret splattered like blood on the cold stone.

"What the devil—"

"Oh, for Christ's sake, have done, Francis. This paltry little tragedy has gone on long enough." He came out of the armchair and stood face to face with his friend, his enemy. The color had drained from his face just as completely as the wine had drained from the cup. "You have failed. Alix is alive. You were careless, Francis. Next time you'd better hire an assassin."

Francis Lacklin didn't move or speak for a moment, but the tension in his big body was plain. At last he said, "I don't know what you're talking about."

"No, of course not. I could be lying. Suspicious and trying to entrap you. Grief-stricken over the death of the woman I loved and wanted to wed." Roger's voice was shaking. "The woman I *love*, Francis! Given what you've meant to me all these years, I could have forgiven almost anything else, but you should have known better than to lay hands on her!"

"You're ranting, Roger. You must be very drunk. Where is Alexandra? Is there something the matter with her?"

"No, Francis. There is nothing the matter with her. Alix? Come here."

Feeling like an actor making a dramatic entrance, Alexandra walked through the archway into the hall and approached the two men. "Hello, Francis," she said.

Lacklin whirled, his silver-gray eyes as large as coins. He muttered something under his breath; then he was coming at her, fast—for what purpose, she couldn't imagine.

Roger shot between them. "Get away from her!" Whipping his sword out of its sheath, he leapt at his old friend. "If you touch her, I'll skewer you here and now." And his blade was at Lacklin's throat, hovering just above the jumping artery.

Francis paid no attention to the sword. He was staring numbly at Alexandra. "You're alive."

"Yes." She was feeling absurdly sorry for him. She wanted to reach out to him, offer him her hands, assure him that he was truly and sincerely forgiven. "As you see."

"But how . . . You can swim?"

"I have always been a good swimmer."

Lacklin's big shoulders drooped and his breath came out in a sound that was almost a sigh. "I'm glad. I regretted it . . . Christ, how I regretted it! I am relieved to find there is some justice in this world, after all." Then, slowly, careful

of the blade that pressed against his throat, he turned back
to Roger. And waited.

"You killed my brother Will." Roger's voice seemed to
come from some great distance.

"Yes."

"And Ned, the village half-wit. You strangled him in
such a manner as to make it appear to be self-slaughter."

"It's true. I take no pride in it."

"You left Priscilla Martin for dead and tried to drown
Alexandra."

Francis didn't reply this time. Neither did he meet his
old friend's eyes.

Roger was floating. He thought he'd been prepared for
this, but somehow, confronted with the reality, confronted
with the *man*, it was proving to be much harder than he'd
anticipated. Nothing was real; he was not in this cavernous
medieval hall ... instead he was riding the deck of the *Argo*
under an arching vault of blue. He was standing at the side
of a gray-eyed man as they plowed through the sun-flecked
sea, laughing as they sailed over the rim of the world.

Trying desperately to re-focus, Roger stared along the
metal of his sword. "Draw your rapier, Francis."

"No!"

Alexandra's protest was joined almost at once by Francis' voice, sounding bizarrely calm and normal. "No. I will
not fight you, Roger. Not today, not ever."

"Then I shall kill you as you stand."

"Do. You have good reason, and I no longer have the
slightest wish to live."

Roger's swordhand trembled. Beneath his blade beat the
pulse of his friend's carotid artery. He imagined it slashed,
his lifesblood spilling onto the floor. . . . No. He lowered
the sword, as if fleeing the gravest temptation. "You have
most greviously offended my honor, sir, and the honor of
my family," he stated in the ancient, formal manner. "I
demand restitution. God will be our judge."

"No, please, Roger," Alexandra cried. She grasped his
arm, her fingers trembling. "In sooth there is no reason for
trial by combat, if that's what you intend. He has admitted
his crimes—there is no dispute to be settled."

"There is my brother's blood, crying out to be avenged."

"I will not stand back and watch you follow Will into the family crypt!"

Lacklin added his own objections to hers. "I'll fight no duel with you, Roger," he repeated. "You cannot force me to take up arms against you."

"No, I cannot force you. But you will fight me, nonetheless. You have unmanned me, Francis. For eleven years you have been there, the dark shadow at my shoulder. My wiser friend. My older brother. My colder, more controlled adviser. The father figure I rejected as a youth."

Francis tried to speak, but Roger jammed the blade against his throat again. "No, damn you, this time you will hear me out. I am not the sort who takes well to domination. I have borne it meekly for far too long. Once I fled from you into a monastery, but I couldn't shake you, could I? You're always there, one step behind me, waiting and watching, the devil at my heels."

"I have been your friend," said Lacklin tightly.

"You have been my master. Friends are equal, and that is something you and I have never been. You have always had me at a disadvantage. You were calmer. More rational. More godly. More secure from the temptations of the flesh. Stronger, and more skilled with the rapier. Until today, Francis. Today the scales will be balanced at last." He lowered the sword and took a step back. "Your rapier, Francis. This is our final conflict. You will fight me—it has been inevitable since the day we met."

There was a long silence. At last Francis said, "You would risk your life so recklessly just to prove yourself my equal?"

"Not to prove myself, Francis. To free myself. To free myself once and for all of the long shadow you have cast upon my life. Anyway"—Roger actually smiled—"it may not be as much of a risk as you think. I have been in constant practice. And your shoulder is no longer what it was."

"My shoulder is fully recovered."

"Good. I would not wish to feel that I had an unfair advantage over you."

"You mean it, don't you? You're looking forward to this."

"I've been looking forward to this for a long, long time."

"Very well." Lacklin's voice was heavy. "I shall fight you, Roger."

"No," Alexandra said once more, but her voice was low, despairing. They did not so much as glance in her direction. It was, she knew, already decided.

39

THE GREAT hall at Chilton flickered with the light of a dozen extra torches as the servants moved the trestle tables and benches and prepared the room for the first duel of honor to be fought in recent memory. The two participants had stripped to shirt and hose and selected their weapons, fine Florentine rapiers of flexible tempered steel. Up on the dais, from which the family and retainers were to observe, Alexandra stood gripped by apprehension.

Roger also was nervous. He tested the strength of his blade against his boot and wondered if he would be alive an hour from now. He hoped so, for the sake of Alix and the babe.

Francis approached him, looking fit and strong and entirely at ease. And why not? When had he last been defeated in a trial of this particular weapon? Had he ever been defeated? Recently, in practice, Roger had scored several hits against him. But they had never had a bout in which Francis did not also score, usually in *quarte*—the line that guarded Roger's heart.

"You are certain you wish to go through with this? It's not too late to call it off."

"Worried, Francis?"

"Of something you and I have done so many dozens of times? No, my friend. In this you are my partner. In this I know you as well as a lover knows his longtime mate."

"An apt allusion, if somewhat imprecise," Roger said scathingly.

Francis smiled. "If I defeat you I will not kill you. I will, however, demand another forfeit."

"Another sheath for your sword?" Roger tossed the words off as if in badinage, but inside he was shaking. He felt fifteen years old again, and threatened. "If I defeat you, you will certainly die."

"I would hope so. Life holds little joy for me now."

Shortly thereafter, the two men faced each other in the ready stance. George Dawes, the baron's master-at-arms, stood beside them, his arm raised over his head. "Any special rules?" he asked the two men.

"First blood decides it," suggested Francis.

"No," said Roger. "To the death."

Francis shrugged and flexed his sword. "As you wish."

They saluted each other formally, then took several steps back. Roger glanced over to the dais and saw Alexandra, her eyes huge and round, her expression one of ill-concealed despair. But as he met her eyes, she smiled, and he cherished her spirit, knowing the smile was one of the braver acts of her life. He gave her a reassuring grin. Another man-at-arms had positioned himself just behind her. Roger had ordered him to restrain her if she tried to interfere with the duel. *I love you, I love you,* he told her silently. *Forgive me, but this is something I must do.*

He turned back to Francis. The referee lowered his arm, and the match began.

Roger opened aggressively. He hoped to set a quick pace and tire his opponent. He was younger; he believed he could make up in stamina what he lacked in skill. His plan included a constant, unrelenting attack on the high lines, where Francis should be weaker now, because of his chest injury.

As Roger attacked, Francis parried effortlessly, smiling slightly as their swords played, the blades flashing silver in the torchlight, clicking and sparking with the contact. They circled once, twice, three times, taking each other's measure as if they had never fought before. Francis' silver-gray eyes were wary and intent. Respectful, too, Roger realized. Despite his skill, Francis was making no assumptions about the outcome. Yet he was confident, as he had every right to be.

They circled yet again. It was Lacklin who was retreating before Roger's advance, but Roger could detect no weakening in his technique. Every attack was met with a smooth parry and riposte, and every counterriposte of Roger's was coolly and easily repelled. It took Roger several minutes to realize that Francis was conducting no offensive of his own. Experimentally, he feinted off-balance, leaving his right side momentarily undefended and eliciting a gasp from Alix. Francis' eyes were perfectly bland as he ignored the opening and fell back.

"You bastard," said Roger softly. "Fight!"

"I am admiring your style."

"Torment me, if you will. But this is unfair to the spectators, and Alexandra has suffered enough. Let it be decided, one way or the other, without undue delay."

"Very well," said Francis, beginning to move with the skill of a master.

From the dais, Alexandra watched the two men with growing, albeit reluctant, admiration. She had not caught their words, but she had heard them speak, and then something had changed. The bout that had been careful, measured, almost dull, transformed itself into an elegant, stylized dance of death.

They were well-matched. Better matched, somehow, than they had been last summer in the forest. Then Roger had been clearly on the defensive. Now he was more confident, more determined, and infinitely more threatening. A certain dramatic flair characterized his movements as he beat, parried, thrust, riposted in perfect synchrony with Lacklin's identical movements. Tall and slender as he was, his grace was evident, but so was the power in his strong shoulders and long arms, the subtlety in his firmly flicking wrists, the palpable masculine force in his lunging thighs. Francis Lacklin is not so beautiful, she thought idiotically as they wove a trail of silver ribbons through the air around them.

And she wondered at the perversity in human nature that could create such an illusion of beauty at the very borderline of death.

They fenced with this beauty and precision for many long minutes, moving back and forth across the hall, up and down and around. But such perfection could not continue indefinitely. Sooner or later, one of them would make a mistake. And when he did, the other would strike.

The thought had barely run through Alexandra's mind when Roger missed his footing. He recovered instantly, but the moment cost him. Alexandra's heart nearly choked her when Lacklin feinted once, twice, and then lunged, unexpectedly, catching Roger's right shoulder as his sword dropped to defend the low inside line. Blood welled up instantly, and the spectators groaned. The heir of Chilton could bleed. He could die.

It was a trifling wound, but Roger felt slightly ill as he acknowledged it. Francis had disengaged. His face was taut with tension. "First blood to me. I am satisfied if you are."

"No," said Roger. He felt a stinging; no real pain and, more important, no stiffness. "We will continue."

"We have fenced scores of time, but always with blunted tips. It gives me no pleasure to watch your blood flow. Let us end this folly now. You may do whatever you want with me—whatever you believe to be just. Turn me over to the crown. Hang me. It matters not. But please don't make me kill you, Roger."

"You're not going to kill me. 'Twill be the other way around." Roger raised his blade to reengage. "Defend," he insisted, and attacked.

It was as if his wound served to increase his energy, for Roger fought ferociously now, forcing Lacklin to retreat. Alexandra pressed her hands together, praying inarticulately. The pace increased, and soon both men were breathing rapidly and sweating. Roger drove Francis back against the tapestries that hung upon the walls, where, for an instant, the older man faltered. But he defended himself adequately against Roger's lunge, pressing him back in turn while he swiftly recovered, finding an opening and lunging. Another ring of steel, another parry, high this time as for a moment they grappled body to body. Alexandra moaned, unable to see, in the tangle of thrashing limbs, precisely what was happening.

They sprang apart, blades cutting wildly as the fine art of the sport was briefly abandoned. The referee yelled something and they disengaged, backing a few steps away from each other, both gasping air, both running with sweat. They eyed each other warily and circled again, engaged only at the tips. There was anger between them now. Alexandra could feel it. Control—both bodily and mental—was dissipating as the raw passions that moved them built toward the flash point.

They fenced uneventfully for several minutes more, both slowing, growing tired. Then, unexpectedly, Lacklin attacked again, driving Roger backward at the speed of a run. Roger missed a parry and Lacklin's blade instantly took the opportunity to snake through his weak *quarte* defense. Alexandra cried out as the steel shot toward her lover's heart. But instead of falling to the floor in a heap, Roger did an astonishing twist in the air and somehow avoided the thrust. Lacklin's immediate retort sent Roger to one knee, his blade thrust up like a crossbar, protecting his throat and chest.

There was utter silence for a moment; then Francis fell back. "Get up," he said.

Roger's eyes blinked closed for a moment as he acknowledged the fear within him. Again, as usual, he was going to lose to Francis, and this time he would die. It had been foolish to think he could turn this particular tide. Here, at least, Francis would always be his master.

His dismay startled him. He had faced death before without faltering. But it was different today; he was not ready to die. Why had he allowed Alexandra to watch? He could not bear the thought of her witnessing his death.

He glanced toward her as he rose, noting her pale face. *Take heart, I'm not dead yet.* Then he saw something else. Behind Alix, leaning on Dorcas' arm, was the baron, his father. He had risen from his sickbed to see the outcome of this fight.

Body of Christ! He was amazed that Dorcas had allowed it. Surely this would qualify as precisely the undue excitement that his father was supposed to avoid.

Grimly Roger engaged blades with Francis once again. His father was dying. There was no love between them, it was true, but there was the family honor. His father's eldest son had died at Francis Lacklin's hands, and Roger was determined that the baron should not go to his grave grieving over the loss of yet another son and heir.

Steel clashed and rang as they attacked, parried, feinted, and lunged, neither of them exercising much style now because they were both so exhausted. Roger's shoulder was hurting, although the bleeding had stopped. His wrist was losing its power. And so far he had not penetrated Francis' guard, not delivered even so much as a scratch. He tried to concentrate on strategy, but all his plans seemed to have disappeared in smoke. He battered the high lines, watching intently for a slip, a momentary falter, an opening of any kind. But there was nothing. And his own defense was working on instinct alone, as he relied on his arm to act without his conscious direction.

Suddenly it occurred to him that his original strategy had worked. Francis was even more weary than he. Roger forced his gritty, burning eyes to study him. His adversary was breathing heavily, his shirt was soaked with sweat. There were dark shadows under his eyes, the like of which Roger remembered from those days when he and Alix had hovered over Francis' bedside on the *Argo*. For the first time ever, his swordplay was loose, careless. And once, as he raised his arm for a lunge, his arm trembled and his face contorted for an instant in pain.

Jesus. Roger feinted skillfully, then again, and watched in disbelief as Francis dropped his blade to parry the second feint, leaving, at last, an opening. Roger lunged; for an instant, gray eyes met brown.

"Very good, my friend," Francis said softly, pivoting so quickly that Roger's tip caught his arm instead of his chest. Cloth ripped and Roger felt the sickening jar of flesh giving way beneath steel. There was blood; more blood than there had been with Roger's shoulder wound. And this was Francis' sword arm.

Roger leapt back, disengaging. "You may bind it up."

But this time it was Francis who said, "No, we will continue. Let's get this over with, shall we?"

Once again their blades clashed. It was apparent to everyone that this would be the last phase. Both combatants were wounded, both were too tired to fence with any art. Alexandra watched in growing horror as they fought with obvious desperation, their faces pale and set, their arms heavy, their movements slow and vicious. When Lacklin's blade cut through the air where an instant before Roger's bare throat had been exposed, Alexandra averted her eyes, only to look up and discover that her lover had ducked in time. Beside her Roger's father groaned as he watched; his breathing seemed as hard as his son's. Alexandra signaled Dorcas with her eyes to get the baron away, but with tears streaming down her cheeks Dorcas whispered that he was determined to see this through. The baron heard.

"I owe him this," he told her. "I've never stood by him, never encouraged him, never shown him my love. Dorcas has told me why you came back to England, and why he followed. I have misjudged him. I'll be here for him now, though it be the final act in my wretched life."

Alexandra squeezed the baron's hand. "He appreciates your presence, I'm sure." But in fact she didn't know whether Roger was even aware of it. He was fighting for his life, and Francis seemed stronger once again. He forced Roger back until they were directly in front of the hearth. Its blaze threw their silhouettes high on the walls, two grappling shadows, dark as death itself, each trying to lay the other low.

And suddenly Roger misinterpreted a feint. Off-balance, he parried wildly as Lacklin lunged in *quarte,* striking for the heart. At the last moment, miraculously, Roger's blade whipped up to defend, the force of his desperation jarring Francis' injured sword arm. Then Lacklin, overextended at the end of a lunge, off-balanced also, and Roger's savage riposte wrenched the blade from his hand. It clattered to the floor. Francis straightened, empty-handed, disarmed. And the edge of Roger's rapier followed, lodging against the hollow of his opponent's throat.

There was complete stillness in the hall. They stood less than two feet apart, two friends, two enemies, heaving for breath and staring into one another's eyes. "My victory," said Roger. His ribs were burning; he could hardly speak, but he managed to get the words out: "For the death of my brother, for Ned, for Priscilla Martin, and for Alexandra, I call your life forfeit."

Francis showed no trace of fear. He half-smiled. "I congratulate you. You're the first man to defeat me in nearly fifteen years. You're your own master now." He paused for an instant, then added, "I am ready. Good-bye."

Oh God! Roger's trembling hand jerked the blade a couple of inches back. He could not. At the end of a thrust... perhaps. But like this?

"Do not falter," said Francis in a voice so low only Roger could hear. Silver-gray eyes stared into his, wanting nothing, waiting for nothing but surcease. "Do it. It's what you want. It's what *I* want. End it, Roger, now."

Roger tried again, scraping the blade across his old friend's skin, but unable to press, to cut, to kill. Jesus! The *coup de grâce* is given swiftly, kindly, surely. 'Tis monstrous to make him wait.

The hot sweat that had been steaming from Roger's skin turned icy cold. The world darkened around him and he was back on the riverbank at Greenwich, watching Francis deliberately thrust himself in the way of a blade that was intended for him. No, he thought. No. "I cannot. God help me, I cannot." And he threw down his sword.

There was more stunned silence; then several things happened at once. People began shouting, cheering. Alexandra burst from the dais and ran to Roger, flinging herself into his arms. Francis swayed, and had to support himself on the mantel by the hearth. The baron bent over in his chair, burying his face in his hands.

"You did it," Alexandra was saying, cradling her exhausted lover in her arms. "You fought him and survived.

You won! Do you realize what you've done? You've actually defeated one of the finest swordsmen in Europe." She let out a whoop of pure delight. "You defeated him, and you're both still alive!"

She kissed his lips, then let him go, for the others were beginning to crowd around to congratulate him. She checked his shoulder briefly, and was relieved to see that the bleeding had entirely stopped. The same was not true of his opponent, whose sleeve was crimson with still-flowing blood. She went to Francis, who was alone, his forehead pressed against the mantel, his shoulders heaving as he continued to fight for breath—unwanted breath. "Francis?" It mattered not a jot that this man had tried to murder her. "You're bleeding. Let me see your arm."

But he twisted away from her, not wanting to be touched. She desisted, saying softly, for his ears alone, "I know. You'd rather be dead. But for his sake, be grateful you're not. How do you suppose he would feel, going through the rest of his life knowing he'd cut your throat?"

Then gently, impersonally, she examined the gash on his arm. It was nasty, far nastier than the wound on Roger's shoulder. She quickly tore a piece from the bottom of her shift and bound it around the seeping wound. "That'll stop it temporarily, but it must be properly cleaned." She called out to one of the servants, "I'll need hot water and bandages, if you please."

But the woman called back, "Mistress, I think you'd better look to my lord the baron. 'E doesn't look so good. 'E's clutchin' 'is chest and 'is breathin' sounds funny."

Both Alexandra and Roger rushed to the dais, where the baron was still bent over in his chair. Dorcas was holding his head, her eyes round with fear.

"I'm all right," the baron was insisting, even as he fought for breath. Alexandra noted the bluish tinge around his mouth.

"Where's his physician?"

Roger was cursing, his victory temporarily forgotten. "Probably drunk in some corner, as usual. Christ Almighty, Father, why didn't you stay in your bed?"

The baron looked up and met his son's eyes. "I wanted to be here for you. I vowed to be here even if it was the last thing I ever did."

"As it may well have been," Roger snapped, but there was a gentleness in his eyes that Alexandra had never seen him betray to his father. "You thought he was going to skewer me, didn't you?" He glanced around at the others, who avoided his eyes. "You *all* thought so, didn't you? 'Tis most certainly true that a prophet is without honor in his country," he added ruefully.

Alexandra had loosened the baron's collar. She was taking his pulse, which was rapid and irregular. He seemed to be breathing a little more easily, but the cyanosis around his lips had not receded. "Let's get him back to bed, please. Now."

The baron tried to rise, but Roger cursed and pushed him back down. "You're not walking. Here." He bent over. "Put your arms around my neck."

"You cannot carry me, my son. You are exhausted."

Roger gave his father a jaunty grin. "It's just sinking in that I've actually fought Francis and lived. I could carry the world at this moment, I think. Come." And with no apparent effort, he lifted his father's wasted body into his arms.

"What about him?" one of the men-at-arms demanded, pointing to Francis, who hadn't moved from the fireplace.

Roger spared a glance at his old friend. "Lock him in a cell. His fate will be settled on the morrow."

"Settled? How?"

Roger bore his father toward the stairs that led to the upper reaches of Chilton Hall, taking care not to jolt him too much. "He is guilty of murder. You may construct a scaffold. At dawn tomorrow, he will be hanged."

40

ROGER'S FATHER slept all day after the duel, gravely ill but still clinging to life. He woke that evening and asked to see his son. Roger was about to enter his father's chamber with Alix when he was called aside by the baron's master-at-arms.

"I've just had a report that there's a troop of armed men riding up the road toward Chilton. 'Tis the queen's men, the lookout believes. Led by Sir Charles Douglas, whom he recognizes by his red hair and beard."

"Oh sweet Jesu," said Alexandra. "Not my father. Not here, not now. You must hide, Roger. Or flee. He'll take you back to London to stand trial."

Roger scowled. "No. Let him come."

"Roger, please—"

"My father is sick, perhaps dying. He wishes to talk to me, he says. Have done, Alix. We are hundreds of miles from Queen Mary Tudor, and I've known Charles Douglas for most of my life. He isn't going to arrest me."

"He's still angry for what he imagines you did to me. He didn't believe me when I swore I was willing. If you think he won't act, you're deluding yourself, Roger."

"When he finds out you are carrying my child, the worst he will do is drag us both in front of a priest."

Alexandra grimaced. She wasn't at all sure what her father would do.

"Trust me." He touched one finger to the side of her cheek, then walked into the room to find Master Theobald fussing with his father. "'Tis passing strange," he added softly. "I told you once I would not care if the old bastard fell down dead at my feet. Now I find that I do care."

"Roger?" The baron's voice was thin but urgent. Both Roger and Alexandra hurried to his side. Richard Trevor gestured at the physician. "Get rid of him," he said to his son. Roger looked at Alexandra, who nodded. Theobald was incompetent; she'd always thought so. Besides, at this point there was very little anybody could do.

"If I don't attend him, I won't answer for the consequences," Theobald said. "He will die before the night is out."

"Get thee gone!"

Theobald went.

"He wants to keep me alive so he can retain his post here," the baron said. "Dorcas has been fool enough to provide him with an unlimited supply of food and drink." He smiled at Roger. "Your first act as baron should be to send the blackguard packing."

"Don't talk like that." He had sat down on the mattress of the big four-poster, his tall, powerful body in dramatic contrast to his father's shrunken form. Leaning over, he lifted the baron's head and rearranged the pillows. His hands were gentle, Alexandra noted. As gentle as they were on her own body during the act of love.

"Why not? You faced your own probable death with courage and dignity this morn; I ought to be able to do the same." He paused a moment. "I am glad you returned. I did not expect to see you again, and my greatest regret would have been to die without first making my peace with you."

"Is that what you wish to do?"

"Aye, my son. 'Tis rather late to ask for your forgiveness," he went on. "But it's odd ... when you lie abed all day and all night, your body a traitor to a mind that is still vigorous, you have nothing to do but review the past and note—too late—all your mistakes. The things that seemed to matter no longer do: power, position—they are chimeras. Religion doesn't even matter—I haven't been lying here contemplating God. Instead I am thinking about my family, and how miserably I have failed them. You, Roger, in particular. And your mother."

Roger hesitated, then said, "She used to come to me and complain of her unhappiness. She used to rage, and cry, and charge you with violence toward her, a charge I had every reason to believe, since I was the victim of your violence on such a frequent basis myself."

Richard Trevor's head shifted restlessly, and his eyes, when they opened, were dark with pain.

"Roger," Alexandra interrupted. She noted the way the baron was pressing one hand to the center of his chest, the obvious lines of agony about his mouth. "Perhaps you shouldn't . . . it is too much—"

"No," the baron said, his voice almost fierce. "We must have this out."

"Would you like me to leave you alone together?" she asked.

"No." Roger's voice was equally emphatic. "Stay."

And so she pulled up a stool and sat down beside him, close by, to offer what support she could.

Roger steeled himself for what was to come. When he spoke, his voice was carefully expressionless. "If you would make your peace with me, you must explain why you treated me as you did. Why you gave me hatred instead of love. Why you beat me—not Will, not Alan, only me. And what it had to do with my mother."

"You are hard, Roger," the baron said, his lips curling in a smile. "I had hoped to get off more easily."

"I am like you."

"Aye, that you are. Like me you are stubborn and passionate, ridden hard by your emotions, quick to jealousy and anger. Catherine was the same. Both your mother and I were very wrong—poor parents, if you will. We were too selfish to realize what we were doing to you. She made you her confidant, something no adult should ever do to a child. And I, resenting the way she turned you against me, made you a scapegoat, a whipping boy. You are perfectly justified in hating me for that."

"What I don't understand is why. A scapegoat for what? When you beat me, you were hurting her—I well remember how she used to cry and plead with you in my defense." Roger shuddered. It was no easy task to talk about these memories; it made all his bitter resentment flare up again. He had to focus hard on the frail, dying man before him in order to drive out his mental image of the fierce, violent giant roaring after him with a leather strap.

"What did she do that you had to punish her so? Was my mother unfaithful to you?"

The baron stared at him, obviously taken aback. He passed his tongue over his bluish lips and did not answer.

"Father, forgive me, but it has recently occurred to me to wonder how much of your anger toward me sprang from doubt that I was indeed your son."

The baron smiled thinly. "You are my son. You resemble me in looks as well as in passions."

"That is apparent now. When I was a lad, it might not have been so obvious. Is that what you meant one day last summer when you referred to the 'truth about my mother'? Was she adulterously involved with another man?"

There was a long pause. The baron's breath was coming hard. "Catherine died wretched and unhappy. Whatever wrong she may have committed, she dearly paid for." Richard Trevor's hands folded themselves into one another, unfolded and folded again. He met no one's eyes; he seemed to be staring into the distance, seeing something that was not actually in the room. He did not speak.

Roger and Alexandra exchanged glances. It had been a guess on his part, but it seemed that he had guessed correctly.

"Beware a jealous heart, my son. Suspicion can destroy love, especially when it is unjust and unfounded."

"Was it unfounded?"

"No." It was clear that the admission still tormented the baron, even after all these years. "She had a lover, yes. In the last weeks of her life, Catherine was an adulteress. But I drove her to it, I fear. For years I suspected her of faithlessness—I do not know why; I had no cause. But she was beautiful, high-spirited, and willful, and I never quite believed that such a woman as she could be in love with me." He seemed to be looking into the past. "She did not wish to wed me; she was enamored of another, a handsome young knight of whom her parents disapproved. She came to me grudgingly, and I was jealous from the start. Even when passion bloomed between us, I continued to mistrust her."

"Surely if you loved one another, you could have learned to trust," Alexandra put in. She was appalled at the note of tragedy in the baron's voice.

Roger shot her an ironic smile. "You are adept at that, I suppose, Alix?"

She flushed to the roots of her hair. For an instant she was enraged; then the feeling left her so completely that she sagged slightly on her stool. "You are right. I ought not to criticize someone for the failing I share. I have never trusted you as you deserve to be trusted." Her voice sounded strangled as she added, "Forgive me."

He reached over and squeezed her hand. "I nearly killed Alexandra because I believed she had given herself to another man," Roger explained to his father. "And the crimes she has suspected me of committing over the past year would truly boggle the mind."

The baron looked from one of them to the other and nodded faintly. "Still, you are well-matched. She is more open-spirited than your mother was, Roger, and you are more tolerant and less of a tyrant than I. You do have my blessing, you know. Whether you wish it or not."

"We do wish it," Alexandra said. She glanced at Roger, then added, "We shall marry, and you will have a grandchild. In sooth, I already carry Roger's babe in my womb."

"Praise God," the baron murmured. "And what a child it will be! Thank you, Alexandra, for telling me. I will go to my rest more easily now, knowing that despite my mistakes as a father, my line will continue."

She bent over and kissed him. His lips were cold, his pulse an irregular flutter. His fist, once again, was pressed against his chest. She trembled slightly. He was dying. Theobald, after all, was right. He would not survive the night.

She rose, touching Roger's shoulder gently. "There isn't much time," she mouthed. "I'm going to call Dorcas." She slipped quietly out of the room.

As if he sensed the need for haste, the baron's eyes darted up at Roger. "About your mother. I didn't finish."

"It doesn't matter."

"Aye, it does. I want you to know, to understand. Catherine and I were at court the winter before you were born. We were not on the best of terms. There were several young gallants who enjoyed her company—one in particular, a musician, whom I suspected her of meeting clandestinely. When she became pregnant, even though I myself had taken her nightly, I wondered if he might be the father of the child. She denied it fiercely. But she was lovely and I was wildly jealous. I brought her home, refusing to allow her to visit the court again. And although she swore on the Holy Scriptures that you were my true son, for years I was tormented by the suspicion that you were not."

"A musician? That, I suppose, explains why you smashed the lute I was attempting to learn how to play when I was six or seven years old."

"God forgive me. I was a blackguard and a fool. I treated you badly, and naturally enough, you grew up with such an obvious preference for your mother that I only resented you all the more." He sighed. "Things seemed to grow worse and worse. In the end, Catherine must have decided that since she was suffering all the recriminations of adultery, she might as well know the pleasures of it, too. She took a lover. But her guilt was heavy. Adultery, she had always believed, was a terrible sin. She punished herself far more than I could have punished her. Indeed, she took her own life."

Roger made a faint sound in his throat and rose to pace the chamber. The death of his mother had haunted him for years, all the more because he himself had had some trivial argument with her on the morning of the day she had flung herself from Thorncroft Overhang. He had had no idea then of the terrible pressures she had been under.

"You accused me of killing her. It was not true, of course. Yet I hated you for saying it, because I did feel responsible.

I had hounded her for years. I had destroyed the love she felt for me and driven her into the arms of another man. And even so, when she confessed, I could not find it in my heart to forgive her. I threatened to divorce her and publicly expose her sin. She could not live with the shame of it, I suppose. She left no note, but that must have been why she died. She could not bear the thought that her sons would know, that you in particular would grow up to condemn her. So you see, you were right—her blood *was* on my hands."

Roger groaned. He was remembering his dark-eyed, wayward mother... her laughter, so joyful sometimes it bordered on wildness. He had adored her, yet she had frightened him a little, he realized now. She was so intense. She burned like quicksilver—bright and beautiful, but impossible to hold. He suddenly had an inkling of the pain his father must have suffered on her account.

Before either of them could say more, the door opened and Alexandra reentered with Dorcas, who rushed to her husband's side. "My father and his company are at the gate," Alexandra said, low. "You must go now, Roger."

He stopped at the window, which looked out on the Chilton road. In the dim light of dusk he could see the horsemen demanding that the gates be opened to them. George Dawes and the baron's men-at-arms were stalling, but that would not last long. There could be no fight, of course. Chilton's defenses were not what they had been a few hundred years before, and Roger had no intention of allowing men to die for his sake.

He was about to turn away from the sight of the red-haired leader when another of their besiegers caught his eye. Golden hair and a languid body. A pretty face looked up toward his window, a serpent's mouth seemed to smile at its cornered prey. And Roger knew he was trapped.

Sir Charles he could have dealt with—he was, after all, the grandfather of the child in Alexandra's belly. They were far from London; they could have struck some sort of bargain. But if Geoffrey was with him, it could only mean that the queen did not entirely trust Douglas. Geoffrey's presence would assure his arrest.

In that instant of illumination, Roger yearned to take

Alexandra's advice and flee while there was still time. If
he allowed himself to be taken, he would be conveyed to
London and condemned to certain death. Yet how could he
leave? He glanced, agonized, at his dying father. He and the
baron had only these few minutes left to them; it was the
only chance they would ever have to redeem the past. And
to answer the questions that still remained.

His voice was urgent as he once again approached his
father. "Who was her lover?"

The baron had closed his eyes again. Dorcas was bathing
his forehead with a rag. "In faith, I do not know. That, she
did not confess. Roger, listen to me: Alexandra is right—
you are in danger and must leave. Go out the postern gate
and down into the woods. Even Douglas would have difficulty finding you there."

"I'm not going anywhere while you lie dying! You came
downstairs to the hall this morn to be with me. Now I would
stay here and be with you."

"I order you to leave," said his father.

Roger sat down on the bed. "And I, as usual, defy your
orders. I shall not abandon you while you live."

The baron grimaced in frustration. "Then I must be quick
about this business of dying, I think. You have always been
infuriatingly stubborn, Roger." He paused briefly. "Can you
forgive me for all the wrongs I've done you now that you've
heard the truth?"

Could he? His bitterness and anger were still warm within
him; he felt no upsurge of peace or filial love. He did not
know exactly *what* he felt. Too much had happened . . . too
much had hurt him. But his father was waiting with eyes
that pleaded—dignified eyes, and proud, yet they pleaded
all the same. *Christ!* He had to speak.

But he could not.

The baron sighed. He reached out a thin and bony hand;
Roger stared at it for an instant, then slowly took it in his
own. It was cold, fragile. Roger had a vague image of this
same hand, then big and strong and hearty, holding his small
boy's fingers, pulling him up and into his lap, throwing him
high in the air and catching him. A man laughed, a child
squealed in delight. He swallowed hard. Had it happened?

Or was it only a long-buried, unfulfilled longing for a father's love?

Roger's eyes filled. His fingers tightened around his father's hand as he took a breath and said, "I forgive you, yes."

And a great weight seemed to slide away from his heart.

"Thank you, Roger," said the baron. He closed his eyes. Continuing to hold his hand, Roger looked across at Alexandra. Her face streaked with tears. She hugged Dorcas to comfort her; she kissed the baron's gray and tired face. Her grief was as sincere as her love.

After a few moments Alexandra withdrew to the window. Roger watched her, and a moment later he knew that she too had spotted Geoffrey. She whirled back, appalled, covering her mouth to restrain her obvious urge to scream at him to run, to escape while he could. Roger shook his head once at her, then looked away from the agony in her brilliant eyes. She understood; of course she understood.

The baron was smiling faintly, looking free of tension, serene. Roger clenched his jaw. Nothing, he decided grimly, was going to be allowed to interfere with that serenity. Nothing. If his arrest was the price he had to pay for these last few moments of domestic peace, so be it. That much forgiveness, that much filial love, he could render to the man who had given him life.

Somewhere far below he heard shouts and a pounding on the gates, but he paid no heed. He simply sat there clasping his father's hand tightly in his own until Richard Trevor's tired heart very gently, very peacefully, ceased to beat.

41

"*I* ARREST you in the queen's name."

Roger Trevor stood silently before Sir Charles Douglas and his men downstairs in the great hall at Chilton while Alexandra's father read out the charges against him. He was accused of heresy, treason, abduction, and rape. The terms of the indictment were long-winded and formal; Roger hardly heard them—he was staring into the angelic eyes of his enemy, Geoffrey de Montreau.

If he had known that Geoffrey was traveling with Alexandra's father, Roger would certainly have taken some steps in his own defense. Geoffrey had become a trusted agent of the crown, more trusted, evidently, than Charles Douglas himself. Roger had seen that the men who had accompanied Sir Charles were not wearing his badge, but that of the queen. Alexandra's father was under scrutiny. He had no choice but to obey strictly the letter of the law.

"You are ordered to make yourself ready," Sir Charles finished, rolling up the document again. His florid face was tired and grim and his eyes were genuinely regretful. "You will accompany me back to London to stand trial. I'm truly sorry this coincides with the death of your father." When Roger merely gazed at him blankly, he added, "Don't you have anything to say for yourself, lad?"

"My lord," Roger corrected.

"What?"

"I am Baron of Chilton now. I expect to be treated with the respect to which my rank entitles me."

"Well, I never knew you for one who used to stand upon ceremony, but it makes not one whit of difference to me, *my lord.*"

"I have one request before we leave. It concerns your daughter." He met Alexandra's eyes and sent her a smile. She was standing nearby with Alan and the resurrected Priscilla Martin. It would have been impossible to determine now that the two women had ever been rivals in love. On Priscilla's arrival they had thrown themselves into each other's arms in a paroxysm of relief and thanksgiving.

"What about her?" Douglas growled. "You've done enough damage there, as it is. If I were not under such strict orders to return you to London for trial, I'd call you to account for besmirching her honor right here and now."

"I think not, Douglas. I wish to marry her. I ask that a priest be summoned so the ceremony can be formalized before you take me away. There may be no opportunity after the trial."

"Indeed there will not—after the trial they'll hang you. And I've no desire to have my girl married to a notorious criminal, even for the few short weeks until she becomes a widow!"

"Your daughter will be the wife of the Baron of Chilton. And the child she carries in her womb will be my heir. I wish the child to be born legitimate, Douglas. I feel certain you'll agree."

Everyone within hearing began to buzz and stare at Alexandra, who held her head high. Her father turned to glare at her. "Daughter, is this true?"

"Yes. Your grandchild will be born in April, Father."

Sir Charles Douglas spewed out a colorful collection of expletives. "The devil take you, Trevor! 'Tis bad enough that you abduct my lassie and ensnare her affections without getting your brat upon her as well!"

"No doubt it's a lie," Geoffrey said dispassionately. "The poor misguided girl will say anything that she thinks will keep her by his side."

"It is no lie." Alexandra turned furious green eyes on Geoffrey. "And the poor misguided girl is likely to borrow someone's sword and stick it down your throat, monsieur, if you make one more disparaging remark."

Sir Charles looked slowly from his daughter to the man she loved. He sighed. "You shall have your wish, my lord. I shall summon a priest."

Two days later Alexandra stood by Roger's side in front of the altar in the chapel at Chilton and repeated the vows that would make her his wife. In the interests of haste, the ceremony followed directly upon Richard Trevor's funeral. The mourners were now the wedding guests.

"'Tis bad luck," Lucy Douglas moaned. "You do not hold a wedding on top of a burial—shovel in the corpse, then pull out the ring! Nor should you marry in black!"

"I certainly can't marry in white."

"Neither could half the brides in this county. At least you're not showing. Your belly is as flat as an unleavened loaf."

"It hardly matters, Mother. Everybody knows."

And indeed, as she stood up with Roger she remembered Merwynna's words: *Ye shall not come a maiden to yer bridal bed*.

But there was not to be a bridal bed. Her father and his men were taking Roger away right after the ceremony. "There's no need for consummation with the bride already pregnant!" he had roared when she'd pleaded for a wedding night with her husband.

"Have some pity, for God's sake, Father. You're taking him to his death!"

But he would not be moved. "You've had your sport with that blackguard; 'tis time to pay the piper now, girl."

In the end Alexandra married in a gown made from the green silk Roger had brought her last summer from Turkey. In her hair she wore the ivory-and-gold comb. He was dressed more simply in a dark doublet and hose with no ornament of any kind.

She and Roger stood listening to the sonorous flow of the Latin Matrimonial Mass being said in the chapel from which Roger's father had sought to have such ceremonies banned. The rites for his father had been Protestant, as the baron had requested. But Roger had been content to be married with the traditional liturgy of the Holy Church. "I am no heretic, despite your long-winded indictment," he'd informed Sir Charles. "I'll say any damn vows you please, as long as my marriage is fully recognized by civil and canon law."

To Alexandra he said privately, "It does not matter what words we speak, sweetling. God has already joined us, and not even death shall put us asunder."

Alan and Pris Martin served as attendants. Alan was very pale, but he spoke not one word against the marriage. It had not escaped Alexandra's notice that Alan was almost constantly at the side of Pris, or that Pris would occasionally look upon Alan with a warm expression in her lovely blue eyes. She had been generous in her praises of him, telling Alexandra that she surely would have died had Alan not found her and succored her. "He's very gentle. And so solicitous in his care of me."

Was it possible that Pris could fall in love with Will's younger brother? Alan was handsomer and more sensitive than Will, and like Pris, he had adopted the Calvinist teachings. Why not? Had it not been a time of mourning, Alexandra might have attempted a little matchmaking. Perhaps the experience of standing up together in front of the altar with herself and Roger would inspire Alan and Pris to think in similar terms.

Dorcas remained after her husband's burial to witness the wedding, even though Alexandra urged her to go home and rest. Lucy Douglas was there with Charles, her caustic tongue making an occasional comment that was echoed by the bare walls of the chapel. Geoffrey de Montreau was not present, largely because Alexandra had threatened again to skewer him if he approached her on her wedding day. Roger had made no such threat, but the look in his eyes when he regarded Geoffrey would have intimidated many a hardier soul. And Merwynna, of course, was not present. The wise-woman would not under any circumstances enter a church. But she was waiting outside, Alexandra knew, with the cotters and villagers to wish the bridal couple prosperity, fecundity, and good fortune.

There was one other person missing from their wedding. Francis. A satisfied smile flitted over Alexandra's lips as she thought of Francis. Out of the debacle of the last two days, one thing, at least, she had salvaged. She had had the presence of mind to go directly from the baron's deathbed to the cell below the great hall where Francis had been imprisoned. She changed the dressing on his arm while telling him concisely all that had happened. He bowed his head over her account of Roger's father's death and grimaced at the news of Douglas' arrival with a troop of men. "The only question that remains to be answered is which of them will hang me first—Roger, Douglas, or the queen."

"Suppose I were to give you the opportunity to live?"

"I would rather you gave me a dagger so I might cut my own throat."

"I am serious, Francis. Roger could have escaped, but he refused to leave his dying father. Now they will take him to London to be condemned and executed. Who will help him then?"

Francis stared at her. "What are you saying?"

"I'm saying that you are the expert at saving people from the so-called justice of the courts. If Roger is to be arrested, I would breathe easier to know that you, at least, were free."

"Those were nameless, faceless dissidents, Alix! And most of them were not yet under indictment, but simply at risk. Roger is a celebrated felon. If he is arrested and brought to trial, nobody will be able to save him."

At which Alexandra, thoroughly overwrought, had finally broken down. But instead of sobbing, she'd screamed at him, "I am going to leave this cell unlocked, Francis! There's a passage through the cellars that leads to the postern gate, and from there it's a short walk to the shelter of the woodland. If you're still here in the morning, damn you, I shall return with a dagger and cut your throat myself!"

But in the morning, Francis Lacklin had been gone, and an innocent man-at-arms was fiercely reprimanded by Charles Douglas for failing to lock the door to his cell. Alexandra had watched the poor fellow insist that the door had been

securely bolted, and listened to her father's scathing reply.
For once she'd felt no trace of guilt at all.

Roger, she suspected, guessed the truth. But he did not
question her. Roger was obviously determined to exorcise
from his mind all thoughts, all feelings concerning Francis
Lacklin.

Roger. She felt his hand touch hers. She was being asked
to repeat the wedding vows. Looking into his eyes and
smiling, she did so, speaking the words clearly and distinctly
as she formally bound herself to her beloved in the eyes of
God and man. He smiled at her also, and the world narrowed
to include themselves alone. It was not happening the way
she'd wished or imagined, but it was happening. He placed
the ring on her finger, his hands warming hers as he did so,
and the priest pronounced them husband and wife. Then
Roger took her in his arms and kissed her. When she felt
the sweet pressure of his mouth upon her own, she forgot
all the looming dangers that threatened them. God had given
them to each other. Surely He would not divide them.

When the Mass was completed and the final blessings
had been invoked, Roger did not march out with his bride
as was customary. Keeping her hand tightly clasped in his,
he said to Charles Douglas, "We wish to have a few minutes
here to say good-bye to one another."

Douglas could scarcely refuse. "Be quick about it, then,"
he said gruffly. "Our horses await us outside, and I would
start our journey immediately." He paused a moment, then
added, "I have no great liking for any of this, Trevor. If it
were not for that snake de Montreau . . ." He allowed his
voice to trail off.

"I know," said Roger. "I do not envy you your predicament."

"I have my duty. This queen'll not last long, I warrant,
but while she's alive, I'll not cross her."

"Enough. Just give us a few minutes alone."

Douglas touched his daughter's hand. "You're a lovely
bride, lassie," he said, and left them.

"Come here, wife." Roger slid his arms around her waist
and pulled her close. He pushed back her veil and threaded
his fingers through her burnished hair, which she had worn

loose, in the manner of a maid. "Your father's right—you're looking exceptionally beautiful today," he told her, smiling into those honest green eyes that were so naked with her love for him. Her skin seemed translucent, more radiant than ever since her pregnancy. Her turned-up nose had an impish quality about it, but her wide, full-lipped mouth was sensuous and womanly. He bent his head and kissed that mouth. She sighed against his lips, then responded with a fervor that both delighted and tormented him. "Sweetling," he murmured, sliding his hands down her spine to cup her thighs and crush her intimately against him. "D'you suppose God would strike us with a thunderbolt if I pressed you down upon the altar and consummated our marriage in the church?"

She laughed, the bright sound of her mirth filling the gloomy corners of his soul with sunshine. Most of all, he thought, he would remember her laugh. He would hold it close to him and cherish that joyful, hopeful sound during the long weeks of hell that loomed ahead.

"I know not, but I think it might be just as well not to do anything to offend God at this point. I suspect we're going to need Him on our side." She paused, then added, "Despite my pleading, my father refuses to allow me to accompany you to London. I will come, though. Alan will bring me in a few days, and perhaps Pris Martin too. My mother is also considering making the journey. She says she is tired of missing all the exciting things that happen to everybody else while she is stuck up here in the Yorkshire countryside. And she intends to convince Dorcas to come too, in an attempt to lift her spirits as she adjusts to being your father's widow." She smiled and ran her fingers through the dark hair that framed his face. "So you see, my love, you shall not be alone. We will all be there to support you— your wife, your family, the people who love you best."

Roger closed his eyes in agony. She apparently did not know what to expect of a state trial for heresy and treason. He did. Although the law did not provide for it, they would almost certainly torture him first, seeking a full confession. The trial itself would be a mockery of justice. It was possible that he could get the heresy charges thrown out, since he was not a Calvinist and had no qualms about saying so. That should save him from the ecclesiastical courts and the stake. But the crown would go ahead and try him for treason, and that charge, no doubt, would stick.

The manner of his death was really the only issue to be decided. Someone of his rank was usually dispatched by an ax-wielding headsman. But depending on the whim of the court, he could legally be killed far more hideously—hanged by the neck, cut down while still alive and disemboweled, his entrails burned before his eyes, then bound limb by limb to horses and divided into four pieces—mutilated, ripped apart.

He shook his head to clear it of such hellish images. "I wish you would not come. There will be nothing but pain and torment for you in London, I fear."

"Roger, you must have hope. All is not lost. All is never lost as long as there is life in our bodies and love in our hearts." She took his hands and pressed them to her still-flat belly. "You are my husband, the father of my child. I have no wish to be a widow, to raise our babe alone. I will fight for you. You must do the same. Promise me. Promise me you will never surrender to despair."

"Alexandra, I beg you to be realistic. I don't think you understand the seriousness of the charges against me."

"I do understand," she said with a shudder that convinced him that she did. "But something may happen, something *will* happen to save you. I feel, I *know* that you and I will live for many years together." She smiled cheerfully into his brown eyes. She had ordered herself to banish terror, banish despair. She would not give in to mournful speculation. She would concentrate on the image of Roger free, Roger safe, Roger alive and in her arms.

He looked down into her brave, determined face and felt a fierce upsurge of love. There was no one to match her. She was his Amazon, his guardian angel, his bright and beautiful love. If she could face the future with such hope and courage, so could he. For her sake he would fight his fate with all his wit and skill and strength. For her sake he would try to stay alive.

"Come here," he whispered once again, pulling her tight

against him and kissing her deeply. Her arms wound around his neck, her sweet breasts nestled to his chest. She was soft and fragrant, his wife, his lover, his soul's true partner until the end of time. "I adore you, Alix. We will be together again."

She tilted her head back slightly. "Swear it, Roger. Promise me."

He pressed her to his heart. "As God is my witness, I do so swear."

They held each other close until her father came to insist that it was time for them to part.

As Roger Trevor rode down the road that led south from Chilton, a prisoner surrounded by a troop of twenty men-at-arms, he turned his head to see Alexandra smiling and waving to him from the church steps. He waved too, until he rounded a bend in the road and could see his beloved no more. So he missed the sight of Alexandra's jauntily waving hand falling limply to her side; he did not see her sway and fall, nor did he hear her heartrending whimpers of terror and grief. He did not see her mother kneel beside her and take that shining red head into her lap, nor was he aware of Merwynna slipping out of the crowd around the church to touch Alexandra gently and press an herbal potion to her lips. No, he remembered her brave and strong and smiling, which was exactly what she had hoped. That cheerful image, delivered at great cost and taxing her acting abilities to the utmost, had been her parting gift to him.

IV
London, January 1558

But true love is a durable fire,
In the mind ever burning,
Never sick, never old, never dead,
From itself never turning.
                    —Sir Walter Ralegh

42

ALEXANDRA touched an anxious hand to the front of her gown as she awaited her summons from the queen's chamberlain. When at last it came and she was allowed to enter Mary of England's private chamber for the audience she had requested weeks ago, she was outwardly calm, but inside she was trembling. As if in sympathy, the child within her kicked and rolled. "Oh, love," she murmured, "we must do our best now, mustn't we?"

The queen was sitting at her desk, with piles of documents in front of her, as always. A tireless worker, she was completely dedicated to the task for which she believed herself chosen by God. If He was failing to reward her devotion in any obvious manner, surely her spiritual goods must be piling up in heaven—was that what Mary was telling herself these days? Alexandra wondered. Her life, certainly, had been joyless and cruel.

Although Alexandra had been announced, Mary ignored her slow approach. She was hunched over her papers, scribbling something with her quill. The same quill with which she had signed the warrant condemning Roger? Alexandra drew a deep breath and prayed for calm, for courage, and for eloquence.

The queen raised her head and Alexandra sank in a deep curtsy. It was a move she'd practiced. She was not yet ungainly, but still, a six-month child created certain problems, particularly since she was doing her best to conceal her pregnancy from the queen. Her farthingale had been skillfully positioned to hide as much of the evidence as possible.

"Ah. Alexandra," said Mary without inflection.

"Your Grace."

"It has been some time since we have looked upon your face."

"Yes, your Grace." She moved a little nearer, startled at the way her monarch had changed. She looked old. She was meticulously dressed, as always, but her face was lined and sunken about the eyes, and her skin had an unhealthy pallor. Her eyes were dark and tragic, and something was gone from her—that old spirit that had held her stalwart and strong, no matter what adversities were haunting her. She was indeed a haunted woman, the gossips whispered, since her husband had left her again last summer.

"I have thought of you often," the queen went on, lifting her quill from her papers and tapping it against the fingers of her other hand. "I have particularly missed the potions you so kindly used to brew for me. My physicians are fools. I feel almost constantly unwell."

"I am sorry, your Grace."

There was a pause, and Alexandra wasn't sure whether to break it or wait for the queen to speak again. Surely she knew why she was here.

"Your father is well, I presume?"

"Aye, your Grace."

Mary's sharp eyes looked right through her. "And your husband?"

Alexandra straightened her shoulders. "As you know, he is condemned to death. You signed the warrant last week."

"Last week? And sentence has not yet been carried out?"

Alexandra's voice seemed to come from someone other than herself. "It is due to be carried out two days from now. Unless you cancel the warrant, your Grace. Which, as you must realize, is what I have come to plead for you to do."

The queen shuffled her papers. "I have read my clerks' accounts of his trial. He has been condemned of treason;

there is no question in my mind of his guilt. Charges of heresy were dismissed, since, unlike most of his hellbound friends, he lacked even the courage of his convictions and declared himself no follower of such archfiends as Luther, Calvin, and Knox. Charges of abduction and rape were dropped when the chief witness against him—you—refused to testify. Indeed, this complex case has caused a tangle in my courts. But of his treason, there has never been any doubt, although he did, I understand, defend himself quite skillfully during his trial. An interesting man, your Roger Trevor. It is sad indeed that he chose to put his considerable talents to such villainous use."

Alexandra moved closer. "Your Grace, I love him. He is not a heretic, has never been a heretic. And his only crime was to help some people whom he misguidedly considered less fortunate than himself. He was not disloyal to you; the man he worked with—the same man with whom he later fought a duel of honor—had a hold over him which has now been broken. He is no threat to you. If you cancel this warrant and let him live, he may one day prove of great value. You need a man like him to broaden England's Mediterranean trade. The war with France has been costly... Roger can sell good English cloth and tin to the East for the silver and gold that are sorely needed in the coffers of state, he can—"

"Enough," the queen interrupted. "He is one of many mariners, and besides, I do not employ traitors for such missions. No, Alexandra. There is nothing to be done. The warrant is signed and your husband must die. Now, leave me, please; my head is aching. I will pray for you."

She could not fail. She *could not*. To attempt her next argument was to move into treacherous waters indeed, but she had nothing left to lose. "Your Grace, wait. Hear me out, please. Hear me not as a monarch, but as a woman. You too have loved a man. You too have lost him; not to death, thank God, but to his duties, as they were ordained by God." She noted, with trepidation, the look that came over Mary's face as she raised the subject of Philip of Spain. "Please God, he will soon return to give you a child," she added, although she knew, as no doubt did the queen, that this was highly unlikely. "But in the meantime, you have known the unhappiness of yearning for your husband. You know what I suffer; you have shared my pain." She raised her eyes boldly to the queen's face. "You once asked me for a beauty enhancer, which I concocted for you. You told me then that you would grant me any boon. I asked for nothing at the time, your Grace. I ask you now for Roger Trevor's life."

There was a deathly silence. The pitfalls in this were legion: the reminder that the queen had once required a beauty enhancer, the memory of happier times with Philip, times that had not lasted, beauty enhancer or no. The only thing that was working for her, Alexandra knew, was the queen's highly developed sense of honor. She had promised Alexandra a boon. Would she keep her vow?

"I should have had you put on trial with him," Mary said harshly. "Do you have any idea how much evidence I have against you? You could be dying at his side."

"I would gladly die at his side!"

Another silence. Then Mary said, "Yes, I believe you would." Her eyes ran over the front of Alexandra's gown. "But we could not execute you, of course, until the innocent life within you is delivered."

Alexandra swallowed uneasily. There was a good chance Mary had heard of her pregnancy, of course. She had hoped that with her preoccupation over the war on the Continent Mary might have failed to take in the most recent gossip. The queen's own failure to achieve pregnancy and give England an heir was perhaps the greatest tragedy of her life, a sad fact that was very likely to make a mockery of her lifework. With no Catholic heir to the throne, Mary's sister Elizabeth would be the next Queen of England. And Elizabeth, though she now diplomatically attended Mass, had been raised as a Protestant.

"My child is innocent, as am I," she stated. "I am guilty only of loving one man too much. But 'tis a sin I will never regret. My boon, your Grace? Will you grant it, or not?"

"You ask too much, mistress." The queen's voice rang with undammed passion. "Trevor must die. His child will live, and you will be permitted to retire with the babe to your home in the north. Be grateful that God has been so merciful. Now, get thee gone from my sight."

It was her pregnancy that did it, she told herself later. She was overwrought, weakened, and greatly dispirited after suffering through the long weeks and months that had marked Roger's imprisonment and trial. Mentally and physically she was at the end of her endurance. Her lips began to tremble and she flung herself to her knees at the queen's feet. "Please, your Grace. *Please!*" She said it quietly at first, but soon her voice rose. "Tear up the warrant, I beg of you!"

"Control yourself, Alexandra," Mary said stiffly. "Unless you would have me order up one of your own potions to calm your nerves?"

Oh God. Alexandra sobbed out her fear and grief, hating herself for her weakness, yet helpless to repress her feelings anymore. She had tried every ploy imaginable to save her husband—from rallying his friends to testify at his trial to offering discreet bribes to people in high places. The queen was her last remaining hope; yet here too she had failed.

Mary reached down and stroked her hair very lightly, very tentatively. "I will pray for you," she repeated. "There is nothing more I can do."

Setting her jaw, Alexandra managed to say, "Since you will not grant me that boon, I ask another. I have not been allowed to see Roger since he was condemned. I wish to visit him in prison before he dies."

"You may do so. I shall give the order."

"I want a writ, signed and sealed by you." She nodded at the table, the quills and ink and papers. "Please write it out for me now."

"You command *me*, mistress?" the queen said in a dangerous tone.

"No," said her former lady-in-waiting. "As you see, I am begging you on my knees."

Mary snatched up a quill and wrote. "Take it and be gone."

They were keeping him in a cell in the Tower of London, the same place where many more illustrious prisoners than he had been sequestered before their deaths. Anne Boleyn and Cat Howard, two unfortunate wives of Mary's father, Henry Tudor, had died here on Tower Green. The honorable statesman and scholar Sir Thomas More, another of Henry's victims, had also met his doom within these walls. As had Lady Jane Grey, who had so unwisely agreed to be a puppet queen for nine days at the beginning of Mary's reign. Elizabeth, current heiress to the throne, had been imprisoned here too, after Wyatt's unsuccessful rebellion. Alexandra tried to take heart from the fact that Elizabeth had later gone free.

She had heard that there were various kinds of accommodations in the Tower; depending upon his or her rank, the prisoner might be housed in anything from a relatively pleasant chamber to a hellhole. Roger, who had both lineage and wealth, was accorded one of the better cells. On an upper level, it was large and relatively clean, although there was a musty smell, arising, no doubt, from the proximity of the River Thames, which flowed alongside the ancient fortress.

The queen's writ had conveyed Alexandra through the various gatehouses, past the administrators and guards. Everybody seemed to know who she was. Even her pregnancy was no secret here. "You want to watch yourself with 'im," she was told by Harry, the cheery potbellied warder who led her along a dark, narrow passageway toward Roger's cell. "A man who's about to die often wants some last crumbs of earthly pleasure, and you've got a babe to protect inside you. You want me to stay nearby and interrupt the poor sod if 'e tries anything with you?"

"Of course not," she told the guard with equal frankness. "He is my husband. Why do you suppose I'm here?"

Harry guffawed loudly. "Out of the mercy of your 'eart, 'ey, mistress? May the good Lord give me such a woman at the time of me own death!" he said as he unlocked the door to Roger's cell.

He was stretched out on his pallet, squinting over a book in the dim light from a guttering candle. "Now what?" he asked laconically. "Not another blasted priest, I hope. Harry,

I've told you..." His voice trailed off as he saw her. He dropped the book and rose jerkily to his feet. "Alix?"

She ran into his arms.

"Alix, good God, what are you doing here? How did you get in? They told me I was allowed no visitors, and God knows I've had none, despite my various attempts at bribery... Oh, sweetling, let me look at you." He pushed her back and ran his hands over her swelling belly. "The babe's growing. You're beautiful, lass, more beautiful than ever." He hugged her, kissed her, his hands and lips trembling. "Body of Christ, I thought I'd never see you again!"

He was thinner. The angular cheekbones stood out now, giving a lean and hungry cast to his face. There were shadows around his beautiful dark eyes, and tracings of silver in his hair. She ran her hand over his chest and stomach. "You're getting thin and I'm getting fat," she whispered.

"A shadow of my former self, 'ey?"

She held him closer, her embrace convulsive. "Have they tortured you?" she asked, thinking of all the nightmares she'd had since the day of his arrest at Chilton in September.

"Not lately." He brushed back a lock of burnished hair that had pulled loose from her intricate braiding. "In the beginning they did." He shuddered slightly, then controlled it. "But since the trial they've been perfectly decent and civilized. Keeping my strength up, I imagine, for the final ordeal."

A fine shiver stole over Alexandra's skin. Convicted of treason, Roger had been condemned to be hanged, drawn and quartered. It was a savage, gruesome death. "You've sufficiently bribed the executioner, I trust?" 'Twas common practice, she knew. For a certain sum of money, the hangman would make certain that death came speedily, at the end of the robe. Otherwise, a traitor's death was lingering and brutal.

When Roger did not answer, Alexandra leaned back in his arms to see his face. His mouth was set in a grim line. "Let us talk of pleasanter things, my love."

"You *haven't* bribed the executioner?" she cried in horror.

"I tried." His voice was grim. "But it seems he's had

special orders concerning me. I am to be kept alive until the bitter end, like a worm writhing on the end of a pin. They want to make an example of me."

"Oh God!"

"Shh, sweetling." He gathered her close, pulling her down with him upon the bed. "Hush, my darling, I'm not afraid. Well ... that's not precisely true; I am afraid, of course, but no doubt I shall rise to the occasion. I usually do, and how long can it last, at the worst? There will be an end. And the fire would have been just as bad."

Alexandra began to tremble and couldn't stop.

"Promise me something," he whispered. "Promise me you won't be there. I could not bear to have you watch."

"I thought to be close, where you could see me. To give you something to hold on to. To send to you my love at the moment when you need it most."

"Send it from afar, then, sweetling. Have you ever witnessed a traitor's execution?"

She shook her head.

"It is a spectacle fit only for savages. You are pregnant, love. Stay away, lest you lose the child." He touched her belly again; the child rolled beneath his hands, making him smile. "Listen, sweetling. This babe is all that will remain of me. She is my final gift to you. I want you to leave this prison and return to Westmor to await her birth."

"But Roger, you may need me."

"No, love." His voice was intense. "What I need is to be assured of your safety, your peace of mind. I would not have you suffer more; I would not have you see what they are going to do with my body. Rather I would have you remember me as I am today, whole and alive and full of the joy that comes with loving you." He touched her breasts, her thighs. "Remember me as your hotly passionate lover." He touched her distended belly. "And as a proud father and husband." He bent his head and tenderly kissed her lips. "For I am your husband, though we have never lived together in our married state. Before God, you and I are joined. And you will be with me, at the end, in spirit. As I will be with you, ever after." He paused. "Promise me."

Tears were pouring down her cheeks. She pressed her

face against his throat, feeling his warm living flesh, hearing the throb of his pulse beneath her ear. She could not believe that his heart would soon be silenced, his body mutilated and destroyed. "Oh, Roger, I love you so. How can this be happening to us? How can God let it happen? You're all I've ever dreamed of, all I've ever wanted. I've tried so hard to be brave, I've done so well ... but you were alive and there was always hope. When you are gone, there will be nothing. How can I live without you? From where will I draw my strength?"

"You will find the strength." His voice was calm, authoritative. "You will remember all the joy between us— all of it, from the years when we were children, to the recent months when we have loved each other as man and woman. You will hold those moments close; they will expand to fill your life. And someday, when the time for grief has passed, they will recede to linger in the background as you discover other sources of happiness and joy. For there will be others, my sweetling; you are still young. You will have our child to make you laugh, and perhaps, in time, another man."

"No!"

"Hush—I do not begrudge you that. You must take what life offers you. I shall not mind—it is only bodies that are sexually jealous, not souls. Bodies need other bodies; that is natural. But souls fly free, and one day yours will join me; I have no doubt of that."

"Yes, that is true," she said fervently. "Our souls are one and have been so since childhood."

His hands moved more insistently over her bodice. He kissed her deeply and stirred against her. "In the meantime, since I'm still in my body ... " His voice trailed off with a slight chuckle as his fingers sought the fastenings of her gown. "D'you mind? Once more before I leave all fleshly cravings behind me forever?"

She shook her head, smiling bravely, and helped him untangle the intricate bindings of her gown. He jerked the fabric down to her waist and parted the ribbons of her delicate lace chemise. As she felt his cool, deft hands moving on her breasts, she melted instantly, glowing for him as she always did with the fires of life. He reached up

and loosened her hair, raking his fingers through it until it
fell in fiery waves upon her naked shoulders. He took a
lock and wrapped it around his fingers, then teased the rosy
peak of her breast with the strands of hair until she moaned
and arched toward him.

"My love." He bent his head and kissed her sweetly.
"Look at you, burning, shining. You are life at its best, its
bravest, its most noble. You are my candle in the dark. We
will be together always, never doubt that. As long as there
is fire in the heavens, my soul and yours will burn with
love. Do you believe me?"

"Yes," she whispered. And she did.

43

"*I* WISH to speak with the head executioner," Alexandra said to the guard, Harry, as he led her down the corridor away from Roger's cell.

"Do ye now?" Harry looked at her sympathetically. "I warrant I know why. 'E's bein' particularly stubborn in this case."

"Why? My husband has offered him gold, lots of it. What does he want?"

"'E wants to keep 'is job, I reckon. I've 'eard 'e's been pressured from somewhere on 'igh to make your man's execution an event to remember."

"By someone on high? Who? Not the queen, I know; she is not so cruel."

"I know not, unless it be that Frenchman."

"What Frenchman? Describe him."

"A true peacock the wight is, yellow 'air, slender as smoke, and as foppishly clad as one of them fancy-boys down at Madam Nan's riverside establishment."

"Geoffrey," said Alexandra grimly.

"I don't know 'is name. All I know is, 'twas after one of 'is chats with Master Simon—that's the 'eadsman, dearie—that we 'eard that 'e wasn't gonna take a bribe from your man to keep 'im from dying slow."

"The Frenchman, apparently, already paid his price."

"Looks like it."

Alexandra cursed under her breath. Geoffrey again, always Geoffrey. He'd been there throughout the trial, gloating. He'd laughed with triumph over the verdict, and rubbed his hands together in glee when sentence had been pronounced. Now he was making certain that Roger would die horribly, in unspeakable pain. Was there no end to the man's malice?

"What sort of bribes does this Master Simon usually take?" she asked. "Money, of course; we can assume the Frenchman's given him that. What else? What if the prisoner has no money?" She deliberately hardened herself. "What if the prisoner is a woman? What bribe does she offer?"

Harry touched a solicitous hand to her arm. "Look, young mistress, you're not thinkin' what I think you're thinkin', I 'ope? Simon's an ugly brute. Oh, 'e's a master with the ax and the gibbet, that's certain, and 'e can put out an eye or mangle a foot in the Boot with the best of 'em, but 'e's no gentleman with the wenches, I assure ye. You're a fine lady, too good for the likes of 'im!"

"Does he like women," she persisted, "or might there have been another reason for his favoring of the foppish Frenchman's suit?"

"'E likes women, all right. 'E's got a wife, a wig-maker, but she's a shrewish bitch. Simon takes what 'e can get round about these parts, you need not doubt that."

"Take me to see him, then, please, Harry."

"I ought not. Your man and me, we got to be friends lately. As much friends as a man of 'is station can be with a bloke of mine. 'E told me about you. 'E loves you. 'E'd not appreciate this, I can tell you."

"He won't know," Alexandra said calmly.

"But you—is not honor more important than anything else to fine ladies like yourself?"

"Honor is a man's word," she said to Harry, as she had once said to Roger. "We women care less for honor, and more for love."

"'E's a rough man, my lady," Harry repeated with a sigh. "'E'll 'urt you."

"Nothing that your Master Simon can do to my body will compare with what he will do to Roger's if I do not persuade him to kill my husband quickly with the rope. Take me to him. Now."

Master Simon was not what she had expected from Harry's description. He was no giant, but a man of medium height and build, well-muscled, but not brutish. He occupied a small apartment in the Tower while waiting to carry out his duties, and when Harry somewhat hesitantly showed her in, he rose and greeted her with respect.

"Lady Trevor?" His eyes flicked over her. They were small eyes, set close together. "I have heard of you."

"Everybody has heard of me, Master Simon. May I sit down?"

There was a small stool in front of a nearly lifeless fire. He nodded, still staring closely at her body. She sat. She could not decipher his expression. Her legs were aching and the babe was kicking vigorously. Jesu! What if Master Simon had an aversion to pregnant women?

"If you've come to offer me a bribe, I cannot take it," he informed her.

Vaguely grateful that they weren't going to dance around the subject, she asked him why not.

"Roger Trevor is no ordinary traitor," he told her. "His trial, with all its excitement, attracted almost universal attention. He has become a romantic figure of sorts. His death will be a rare event, a spectacle. And the people are jaded, my lady. They have witnessed too many burnings. But a good old-fashioned traitor's death, with slow strangulation at the end of a rope, disembowelment and burning of the entrails before the victim's still-living eyes, and dismemberment by four horses, each driven toward a different compass point—*that* they have not seen for some time."

Alexandra had to fight to catch her breath. She knew the details, of course, but hearing them so coldly described from the lips of the man who was going to torture and kill her husband was brutal beyond belief. She felt a line of sweat break out along her backbone and there was a roaring in her ears. *I cannot bear it. I cannot.*

"My lady?" He sounded genuinely concerned. "Is aught amiss?"

"No," she whispered. "No." She sucked air into her lungs and straightened her spine. "Hanging is tricky," she stated. "The victim's neck might break; he might suffocate more quickly than you imagine."

"Not in the hands of a master hangman."

"That you are a master I have no doubt. But accidents will happen, and no one could blame you if one did." She paused. "You have refused the money Roger offered you because you had already been bought by Monsier Geoffrey de Montreau, is that not so?"

The small eyes hardened, but the executioner neither confirmed nor denied her charge.

"I will pay you twice what Geoffrey has promised you. And believe me, you will take no risk with me. I have the complete and unlimited funds of both my own estate and Roger's. De Montreau is an expatriate French traitor. He is not wealthy, and he is far more likely to pay you off with six inches of steel in your belly than with the agreed-upon silver."

"I am not greedy for wealth, my lady," Simon said complacently. "The Frenchman merely offers to pay me to do my job well. You, on the other hand, wish me to bungle it. I have my pride. And, as I've explained, this is no back-street execution. Hundreds, perhaps thousands of people will be present to watch me perform. They will expect me to keep the prisoner conscious and screaming for mercy for several hours before I dispatch him. 'Twill be a triumph for me. Twice what the Frenchman paid me—even three times that amount—would not compensate me for the loss of face I would suffer should he die too fast."

Once again Alexandra had difficulty holding on to the contents of her stomach. "What did he pay you?"

He named an exorbitant amount. A lie? Alexandra neither knew nor cared. Without blinking she offered him three times as much. "In gold," she added. "Payable immediately—tomorrow, that is. I will go home, notify my bankers, and return in the morning with a coffer full of gold."

"No," said Master Simon. His small eyes were hot now,

with an expression she could not mistake. "Your gold is not enough."

Her skin crawled, but she forced herself not to betray her repulsion. She allowed her eyes to meet his; she reminded herself of the tricks she had first learned at court, the simpering come-hither behavior of the practiced coquette. If this was the way it had to be, she might as well give a good performance. She also had her pride. "What, pray, might I add to my gold that would persuade you to change your mind?"

Master Simon approached her slowly. Something had changed in the air between them; his air of respectfulness had vanished. Suddenly the brutality Harry had referred to was out in the open, and Alexandra was afraid. "Stand up," he ordered her. "Remove your cloak; I wish to look at you."

Alexandra did as he required.

"You carry a child."

"I assure you, I am agile despite that limitation," she said dryly.

He walked slowly around her, staring at her breasts, which were partially revealed by the low neckline of her gown—the gown she had worn deliberately for Roger's pleasure.

"Yet you are still slender, and your skin is fresh and white," he muttered. "And clean. Female prisoners are usually filthy and infested with vermin. How old are you?"

Alexandra wanted to scream, but somehow she managed to simper and say, "I am but nineteen."

"My wife is thirty-nine, and fat. She reeks of beer." He reached out and fingered her hair, which she had inadequately rebraided after Roger's lovemaking. "My wife is a wig-maker. She does excellent business making wigs from the hair of my victims. Their heads are cropped before execution and I take the tresses home to my wife. She complains, though, because it is often dirty and befouled with lice. Take down your hair, mistress. I wish to examine it."

As if in a daze, Alexandra obeyed. Merwynna, she was thinking, be with me.

Master Simon stroked her hair, then gathered it in his

hands and sniffed it. "It is good," was his opinion. "Thick, slightly waved, and a most fashionable color. Aye, I believe my wife would be most pleased with your hair."

Her patience had reached an end. "I am not one of your victims," she reminded him, jerking her head away. "You know full well what I am offering you, hangman. A coffer of gold, and my willing body for an hour in your bed." She pulled her cloak around her once again. "In return, you will ensure that Roger Trevor dies an instant, painless, and merciful death at the end of a rope. And I warn you, if you betray me, if you take my gold and my other offerings and then fail to kill him precisely as I have demanded, you will not live to see another dawn. I have powerful friends, Master Simon. 'Tis your neck as much as my husband's that is at stake here." She paused; they glared at each other. "Well? I await your decision."

"I will take your bribe," he told her calmly.

She nearly sagged with relief. Her threats were empty, or nearly so. That she could have Simon killed after Roger's execution, she had no doubt, but that would not save her husband from his agony.

"With one addition," he went on. "I want your hair. All of it. You will return here tomorrow evening at eight o'clock, asking to see the prisoner one final time. You will bring one coffer full of gold and another filled with those thick red locks. I will take you then, your head shorn like a lamb's. I fancy it that way. Do you understand? It is my price."

Her hair. Once it would have meant nothing to her, the loss of those flamboyant red tresses. But because Roger loved her hair, cutting it seemed almost as much of a violation as the other thing he demanded of her.

And yet it did not matter. Roger would never see, never touch her fiery hair again.

"It is a bargain, hangman," she agreed.

When Alexandra passed through the inner gatehouse to the courtyard of the Tower of London, she ran down to the edge of the moat and vomited. She didn't notice the dark shadow that slipped through the gates, following her. She was still coughing and wiping her mouth with a handkerchief when a man came up behind her and touched her lightly on the shoulder. She whirled and found a black-robed priest behind her, offering comfort, she supposed.

"Never mind, Father, I'm better now."

"Are you?" asked a familiar voice.

She stared. She was looking into the face of Francis Lacklin. For one shocked instant she simply gaped at him. Then, without having the slightest idea how it happened, she was in his arms.

She felt his hands gently patting her head while she sobbed out her grief on his broad shoulder. It did not occur to her to fear him, though he had once tried to kill her. That was behind them now. All that mattered was that the man they both loved was due to die on the day after tomorrow, shortly after dawn.

"What are you doing here? And dressed like that?"

"I've been here for some days. It seemed the only reasonable way to get into the prison."

"But a priest, Francis! You mean you're actually saying popish prayers?" In spite of herself, she was tempted to smile at the image. "I can't believe it!"

"Did they allow you in to see him?" he asked.

"Yes, yes. And you?"

"'Tis he who won't see me . . . see a priest, that is. Do you suppose he's actually turning toward the reformed faith? How is he?"

"Oh, Francis, they're going to kill him slowly; Geoffrey has arranged it. I've tried to bribe the executioner myself, but what if he changes his mind and goes through with the torture anyway? Up there on the gibbet, Master Simon will be able to do whatever he pleases. 'Tis his pride that's at stake, he informed me. His *pride!* He takes pride in extending the suffering of his victims, making them sweat and writhe and scream for surcease—"

"Sweet God, Alix, hush!" He jammed her face against his gown. "It won't be like that, I promise you."

"I've done my best to stop it. The hangman wants gold, which I've promised to bring him tomorrow night. And my body, of course—that's nothing to me now. And my hair—can you imagine, he wants my hair! His wife is a wig-

maker, and red has become a fashionable color, he claims.
I have to go home now and cut off my hair."

"Alix, you're raving."

"No, Francis, I'm not. This is happening." She repeated
it, trying to drum the reality into her head. *"This is happening.* They're going to kill him. The only thing I can
hope for now is that they kill him swiftly."

"No, Alix, you must hope for more than that. Listen to
me." He pushed her back to arm's length and shook her
slightly. "We're going to save him. It's what you freed me
for, remember? We're going to get him out."

"Are you mad?" She jerked her head toward the black
walls of the ancient buildings behind them. "This is the
Tower of London! It would take an army to get him out of
here!"

"Perhaps. But years ago when Roger and I were sailing
together in the Middle Sea, he got me out of a Turkish
fortress that was considerably more formidable than this
one. We shall use guile. I have already made certain plans
and arrangements, but I needed a lever. You may be able
to provide it. Come away from here." He slipped her arm
through his and pulled her in the direction of the outer gate
of the fortress. "It is dangerous to talk here. We will go
somewhere more private and you will repeat everything
you've so incoherently told me about your attempt to bribe
the executioner." He glanced up at a guard patrolling the
battlements. "Bow your head. You are a grieving lady and
I a priest offering you support and comfort. We wouldn't
want anybody to draw any alternative conclusions."

They identified themselves to the guards in the outer
gatehouse and were waved through. "Oh God, Francis, do
you think there's a chance?" she asked when they safely
gained the city streets.

"As long as there is life in his body, there's always a
chance. Come. I will tell you my plan."

Deep within the walls of the Tower, Roger Trevor had
another visitor that night. He was lying lethargically on his
cot, thinking of Alexandra and wondering if there was in
truth a life hereafter, when Harry the warder came again to

his cell. This time he brought Sir Charles Douglas, Alexandra's father.

"Hello, my lad."

"Charles." Roger sat up, but made no effort to be formal. He and his father-in-law had an odd relationship. During the early part of his captivity, when Charles had escorted him to London to stand trial, they had developed an uneasy respect for one another. Douglas had indicated that although he was doing his bounden duty, he took no pleasure in arresting his own daughter's husband. Indeed, he made it clear to Roger that were it not for the hostile presence of Geoffrey de Montreau, he might have looked the other way while Roger made an effort to escape.

During the trial, when Douglas had been called to speak against his son-in-law, he refused to do so. This had caused a certain amount of comment at the time. Roger had heard that Douglas' fortunes at court were no longer as high as they had once been, and there was no doubt that his daughter's marriage to an infamous traitor had done his career considerable harm. Sir Charles would have been wise to dissociate himself from the scandal by condemning Roger in suitably scathing terms and disowning his wayward daughter, but he had not. For Alexandra's sake, Roger was grateful.

"You haven't come to gloat, I trust?" he said.

"No, of course not. Although, now that you mention it, I recall swearing, wild lad that you were, that one day you'd come to a bad end."

Roger grimaced. "So why are you here?"

"Two reasons. You're my daughter's husband. I wanted to be certain she and her child were to be adequately provided for."

"You imagine I have not taken care of that myself?" Roger's voice was harsh. "I have spoken with my bankers and drawn up all the necessary legal documents. I assure you, the matter has been dealt with."

"I only ask because you were arrested on the day of your father's death. You had no time to straighten out his affairs, let alone your own."

"I've had plenty of time lately, since the trial. As you

may or may not know, in addition to my father's resources, I have considerable funds of my own. All this will come to Alexandra." He paused, then added, "How does it feel to be the father of a woman who owns three trading ships that sail the Middle Sea?"

"I'll worry about that when she runs off to sail them. Which, knowing Alix, she will probably decide to do."

Roger smiled as he briefly envisioned his red-haired lady commandeering the quarterdeck of a full-rigged vessel in the Mediterranean. His heart twisted inside him. If there *was* an afterlife, how could he bear to experience it without her?

"Will you do something for me, Douglas?"

"Aye, lad. Name it."

"Get her out of London before the execution. I have ordered her not to watch, but she may decide that I need her presence, and you know how stubborn she is. I do not need her presence; in fact, nothing sickens me more than the idea that she might witness the barbarism the crown has planned for me. Anyway, there's the child to consider. She must not be there."

"Of course. I have told her so already."

"You must do more than tell her. I am counting on you, her father, to make sure she does not share in the spectacle of my death."

"Very well. You have my promise."

Roger let out a long breath. "And you have my thanks."

For several moments neither man spoke; then Roger ran a hand through his hair and said, "And the second reason?"

"What?"

"You said there were two reasons why you had come. You have mentioned only one."

"Ah, yes." Douglas looked strangely uncomfortable. "There is something else. A confession of sorts. I have debated this greatly within my heart, uncertain what to do, and at last I have decided to tell you. But it may be a mistake. I would not add to your troubles, lad, and that's the truth."

"Now that my curiosity is piqued, I think you must continue."

"Aye. Well . . ." He stopped again, then continued, "This

is the way of it; many years ago I fell in love with a beautiful woman." Douglas sounded dreamy, as people do when speaking of the past. "I was unwed at the time, but she, unfortunately, was married. It seems her husband was a difficult man and she was not happy with him, so I had some small degree of hope. I pursued her for several years, but she would not grant me any favors. At last, resigning myself to the belief that she would never love me, I also married. But my own attempt at holy matrimony was no more successful than hers."

"Charles..." Roger interrupted. Body of Christ! He knew what was coming.

"Hear me out. One day, years later, I met this woman in the forest. She had been thrown from her horse and was slightly injured. I took her on my own mount and attempted to convey her to her home, but we were caught in a violent storm. We took shelter in a cave and she confessed that she had loved me for years. The cave, the storm, the heady atmosphere, the powerful feelings between us all seemed to make it inevitable that we should become lovers at last." He looked wryly at Roger. "Yet we did not. The lady was adamant about it, you see. She was married; she would not commit adultery."

"It was you?" Roger was staring at the passionate coloring and vigorous physique of Alexandra's father, who was so well known in London for his success with the ladies. "You were my mother's lover?"

"I loved her, yes. I loved her deeply and sincerely, and I do not apologize for that. But Alexandra has told me the reason we took you at Chilton... the tale of his unhappy marriage that your father insisted on telling you on his deathbed. My daughter did not know, of course, that it was I who had been Catherine's mysterious lover. Indeed, no one has ever known. For the truth is, she never came to my bed. Your father was wrong, you see. Your mother was not an adulteress, not even at the end."

Roger's head was spinning. "But she confessed adultery to him."

"Perhaps, but what she was confessing was the intent, not the commission of the sin. For we did intend it, Roger.

That day of our meeting in the woods it nearly happened. I pressed her afterward, relentlessly, giving her no peace until she finally agreed to meet me once again in the same place. But she died, poor lass, before the deed was carried out. And her death was accidental. 'Twas no suicide, and that's the chief reason I tell you this tale. I decided you had a right to know, before you die, that your beloved mother was chaste, and that she died by misadventure, not by her own hand."

"How do you know?"

"I was there," said Charles. "I was there in the cave atop Thorncroft Overhang on the day she died. She had come there to meet me and consummate our love."

"Sweet Christ!" Roger well remembered the strange feelings he had experienced on that stormy day when he and Alix had confronted each other in the cave on Thorncroft Overhang. It was a cursed place. Ned, the half-wit, had died there, and he himself had wrestled Alexandra to the ground, and barely restrained himself from hurting her. "What happened?" Roger asked. "How, exactly, did she die?"

"May I sit down?" Without waiting for an answer, Charles dropped onto the end of the cot and buried his red head in his hands. "'Twas a bad day, wet and foggy the way it often is in Westmor Forest. The path up the cliff was slippery. We got to the top and a storm broke. Catherine was frightened of thunder, as you may or may not remember. There was very little else in life that scared her, but in thunder, she used to say, she felt the power and wrath of God." He broke off for several seconds.

"In sooth I grew impatient with her," he went on heavily. "Instead of entering the cave with me, she pointed up at the sky, declaring the storm to be a sign from God that she should not break his commandment. It began to pour rain, and I had had enough. I put my arms around her, kissed her, tried to coax her into the cave. She broke away, enraged. It happened very quickly, Roger. I can still see it, even now, so many years later. Thunder cracked and a great fork of lightning came down. She shied and lost her balance. She was too near the edge. Her feet slipped on the wet ground; she slid and fell. I tried to grab her; I nearly went over myself trying to save her. And when I realized she was gone, I almost jumped to join her . . . I went a little mad . . . the storm itself was drowned out by my howls of grief." Douglas shuddered visibly. "It makes me cringe to remember."

"You told no one!"

"How could I, man? She was the baron's wife. No one would believe her innocent if they knew she had met me alone in the forest. And I had promised her that no one would ever know the secret of our love." He met Roger's eyes. "I do not break that promise lightly. But I loved your mother and I would see you at peace with her. Alix says you forgave your father at his deathbed. I would ask you to forgive Catherine too." He paused, adding heavily, "And me. For this, and for all the other wrongs I've done you."

Roger closed his eyes. His father's pleading for forgiveness haunted him still. Had he truly forgiven him? If forgiveness meant the giving up of all anger and bitterness, he feared he'd failed, for he was bitter still. "You ask too much of me, all of you." He rose and paced, his steps rapid and jerky. "Damn you! Am I supposed to turn into some sort of saint because I've been condemned to die? What am I supposed to say, to feel? If you had told me this story at some other time, it would perhaps have been different. I would have felt something more, done something more. But my mother is dead, Charles. My father is dead. And despite what I know will happen to me two days from now, I am still alive!"

He slammed his fist against the stone wall. "I'm alive and I'm not sitting here thinking about sin, guilt, and forgiveness. All I really care about is my wife, whom I love, and my child, whom I will never see. The truth is, I don't give a damn about your tragic lovers' triangle. It's nothing to me now. All I can think of is Alix, my own sweet love, whom you have cruelly pulled, time and time again, from my arms!"

Charles bowed his head in silence. Roger rubbed a hand across the moisture on his cheeks and added, "I am not reconciled to death, you see. They tell me I'll go straight to the devil, but I don't believe that. For I swear to you, when I am dead and my spirit is free, no demon's chains will keep me from my beloved's side. Other folk may wing off to heaven or to hell, but not me, Douglas. I'm staying here, with her, for the rest of her earthly life. And when at last she dies and joins me, I defy both God and Satan to separate our immortal souls!"

Douglas shook his head under the force of this declaration. "I warrant they ought to have tried you for heresy after all," he said gently. He rose. "I have said what I came to say." He held out his hand. "Farewell, my son." His voice quavered a little, then came once again under control. "God give you the strength you need."

Roger clasped his hand, then moved closer and embraced the man who had loved his mother. "If the affection and respect I feel for you constitutes forgiveness, then you have it freely of me. Go now. I've been unmanned enough for one night."

Douglas clapped him on the shoulders once and left.

44

DRESSED in a long loose gown and high-heeled slippers that added several inches to her height, Alexandra was getting ready to meet her co-conspirators the following evening when one of the Chilton House servants came into her chamber to announce the arrival of her father. Reluctantly she went down to meet him, covering her head with a cap so he could not see the pitifully short curls that were all that remained of her hair.

"Father? I did not expect you tonight," she said uneasily as she embraced him. "How is Mother?"

Her parents had been living together at her father's town house for several months now while Alexandra maintained her own residence at Chilton House. When she had come to London, they had pressed her to stay with them, but she had refused, insisting that she was the head of Roger's household now and intended to behave as such. The dowager baroness Dorcas was with her at Chilton House, as were Alan and Priscilla Martin. They would have made a merry group, Alexandra suspected, were they not all so heartsick about Roger.

"Your mother is well, but she misses you. I've come to take you home," her father informed her. "Lucy and I don't want you to spend this night alone."

Alexandra was touched; she could see the love and sympathy in her father's eyes. Roger was to die; her parents wished to comfort her. She was grateful, yet she must convince her father that she did not require their help. She must convince him to leave so she could go about the business of saving Roger's life.

"I thank you, but I do not need you yet," she said gently. "Tomorrow I will need you."

"We want you with us tonight," her father repeated. "And in the morning, early, we will set out for Westmor together."

"No!"

"Roger was right," her father said slowly. "You have every intention of going to watch the execution."

"I have no such intention!" Alexandra said in perfect honesty. There wasn't going to *be* an execution.

"Daughter, I have spoken with your husband. I have promised him that you would not be in London to witness his death. 'Tis the least I can do for him. So get your things together. You are coming with me now."

Sweet heavens, this was Roger's doing! Her father was looking quite determined; it would not be easy to be rid of him. And yet, she must.

But before she could say more, there was another commotion at the front entrance, and Alan entered with Richard Bennett, the mariner-adventurer whom they had met at Roger's house last summer. He was a close friend of Roger's; he had offered to help in any way he could. Alexandra had taken him up on his offer; 'twas his ship, waiting in the river, that she and Francis intended to utilize for Roger's escape.

"Here we are, Alix. Are you ready? Francis will be below by now, waiting in the cellars—" Alan began, abruptly cutting himself off when he saw her father.

Sir Charles Douglas looked with narrowed eyes from his daughter to the two men, who were dressed in dark clothes for concealment and armed to the teeth. "What the bloody hell is going on here?"

Alan flushed and began to stammer a reply, but he was interrupted by Richard Bennett, a dark and handsome man with quick wits and a smooth tongue: "We've come to abduct the lady and make merry with her. To force her to forget her troubles, if you will. Indeed," he added, winking an extraordinarily blue eye at Alexandra's father, "we mean to get her so blind drunk that she will sleep around the clock tomorrow." He slipped an arm around Alexandra's waist and pulled her to his side. "Come, lovely lady, and we will sing and dance before we mourn."

Douglas blocked his path to the door. "D'you take me for a fool, man?" he said, his tone low and dangerous. "You're up to some scheme, the three of you. Suppose I were to call in a troop of the queen's guards to accompany you on your night of revels?"

Alexandra freed herself from Bennett's arms and stood stubbornly facing her father. Her voice was equally as hard as his as she said, "You have done enough to destroy my happiness. This time, Father, you will not interfere. Do you hear me? You will leave my house, return to your own, and *tell no one*."

"Are you mad, lassie? You are six months gone with child!"

"Yes, and I would have more children! And a husband to father them!"

"You cannot extract your husband from the Tower of London! You will be arrested and condemned to die yourself!"

"Nevertheless, I am going to try, Father." She reached under her cloak and drew her dagger from her girdle. She held it poised and ready, her will as firm as that of any warrior. "If you attempt to stop me, I will kill you."

Douglas cursed loudly, but made no move toward her. For several seconds there was utter silence in the room. Alan and Richard Bennett closed around Alexandra; their hands hovered near the hilts of their swords. Alexandra was rigid, her green eyes hard and implacable. "I mean it, Father," she said, low.

The tension broke as Douglas unexpectedly flashed a smile. "God's blood! No wonder that young devil loves you. You're a rare fine woman, daughter, and that's the truth." He sighed. "The queen is finished, you know. We've just had word that the French have taken Calais. Rarely has the new year been rung in with so disastrous a loss. The war will end in ignominy for England and her queen, who is sick at heart and weak of body. She will be dead, I doubt not, before many months have passed; those who have supported her policies will fall."

"And you do not intend to be one of them?"

"The Lady Elizabeth, I am told, has expressed secret admiration of your husband. If we could keep him alive until she takes the throne, I believe she could be convinced to grant him a full pardon."

Alexandra hardly dared to breathe. "If *we* could keep him alive?"

Sir Charles laughed heartily. "Aye. I've decided to help you, daughter. Your rogue of a husband has won me over at last. Tell me what I can do."

Alexandra sheathed her dagger and threw her arms around her father.

A little more than an hour later, Alexandra stood with her head bowed in the executioner's gloomy chamber while he opened the coffer she wordlessly presented to him. A wild profusion of burnished red hair greeted him. Alexandra had cut it off herself, braided it together at one end, and laid it in the chest without a second thought. But now as Simon lifted her hair from the coffer, stroking one coarse finger over the bright luxurious waves, she felt herself tremble with rage. 'Twas a rape of sorts, and she hated him for it.

"Very good, my lady," he said as he weighed the thick hair in his hands. "'Tis full four feet long and will fetch a high price. My wife will be pleased."

"No doubt," she said dryly.

He laid the hair aside and examined the rest of the contents of the coffer, which consisted of gold coins adding up to even more than the amount he had demanded. "Excellent," he said, allowing a few pieces of gold to trickle through his fingers. "You have done well." Smiling, he turned to look at her. "Now there is but one part of our bargain left to fulfill."

She shuddered inwardly but took care not to betray her revulsion. "Shall we get on with it, then?"

"Aye," he said, running his tongue over his lips in lustful anticipation. "Remove your cloak, please. I wish to see how you look now that your crowning glory is gone."

Alexandra threw back her hood, revealing her shorn head. It felt strangely light without all the extra weight. Her hair was cropped just below her ears. It curled up gently, looking even shorter than it was. She would have resembled a boy, had it not been for her full belly.

Simon walked around her once, examining her as if she were a horse he was considering buying. She flushed in misery, wondering how much of this she would have to endure. Where was Francis? "You must distract the fellow," he had told her. "There must be no opportunity for him to give the alarm."

"Now your gown," said the executioner, his voice harsh and husky. "Are your breasts as soft and white as your shoulders, mistress?" He stepped close to her and tore at her laces himself when her own fingers stumbled over the unwelcome task. He shoved one hand in against her bare skin and squeezed her nipple, making her gasp. "Ah, your pregnancy makes them tender, does it? What a pity." He squeezed again and Alexandra realized sickly that he was the sort of man who found pleasure in hurting his women as he took them. What other sort, indeed, could she have expected to ply such a trade as his? Sweet God! She knew a sudden fear for the babe in her belly as Simon pushed her down roughly across the bed. *Francis, please!*

She felt him climbing on top of her, dragging her skirts up her legs, his harsh, bad-smelling breath hot on her face. She squirmed and he slapped her. "Hold still, wench. Fine lady you may be, but between your legs you're a bitch like any other." He was tearing at his clothes, so crazed with lust that he neither heard nor saw the dark shadow that crept up behind him. But Alexandra did. She saw both the shadow and the glint of steel. She closed her eyes as Simon bared himself, and he laughed at her. Then the laugh turned into a groan, a strange gurgle in his throat as he collapsed limply upon her, a look of stark amazement on his coarse features.

Francis Lacklin rolled the body to the floor and averted his eyes as Alexandra jerked down her skirts, sat up, and tried to refasten her bodice.

"Are you hurt?"

"No." She forced her voice not to quaver.

"I'm sorry I had to wait so long, but it seemed the only safe way."

She nodded, rising quickly to her feet and stepping away from the bleeding lump of once-human flesh that was lying there. She didn't have to ask if Simon was dead—of that there could be no doubt. Francis Lacklin could kill very thoroughly when he had no qualms to impair his efficiency.

"Come quickly. Your hair; don't forget your hair." He helped her into her cloak and pulled the hood tightly over her head. Her thick red locks she clutched to her breasts, hiding both arms under the voluminous folds of the cloak, and followed him out into the dark corridor that led toward Roger's cell.

Harry, the kindly warder, suspected nothing as he showed Alexandra and the priest in to see his prisoner. He must have seen Francis lately with the other prisoners, for he questioned his presence not at all. "You'll do more good for the lady than for 'er 'usband, I warrant, Father," he said. "That one takes no comfort in religion. 'E'll very likely toss you out afore you get a single blessing past your lips."

Roger was stretched out on his cot when they paused outside his cell. He sat up slowly as the door swung open, blinking into the light of the warder's torch. He saw Harry and a black-gowned man—oh Christ, not another priest— then a third person, a woman. "Alix?" She ran toward him; he threw out his arms and she flung herself into them. He held her tight, his hands stroking over her body in disbelief. He hadn't thought to see her again. He'd believed her visit of yesterday to have been their last farewell. He pushed the hood back from her face to kiss her and saw in confusion her close-cropped curls. He swore softly. "Your hair, lassie, what have you done to your hair?"

"Nothing," she said sharply, and he caught the warning in her eyes. Behind her the priest closed the cell door with the warder still inside. Harry was smiling benevolently at the embrace of husband and wife when the priest raised his arm and struck him from behind.

"What the—" Roger stared as the priest flung back his hood. "Francis?" he gasped as Harry fell.

"Hello, my friend."

"Body of Christ!"

"I asked you not to kill him!" Alexandra ran to kneel beside Harry. "He was kind to me."

"Shh, calm yourself. He's not dead," Francis told her. He bent over and began tearing at the warder's clothes. "He'll have a lump on his head, that is all. Hurry, now. Do as I've instructed you."

"What the bloody hell is going on?" Roger demanded.

Francis sent him a grin. "What do you imagine, you thickhead? We're saving your miserable life."

"You'll forfeit your own. And hers!" Roger's voice was a whiplash. "Have you lost your wits?"

"My wits are in excellent condition, thank you. Here." He lifted his priestly robes and tossed Roger a knife and a sword. "Arm yourself. Then, as soon as your wife takes off that gown and changes into Harry's clothing, you're going to array yourself like a lady. 'Tis a mercy Alexandra's so tall. The couple of extra inches you possess won't be noticed in the dark, I warrant."

"Why, Francis?" Roger asked, even as he took the weapons and jammed them in his belt. "Nothing's changed between us. I would have hanged you, had Douglas' men not arrived so opportunely at Chilton in September. You call me friend, but there can be no friendship between us now, not again, not ever."

"Never mind that. We haven't time for such fine distinctions of rhetoric and honor. You can hang me later. Or cross swords with me again, if you dare."

"If *I* dare! I bested you!"

"But could you do so again? Escape, and find out."

There was a pause while Roger stared at his old shipmate, a rapid succession of emotions storming through his brain. Francis here, free, alive. He had thought of him often during the last few months. Never expecting to see the man again,

he'd tried to make his peace with Francis, to understand
and forgive him. Had he done so? He feared he had not.
But perhaps it would be possible now. And so he said slowly,
"If I ever cross swords with you again, 'twill be with blunted
blades, I think. Once such match with death riding on every
thrust is all I care to venture. I doubt I would ever wish to
tempt the fates so sorely again."

It was a beginning. Alexandra could almost feel the ten-
tative peace being forged between them—the feelings of
good fellowship and loyalty and trust that ran far too deeply
between these two men to ever be completely destroyed.
She smiled as they spontaneously moved toward each other
and clasped hands.

"You and Alix, working together?" Roger said in wonderment.

"And the lion shall lie down with the lamb. Stranger
things have happened."

"The question is, which is the lion, and which the lamb?"

"At present, we're both lions," Alexandra said tartly.
"Now, hurry up!"

"I've missed you," said Roger to Francis.

"And I you. I would have died in your place. But since
they would not allow it, rescuing you seemed the best alternative."

"We may all die."

"So we may. But not at the whim of a vicious executioner."

"No," said Roger, heaving a sigh of relief. He touched
the dagger Francis had given him. He would kill himself
rather than be killed the way the crown had planned.

Quickly Francis explained the plan to Roger. They were
to walk out coolly past the guards and get to the bank of
the river, where Alan and Richard Bennett were waiting
with a boat. Charles Douglas had undertaken to see to it
that the queen's guard would be slow to respond should any
alarm be given; if they could get past the Tower guard, they
should be free and clear. And Richard Bennett's ship, waiting in the river, was ready to sail at the turning of the tide,
leaving England far behind.

Alexandra pulled off her gown and threw it to her husband, then scrambled into Harry's doublet and hose. The extra fabric in the front that had cradled his potbelly was more than enough to cover the swelling of her pregnancy. Indeed, with his helmet, which fit easily over her cropped hair, and his cloak of office, Alexandra looked very much like the wide-girthed Harry. And Roger, thin from months of prison fare, fit into her large-size gown alarmingly well.

"Couldn't you have chosen some other disguise?"

"You don't fancy life as a woman?" she asked archly.

"I don't fancy having to flee in skirts. Good God." He paced a few steps. "How do you manage?"

"Don't take such large strides. That's better. Here. Now for the best part. Bend your head down." She unfolded her thick mantle of hair and began pinning it to his own. "No one will recognize you now."

He touched her shining locks with one finger. He seemed stunned. "How could you do this, Alix? Your beautiful hair—it must have taken you years to grow it."

"'Twill grow again. And you will be with me to watch it."

"Oh, my beloved." He pulled her close. "I am so frightened for you." He touched his hands to her belly. "For the babe. Dammit, Francis. Couldn't you have done this without her?"

Francis shook his head. "No. She insisted, and there was no arguing with her. You know how stubborn she is."

"Aye," Roger said with a sigh.

Alexandra finished fastening the hair and skillfully fashioned a wimpole, then slipped the hood over his head, allowing the long locks of hair to drift down over his shoulders. "You're beautiful, ducks. Almost as fair a woman as you are a man."

"Stop laughing. There's nothing funny about any of this."

"On the contrary, we must treat it as a great adventure. I think a joyful attitude will help us all immeasurably. There, now. Are we ready?"

Francis had bound Harry hand and foot and laid him on Roger's cot. He covered him with the blanket and turned him toward the wall. "If anyone should pass, 'twill look as though the prisoner's secure." He appraised them both and nodded. "We look like the same trio we were when we entered—a lady, a warder, and a priest. Excellent. Let's go."

It was absurdly easy. They walked down the corridor along which Harry had led them, Alexandra boldly leading the way, swaggering a little as she imitated Harry's walk. No one saw them or tried to stop them. They turned right, moved past the turnoff that led to the executioner's apartments, around a corner, then down two flights of stairs. At the bottom, they paused briefly.

"Now for the tricky part," Francis whispered. "We've got to get past two sets of guards, and Alexandra cannot speak lest her voice betray her."

"Neither can I," said Roger wryly.

"No, but you can make as if to weep so your softhearted friend Harry the warder will be hard put to comfort you."

"And stop taking such tiny, mincing steps," Alexandra added. "I don't walk like that!"

"Complaints, complaints." Grinning, Roger took several steps, swaying his hips outrageously. "Why don't I just seduce the guards?" he simpered *sotto voce*.

Francis cursed at him, but Alexandra laughed. She threw one arm around Roger. "Cry upon my sturdy shoulder, dearie."

Just then two guards came around the corner, heading for the stairs. They both greeted Harry, who grunted a low reply while Roger let loose a convincingly high-pitched sob and clutched at the "warder's" shoulder.

"The Lady Trevor," Francis said smoothly to the guards. "She's just seen her husband for the last time."

"Aye, I recognize her by her red hair," said one as he passed them by.

"Poor lady," said the other.

"Poor husband!"

They disappeared up the stairs.

"We're hot," Roger exulted. "Come on, let's do it."

With a similar performance of grief, they approached the gatehouse that led into the grassy courtyard of the fortress. There were two burly queen's guards in the stone archway.

They seemed to know Francis, whom they greeted civilly; and they, too, apparently recognized Alexandra's red hair, for they made no move to halt the mournful little procession that stepped through the gate and out into the night.

"I can't believe this," Alexandra muttered under her breath as they mounted the stone bridge that led across the moat toward the outer walls. "Only one more gatehouse to go. We're going to walk right out under their noses."

"Don't get cocky," Roger warned. He glanced up at the walls that towered over them, nodding at a guard. He was armed with a crossbow. "From that height he'll have a range of a couple of hundred yards. Even if we get safely outside the walls, they can still kill us."

"I will not dwell on such unpleasant possibilities."

They wended their way slowly on to the outer gate, the Lady Trevor weeping, sturdy, potbellied Harry comforting her, and the priest murmuring prayers. There were two more sentries, and the gates were closed.

"Open the gates, please," said Francis pleasantly.

"'Tis a bit late for visitors, Father, is it not?" one of the guards said.

"The Lady Trevor has been with her husband until the last possible moment. He dies on the morrow, as you know."

"In sooth, the brash traitor will swing for his crimes."

"The Lady Trevor" let out a sob when she heard this and turned her face more securely into "Harry's" neck. "Have you no pity, my son?" said Francis. "The lady is sorely distracted, as you can see. Now, open the gates quickly before she swoons."

The tactless guard turned laconically to do so, but his partner took a long look at "Harry" and stepped forward into Alexandra's path. "Just a minute. Your pardon, Warder, but I don't think I know you. My orders are to open the gates to no one whom I do not personally recognize. Tonight in particular."

"Most particularly tonight," said a third voice. A slender golden-haired man stepped out of the darkened doorway of the gatehouse, his rapier poised in his hand. "Ah," said he, "I am not surprised. I have been expecting something like this for days. My only astonishment is that you wait until the last possible minute to make your attempt, *mes amis.*"

It was Geoffrey de Montreau.

"Seize them," he ordered the guards. He pointed to Roger. "This is no lady, but the prisoner himself."

Roger did not hesitate. He thrust Alexandra behind him and drew his sword out from under the cloak. "The gate," he whispered to her as he and Francis, now similarly armed attacked the two astonished guards. One guard fell immediate victim to Francis' blade. While he battled the other, Roger took on Geoffrey.

"You!" he snarled. "Everywhere I go, it's you, Geoffrey, it's you. This time you go too far." Wild with rage, he drove the Frenchman back against the wall.

"For Celestine!" Geoffrey gasped, fending him off with practiced skill. "I swore vengeance, and I *will* have it."

"For the last time, I did not kill her!" Roger parried a violent lunge. "And your convent-educated sister was no paragon of virtue—she seduced me, as a matter of fact. And she had known other men before me. So have done with all this talk of revenge."

"You lie! She could not have wanted you, Trevor!"

"As God is my witness, she did. She was no virgin. You carry the loyal-brother act too far!"

"I was more than a loyal brother to her, do you hear me—more," Geoffrey cried, hard pressed now as Roger attacked him over and over again. He was an excellent swordsman, but Roger was better. Even Francis, who had dispatched the other guard, acknowledged this—he put up his own sword and let them fight.

But there was no time. Alexandra was pulling at the heavy gate. It creaked open, but not fast enough. The noise had attracted attention and other guards were running in their direction, armed with pikes, crossbows, swords. Sweet Jesu, there was no time!

"Hurry up and kill him," Francis snarled at Roger.

"No!" Geoffrey gasped. "*He* must die, Trevor must die! You murdered her, Roger. And you murdered our child."

Roger disengaged, his face pale. "*Your* child?"

"I loved her!" Geoffrey was shouting. "I loved her, you bastard, and you took her away from me!"

"You loved her? Body of Christ! Are you telling me you slept with your own sister? You seduced the flesh of your own flesh and got a child upon her? And then you foisted it on me?"

"I adored her," Geoffrey was mumbling, eyes wild. "She was perfect and sensual, more beautiful than the sunrise . . . no woman has ever been her match . . . she leaves me cold for other women . . . dead for other women! Damn her! She never leaves me, even now. Celestine!"

"He is distracted," Alexandra cried. "Leave him, Roger, they are almost upon us." She had the gate wide open now.

"You whoreson!" Roger exploded. "It was your child in her belly? A child created in incest? No wonder she died! Your misbegotten babe took root outside her womb and killed her. You killed her, Geoffrey. You!"

"No!" the Frenchman groaned. "I loved her. I would never have hurt her. I took her to my bed because I could not bear to think of another man taking her maidenhead, hurting her . . . she was mine, Trevor! Never yours, only mine!" Like a man in a frenzy, he continued to fight, taking up the precious seconds they should be using to make their escape. Roger had no choice but to continue to duel—his enemy's movements were ferocious; if he tried again to disengage, he would die. And he was hampered by the long skirts of Alexandra's gown. Her cascading wig of red hair had already fallen into the dirt, victim of the violence of the fight, and it was fully obvious to anyone who cared to watch that this was no woman fighting for her life just inside the walls of the ancient fortress; this was Roger Trevor himself, notorious criminal and condemned traitor.

"Run, Alix!" he shouted at her. "Remember the babe. Now. Obey me, blast you, for once in your life!"

But babe or no babe, she could not leave him. Francis was cursing. And above them on the battlements, a sentry with a crossbow was taking aim at her husband. Geoffrey de Montreau was just in front of her, and the angle of the duel gave the archer a clear shot at Roger's chest. She saw the guard tense, ready to release the arrow. "No!" she screamed. Rushing forward, she shoved Geoffrey toward Roger with all her strength. His sword arm flailed and Roger ducked. There was a whirring sound and a thud, then Geoffrey crumpled to the ground, an arrow embedded in his back.

"Jesus," Roger muttered, looking up at the archer, who was rearming his instrument. He seized Alexandra's long skein of hair from the dirt as he took her elbow and flung her through the gate, following quickly, at a run. "Make haste—into the shadows!"

"Is Geoffrey dead?" Francis asked as they fled.

"Aye. Shot cleanly through the heart. I thank you, sweetling, for my life. If you had not acted, my heart would have been that arrow's sheath."

Alexandra made no reply as they tore through the walls, across the road, and down the embankment where the rowboat was waiting to carry them downriver with the tide to Richard Bennett's ship. Geoffrey, whom she had once vowed to kill, was dead. *One who dies*. But Geoffrey was *one who cannot*. And she remembered the Voice's qualification: *In sooth, two will die. In a hail of arrows shall they fall.* Oh God, she felt sick inside. Which two? Another arrow whistled by her head and behind them they could hear the loud pealing of the alarm bell.

"How much farther?" Roger demanded. Ahead of them they could see several figures calling and gesturing to them from the riverbank. "Dammit! We're still within range."

This was dramatically confirmed a moment later by a sharp burning in Alexandra's shoulder. Pain shot down her arm, curling her fingers into a fist. A cry escaped her, and her legs suddenly seemed to lose their power. Me? she thought in wonderment. Why had she never expected that it would be she who would die?

She would have fallen, had Francis Lacklin not scooped her up from behind and swung her into his arms. "She's hit," he replied to Roger's frenzied query. "Grazed only, her shoulder—'tis benign . . . not much blood. Keep going. I've got her." But he staggered under the extra weight.

Alexandra struggled weakly. "Leave me. I'm hindering you. Please. They won't kill me, not while I carry a child within my womb. I'm safe, but you and Roger—"

"Be still. I've had your death on my conscience once already, Alexandra. 'Twas unbearable. I would willingly give my life for yours if it would erase that blot upon my soul."

"It is erased already. By your unselfish actions tonight you have undone all your evil, I am sure."

She was glad afterward that she had said it, for the next arrow to strike was not benign. They were nearly at the boat, out of range of all but the strongest, most skillful archer, when Alexandra felt a jarring impact, but this time it was not she who was hit; it was Francis. He made no sound, but suddenly the ground was heaving up at her as they both fell. She whimpered in horror, for she felt his blood, warm and wet and alarmingly profuse. The arrow had struck him in the throat, severing the artery. She knew at once it was a mortal wound.

"Francis?" She scrambled out from under his body, her awareness of her own injury totally gone.

There was no reply. She heard a cry, but it was not from him. It was Roger, throwing himself on the ground beside them. "Francis? Francis! Dammit, Francis!" He was shaking the body of the man who had been his closest friend. But Francis was motionless. His lifeblood coursed out like a river. Alexandra turned away, sick. No one could lose that much blood and live.

Time passed; she wasn't sure how much. Then the others were gathering around them, trying to drag them away. She dimly recognized Alan's voice, Richard Bennett's. "Come quickly," said the latter, "the boat is here; we must be swift; there's no time for mourning now."

She looked back at Francis. The artery was already ceasing its frightful spurting. His heart, she knew, had ceased to beat. Oh God! She gazed into his face. Unlike the usual death mask of those who die suddenly, there was no surprise, no rebellion. His features were peaceful and relaxed; his soul, she sensed, was flying free. Tears crowded into her eyes. He had died saving her, saving Roger. Surely God would accept his sacrifice and forgive him for Will and Ned.

Another arrow struck the ground near the place where

Roger knelt. She glanced at him; tears were streaming down his cheeks. She slipped her hand into his. "Roger," she whispered. "We must go or his death will have been in vain."

But Roger grabbed Francis' shoulder and made as if to pull him toward the boat. "I won't leave him. He needs a surgeon. We must take him with us. We must try to save him—"

Alexandra pried his fingers away from the body. "He's dead, Roger," she said gently. "We cannot save him. Not now, not ever. You must accept it—Francis is dead."

Roger's face was a mask of pure agony. "No, Alix. I have to tell him I forgive him. Don't say he can't hear me. I can't let him die still thinking I hate him. I never really hated him, you see. He's got to understand that!"

Fresh tears gushed out of her eyes. "He knew you forgave him. Some things are clear without words."

He didn't seem to hear her; he wouldn't leave; he wouldn't turn away from Francis. Desperately she drew his hands against her belly. The babe, who was moving excitedly within her, rolled beneath his fingers. Roger's hands were impersonal for several seconds; then they clutched at her, at the evidence of new life burgeoning within her. She felt him shudder, heard him groan.

"Francis is dead, but we are not. This is your child. She needs you, Roger. I need you. The ship is waiting to take us safely from here, and Francis would want us to be on it. Now, come with me, beloved. Come."

Roger regained his senses then. He lifted his head and looked around him, saw Alan and Richard, understood the expressions of haste and desperation on their faces. Quickly he pushed Alexandra into his brother's arms. "Get into the boat," he ordered in his usual voice. "I'm coming."

They obeyed while Roger bent once more over the body of the man who had loved him. *Francis*. He stared at his peaceful face, trying to memorize it, imprint it deep upon his brain. Despite the tragic circumstances that had arisen this past year to divide them, only one human spirit had ever been closer to him. And Francis had just laid down his life for hers.

"Farewell, my friend," he whispered. He was crying; he did not care. Francis would have wept for him, too, if it had been his body lying bloodless in the dust.

Gently he closed those silver-gray eyes forever, and then he did something he had never done, something he would never have dreamed of doing, although if he could have seen it, Francis would doubtless have been gratified. He kissed him full upon the mouth. "God grant you peace." He covered his friend's body with Alexandra's hair, a living, shining shroud. And then he straightened and ran—to his wife, to his child, to freedom.

Epilogue
Chilton, June 1559

The small procession winding up the road to Chilton halted when the gates of the fortress were flung open and a man came running out into the road. "Alix?" he cried, extending his arms to a slender red-haired woman seated sedately upon a horse.

"Hold the baby, husband," she said, thrusting a bundle into the lap of the man at her side. Then she slid from her horse and threw herself into Alan Trevor's arms.

"Very nice," said Roger Trevor dryly. He too dismounted, carefully cradling his child. "I shall expect an equally warm embrace from *your* wife, little brother."

"And you shall have it," said the quiet voice of the elegant woman who had followed Alan through the gates. She embraced him as closely as her heavily pregnant state would allow. "Welcome home, Roger, Alexandra," said Pris.

Alan released Alexandra, who turned to hug Pris. He offered his hand to his elder brother. "Indeed, welcome to your lands, your castle, my lord," he said with a grin. "'Tis high time you returned to attend to the running of them."

Roger shaded his eyes and considered the newly repaired fortress walls with satisfaction. "I do believe you've found your calling in life, lad. Restoring ancient wrecks. Perhaps I'll take my wife and child back to London and leave the running of the place to you."

Alan waved his suggestion away, but Alexandra met her husband's eyes with a smile, knowing that this was exactly what he intended to do. Roger's place was at the court of the intelligent and farsighted new queen, Elizabeth. And she, his wife, meant to be right there beside him.

"Come within," said Pris. "You have much to tell us . . . and show us." She glanced at the fourteen-month-old infant in her father's arms. "May I take her?"

Roger had his hands full as the little girl began to squirm to wakefulness. He cuddled her, crooning. It was obviously a task he was well accustomed to. His daughter responded instantly to his voice, giving him a sleepy smile and murmuring "Da-da."

"If she'll go to you. She's a little wary of strangers." He held his daughter up so she could see his brother's wife. Pris smiled and clucked at her; the little girl tentatively smiled back. She had thick black curls, fair skin, and blue-green eyes that were turning greener week by week.

"She's beautiful!"

"Her parents believe her to be the most comely child ever born," Alexandra laughed. "And the cleverest, of course."

"You darling," Priscilla murmured, taking the child. "What is her name?"

"We call her Frances," Roger said.

Pris met Alexandra's eyes briefly. "It is a lovely name."

An hour later, Alexandra and Roger sat on the dais in the great hall at Chilton with Alan, Pris, and Dorcas, eating, drinking, telling tales of their adventures, and explaining the circumstances that had brought them home to England after a year and a half of exile abroad. "Last November when Mary Tudor died and her sister Elizabeth took the throne, we could but wait to see what she would do about the religious strife that has plagued our country for so many years," said Roger. "It is apparent now that all sectarian prosecution has ceased. Elizabeth has declared that she wishes to open no windows into men's souls."

"She *is* wise," Pris agreed. "All the soothsayers are predicting that Elizabeth will rule for many years. They say the new queen will lead England into a golden age."

Soothsayers. Merwynna. Alexandra had not seen her yet. It was her intention to ride into Westmor Forest after the midday meal to visit her beloved old mentor and friend.

"After Queen Mary's death, my father petitioned Elizabeth for a pardon for Roger," she told them all. "We finally heard this spring that it had been granted." She smiled and touched her husband's sleeve. "He returns to England a free man."

"Thank God!" said Dorcas. Although she still wore mourning for her dead husband, the dowager baroness looked happy and content, her expression more carefree than it had been when she had worried so constantly over Richard Trevor's illness. "I had a feeling it would happen, that we would all be together again."

"Did you? I had no such confidence, I'm ashamed to report," said Alexandra. "I had begun to despair of ever seeing my home and family again!"

"Have you seen your parents yet?" asked Alan.

She nodded. "They were in London. After Roger's escape from prison, my father suffered the consequences— he was dismissed from his post at court. But it turned out to his advantage, since Mary sickened not long after and slowly died." Alexandra had a momentary pang of sorrow for her dead mistress, whose last few months, by all accounts, had been as joyless as the rest of her life. "Being dismissed by Mary proved to be a boon for my father when Elizabeth took the throne. He is now advising her."

"Good old Charles," said Roger. "He is a clever man, with brilliant political instincts." He bounced Frances upon his lap and attempted, with limited success, to feed her an occasional spoonful of Yorkshire pudding. "He knew Mary's ship was sinking when he declined to interfere with my escape. If anyone will rise to greater power within this realm, it will be Charles Douglas, I am full certain."

"I think not," Alexandra argued. "Oh, he *could*, that is true, but when we spoke in London last week he told me he had given over his quest for power. There are personal quests more important, he told me."

"Meaning what?"

"My mother is with him. They have made peace with one another, and are happy for the first time in years, I think."

"You, my love, have a romantic soul."

"No, truly, they are reconciled. She told me so herself. She even told me..." She paused, sending a mischievous wink to Pris and Dorcas. "... that lovemaking is even more pleasant at her age than it was when she was a girl."

Alan cleared his throat, looking embarrassed, but everybody else laughed.

"I sincerely hope that twenty-five years from now I may say the same thing!" Alexandra added.

Roger groaned as his daughter dumped a dollop of Yorkshire pudding into his lap. "You'd better pray for a miracle, then, sweetling, since at this rate I'll be dead of exhaustion long before twenty-five years is up! Where the devil is her nurse?"

"I'll take her," Alexandra laughed, and did so, even though her little daughter squalled briefly at being removed from her beleaguered father's arms.

"She's Daddy's girl," said Roger, proudly patting his daughter's head.

"You are happy, Pris?"

Alexandra and Priscilla were alone briefly while Alan took his brother on a tour of the renovations of Chilton Hall.

"Very happy, can you not tell?"

"In sooth, you look it. Alan too."

"Life is wondrous strange. I have loved two brothers. When Will was alive, it never occurred to me that Alan and I would ever suit each other. Yet we do, exceedingly well. He is gentle and loyal. He composes poetry, did you know that? And he plays sweet music on his lute that deeply touches my soul. He sang to me at our wedding. I wish you had been here for that."

Alexandra smiled. "Indeed, we were sorry to miss your wedding. 'Twas at Christmas, was it not?"

"Yes. We wanted to wait for you, but we were not sure when you would return, and... well..." She touched her full belly and laughed. "We could wait no longer, I'm afraid!"

"No, I imagine not! So it was Alan's gray eyes that struck you to the heart?"

Priscilla's expression sobered slightly. "Yes. You were right about that. You said it was a metaphor for love, not death." She paused. "I heard that Francis Lacklin gave his life to save yours. Is that true?"

"Yes." Alexandra sighed at the memory of the eventful night of their escape and the long period of grieving that had followed. For Roger especially those weeks had been sad and cruel. "He saved Roger from the gibbet and me from certain death at the hands of the Tower guards. 'Twas the final act of his life. God will forgive him, surely, for everything else."

"Do you forgive him?"

"With all my heart."

"So, then, do I."

Later that afternoon, Alexandra dismounted in front of Merwynna's woodland cottage. It looked just the same—the trees rose dark behind it, and before it the bright water of the lake shimmered. Roger, with a wakeful Frances seated on the horse in front of him, rode down to the water. His daughter loved water of any kind—the sea, in particular. He was sure she would grow up to be an indefatigable explorer.

Just as Alexandra raised her hand to rap on the door, it opened. An old woman with white braids, and fierce black eyes hovered on the threshold, her forbidding face cracking in a grin.

"So ye have come home at last. I saw ye in my dreams, crossing the sea, wending yer way to the north. I prayed to greet ye once more again before I laid my sorry carcass down in the earth forever."

"Merwynna." Alexandra opened her arms and hugged the wisewoman tightly. "How I've missed you! And don't talk of dying! You look hale and strong as ever, God be thanked."

Merwynna held her away and looked into her eyes. "Aye, lass, and so do ye." She glanced at Roger, who had also dismounted. He was trying to coax Frances away from the lake.

"So." Merwynna strode over to the little girl. "And this, I warrant, is the daughter who insisted upon getting a start in her mother's belly long before her parents were wed?"

"She's a spirited lass who knows her own mind, just like her mother," said Roger with a grin. He lifted the child so Merwynna could get a better look at her.

"Who-dat?" Frances demanded, pointing a chubby finger at Merwynna.

"That, my girl, is a witch."

"Roger, you'll frighten her!"

But Frances obviously shared her mother's mettle, for she tilted her head to one side and examined Merwynna carefully with her round green eyes, not seeming the least bit intimidated at the idea of coming face to face with a witch. Merwynna crooked a finger at her and Frances laughed.

"When ye're older, lass, come to me in the forest and I will teach ye as I taught yer mother."

Roger gave a long-suffering sigh. "I can see it now. The three of you, dancing wantonly around a steaming caldron. Body of Christ! We should have stayed in the Mediterranean."

"Hush, husband, or I shall put a spell upon you."

Roger handed his daughter to Merwynna, hooked a hand around his wife's shoulder, and jerked her against him. "I'll match my magic to yours any day, woman," he growled. He bent his head and kissed her soundly. Frances squealed delightedly. It was apparent that this was a game she had witnessed many times before.

Inside the cottage, Roger played with his daughter on the floor while Alexandra sat at the herb table with Merwynna and caught up on all the local gossip. "And the birth?" Merwynna asked, casting a knowledgeable glance at Alexandra's once-again slender figure. "I had hoped to be with ye for that. Did all go as it should?"

"It was horrible," Roger said feelingly. "She insisted on coming on a short voyage with me and gave birth at sea, if you please, three weeks early, with no woman to attend her. There was only me and my physician, Tom Comstock, to assist in the birthing. I was terrified she would die."

Alexandra laughed. "In sooth, he suffered more than I. 'Twas easy, Merwynna. And Tom was very skillful, for a man."

The wisewoman muttered her disapproval. Men were useful for getting a babe into a woman's belly, she declared, but good-for-nothing when it came to getting it out.

"The Voice was right about everything, Merwynna," Alexandra mused. "All the prophecies came true. There's only one thing I still don't understand."

"And what might that be?"

"What saves us? Do you remember? You said I would have to learn that for myself."

"Ye have," the wisewoman said. "Ye know the answer now."

"No, I don't. It is not reason. It is not self-knowledge. What then? Faith? Hope? Courage? Fortitude? Or perhaps the ability to forgive?"

"All those things," suggested Roger, listening to the conversation from the floor. "And children, too. Watching the joy my daughter takes in life has certainly given me a new outlook on things." He smiled as Frances toddled aggressively to the doorway, pointing excitedly at a bird that was pecking at the ground in front of the cottage. The child made clucking sounds in imitation of the bird, and laughed delightedly at her own voice.

"Look at her—so young, so eager to discover all that life has to offer. We were all like that once—proud, determined, unafraid. And we have the capacity to be like that still." He paused, then added, "One thing I've learned is that nothing is ever lost. We grow and change, but we need not be alienated from our former bright and carefree selves." He reached for Alexandra's hand. "With you, pretty lady, I am able to recapture that early confidence and joy."

"And I with you," she told him, leaning down to steal a kiss.

"The babe is fleeing out the door," Merwynna pointed out. "Never mind," she clucked, as both parents reluctantly started to their feet. "I will play with her for a time. Try my mattress," she added with a rare smile. "It is fully as soft as it was the first time the two of ye made carnal use of it."

"Merwynna—" Alexandra was blushing.

"Go to it," the wisewoman advised, chuckling. "The time is ripe for ye to conceive again, and I would deliver yer next babe myself. 'Twill keep me alive for at least another nine months!"

Then she chased out after Frances, closing the cottage door securely behind her.

"Well," said Alexandra, grinning at her husband, "how can we refuse?"

Roger wasted no time in dragging her over to the mattress in question. He loosened her thick red hair, which had grown down below her shoulders again, and caressed it in his sweet, hot way. "I wouldn't dream of refusing," he whispered as he pressed her down beneath him.

On the way back to Chilton Hall, they stopped briefly at the old Norman church where the Trevors had buried their dead for centuries, the church where they themselves had been wed. They were surprised to discover the changes there. Although Alan and Pris were Calvinists who did not worship here, this had not prevented them from restoring the interior to its former grace and beauty. Alexandra was deeply moved to see that the tapestries, altar cloths, and sacred hangings had been replaced, some embroidered, she would swear to it, by Pris's skillful needle. There were fresh flowers on the altar, and no dust at all in the cracks surrounding the stone that led below, to the burial crypt.

"Look, Roger." She laid the napping Frances gently on one of the front pews. "Alan has found his calling indeed! This place is immaculate."

"He's certainly dusting off the Trevor family name," Roger agreed. "'Tis a pity he's not the lord of the manor. He obviously cares a good deal more about all this than I do. Maybe I ought to have let them hang me, after all."

She elbowed him sharply in the ribs. "No, my dear baron. The arrogant title suits you, I warrant. But while you are lording it about in London and—knowing you—on the high seas, Alan can live here at Chilton performing all the mundane tasks that you despise."

"And you, I suppose, are going to remain here in the country like a dutiful wife, breeding yearly and raising my children to be proper little lords and ladies?"

She laughed and the stone walls echoed the merry sound. "Do you truly expect to turn me into a dutiful wife at this late date?"

His brown eyes were twinkling as he feigned despair. "I seem to have made a tactical error with you somewhere along the way, poppy-top. You have obviously lost sight of the fact that a woman's husband is her lord and master. 'Tis scandalous. Even Mary Tudor bowed in submission before Philip, her husband."

"Perhaps. But Mary Tudor never rescued her husband from prison, and I doubt very much that she had occasion to hold a knife to his throat and order him to pleasure her. 'Tis difficult," she teased him, "to bow down in submission to a man you have raped!"

He gripped her wrist and jerked her none too gently against him. "You, wench, are going to get your comeuppance." He pressed a rough kiss upon her lips, then let her feel his teeth on the side of her throat. "Now that our travels are over for a time, I intend to devote myself to taming the shrew I have married."

"Indeed, sir? How?" She rubbed against him and raised her eyebrows wickedly at his response. "Sweet Jesu! Ready again, are you? And I thought I'd had the best of you not an hour ago in Merwynna's cottage!"

"You'd best stop that, sweetling, before I commit a highly disrespectful act right here in the church."

More soberly she said, "It might not be as disrespectful as you suggest. The church could use more acts of love, I think. And fewer acts of pride, cruelty, and intolerance."

"You are right in that, Alix." He slipped her hand into his as they walked up the chancel steps to the altar. "Do you remember meeting me here three summers ago? You were praying for Will."

"And you had just returned after ten years' exile. I thought you were a ghost."

"And I thought you were an angel. A lovely flame-haired angel with a body far more temptingly lithe and slender than any I had ever seen before. I desired you immediately, you know. You, an innocent Amazon virgin. For months you tormented me."

"I wanted to be your wife, while you thought of nothing but bedding me."

He grinned. "That, my lady, is the way of the world."

"I got you anyway, my Lord Lechery. You married me, right here in the place where you had first lusted after me."

"It happens to the best of us, I fear."

She squinted at the tablet honoring the dead. Alan had seen to that, too. Two names had been added since that day of Roger's homecoming. Below the name of Catherine Trevor were those of her son William and her husband, Richard. "Your parents, Roger. I wonder if they have made peace in heaven the way my parents have made it here on earth? And Will and Francis? Are their spirits reconciled with one another, do you suppose?"

"Who can tell? I think it wiser to reconcile while we are here on earth, Alix, since none of us knows what may or may not await us beyond the grave."

She knelt and bowed her head to pray for those whose bodies lay beneath them, and for others, like Celestine and Francis, who lay they knew not where. Roger knelt beside her and added his prayers to hers.

"'Tis strange," he observed after several minutes of silence. "I feel light of heart suddenly. Perhaps I have finally forgiven them—my father and mother for tearing me apart between them, Will for being first in their hearts, Francis for putting me first with such a vengeance, Celestine for dying, even Geoffrey for his own tragic obsession with her."

"So many deaths. What, I wonder, has preserved us, who are no less sinful than they were?"

"What saves us?" he said wryly. "You do know the answer, Alix. 'Tis all the things you mentioned to Merwynna, and something else." He looked into her green eyes. *"So faith, hope, and love abide, these three, but the greatest of these is love."*

"Love saves us?"

"Does it not? Not simply sexual love, nor love of one's fellowman, nor love of country, nor love of God. Not even"— he cast a glance toward their sleeping daughter—"the love of a father and mother for their child. But all these things taken together, with all the joy and pain that they confer— they can save us. Love of life, Alix. You have it. And since I've found you, so do I."

He was right, she thought. The simple pleasures of drawing a breath, crunching leaves underfoot, smelling the tangy scent of wildflowers, and watching the gray-green heaving of an angry sea—these were the little things that gave her strength and filled her spirit with joy. And Roger, of course. Being close to him, touching his warm, living flesh, hearing his well-beloved voice, meeting his mind and soul in a union that transcended earthly time and space. "We are blessed," she said softly. "My heart is full. I feel as if I'm going to cry."

He slid his arms around her. "No, love. Laugh, as you always do, my sweetling. Your laughter and your light have saved me, and will save others, I expect, in the years ahead. Now, come. We've tarried in this dark place long enough."

Carrying their daughter, they left the church, walking hand in hand together into the sunlight.

Linda Barlow has been addicted to inventing characters and writing stories about them for most of her life. Fires of Destiny is her first historical novel; she created the hero and heroine twenty-five years ago when she was in seventh grade! A former lecturer in English at Boston College, Linda lives with her husband and daughter in a suburb of Boston. She is also the author of several critically acclaimed contemporary romances.